D0956093

THE FIVE GATES
OF HELL

THE FIVE GATES
OF HELL

RUPERT THOMSON

ALFRED A. KNOPF   NEW YORK   1991

For Robin and for Kate

Let the wicked fall into the traps they have set,
whilst I pursue my way unharmed.

— PSALM 141

And they all went to heaven in a little row boat . . .

— AMERICAN CLAPPING SONG

CONTENTS

ONE
THE JETS   3
MOSCOW, BRUSSELS, HELSINKI   17

TWO
THE WOMB BOYS   33
TOMBSTONE TATOOS   46
THE SHARK RUN   58

THREE
COLOURS EVERYWHERE   75
KNOW YOUR ENEMY   91
HARD WATER   110
LOYALTY IS SILENCE   123
TEETHMARKS   145
YOU, ME, AND THE CHAIRMAN   153
CATS FOR DROWNING   169

FOUR
THE FIRST DROPS OF RAIN   181
HEAVEN IS A REAL PLACE   204
SKULL CANDY   227

FIVE

OLD FRIENDS   245

AND SPRING CAME FOREVER   256

THE OCTOPUS MANOEUVRE   267

THE SUIT OF BONES   273

ALL WINS ON LIT LINES ONLY   284

RED FLAGS   296

YOGHURT, ICE-CREAM, MINESTRONE   307

THE OCEAN BED MOTEL   316

MACKEREL STREET   325

3UR IAL   341

DEAD ENDS   362

AKNOWLEDGEMENTS

During the past three years several people provided me with
places where I could live and work. I'd like to thank Jean
Bedford and the girls, Prue Hawke, George Papaellinas and
Cathy Murphy, Polly Whyte, and Martha Crewe. I'd
also like to thank Rod Parker, and this book is, in
some sense, dedicated to his memory.

Lastly I'd like to thank Imogen for all the support and
encouragement she's given me since the beginning, and for
the use of her bath when mine was unexpectedly destroyed.

ONE

THE JETS

The first time Nathan had the dream, he was staying at his aunt's house on the Cape.

He was standing on a barren plain with his sister, their hands linked as if to cross a road safely, the way they'd been taught. There were no roads, though, not in this place, no human markings of any kind. No trees either. No scrub. Just dust and stones, distant mountains, brutal sun.

Then, in the distance, a mirror-flash of silver and the jets came tearing through the membrane of the sky. The air turned to sound, there was nothing left to breathe, and in his ears the stammer of machine guns as the bullets scuffed the dust around their feet, raised rows of ghostly plants that grew one after another in the dry ground, hung in the air, then crumbled, and their hands were pulled apart, and they scattered, screaming, limbs of water, breath like saws attacking wood.

He woke up. Listened for his sister's breathing through the half-open door. Couldn't hear anything. Listened for his father's slightly faster breathing through the thin wall to the right. Couldn't hear anything. He could hear another kind of breathing. A breathing he didn't recognise. Rasping, sucking, rattling. Lungs like chains. The sea.

He opened his eyes. Everything was white and pale-blue. Curtains decorated with anchors and mermaids, the steering wheels of ships. The skull of a seagull above the bed, a silver coin winking where the right eye used to be. A heap of shells unsorted on the rug, the shells he'd found only the day before. He was in the wrong house. He was staying with his Aunt Yvonne. 121 Ocean Drive, Hosannah Beach, The Cape. He repeated the address to himself, scarcely moving his lips. Dad had told him to learn it, in case he got lost.

Dad.

Nathan's mind slipped back to the sunlit afternoon a month ago, the reason he was here now. He saw himself halfway up the hill. He smelt the melting road, the tar as soft as fudge, you could leave a footprint if you pressed hard enough. The melting road, the trees heavy in the heat. He could even feel the sweat trickling under his grey school shirt. He looked back down the hill, and shouted, 'Georgia, come *on.*'

He walked home from school with Georgia every day. It usually took about half an hour, but that was her fault. She was so slow. Alone he could've walked it in fifteen minutes. He stared back down the hill. Look at her. She wasn't even trying. She was just standing there, one fist pressed to the corner of her mouth. She was probably crying. He supposed he must've upset her or something. The hill, it was always the worst part.

He muttered 'Jesus' under his breath, a new word and just about strong enough for what he felt, and, heaving a sigh, began to retrace his steps. He wished he could just leave her behind, it wasn't far to the house now, another five minutes, but he'd promised, Dad had made him promise, and what if something happened? There were people called strangers and you talked to them and then something happened. He didn't know what that something was. It was too bad to even talk about. He reached Georgia and stood looking down at her. He could only see the top of her head. 'What's wrong now?'

'You left me.'

He didn't say anything. Instead, he watched a thick chalk line grow longer in the sky. When you screwed up your eyes you could just make out the tiny silver speck of the plane. He tried to imagine the man inside that tiny silver speck and a shiver slid up his spine and vanished into the short hairs at the back of his neck. He wondered how fast the plane was going. Five hundred? A thousand? He looked down into Georgia's face, her wet eyelashes, her trembling lower lip. If you were a plane, he thought, we'd be home by now. We'd've been home hours ago. He looked at his sister and wished she was a plane.

'You left me,' she said again.

'I didn't mean to,' he said. 'It's just you're so slow.'

'I'm five. If you were five you'd be slow.'

'Not as slow as you.'

Georgia scowled. She wiped one eye with her sleeve and turned and stared back the way they'd come.

'I hate this road.'

He took her hand. 'Come on, George. Just walk.'

'My legs hurt.'

'Don't think about your legs, just walk. It's not much further now.'

He played the game where you have to step in between the cracks on the sidewalk, except he invented a new forfeit: if you stepped on a crack you had to run three paces. He knew that in games Georgia always did the things you weren't supposed to do; she couldn't resist treading on the cracks and so she kept having to run three paces and they reached the top of the hill without her even noticing.

That was the hard part over. From the crest of the hill you could see the corner of Mahogany Drive, which was where they lived. Another hundred yards and they'd be home. Still, he must've let go of her hand again, because he was alone when he turned into the driveway and saw Aunt Yvonne's station wagon parked outside the front door.

He ran back to the gate. 'Guess what, George.'

Fifty yards away, Georgia stopped, looked up. She was too tired to guess what.

'Aunt Yvonne's here,' he said. 'Come on.'

But he couldn't wait for her. He ran into the house through the back door, and it was like running from day into night, his voice sounded far away and he couldn't see, only the dim shape of Dad with his head in his hands, and his aunt's voice somewhere overhead.

'Your mother's dead,' she told him, and he cried because the word had such a dull, empty sound.

She tried to explain. 'When someone dies,' she said, 'they go away.'

'When do they come back?'

'They don't,' she said. 'They don't come back.'

She seemed to want him to ask more questions, but he couldn't think of any. He stared at his shoes, the toes pale from kicking stones.

'Auntie?'

'Yes?'

'Can I go and play in the garden now?'

A sigh came out of her, and her face crumpled up. He stared at her for one long moment and then ran out of the house. Someone called his name. He ran down the garden, the inside of his head all blank and hollow, smooth as the lawn beneath his feet. He didn't stop until he reached the wild part of the garden, the part he called the Jungle. He stood still, in gloom that was almost green. He looked up, past branches tipped in orange, into the deep blue sky where the chalk line that the plane had drawn was just beginning to break up.

The next day, after breakfast, Yvonne asked him if he'd like to come and stay at her house on the beach. He'd been before, some other summer, and he remembered the excitement of those words 'house on the beach', but things were different now, with different meanings, so he thought for a moment, then he said, 'What about George?'

'She's going somewhere else.'

A whirl through his stomach as he thought it might be for ever and ever, like prayers. Yvonne put her hand on the back of his head. 'It's only for a few weeks,' she said. 'You'll be back together before you know it,' and he looked up at her, with her copper hair that fitted on her scalp like a magnet and her smile that was bright, missed lipstick and crooked teeth, and suddenly he trusted her again, and could smile back. So it was settled.

The day came for them to leave. Dad called Nathan into the lounge and pressed a silver coin into his hand. 'I just wanted to give you something,' he said, and then he turned his head away. Nathan clutched the coin in his fingers and stared at the table leg, how it had an ankle, and how the ankle curved into a golden paw. How one of the claws was chipped.

Dad waved goodbye from an upstairs room, his face rising in the window like a pale moon, smudged craters for his mouth and eyes. A full moon seen through glass. Bad luck, as Yvonne, who was superstitious, might've said. She wore her special fish brooch that morning. She believed that fish were sacred. 'They're the guardians of the soul,' he'd heard her say, and he couldn't pretend he understood. She'd been wearing the brooch for a week now, ever since her sister, his mother, ever since it happened. It stood for loss, it was so she remembered, it was how you could tell she was sad. You'd never have guessed otherwise. Yvonne dressed like someone from another time. Which time, though, nobody could ever quite decide. Dad was always asking her where the costume party was; it was one of his jokes. For the drive up north she'd fastened her copper hair in a canary-yellow headscarf. Triangles of turquoise swung from the lobes of her ears. She wore dark glasses with tortoiseshell frames and a silk blouse that wrinkled and shimmered like a piece cut out of the ocean. A small box, made from the same metal as her hair, hung from a chain around her neck. Inside the box was a clove of fresh garlic wrapped in a twist of crackly red paper. To thin her blood, she said, and keep the devil on his toes. But it was still the fish brooch that you noticed most. When the man in the gas station leaned one friendly smeared forearm on the window and asked how much she wanted, Nathan watched the fish catch his eye and reel it in, and suddenly the man was stepping back and ducking his head and muttering how sorry he was.

'My sister just died,' Aunt Yvonne said. 'This is her little boy.'

She turned away and stared through the windshield, into the light, and Nathan could see her right eye through the side of her dark glasses, could see the tears shuddering on her lower lid. Back on the highway she rolled her window down and stepped hard on the gas pedal, it might've been a beetle the way she crushed it into the floor. The needle on the speedometer leapt and trembled. Ninety, ninety-five. He thought she was going to cry, but she didn't. He thought she was brave.

It was six hours to Hosannah Beach and he didn't glance at the silver coin that Dad had given him, not even once. All the way he clutched it tight in the palm of his hand and felt the bevelled edge bite into his skin. They arrived in darkness, the headlights trained on a stand of cactus, its leaves a pale chalk green and sharp as the fins of sharks. Waiting in the car while Yvonne unlocked the house, he brought his hand up to his face and opened it. His sweat had the bitter smell of hot metal, hot and bitter, this was what leaving home would always smell like. Through the open window he heard the wind in the pine trees and the ocean, he couldn't tell which was which, he was too drowsy now from the long drive, and then Yvonne's voice, calling him inside.

He woke early and listened. Nothing. He lifted his head. Morning lay against the window in a thick grey fog. He left the warmth of his bed and crept downstairs, thinking he would be the first, but when he turned into the kitchen he found Yvonne adjusting the shoulder-strap on her black swimsuit. Her skin looked dry and brown and crinkly like the paper Dad gave him to paint on when it rained.

'I was just going for a swim,' she said. 'Would you like to come?'

The house stood on a low cliff overlooking a stony beach. A narrow footpath led down steep rocks to the sea. There was a handrail, made out of wooden posts and faded orange fishing rope. You had to hold on tight, otherwise you might fall. He let her lead the way. She held one arm out in the air as if the footpath was a tightrope. The backs of her thighs rumpled and quivered. Once on level ground she became strong again. He liked the way she marched across the beach, as if she was leading an army, the stones chinking under her wide bare feet like chain mail.

The water was colder than he was used to. He swam until his lungs burned, then he wrapped himself in a towel and explored the beach. He found a skull wedged between two rocks and managed to prise it loose without breaking it. He showed it to Yvonne.

'It's some kind of gull,' she told him.

'Can I keep it?'

She laughed. 'What would you do if I said no?'

He smiled, but was uneasy.

Then he looked down at the skull again, his skull, and a strange pleasure eased through him. Everything spread outwards from the object he held in his hand, everything spread round him, unlimited, available.

Back at the house, after their swim, they ate a breakfast of eggs speckled with fresh herbs from the garden and waffles soaked in maple syrup and tall glasses of cold milk.

'You know, I think it's the first time I've ever seen you swim,' Yvonne said. 'You're pretty good in the water, aren't you? You were made for it, I'd say.'

'Dad says it's in my blood.' Nathan licked a trickle of syrup off his finger. 'You know when you get hot and sweat? That's how you can tell. You taste it and if it tastes like salt, it's because the sea's in your blood. Dad's got the sea in his blood too. He told me.'

She was smiling down at him. Sometimes, when she smiled, her whole face seemed to wobble, like a drop of rain just before it falls off a twig.

For the first few days the weather stayed damp and grey. In the early afternoon the sun would almost burn through, you could sense the blue sky somewhere high above, the blue sky planes fly through, and then the light would fade and the mist would come ghosting in off the ocean, over the dunes and the marshland, over the withered silver bushes that looked like bits of witches, over the old coast road, and you had to switch your headlights on if you drove to the store, even though it was still daytime, otherwise some tree'd step out and put an end to everything.

Yvonne told him about the walk out to the headland. She had cut the path herself, she said, with her own two hands and a machete, and nobody must ever know. It was their secret, other people would ruin it, you must never tell, she said.

'Who would I tell?' he asked her, and saw that smile on her face again, that smile that was like a drop of rain, and then she took his head in one hand and brought it to her breast and held it there.

He went on the walk every day. You left the house through the sliding doors at the front, crossed a garden of tangled shrubs and plants and, when you reached the cliff edge, you pushed your way through a bush and there was the hidden entrance to the path. You followed the cliff edge for a long time, the sea sleeping way below, that rustle as it rolled over in its bed, that sigh. Eventually you were forced inland, through a forest of twisted black trees and green grass, and it was this forest that delivered you out on to the headland. It was sixty feet high, but still the spray came vaulting over the edge, a fright every time because you couldn't hear it coming, it was like someone jumping out from behind a door. He found a flat rock near the edge and sat and watched the wind lift clouds of fine spray off the top lips of the waves.

One day Aunt Yvonne followed him out. He heard her as a movement in the grass behind him and didn't need to turn. He'd known that, sooner or later, she would come. She sat down next to him and locked her arms round her knees.

He'd been thinking, and now he turned to her. 'When my mother died, where did she go?'

'She went into the ocean.' Yvonne took his hand in hers. 'She loved the ocean. It was in her blood, just like it's in yours.' She lit a cheroot and suddenly the world smelled like the inside of a cupboard that hadn't been opened for years. 'When you go back to the ocean,' she said, 'all the bad things you've ever done, they're washed away. You're purified, cleansed, ready for the next life. You know that skull you found?'

He nodded.

'Remember how pure and white it was?'

He remembered.

'Well, that's what the ocean does,' she said. 'Takes out all the dirt, all the stains of having been alive.'

'You mean, like a washing machine?' he said.

She laughed. 'Just like a washing machine.'

That night, in his room, he took the bird's skull and held it under the lamp. Aunt Yvonne was right. There was only pure white bone. No trace of anything else. Slowly he raised the skull to his nose and sniffed. There was no smell. He wished he could dive down to the ocean bed and watch his mother's soul rising from her pure white bones. But it struck him suddenly that he could no longer remember what she looked like. He wouldn't have known how to recognise her.

During the second week, the weather changed and all the pale colours he remembered from two years before came back. The yellows, the whites, the eggshell-blues. Yvonne began to paint again. After their dawn swim together, she would retire to her studio in the east wing of the house, her hair wrapped in a twist of bright silk, a box of cheroots under her arm. Once he heard the click of her studio door he knew he'd be alone till noon. There were no rules for how to use the time; she expected him to make his own. He filled the first days searching the dunes for shells and skulls or curling into their soft hollows with a book. He was lying on his back one morning after swimming, one hand draped against his belly, the other bent behind his head. His trunks had slipped down and the sun seemed to tug on his blood, he felt his penis swell and push against the damp wool and then, like someone in a trance, he didn't know what he was doing and yet he knew what to do, he built the hot sand into a mound beneath his towel and, turning on to his stomach, began to rub himself against the mound, his legs like scissors, his eyes tight shut, and then that part of him seemed to leap, the sun's red through his eyelids vanished, he saw green, cool green, water fathoms down, the gloom inside a wood, the stalks of plants, and the breath came out of him ah-ah-ah-ah-ah like something tumbling down a flight of stairs. When he opened his eyes again, the air was blue glass, and a man in a tall hat and a black coat stood on the sand, between him and the ocean. The man raised his stick in greeting, then walked on. Nathan watched until the man grew thin and warped in the fierce air, then he let his breath out and stood up, legs shaking. As he rinsed his towel in the ocean he wondered who the man was. Could he be one of the strangers Dad had talked about?

Walking back to the house that afternoon, he looked up through the bushes and saw Yvonne standing on the verandah. She wore a dress that was as green as an empty bottle of wine and her hands were smeared with red, he thought for a moment that she'd hurt herself, then he knew that it was just paint. She was leaning forwards from the waist, her head straining on her neck, as if her house was an island and she was scouring the horizon for a wisp of smoke, as if she was hoping she might be saved. He stood below her, unseen. It was a still day. All he heard was one gust of wind passing through the chimes like something breaking slowly, beautifully, inside her. He entered the house through the back door and began to prepare some sandwiches for lunch. 'Well,' Yvonne said, when she walked into the kitchen a few minutes later, 'at least they won't have paint on them for once,' and he smiled at her over his shoulder and, if it was a stranger that he'd seen on the beach, well, he thought, at least I didn't talk to him, at least nothing happened.

The next day, towards sunset, he knocked on the door to her studio and walked in. Aunt Yvonne stood in front of her black easel, palette and paintbrush in her fists like sword and shield, her body concealed inside a pale-blue tent. She always worked with the windows open and, that evening, a wind had lifted off the ocean. Nothing in the room was still. Everything fluttered, flapped and rattled. The dried flowers, the drawings on the walls, her hair. The effect was less one of walking into a room than of suddenly finding oneself travelling at high speed in an open car. He had to shout to make himself heard.

'Yvonne?'

She waved him over. When he was standing beside her, she jabbed at the easel. 'What do you think?'

He looked at the picture. Lots of white and blue balls, trapped between lines. At first he thought of noughts and crosses, and then he realised there weren't any crosses. Then he didn't know what he thought.

'What's it supposed to be?' he asked her.

'It's whatever you want it to be.'

'Don't you know?'

She shook her head. 'Have you got any ideas?'

He looked at the picture for longer, then he looked at the others, stacked in piles against the wall. In some of the pictures there were lots of balls, in others there was only one: a white ball on a blue background, for instance; a red ball on grey. He thought he understood these better. He went back to the picture on the easel and suddenly he had it. 'It's moons,' he said, and felt sure that he was right.

'Moons,' she said. And folded her arms across her chest and tilted her head on one side. 'Moons,' she said again and, walking round to the back of the picture, she wrote MOONS on it, and the date. There was her grin and then there was his. Hers wide and delighted. His still uncertain, but slowly becoming less so.

September came and still the weather held. Nights when even a single sheet seemed too heavy on his skin. Yvonne took to sitting on the kitchen floor with the fridge door open and a tall drink clinking in her fist. He could tell that time had passed by looking in the mirror; his blond hair had bleached almost white, his nose was powdered with freckles and he could see pale half-moons in the bays between his fingers. He felt his weeks with Yvonne had washed everything clean out of his head. It was almost as if he'd gone to the bottom of the ocean too, he could imagine what that was like now, he could almost imagine his mother there. His head felt like the gull's skull he'd packed so carefully in his case. It felt empty, picked clean, pure. Leave it outside and it would whistle in the wind. Drop it into the sea and the fish would swim through its eyes and ears like a game. He could hardly remember what he was returning to. On the drive back down to Moon Beach, Yvonne reminded him.

'Your father's not very well, Nathan,' she said. 'He's going to need help,' and she peered at him over the rims of her dark glasses, 'especially from you.'

'I know.' He looked out of the window. The sun was so bright that day. Like a razorblade it cut round the roadside diners, the billboards, the trees. Such sharp edges to everything. But thinking of Dad, Dad's sadness and Dad's wounds, that thought was like shadows. He saw the place where he'd grown up. Somehow there was shadow even in the yellow of the sunlight on the lawn. As if all colour, even the brightest, held darkness. Nothing was safe. Everything could turn, give way. Fifty miles north of Moon Beach they drove into a gas station and he couldn't see anything for a moment. It was just being in the shadow after being in the sun. But that was what it felt like to be going home.

When they turned into the driveway, Dad was leaning against a pillar, almost shy. He ran into Dad's arms. Smelt the wool of his cardigan, smelt the talcum powder he used. He remembered the skull and how it smelt of nothing, and he was happy then. Dad smelt of things. Dad was alive.

Dad spoke to Yvonne. 'He looks well. Was he a good boy?'

'He was very good.'

Nathan touched Dad's arm. 'Is Georgia back?'

'She'll be back tomorrow.'

That night Nathan spent an hour arranging his trophies on his bedroom windowsill. He gave the bird's skull pride of place, the silver coin shining in one of the empty sockets like a brand-new eye. It was a kind of reminder: if his life was a book, then the skull marked the place that he'd got up to. He sat on his bed. Heard a car grind up the hill in low gear; a distant siren; the hum of someone talking downstairs. It was so quiet. He moved to the window. Tilted his head back on his neck. A soft crunching sound, like gravel shifting in water, like a finger pushed into sand. He undid the string on his pyjamas and, rolling over, pushed against the hard part of the mattress and then, as if by magic, it was morning.

She'll be back tomorrow, Dad had said. And she was. One front tooth missing and her black hair twisted into two short plaits. It was a relief to see her, he felt he'd been holding his breath until she arrived. Since his dream about the jets, he didn't feel he could trust anyone with her. He knew he couldn't bear to lose her. That moment in the dream when the gap opened up between their hands, that was such panic. He could see their fingers separating in slow motion, like pieces of a space capsule. It was a relief and a reprieve. He'd learned something. Life was booby-trapped and there was no easy passage through. You had to jump from colour to colour, from happiness to happiness. And all those possible explosions in between. It could be all over any time. Those movies where the hero runs against the constant red and orange blooms of fire, where all the bullets noisily fly wide, that just wasn't true. Or true, but very difficult. Or just plain lucky. He'd be more patient with her in the future. Even walking home from school. Even on the dreaded hill.

In the past Dad had sometimes rested in his bedroom after lunch. Now he rested every day, often for two hours. If Nathan and Georgia stayed home they had to be quiet till he came downstairs again. It wasn't easy. Silence didn't come naturally to Georgia, it never had, and Dad slept so lightly he could hear the handle on the back door turn. Nathan invented a new game. He called it Red Indian Feet.

'You've got to have Red Indian feet,' he said, 'like this,' and he went into a sort of crouch, with his knees bent and his fingers spread in the air.

You had to talk in a whisper or, better still, in sign language, which they learned from a book about deaf people. You had to walk in a special way: your heel touched the ground first, then the hard outside edge of your foot, then the ball of your foot and, finally, your toes. You had to make devilish Red Indian faces. It was the simplest of games, yet it worked like a charm. Georgia crept through the house, shoulders lifted on a level with her ears, hands spread in front of her, eyes wide. She'd turn a corner and there he'd be, a hunchback with a twisted face, and because you weren't allowed to cry out, because everything happened in silence and slow motion, they'd both double up, roll gasping on the carpet, and the only way to hold the laughter in was to run out to the garden and stuff your mouth with mud and grass and stones.

The jets were still flying. High altitude. Sometimes, as he lay on his back and stared into the sky, he saw a glint of silver high up in the blue. But heard nothing. That was what the word dead was. That glint of silver, that speed he could never guess. At night Georgia used to cry out and he'd wake in the next room and see her through the open door, flailing at the empty air like someone waving goodbye with both hands at once. He invented another game, to calm her. Windshield Wipers, he called it. You had to lie on your back and move your head from side to side on the pillow and make a soft droning sound. They did it together, in their separate beds. It wiped the bad dreams away, it brought the deep sleep back. After their mother went to the bottom of the sea, the days would pass in silence, the nights in fear. They walked through their childhood on Red Indian feet. Not a crack from a stick, not a creak from a stair. Not a sound.

On the way down in the car Aunt Yvonne had told Nathan that she'd just be staying a week or two, until they settled back in, but in the end she stayed till Christmas. Nathan would come home from school to find her painting in the garden, an overcoat thrown over her shoulders, lipstick smeared across her mouth, a cheroot burning in her left hand. 'I'm making the whole neighbourhood reek,' she shouted. 'It's your father's fault. He won't let me smoke in the house.'

Nathan spoke to Dad. 'It's not *that* bad,' he said. 'It's only like cupboards.'

But Dad shook his head and fixed his eyes on the corner of the room. 'It gets in my pipes. It makes me cough.'

So Yvonne went on painting outdoors, often until dusk, sometimes even later, by candlelight. The fresh air seemed to inspire her. It was like her studio, she said, only more so. She was beginning to move out of her ball period, though she hadn't made up a name for her new period yet. The balls had gone, it was true. They'd rolled right out of her pictures, and the lines that used to hold them in place were no longer straight, they now wriggled horizontally across the canvas.

'I don't know,' said Nathan, who'd become the leading authority on her work. 'It could be the ocean, I suppose.'

Yvonne turned to him, and her eyes narrowed in the candlelight and her lips stretched wide across her face. He knew the meaning of the look. It meant that things were coinciding in a way that pleased her. He'd seen the same smile earlier that summer when she discovered that sausages tasted good with marmalade.

The day she left, he helped her lash the new paintings to the roof of her station wagon. 'I need to get back,' she shouted. 'My ocean period's just beginning, and it'll flourish up there, I can feel it.'

He glanced at the sky anxiously. 'I hope it doesn't rain.'

She squatted beside him, her back against the wheel, her face close to his. 'Promise me something, Nat.'

'What?'

'Try not to be too serious, OK?'

He nodded. 'OK.'

'Come on,' and she got to her feet and took his hand, 'I've got something for you.'

She led him into the kitchen. There was a painting leaning against the wall. She turned it round. 'There,' she said, 'that's for you.'

It was a ball painting. A ball of marbled grey and white against a background of midnight-blue. It was one of the first paintings of hers that he'd looked at. It was a real moon.

Yvonne stood with arms folded and legs astride, like her own easel. 'What do you think?'

'It's one of my favourites,' he said. 'You knew that, didn't you?'

That evening he hung the moon painting in his narrow room and then he lay down on his bed. He saw Aunt Yvonne driving back up the coast in her old beat-up station wagon and sent his love with her on the passenger seat. She'd told him Dad needed help, though he'd known that already. Dad seemed to be moving through air that was different to everybody else's, it was thick and sticky, built out of cobwebs. When Dad smiled, it looked wrong; it was as if someone had made a joke and he hadn't got it, but he was pretending that he had. He could see that Dad was in some kind of terrible danger, and he wanted to rescue him, but he didn't know how. Instead, he did everything he was asked to do, and did it without complaining. He hid his own fears and wishes, and only took them out in private, under the eye of the moon. He was a good boy.

He tried to keep his promise to Yvonne, he tried not to be too serious, but it was hard because those jets kept coming over. The scream of silver, the ghostly stalks of dust, the hands separating like two parts of a rocket ship. He'd wake up and lie still, waiting for Dad to die. His mother had been strong, that was what he'd always been told, and now she'd gone to the bottom of the ocean, seaweed necklaces and fish swimming through the spaces in her head. She'd been strong and she'd died, so what chance did Dad have?

He lay on his back in the narrow room and listened for his sister's breathing through the half-open door, listened for his father's slightly faster breathing through the thin wall to the right. He lay like a toppled toy soldier, hands pressed tight against his thighs, every muscle rigid. He couldn't move his eyes. Because the jets flew beyond his dream, they were in the room with him, silent and lethal, swooping like birds in the grey air. It could happen any moment.

He listened to his father breathing and waited for it to stop. He listened to his sister breathing and made plans for their loneliness.

Those daybreaks.

He was eleven then.

MOSCOW, BRUSSELS, HELSINKI

Jed's mother said she didn't want him hanging round the beauty parlour after school, it was bad for business, what with him looking the way he did and all, so he'd walk home and climb out through the bathroom window and on to the roof. They lived in Sweetwater, right out near the airport. It was always funny the first time someone came to the house. A plane would go over and they'd duck or flinch. It was that loud. Once someone even threw themselves face down on the kitchen floor like someone in a war movie. Out on the roof, though, that was best. He'd lie on his back and watch the planes fly over. So close they almost grazed the tip of his nose. He liked the way his ears crackled, he liked to feel the house shake. And sometimes there was the sense that his legs were rising into the air, that the roof was sliding out from under him.

If he'd been Tommy, of course, it would've been a different story. Tommy was his brother, but he was twelve years older, more like an uncle, really. He worked as a foreman at a construction site in Rialto. She wouldn't've minded Tommy hanging round the beauty parlour. He had thick shiny hair and he walked with his legs slightly bent so you could imagine a horse between them. Once he did a hundred press-ups with a girl in a bikini standing on his back (Jed saw the photo). He wasn't bad for business. He wasn't bad at all.

That twelve-year gap between him and Tommy, he knew what it meant. It meant he was a mistake. And not only that, but he was ugly too, just so nobody forgot. Only something so unintended could've turned out so wrong. Born in a bottle of vodka one night, his mother had told him once. Poured out of her seven months later like some sickly cocktail. They had to put him in a kind of see-through tent so he could breathe. 'Oh Muriel,' she was fond of saying, 'I don't know *what* you did to deserve it.' She'd be sitting at her dresssing-table mirror, and he'd be standing beside her, watching her put her make-up on. Eye-shadow, mascara, rouge. Made her look just like plastic. And then she'd roll her eyes and sigh. 'Must be someone's idea of a joke.' Someone was God, and she was always flirting with him, same as she did with any man.

These were the good days, when her disgust could seem like a kind of affection. But there were times when it didn't seem like anything apart from what it was.

The year he turned nine he discovered junk stores. He felt at home there. The people who ran them didn't care if he was ugly; most of them were ugly too, and some of them, maybe they were mistakes as well. Old Mr Garbett, he was ugly all right. He ran Jed's favourite store. It was on Airdrome Boulevard. The Empire of Junk, it was called. Old Mr Garbett had a moon face and eyes that seeped. He sat on a leather armchair just inside the door with a brown bottle of beer standing beside his right foot. He wore the same mustard cardigan every day, and smoked cigarettes with wrinkles in them like the legs of elephants. The strangest thing about him was, his lips were the same colour as his face. It was here that Jed found the radios.

That first afternoon he was so excited that he ran all the way home. Along the boulevard, down Mackerel Street, through the front gate, straight into his mother's bedroom. She was sitting at her dressing-table as usual. Instead of turning round, she used the mirror to look at him. 'Do you have to bring those in here, Jed?'

'They're only radios.'

'Yes, but look at them. They're filthy.'

There was something wrong with what she was saying. But she'd thrown him off balance and he couldn't think.

'And what do you want radios for, anyway?' It was sweet, that voice of hers, it was always sweet, somehow, but like all sweet things too much of it could make you ill. 'We've already got a radio in the kitchen.'

'That's different.'

'What's different about it?'

He shrugged. 'I don't know. These ones have names. It's the names that I like.'

A plane went over, and all her tiny bottles jostled and clinked.

'Names?' She frowned. 'What names?'

'You know, the names of the stations. Moscow, Brussels, Helsinki. Those names.'

If only Pop was still around, he thought. Pop would have under-stood. Trouble was, Pop had moved out about a year before. Jed knew it was final when he saw Pop carrying his gun magazines out to the car. Pop had the same passion for collecting as Jed did, only Pop collected guns. He had nineteen of them. Six were special, and hung on the wall in the den. The rest, he actually used. Sometimes, on weekends, he used to take Jed out to the abandoned graveyard on Normandy Hill and they'd shoot at the wooden crosses. The bull's-eye was the place where the parts of the cross joined, but Jed liked to shoot at the arms and watch the bits fly off. Pop loved guns so much, he'd even named his sons after them: Thomas Colt Morgan, Jed Gattling Morgan (if he'd had a girl he would've called her Beretta). He wanted to change his own name to Winchester, but Muriel wouldn't hear of it. Winchester Morgan! He always thought that would've sounded grand. As it was, he had to be satisfied with Pop. Not even Bang. Just Pop.

About every month or two Pop would come back, late at night, a few drinks under his belt. The door would shake, then the windows, then the door again, it didn't seem so strange, it was just like another plane going over, and then his voice would force its way through the mailbox. 'Muriel? Let me in, will you? Muriel? Goddammit, Muriel, let me in.' And Muriel would call Tommy. Or if Tommy wasn't home she'd call the police. 'He's drunk,' she'd say. 'I think he's got a gun.' She didn't like calling the police, though, because the cars'd scream into the street, the lights'd flash and then everybody'd know. She was a beautician, and she had her reputation to think of.

And now she turned to him and it was as if she'd been reading his mind. 'You must get this from your father.'

She banned his radios from the house, but that just drove Jed's passion underground. He became a regular at the Empire of Junk. He'd insert himself into the darkest corners of the store, dust burning in his nostrils, the tips of his fingers grey as if with ashes, and he would often emerge at the end of an hour with radios that Mr Garbett hadn't even known were there.

By the time he was ten he had more than a hundred radios, radios of every size, make, and year. Some didn't work at all; these he dismantled. Others produced only static, but that was all right too; he could still switch them on and watch the lights come up behind the names like some kind of miniature simulated dawn. A few of the old radios still worked, and he was addicted to the way the voices grew in volume as the set warmed up, and how the voices always sounded so muffled, so cosy, like people wrapped up against cold weather; though it was the present he was listening to, somehow it always sounded like the past. Other boys his age had model aeroplanes or toy soldiers or guns. He looked down on them. A model aeroplane had had no previous life, a toy soldier had no soul, a gun couldn't talk to you. But a radio.

One Saturday morning he left the house at around midday and set off up Mackerel Street. He'd seen a radio in the window of the Empire of Junk the day before, but the place had been closed. He bought a quarter of Lemon Sherbet Bombs at the candy store on Airdrome Boulevard. With their fizzy white centres they matched the excitement he felt. It was a hot morning. July, it must've been, or August. The streets smelt of simmering green vegetables and gas leaks. It was the kind of weather where air-conditioners bust and old people just evaporated. He walked in the gutter as he always did, pausing every now and then to poke at something with his toe. He wore his white T-shirt and his old jeans and his red baseball cap on back to front. When he reached the Empire he stopped in the doorway. Something was different. It was a strange kind of different, though. Like when someone starts wearing a new pair of glasses or they shave their eyebrows off or something. At first you don't know what it is. Jed squinted down at Mr Garbett and all around him too, and then he realised. Mr Garbett was sitting on a stained green sofa. The leather armchair had gone. Jed eyed the sofa, then he eyed Mr Garbett. Mr Garbett raised his bottle to his pale lips and drank, as if it was the sight of Jed, and not the weather, that made him thirsty.

'Where's the chair gone?' Jed asked.

'Sold it,' Mr Garbett said.

'Didn't realise it was for sale.'

'Everything in here's for sale.'

Jed looked at the bottle in Mr Garbett's hand. 'How much for the beer?'

Mr Garbett smiled faintly on his stained green sofa. 'You know anything about tape recorders?'

'Tape recorders? What's that?'

Mr Garbett stood up. It was the first time he'd ever done that. His belly pushed against the inside of his cardigan. 'I'll show you,' he said.

Jed followed Mr Garbett towards a small room at the back of the store. When he reached the threshold he stopped in his tracks. Inside the room was such a concentration of junk as he'd never seen before. There seemed to be something from every place in the world. You could single out one object and imagine the church or mansion or garage that had once surrounded it. That was the thing about junk.

It had been places, seen things you could only guess at. He put his mother in the doorway and looked at her face and grinned. She'd have a fit.

'Now then,' Mr Garbett said. He bent down and grunted as his belly crushed the breath out of his lungs. He lifted something that looked a bit like a radio on to the table, then he sat down and his eyes swivelled in their slits. 'That there's a tape recorder,' he said.

Jed went and stood next to the table. He stared down at the machine. The top of it looked like a face. Two big round eyes with spokes and an oblong plastic mouth. 'What's it do?'

'You really don't know?'

Jed shook his head.

Mr Garbett handed him a white plastic box on the end of a wire. 'Say something.'

Jed couldn't think of anything.

'Sit down here.' Mr Garbett patted his own knee. 'Easier to think of something sitting down.'

Jed sat on his knee. Mr Garbett smelt like casinos when you walk past their open doors first thing in the morning. Drink and smoke and money that's been through too many hands.

'Now,' Mr Garbett said, 'say something.'

Jed watched him turn a fat white switch. The eyes on the top of the machine began to revolve. A green light glowed.

'Don't know what to say,' Jed muttered.

'That'll do it.' The eyes spun back the other way, stopped, then began to revolve again. Mr Garbett put a hand on Jed's hip. 'Now,' he whispered, 'listen.'

A gritty roaring sound, like the ocean dragging pebbles.

'Hear that?' Mr Garbett said. 'That's the room.'

Jed looked around to see where the roar was coming from, then he heard a small, sullen voice: 'Don't know what to say.'

'What do you think of that?' Mr Garbett said.

Jed knew exactly what he thought. 'That's even better than a radio,' he said, and watched as Mr Garbett's hands fumbled at the buttons on his jeans.

He felt he was spreading outwards, moving outwards fast, like ink being soaked up by a piece of blotting paper. He had no centre and no edges and he was moving outwards smoothly, and there was nothing in his head.

Some time later he heard a voice say, 'Did you like that?' and the voice was disembodied, as if it had come out of the tape recorder.

He opened his eyes. The room had shrunk and turned yellow, but it was piled high with junk he recognised. 'Yes,' he said.

'Really?'

'It was nice.'

'Well,' Mr Garbett said, 'if you don't say nothing about it, maybe it'll happen again.'

'A secret?'

'That's it. A secret.'

Jed nodded and slipped off Mr Garbett's knee. He knew all about secrets. Most of his radios were secrets. One secret more or less didn't make any difference.

'You forgot something,' Mr Garbett said.

Jed turned in the doorway.

Mr Garbett pointed at the tape recorder on the table, but Jed still didn't understand.

'You can have it,' Mr Garbett said.

Jed wasn't used to being given things. 'The tape recorder?'

Mr Garbett smiled. 'I've got hundreds.'

Jed lifted the machine off the table and stood with it in his arms and couldn't think what to say, so he repeated what he'd said before, only with more intensity this time. 'It's better than a radio.' And then he had a moment of clairvoyance. 'It sort of makes my radios dead.'

Mr Garbett nodded. 'Maybe.' He walked Jed to the front of the shop. 'Say you got it from a scrapyard.' He looked around. 'It's the truth, really.'

But Jed never had to say anything. He sneaked it in through his bedroom window, the same way he'd sneaked all his radios in. He hid it under the bed, wrapped in an old curtain.

And then, no more than a couple of weeks later, he came home from school one afternoon to find the radios gone. Every single one of them. A deft glance under the bed told him that she'd missed the tape recorder. That was something. But still. Over one hundred radios. He turned cold inside and something tightened in his head.

'They were garbage, Jed. Most of them didn't even work.'

She had come up behind him, while he'd been staring at the emptiness in his room. He turned slowly. She was fixing her hair up in a soft knot with both hands, so she looked like some kind of vase. If he'd been big enough he would've picked her up and dashed her against the wall. A thousand pieces. No, a million. And no glue, not ever. He took one step forwards and slammed the door in her stupid made-up face.

'Come on, Jed,' she cooed from the other side. 'Don't be like that.' She banged on the wood with the flat of her hand. He knew it was the flat of her hand. She was careful never to scrape her knuckles or break her nails. She was a real beautician. 'Jed?' Her voice had hardened. 'Jed, come on. Don't be boring.'

He sat on the edge of his bed and stared at her through the door. He thought he heard her mutter, 'Little bastard,' and she banged once more, one last time, and then there was silence. Then high-heels across the hallway and the kitchen door clicked shut.

He climbed out of his bedroom window and stamped off up Mackerel Street, his red baseball cap jammed on sideways, as if he was turning left. That woman with the wedges of electric-pink and blue above her eyes. That woman, the beautician. His mother. She'd gone and thrown his radios away. All one hundred and twelve of them. She'd even thrown the Ferguson away, three feet high with wings of polished wood to gather the sound. Two years' work collecting those radios. Two years' love.

He was wearing jeans that concertinaed round his ankles and a black T-shirt that said SUICIDE; he was thinking about changing it to MURDER now. He wedged his hands in his pockets, his thin arms locked and stiff. His head began to buzz like the TV screen when a channel shuts down at night. They call it snow sometimes, but it's nothing like snow. It's nowhere near that peaceful.

She must've been planning it for ages with that nail-polish brain of hers. You'd need a special man to shift one hundred and twelve radios. You'd need a truck. He couldn't believe it. He just couldn't believe it. He tipped his head to the clouds and groaned out loud. An old lady stopped and looked at him, concerned. He glared at her and stamped on up the road, round the corner and into Airdrome Boulevard.

MURDER. That was the answer. Then, when she was dead, he could send her to the embalming studio, plenty of pink and blue, he'd say, don't spare the pink and blue, he'd make her look like she was going to a fucking disco, and then they could put her in one of those viewing theatres on Central Avenue, he didn't know how much it cost, he didn't care, he'd save up. He could see it now:

MURIEL MORGAN
NOW SHOWING
ONE WEEK ONLY

She'd be laid out in her coffin, pink satin it'd be, with blue trimmings, to go with her make-up, maybe some neon too, and there'd be radios all round her, hundreds of radios, all tuned to different stations, all on top volume. He'd surround her with radios. He'd *bury* her in radios.

He walked halfway across the city that day, he walked until night fell. He stood under the harbour bridge and watched the lights come on downtown. He leaned his head back against a pillar and shut his eyes and felt the silver trains shake down through the stone. He'd scattered his rage along a hundred streets and he was almost smiling now. He had a new idea.

The next day he didn't go to school. He went to visit Mr Garbett instead. Mr Garbett was definitely a mistake, he knew that now. One look at him and it was obvious. There was an understanding between them that didn't need any words. And since he had so much in common with this man who smelt like a casino and ruled an empire of junk from a stained green throne, it was only fitting that he should have a part to play in Jed's plan.

'How's the tape recorder?' Mr Garbett asked.

'Great, thanks.'

Mr Garbett shifted on the sofa. 'Sorry, but I haven't got any new radios in.' He grinned. It was one of their private jokes. New radios.

'That's all right,' Jed said. 'I'm not looking for radios any more.'

'Oh?' Mr Garbett gave Jed a curious, almost wounded look.

'My mum chucked them out. The whole lot.'

'Why'd the hell she do that?'

Jed shrugged. 'She said they were dirty.'

Mr Garbett's face slackened. The corners of his mouth drooped. Only one thing could do that to Mr Garbett. The wanton destruction of junk. He took a long draught from his brown bottle, then he let out a soft belch and stared into the road. Finally, and without a change of expression, he said, 'It must've taken her a long time.'

Jed grinned for the first time since it happened. 'Ages, I bet. There were over a hundred.'

'I don't know,' Mr Garbett said. 'Some people.'

He dabbed at one eye with the corner of a handkerchief. For a moment Jed thought he was crying, mourning the passing of the radios, but then he realised: it was just Mr Garbett's eye leaking, like it always did.

'You know that tape recorder?' Jed said. 'Well, I need a longer wire for the mike, maybe about,' and he screwed his face up, thinking, 'about fifty feet long. And I need a smaller mike too. That other one, it's too, I don't know, too clumsy.'

'The wire's no problem,' Mr Garbett said. 'I'm getting some in this week. The mike could take a bit longer.'

Jed dropped into the store at least once a week after that and sometimes he let Mr Garbett take him into the back room and open his jeans and turn him into that slow ink. The memory of the radios was like a sore place on his body that he only felt when he was in a certain position; he had to press it every now and then so he didn't forget. By the end of the month he had the wire and the mike. His mother had found a new man, an embalmer called Adrian who wore grey shoes. The time had come.

He waited until she went to work one morning, then he took out the wire and the new mike from their hiding-place inside the aircondi-tioner in his bedroom. The mike was particularly satisfying; it was round and white, the size of a button, and the top was a minute copper grille that looked like a fly's eye. He ran the wire under his carpet and out into the corridor. So far, so good. The next part was tricky, though. The carpet in the corridor had been secured at the edges with tacks, and he had to prise the tacks loose before he could conceal the wire beneath. It took him almost an hour to run the wire from his bedroom door to his mother's, and most of that time he held his breath, praying that nothing brought her home early. When he opened the door to her room he came to a standstill. The dressing-table peopled by tiny potent bottles, the wall-lights designed to re-semble candles (fake wax drips, flame-shaped bulbs), the double bed fringed with satin dust-ruffles: it gave him the feeling that he was standing in a shrine, that even his presence was sacrilege. He closed his eyes and summoned up the ghosts of his radios. He saw the dawn that came up behind the dial in one, he lingered on the sweeping ocean-liner curves of another. He remembered their names, and heard their voices. He muttered stations to himself like incantations, like curses: Moscow, Brussels, Helsinki. 'Hilversum,' he muttered, 'Reykjavik,' and he saw his radios in the garbage dump, he saw their cases crushed and shattered, their innards ripped out, spilled on the ground, their voices silenced for ever, and when he opened his eyes his mother's room seemed to shrink in the face of his new resolve. Tiny bright explosions pocked the precious air, as if something white-hot had burned holes right through reality. The furniture looked charred at the edges. He noticed the clock beside her bed. Almost eleven-thirty. She sometimes came home for lunch. He had better get on.

He levered up the tacks that held her pale-green carpet flush to the wall and tucked the wire underneath, then he knocked the tacks back into the same holes. It took him twenty minutes to reach the bed. There was really only one place for the mike. He pulled the bed away from the wall and fastened the mike to the back of the headboard with a strip of insulating tape. He pushed the bed against the wall and stood back. After examining the bed from all angles to make sure the wire was invisible, he returned to his room. All set. Now for the trial run. He switched the tape recorder to RECORD and ran back up the corridor to his mother's room. He stood beside her stack of frilly pillows and thought for a moment.

'Testing, testing.' He nodded to himself. That's what they said. But what else? He couldn't remember. 'I hope this works.' He paused, and then fiercely, 'It'd better.'

Back in his own room he wound the tape back and switched to PLAY. Nothing for long seconds, then a rustling, like leaves, then his voice, wrapped up, as if he was talking through cloth. His voice, though. It had worked. He switched the tape recorder off and sat on the floor, his thighs pulled tight against his chest, his chin on his knees.

His mother didn't come home for lunch.

He left the mike taped to the back of the headboard for two weeks. During that time the embalmer came round four times. The first time there was an argument in the bedroom. The embalmer was trying to smooth things over, restore things to normal. But he could only do that with dead bodies, apparently. Something was thrown, something broke. Jed couldn't guess what it was. Probably that blue vase by the window. There was a silence, and then tears. His mother's. It was interesting, but it wasn't what he wanted. The second time nothing happened at all. They just went to sleep. The third time a plane went over right at the crucial moment and ruined everything. He almost gave up. Almost. The fourth time he was in the hall when they came in the front door. It was midnight, and they were both drunk.

'What the *hell* are you doing up?' His mother was wearing a red dress that was stained dark with wine or sweat. She looked the way a rose petal looks when you crush it between finger and thumb. The embalmer hung back, awkward at being observed. White shoes tonight. Pretty fancy. Jed didn't say anything. He just backed into his room and closed the door.

First there was rustling. That would be them kissing, undressing. At least a minute of that. Then five creaks, one after the other, very brisk. The bed, presumably. Then a whimper (his mother) and a grunt (the embalmer). Then voices. Hers first, 'Oh Adrian,' then his, 'Muriel,' then hers again, 'Oh God.' God was three syllables. And then a creak. Not the bed this time. A human creak. The embalmer coming. Bit quick, that. Then, about a minute later, a low flapping rumble followed by a whine as the embalmer, Adrian, began to snore. It was better than he could've expected. It was perfect.

The next day he went to see Mr Garbett and asked whether he could get a copy made. Mr Garbett said he'd take care of it. Jed didn't tell Mr Garbett not to listen to it, and he knew, when Mr Garbett handed the duplicate and the original back a week later, that he had. It didn't matter. Jed doubted whether he'd ever see Mr Garbett again. His days of junk were over.

That night he waited in his room with the tape recorder primed. He looked at his watch. It was six-thirty. She usually got home at around seven. He sat on the edge of his bed and wedged a Lemon Sherbet Bomb in his cheek and turned his head to the street. It had been another hot day. Through the window he could hear the hiss of sprinklers watering small lawns. It wasn't often you could hear the sprinklers. Maybe there was a strike at the airport or something.

It was almost nine when he heard the key turn in the lock. He'd been waiting so long, his heart jumped at the sound. Then he froze. She wasn't alone. He could hear a man's voice. Pop's.

He opened his door and stood in the hall.

'You could at least offer me a cup of coffee,' he heard Pop saying. 'I've been waiting two hours.'

'Nobody asked you to wait, did they?' She was trying to close the door on him, but he was stronger.

'Muriel.' Pop was pleading now. 'One cup of coffee.'

She weakened. 'All right. One cup of coffee and that's it.'

Pop stepped into the light. He'd greased his hair back and he was wearing a clean shirt, but it was no good.

'One cup,' he said, and winked at Jed. He was like one of those salesmen who stick their feet in the door.

Don't you see? Jed wanted to shout. It's no good.

'Your mother and I,' Pop said, 'we're just going to have a little talk.' That wink again. A smirk.

IT'S NO GOOD.

When Pop moved towards the kitchen, he trailed this smell behind him, ashes or rust, old worn-down things, things you normally throw out. Jed was sure his mother could smell it too. Though she had different names for it, of course. She called it weakness, failure, regret.

He went and sat in his room while they had their 'little talk'. He heard the shouting, he heard a plate break. The smell was everywhere, you wanted to hold your nose. No amount of violence or repentance could freshen the air.

And he realised, with a slight shock, that Pop didn't count any more. Pop was just another Adrian. A noise, a pair of feet, an inadequacy. He felt sorry for Pop, but in a distant way, as you might feel sorry for someone on TV. He wanted Pop out of the house, even more than his mother did.

An hour later the kitchen door opened. Jed opened his own door a crack, and listened.

'A second chance, that's all I'm asking.'

'What do you think this is, some stupid game?'

The house shook as the front door banged against the inside wall. Through his window Jed saw Pop stamping off up Mackerel Street, clouding the air with empty threats.

He found his mother standing in the kitchen. Her face had the polished look of a trophy. It was a game, whatever she said, and it looked as if she'd won again. He returned to his room and, leaving the door ajar, turned the tape recorder on. Top volume. And waited.

The tape had only reached the creaking stage when she came and stood in the doorway. 'What's this you're playing?' she asked, light, yet tense, as if she had already guessed.

Jed watched the transparent wheels spin round, one eager, empty, one slow and burdened with knowledge. He watched the slim brown tape unwind, unwind.

When the whimpering began, he looked up into his mother's face. He saw the light shrink in her eyes then, without seeming to move, she unleashed herself, the air a blur of red nails and flailing hands, she was hissing and muttering, she seemed to have eight arms, like that statue that he'd seen in Mr Garbett's store, which Mr Garbett said had come from India. She caught him twice with open-handed blows that made his head buzz like a jam jar of flies, and one of her nails tore the skin at the corner of his mouth, as if he ought to be smiling. He didn't try to back away, he just wrapped his head in his hands and when the beating stopped he slowly took his hands away and peered up at her. She was panting and her arms were fastened against her sides and her

hair had come unpinned and hung in tangled strands across her eyes.
She looked more natural now than ever before. She looked like a witch.
He wanted her to hold him now, he wanted to burn with her, but he
knew it wouldn't happen. And so it was like TV again. Everything was
like TV.

'How could you do that?' she was saying in a strange, flat voice.
'How could you do a thing like that?'

Easy.

'You threw my radios away.'

The embalmer began to snore.

Lunging at the tape recorder, she snatched up the spool and tore
the tape to shreds. When she tired of that she threw it down and
stamped on the top of the tape recorder. Then she bent down and
picked the tape recorder up and hurled it against the wall. It dropped
to the carpet and the casing came away, fractured in two places. There
was a dent in the wall where it had hit.

Jed watched all this impassively, as if he could change channels any
time he pleased. He didn't care what she did. The tape recorder had
already served its purpose, and he had wrapped his spare copy of the
tape in industrial plastic, then he'd locked it inside an old metal
toolbox, and he'd buried the toolbox halfway up the garden on the
right, next to the fence. There was nothing she could do to hurt him.
He felt one side of his mouth grinning where she had cut him. He
watched her turn to him and scrape the hair back out of her eyes.

'You won't do that again,' she said.

He said, 'I don't need to.'

'What d'you mean?'

'I've got a copy of that tape,' he said, 'and if you ever touch any of
my stuff again, I'll send it to Pop.' He paused; it didn't sound enough.
'And the neighbours,' he said. 'And that shop where you work.'

Her eyes were blank now, and her cheeks hung, slack and looped,
from the bones of her face. She turned and walked out of the room.
He heard her bedroom door click quietly shut.

His first taste of revenge. Sweet.

TWO

TWO

THE WOMB BOYS

A light rain was falling on the city, so light it sounded like rats. Jed turned into the alleyway that ran behind the school and stopped to wipe the flecks off his spectacles. Looking up again, through clear glass now, he saw four figures arranged in front of him. Their stillness had an urgency to it and he knew right away that it was him they'd been waiting for.

Three of them perched high on dark-green garbage dumpsters. He knew their names: José PS Mendoza, Scraper O'Malley and Tip Stubbs. The fourth leaned his shoulderblades against the wall, hands folded on his chest. He wore a black leather coat and a moustache. It was Vasco Gorelli. Known as Gorilla, though never to his face. He'd had the moustache since he was ten.

Near silence.

Only the light rain scurrying across the rooftops, and the tss-tss-tss of PS Mendoza's headphones.

It was strange. Normally you couldn't talk to Vasco, you couldn't even get close to him. You had to wait for a summons or an audience. He was like a sort of pope. He had lieutenants – O'Malley, Stubbs, Mendoza – then he had a whole string of runners: Thomas Baby Vail, Slim Jimmy Chung, Cramps Crenshaw and Tip's younger brother, a deaf-mute known as Silence. When you saw Vasco walk down the street you saw the petals of a flower and suddenly a flower seemed strong, a flower seemed dangerous. A small gang, but tight. A flower that closed up for the night. A furled umbrella. And when the rain came, which it did sometimes, one snap, a flick, and the gang sprang open, kept him dry. That was how it worked.

So why the sudden interest?

Jed was used to isolation. His face was like some kind of cul-de-sac. It said NO THROUGH ROAD to most people. Confronted with him, they always turned round, backed away. He wasn't wounded exactly. No, not wounded; not any more. It had planted the seeds of scorn in him. It had bred a curious arrogance. You don't know what you're missing, he would think. If only you knew.

And now this.

Maybe the boys were bored that day. Just lookng for some poor bastard to pick on. And he came along with his pitted skin and his glasses and his knees put on the wrong way round and they thought: This one'll do. Scraper and Tip eyed him from above with a strange, dislocated venom. It was like someone saying, Look, nothing personal, but we're going to kill you now, all right?

Vasco took the cigarette out of his mouth, sent it spinning through the air. One bounce on the wet street. Tss. He pushed away from the wall, hunched his shoulders against the rain. One word was stamped across his back in silver studs: IMMORTAL.

'Christ, Morgan, you're so fucking ugly you're hardly even human.' It was curious, but he made it sound like admiration. It was as if he'd heard about Jed's ugliness and he'd sought it out and it had come up to his expectations.

'I know that,' Jed said. 'I've been told.'

'Who told you?'

'My mother.'

Vasco chipped at a weed with the heel of his boot. 'So is it true what they say about your mother?'

Jed stared at Vasco without blinking. 'What do they say?'

'They say she's a whore.'

Tip joined in. 'Is that true? Is she a whore?'

'They say she fucks people who fuck dead people.' Vasco looked up from the weed he was torturing. 'What about that? Is that true?'

Jed scrutinised them one by one.

PS. Short for Personal Stereo. He'd picked up a pair of headphones somewhere, but he'd never been able to afford a Walkman to plug them into, so he just wore the headphones and made that noise you always hear when you're next to someone who's got one: that tss-tss-tss. PS had been wearing phones for a year now and he could make the noise without even moving his lips.

Scraper. The guinea-pig. Gazing up into the sky, sensing the drizzle on his freckled skin. All Jed could see of Scraper's head was a thick neck and a chin like the toe of a boot. Jed gave himself a knife and drew it calmly across the tight, offered throat and watched blood fountain into the steamy grey air.

Tip was closer, more focused. Leering down from his heap of garbage. Brawny shoulders, swollen eyelids, grease in the wings of his nose. Tip swam freestyle for some city team or other. Big fish, small pool.

They were all, in their different ways, waiting for him to break down: lose his temper, burst into tears, piss himself. But they'd misread his bad skin and his glasses. They'd picked on the wrong person. They simply hadn't understood. He felt almost disappointed. Still, he managed a faint smile.

'She's not as smart as a whore,' he said. 'She doesn't get paid for it.'

He'd delivered the reply in his own time, like a comedian, and it caught all four gang-members off guard. They were too surprised to laugh. They couldn't believe he wasn't defending his mother. His own mother. They wanted to know why. He told them about the radios. They nodded. It made sense to them. Then he casually threw in some stuff about revenge, the tape of his mother, the grunts, the whimpers, and he saw a kind of awe appear. Fear, he sensed, was present in this awe of theirs. Then he knew they were his. Though he'd pretend to be theirs, of course.

With that one story he paid his entrance fee. Suddenly he was one of the Womb Boys, as they were known – the gang that had declared war on Moon Beach, war on death. On long quiet nights, camped round a fire in some vacant lot in Mangrove East, Vasco would turn to him and say, 'Tell us the story of the radios.' And he would tell it. And afterwards the silence would come down and Vasco would hand him a beer. People still looked at him, but their looking was different now, it seemed tempered with respect. He was going through a phase of Cinnamon Hearts. They lasted a long time and they turned the entire inside of your mouth red. This only added to his strange notoriety.

One morning Vasco took him down to Moon River at low tide. Among the slippery rocks, the reeling gulls, the sludge, this was where Vasco did his thinking. Idly they combed the mudbanks for a necklace or a watch, something they could pawn at Mr Franklin's establishment on Central Avenue. Just for a moment, as he prodded and jabbed at one particular rock with his sharp stick, Vasco looked younger, looked the age he actually was, an age that Tip and Scraper were never allowed to see. The three tombstones on his left shoulder, that was how old people thought he was. Jed looked into the tattoos as if they were windows and suddenly, standing in the stench of the river, he had the feeling that he could see into Vasco, see what was coming.

Then Vasco straightened up. 'Tell me something,' he said. 'How did you get the idea?'

Jed shrugged. 'I don't know. It just came to me.'

'You're dangerous,' Vasco said. 'You need watching.'

'Lucky I'm on your side then, isn't it?'

Vasco scooped up a handful of river-mud and flung it in Jed's direction. Jed ducked and, grinning, showed Vasco his crimson devil's mouth. But the grin faded as his thoughts turned to his mother, the last four years, their uneasy truce. She was still bringing men home with her, but defiantly now, as if she wanted him to witness it and disapprove. To Jed, these men of hers were all one man, their boots shifting on the carpet, their bodies too big for the rooms; they reminded him, curiously enough, of his brother, Tommy. He stared at them and ignored them, both at the same time. He'd become an expert at the look. Ten years later it would serve him well.

'It's not easy living there.' He took Vasco's stick and jabbed at a rock.

Vasco looked at him sideways. 'Why don't you move out?'

'Where to?'

'Plenty of room at my place.'

It was winter and the air was sharp. Everything you looked at seemed cut out with scissors. The light fell in blue-and-yellow twists on the surface of the river. Jed could see Sweetwater on the far bank, a plane scorching the air as it lifted over the rooftops. He could almost feel the house shake. He could almost smell the nail polish.

He looked at Vasco. 'What about your parents?'

'I haven't got any.'

'You must live with someone.'

'My sister, but she's hardly ever there. Otherwise there's only Mario and Reg. But they're both senile.'

'Senile? What's that?'

'Means when you're nearly dead. You're still alive, but only just – '

Jed stopped listening. He was thinking of the men who were all one man doing one thing. He was remembering his mother's face in her dressing-table mirror. He was imagining her toss his radios casually into oblivion. And he knew then that Vasco was right. But still something reached across the river, something stretched out like arms and tried to claw him back. He didn't know what it was. He took a step backwards, slipped on the mud and almost fell.

'Course there won't be anyone for you to record fucking. My sister does all her fucking at her boyfriend's. And Mario and Reg, they've probably never fucked in their lives.' Vasco spread his hands. 'So what do you say?'

Jed nodded, grinned. 'Does it need saying?'

Vasco bought a bottle of vodka to celebrate and they drank it in the old sailors' graveyard in Mangrove South. This was where the funeral business had first put down its roots. Over the wall, between two warehouses, Jed could just make out the Witch's Fingers, four long talons of sand that lay in the mouth of the river. Rumour had it that, on stormy nights a century ago, they used to reach out, gouge holes in passing ships, and drag them down. Hundreds of wrecks lay buried in that glistening silt. The city's black heart had beaten strongly even then. There was one funeral director, supposedly, who used to put lamps out on the Fingers and lure ships to their doom. Times had changed. There hadn't been a wreck for years, and all the parlours had moved downtown (their old premises had been converted into speedboat showrooms, fishing-tackle stores), but he could see that, for Vasco, the graveyard might have peculiar significance.

Drunk for the first time in his life, Jed saw Vasco with absolute clarity, as if Vasco was outlined in mercury. Vasco was leaning against a stone, eyes shut, chin tipped, teeth bared. Then his head came down and his eyes opened wide and they were like the windshield of a car that's never been anywhere. No record of any insects or moisture or dust. They were so wiped clean. Brutal without meaning to be, brutal and vague. It was something Jed knew about, knew by instinct, it was a quality that he possessed himself. But Vasco didn't seem to know about it at all. He just had it. He was the dreamer who kills people in his sleep.

The next day Jed packed a small bag while his mother was at work. Just before he left he took a pen and a piece of paper and sat down at the breakfast bar. 'I've gone to stay with a friend,' he wrote. 'Don't worry about me.'

Wishful thinking. He was pretty sure that relief would be her first reaction. One less blemish in her life. He wondered, as he folded the paper in half and taped it to the TV screen, whether Pop had left a note when he walked out on her.

It was pure chance that Nathan ever got to know Tip. The city had worked hard to keep them apart. Nathan grew up in Blenheim, a garden suburb on the west shore. Tip, on the other hand, came from the east, some housing project way past Z Street. Definitely the wrong end of the alphabet. Though their swimming styles were just as diverse – Nathan slipped through the water, leaving hardly a crease behind; Tip thrashed it into an angry froth – it was the water that brought them together. They both swam for a team known as the Moon Beach Minnows. They trained three evenings a week in the outdoor pool on Sunset Drive, swimming lap after lap while Marshal, the team coach, patrolled the poolside in his maroon sweatsuit and his snow-white sneakers, booming their times through a rolled-up copy of the sports paper. Between them, they won most of the junior competitions.

One Wednesday, in practice, Nathan raced Tip over one hundred metres and beat him by almost five seconds. He touched the curved tiles at the end of the pool and, rolling on to his back, watched the planes float down through the soft brown sky. The margin of his victory surprised him. His time had been good, but not that good. Tip heaved his hard white body out of the pool and stood with his towel draped round his shoulders. Then he turned his head to one side and spat clear through the wire-mesh fence fifteen feet away. Part habit, part disgust. Nathan grinned. Somehow Tip never left any spit hanging on the wire, it always seemed to soar right into the darkness that lay beyond.

'I saw you, Stubbs,' Marshal bellowed.

Tip nodded. 'Sorry.'

Down in the pool Nathan still had a grin on his face. Tip noticed it, and winked. Maybe they came from different parts of town, but they both knew an old woman when they saw one.

Later that night Nathan left the building just ahead of Tip. While Nathan unlocked his bicycle, Tip stood on the steps, his towel still coiled around his neck, his lips grey in the sodium lights. Nathan could smell the chlorine on his skin.

'So how come you always ride?' Tip said. 'Most people, someone comes for them.'

Nathan shrugged. 'I like to ride.' It wasn't strictly true. He had no choice. There simply wasn't anyone who could've picked him up. Dad hardly ever left the house, and Fosca, the new au pair girl, didn't know how to drive.

'Where d'you live?'

'Blenheim.'

'Blenheim? Jesus. Long ride.' Tip must've known this already. He was just checking. 'So what's your old man do?'

He'd be expecting millionaire or something. Mention Blenheim, that's what people always thought.

'He doesn't do anything,' Nathan said.

Tip pinched his nose between finger and thumb, flicked his hand at the wall, and then sniffed. 'What d'you mean, he doesn't do anything?'

'He doesn't do anything. He can't. He's disabled.'

'Yeah?'

'Yeah.'

Tip looked at the ground, then he looked at Nathan again, sidelong. 'What kind of disabled?'

Tip was trying to look casual, but Nathan could see he was curious. An old man who was screwed up, that was credentials. It was like that plastic grown-ups had. Amex, Visa, Mastercard. It said something about you, it got you into places.

'He's only sort of got about half of each lung,' Nathan said, 'and he's had most of his ribs cut out.'

'Yeah?'

'Yeah, and he's got an orange disc in his car. Means he can park anywhere.'

Tip nodded. 'Cool.'

Nathan almost pinched his nose between finger and thumb, as Tip had done, but he thought he might get it wrong. He just sniffed instead. 'What's your old man do?'

'He doesn't do anything either.'

'How come?' Nathan said. 'Not disabled, is he?'

This would probably have started a fight if he'd said it a week ago. Now it drew a slack grin out of Tip. 'No,' he said. 'He used to work in the docks. Got laid off a couple of months back.'

'I'm sorry.' Nathan chipped at a weed with his shoe. He hoped it looked sort of sympathetic.

'Yeah, well.' Tip stared off in the direction of the football field. 'I got to be going. See you around.'

The next week, after training, Tip asked him if he wanted to go eat. He hesitated. The nights he went swimming, Dad always waited till he got home and then they ate supper together. But he couldn't say that to Tip, it wouldn't make any sense, so he just nodded.

'There's a pizza joint in the neighbourhood,' Tip said. 'We could walk.'

'Sure.' Nathan had never had pizza before. Dad didn't approve of it.

They didn't talk much on the way. Just the ticking of Nathan's wheels and a flat ring every time Tip swung his damp towel at a streetlamp. The place Tip knew was a biker's hang-out called Pete's Pizza. They sat on stools by the window and watched the bikes rip past the open doorway. The street seemed lit by the flare of a match, and it was loud with cars and screaming. Tip ordered two medium Cokes and a nine-inch Tex-Mex Special, with extra pepperoni. It was like a foreign language, a foreign country. And yet Nathan couldn't help stealing glances at the clock. And every time he looked he could picture exactly what Dad would be doing. Seven-thirty: Dad would be sitting down to supper. Seven-forty-five: Dad would be biting his cornflakes up one hundred times. Eight: Dad would be swallowing his pills. Nathan slid his eyes in Tip's direction. Swollen eyelids, grey lips. Hair that lay flush against his skull like animal pelt. Dad would be worried sick.

Tip caught him looking. 'You got to be somewhere?'

Nathan shook his head. 'No.' He took a bite of pizza and spoke through it. 'This pizza's good.'

Tip nodded. He ate like he swam. He was halfway through his third slice before Nathan had even finished his first, and he was talking too – about his old man who was always on the drink these days, about the swimming trophies they were going to win, about the gang he was in.

'The Womb Boys,' he said. 'You heard of us?'

Nathan hadn't.

'Blenheim.' Tip put scorn into the name. 'Might as well live on the moon.' He explained that Vasco made the rules. Vasco was their president. 'You know Vasco.' It wasn't a question. Everyone knew Vasco.

Nathan had only seen him once. Standing by a car in an alley near school. Black leather coat with IMMORTAL across the shoulder-blades. Face the shape of a guitar. Moustache.

'Sometimes we break into places and rip stuff off and sell it,' Tip explained. 'That's fundraising. Other times we just kick back, drink vodka.' He offered Nathan the last piece of pizza, then bit into it when Nathan shook his head. 'I don't know,' he said. 'Basically what we do's sort of political, I guess.'

Nathan nodded. But it was eagerness. 'What d'you mean?'

'It's what Vasco says. He says we've been born in a place where people come to die. He says he's had enough. He's declared war on Moon Beach. That's what WOMB stands for, see. War On Moon Beach.'

Nathan was beginning to understand.

'Like about a week ago,' Tip went on. 'Vasco picks up a paper on a train and reads something about a new funeral parlour that was going up in Carol Park.' He grinned. 'It went up all right. In smoke.'

'You burned it down?'

'Only the crematorium.' Tip's grin stretched wide across his face.

'You burned down the crematorium?'

But Tip wouldn't say anything else. He was one of the Womb Boys. Probably he was sworn to secrecy.

When Nathan walked in through the back door, he found Dad making his tea for the night. The clock in the kitchen said eight-thirty-five. He was over an hour and a half late.

'Where on earth have you been, Nathan?' Dad said. 'I've been worried about you.'

'I just went for something to eat. With one of the people on the swimming team.' Nathan kissed Dad on the cheek, then he began to undo his anorak.

'You smell funny.'

'We had pizza.'

'Pizza? Who did you have pizza with?'

'Nobody special. His name's Tip.'

Dad screwed his Thermos shut and dried the top. 'I just hope you're not getting in with the wrong people.'

Vasco lived in Mangrove Heights, on a bluff overlooking the river. The first time Jed saw the house, he couldn't help thinking of the Empire of Junk. Towers jostled with gables, beams with columns. Gargoyles leered from the eaves, tongues sharp as the heads of arrows, eyes like shelled eggs. The front garden had been planted with all kinds of trees, so the house seemed to skulk. The path to the front door crackled with dead leaves. He could smell plaster, the inside of birds' nests, river sewage.

'I should've been born in a place like this,' Jed said, but Vasco was opening the door and didn't hear.

Vasco shared the house with Mario and Reg, his two great-uncles, and Rita, his sister. Rita was sixteen. She had a boyfriend who drove a dented white Chevrolet. She spent most nights at his place. Mario was almost eighty years old. He had the high, sloping forehead of someone from history. A Roman emperor, something like that. He had white cropped hair and ears you could've caught butterflies in. He spent all his time in a wheelchair. 'There's nothing wrong with his legs,' Vasco said. 'It's just that, now the wheel's been invented, he doesn't see the point of walking. He thinks walking's out of date.'

On the first evening Vasco and Jed were drinking beer on the porch when the front door opened and Mario rolled across the bare boards of the verandah and parked in a square of late sun. He sat in his maroon wheelchair, one hand cupped to his ear.

'What's he doing?' Jed asked.

Mario looked down at Jed. 'Listen.' And he waited a few moments, his hand still cupped to his ear, and then he said, 'Did you hear that?'

'What?' Jed said.

Mario smiled. 'Money.'

On their way down to the pool hall that night, Vasco told Jed what he knew about Mario. Mario studied law at the university and, during his twenties, he built up an extremely successful practice. In a city like Moon Beach, there was never a shortage of business for a good lawyer, especially one like Mario who'd wisely decided to specialise in wills and probates. He'd also been something of an entrepreneur. While still practising law, he'd run a hearse-rental agency. Then, later, he'd bought into a handkerchief factory in Baker Park. Their most famous innovation was the funeral handkerchief, a plain white cotton handkerchief with a black border. Not long afterwards he patented the first black-edged tissue. He'd made millions, apparently, though nobody knew what he'd done with the money. His only extravagance had been to install an elevator in the house, so he could move between floors without getting out of his wheelchair.

'So what did he mean this evening about hearing money?' Jed asked.

'It's his factory across the river. He claims he can hear the money being made.' Vasco looked at Jed and shrugged. 'I told you. The guy's senile.'

It suddenly occurred to Jed that he hadn't heard anything about the other great-uncle, Reg Gorelli. Vasco showed him a photo of a skinny man with big ears and a handlebar moustache.

'He's religious,' Vasco said, 'locks himself in his room. You'll probably never see him.'

The next night Jed sat next to Mario and strained to hear something. A coin, anything. Once he heard a clinking that could've been loose

change, but then the woman from next door walked past with her dog
on a metal lead. In any case, Mario wasn't listening to loose change.
He was more interested in bills. The larger the denomination, the
better. Jed would never forget the night when, just before nightfall,
the last light catching on his white stubble, Mario turned to him and
whispered, 'Listen. Hear that? Hundred-dollar bill.'

Vasco had inherited the same ears. Scooped out at the top and
tilted forwards, as if they'd been thrown on a potter's wheel. But what
was it that Vasco heard? Jed wished he could record it and play it
back. Would it be sad, like the voices of whales? Or would it screech
at you, like the brakes on subway cars sometimes? On second thoughts,
maybe he didn't want to know.

One Saturday night he was sitting in the kitchen making labels for his
tapes. It was late and the house was quiet. All the lights off upstairs
and Rita out somewhere. He had made a tape of Mario. There was
one classic bit where Mario said, 'Listen, hear that?' and Jed said,
'No, what is it?' and Mario said, 'Money,' and then there was absolute
silence. He'd thought of playing it to Mario, to prove you couldn't
hear money, but then he realised it wouldn't prove anything. The
silence was the same silence. Mario would hear money in it.

Suddenly the kitchen door crashed open. It was Vasco. He stood
in the centre of the room, panting.

'Why don't you use an axe next time?' Jed said.

Then he saw the rips in the knees of Vasco's jeans. And the palms
of his hands, red and black. Blood and gravel.

'I got run over,' Vasco said.

Jed stared at him. 'What?'

'I fucking got run over.' Vasco didn't seem to believe it himself.
He was sitting with his hands held out in front of him, palms upwards,
as if testing for rain.

Then he turned and stared at Jed, and all the skin seemed to slip
down his face. 'Scraper's dead.'

'What?'

'They wanted me, but I got out the way. They got Scraper instead.'
His face began to tighten again.

'Who wanted you?'

'I didn't hear it coming. I just didn't fucking hear it.' Vasco kicked
the fridge twice, denting the door.

'Who was it?'

Vasco just stared at him. 'Who do you think?'

It was only then that Jed realised the full extent of Vasco's obsession. It was death that was after him. It was death, of course. After all, you couldn't declare war on death without expecting a bit of retaliation, could you?

It took Jed almost two hours to dig the gravel out of Vasco's hands. For the last twenty minutes he worked with a needle, the tip blackened in a flame. And when he dabbed iodine into the wounds, Vasco sizzled through his white lips, the noise of a branding iron on flesh.

The next day Vasco showed Jed where it had happened. Both his hands were bound, and blunt as the heads of snakes. Dark spots of blood seeping through from the palms, as if he was some kind of risen Christ. Which in a way he was that morning. Down the hill and into Omega. This was dockland. Old warehouses, uneven streets. One narrow strip of sunlight running down ι.e gutter. The rest in shadow. Parked trucks glittering and clumsy. Winches dipping like the beaks of birds.

'Look,' and Vasco had to punch the air because he couldn't point, 'this is it.'

The skidmarks showed as two loose S-shapes scorched on the tarmac. Vasco walked over, stood in the crook of one of them.

'Scraper's death,' he said.

Jed tried standing there too, and felt an odd sensation. It was as if a shadow had slipped through his body. A different kind of shadow, though. The kind of shadow that the shadow in the street would've been frightened of. He saw Scraper laid out on an embalming table, he saw the blur of ginger hair on Scraper's forearms. Like they were going too fast. But not any more. He heard knives. They sounded like loose change. He shivered.

'You were lucky, Vasco.' He put all this brightness that he didn't feel into his voice. He wanted to be lifted up.

But Vasco wasn't listening to him. He was gazing back along the street. Maybe he heard the car again. Or not again, but for the first time. The way he should've heard it the night before. When he turned to Jed he seemed to have been thinking all the way round something. He was tired, but he was sure. 'They couldn't have killed me. It's not my time.'

'Could you hear it coming?' Jed asked him.

Vasco swung back to face him. 'What?'

'Your death,' Jed said. 'You reckon you could hear it coming?'

'What the fuck are you talking about, Jed?'

Jed turned away. They were standing on the moment of collision, the sun was high and white, and three men were shouting at the end of the street. That was all the world was. A high white sun, some tyre marks, three men shouting. Sometimes it seemed as if he'd always been very old. People said that time lasted for ever when you were young. That was lies. Lies and rosy spectacles. His spectacles had steel frames and time was those tattoos on Vasco's arm. They were more like time than any clock. Once, in the Empire Of Junk, he'd seen an hour-glass. Now that came closest to the truth. Except you could turn it upside down and start again. So that was lies too. The sand should run out the first time, run right out. Once, and once only. Time wasn't outside you, it was inside. What was time for Scraper? Thirteen and a bit years, that's what it was. Time was something that went bad, like fruit. To be used before it was all used up. Though, for most people, the only way to live was to deny that. As Vasco was doing now. And Jed suddenly realised, under that high white sun, on the day after Scraper died; he realised that everyone was scared. His mother was scared. Old Mr Garbett was scared. Even Vasco was scared.

Though there he was, standing on the street, the word IMMORTAL flashing on his coat like a gauntlet thrown to fate. And he was saying something. 'I guess you'll be there to record it when it happens,' he was saying, 'won't you, Jed?'

TOMBSTONE TATTOOS

Dad was lying in bed, propped on his seven pillows, when Nathan walked in. A bottle of eucalyptus oil stood in a basin of hot water in the corner of the room.

'It should be ready by now,' Dad said, 'but you'd better test it first.'

Nathan moved over to the washbasin. It was one of the holy objects, this bottle of oil. It was ancient, made of ribbed green glass, green as seaweed. It had six sides and a cork stopper. Dad must've lost the original top. He'd found a cork that almost fitted and then he'd whittled it down. Now, years later, it looked as if it belonged.

The oil was fine: not too hot, not too cold. He let the water out of the basin and brought the bottle over to the bed. Dad took off his nightclothes, the blue sweater with the holes in, the torn pyjama jacket, and lay face down, his head turned sideways on the pillows. He flinched as the oil ran across his back, then he relaxed and said, 'It's all right.'

It had been hard to touch Dad the first time. Everything looked so injured that he couldn't work out where to start. Dad had sensed his hesitation. 'Just be gentle,' he said. 'Do the shoulders first.' That was a good thing to say. There was nothing wrong with his shoulders. The damage only began further down. One side of his body sagged where the ribs had been cut away, so his spine seemed strangely marooned. The scars shone like pink wax. You could still see the holes left by the hypodermic needles when they'd drained the fluid out of his lungs. The needles were so big, Dad had told him once, that you could actually see the ends.

The funny thing was, he didn't *look* disabled. If you'd seen him walking along the street you wouldn't've noticed anything unusual. There were no obvious signs or clues. No crutches, for instance. No wheelchair. No, it wasn't until you saw him naked that you realised the full extent of the damage. Perhaps not even then. You still couldn't see the lungs. If you watched him closely you could see that he breathed a bit quicker than most people, like a bird, Nathan had always thought, but how many people looked that closely? Dad only had half of one lung and a third of the other. Something like that, anyway. He couldn't fly in planes or swim underwater. He had to avoid elevators, phone booths, cellars. All those places could kill him. Even bad weather could kill him. That was why everything was so dangerous. That was why he had to be so careful.

Dad sighed. 'That's good. Just there.'

Nathan worked the warm oil into the shoulders.

'You've got the same touch as your mother.'

Your mother. He always said that. It made her sound so far away, so high up. It was like your excellency, your honour. Your mother.

But Dad's thoughts had taken a different turning. 'Did I ever tell you how we came to live here?'

'No.'

Nathan smiled to himself. He knew how much Dad looked forward to having his back done, how much it helped, but he also sometimes suspected that it was just an excuse, a chance for Dad to talk to him.

'Your grandmother had just gone into hospital and I'd just come out.' Dad paused, remembering. 'She told us we could have her house. She said she wouldn't be needing it any more.'

Nathan knew this part of the story. His grandmother had put herself in a mental home, that whole side of the family were a bit mad, apparently, and she'd given them the house for nothing. He prompted Dad. 'Then what happened?'

'It was spring,' Dad began, and his voice turned dreamy as he reached back into the past.

He drove up the coast with Kay, his wife of seven months, beside him. Such happiness: he felt it so acutely, it had almost seemed like pain. There was no highway in those days, only an old switchback road. In the dips you found towns, as secret and intact as fossils, towns with names like Peacehaven and Marble Bay; from the rises you could see ships inching along the horizon, and waves so far away they looked, he remembered Kay saying, 'like the creases on your knuckles'.

When they reached High Head they bought ice-creams from a van that was playing 'Moon River' (and there the river, magically, was, hundreds of feet below and to the east), the melody all cracked and jangly and slow, and then they crossed smooth grass to the precipice, peered down from behind a low wire fence, and there was the famous lighthouse, hoops of red and white, it must've been sixty feet high, but it looked like a toy, and he said, 'People come here to jump,' and

Kay took his arm and pressed her cheek against his shoulder and said, 'We're so lucky,' not to have a reason to, he thought she meant, not to even think of it, the misery that might bring you here, though he could never be sure with Kay, she took off in such strange directions sometimes, words seemed to mean different things to her, it was as if she had her own personal dictionary.

They must've stood there for, oh, in his memory it took up more room than some whole years, and then she broke away from him and ran off down the path, and he called out, 'Careful, Kay, be careful,' and he went after her, but he couldn't run, you see, all those years in hospital, they'd sucked the running out of him. When he caught up with her at last, she was standing three feet from the edge in her black ski-pants, they were the fashion then, and her cream wool sweater, rising and falling with her breathing, but three feet from the edge! and there was no fence now, why did she like to scare him so? He took her in his arms, and he kissed the side of her neck and behind her ear, and then he kissed her on the lips, he breathed her in as deeply as his damaged lungs allowed, as if those were his last moments with her, as if he was already beginning to lose her, and he felt he'd never be close enough, even naked, making love, his skin on hers, their bodies joined like hands in prayer, pressed together all the way along, even bellies, even knees, even then he'd never be close enough. Perhaps that was true for everyone, but when he saw her run along the edge like that he sensed the recklessness in her, it had been there all along, but now it frightened him. He had this sudden premonition, that she might leave him behind, alone, but he kept the premonition hidden, he just pulled her tighter to him, his arms were still strong, he pulled her tight against him, so tight that she cried out, 'Jack, stop,' and she was laughing, 'Jack, you'll break me.'

Listening to all the happiness, happiness that had actually produced him, Nathan had felt lulled, comforted, but suddenly the vision of Dad holding his wife, that love and worry, it mirrored his own too closely: his fingers faltered.

Dad noticed. 'Are you tired?'

'A bit.'

'You stop then.' Dad sat up and, reaching behind him, pulled his nightclothes on.

Nathan put the green bottle back in its place on the glass shelf above the washbasin. He wanted to hold Dad tight and stop him dying. He didn't want to be left behind, with everything to do. He just hoped he died first. One silent jet looped through the room. Or almost silent. A sound like tyres in rain. He ran the hot tap fast and reached for the soap.

'Are you all right, Nathan?'

'Yes. I'm fine.'

'Nothing's worrying you?'

The water was almost too hot for his hands. He shook his head. 'No.'

'If you're worried about something, you'll tell me, won't you?'

He nodded. He switched the tap off, dried his hands.

'Thank you for doing my back.'

He turned at last and smiled at the sight of Dad propped on seven pillows in his ragged clothes.

'That's all right,' he said.

The day before Scraper's funeral Vasco took Jed with him to the tattoo parlour. 'You'll meet Mitch,' he said as they jumped a bus on Central Avenue. 'Mitch does the best tombstones in town.'

Central Avenue had always been Jed's favourite street. As its name suggested, it ran straight as an arrow through the heart of the city. Aloof in the west, accustomed to the tick-tock of high-heels and the trickle of limo tyres, it hit mid-town and slummed it, movie-theatres, fast-food stands and go-go bars, neon and slang, then it moved further east, turning sullen and jangly, stained with cheap wine and bad blood, only to end its life under the concrete pillars that supported the Moon River Bridge. Mitch's tattoo parlour was just west of here, in a section known as the Strip. Wedged between a sex cinema and a liquor store, it had a window that was opaque, pasted over with skulls and knives and snakes. The sign above the door said TATTOO CITY in old cracked gold paint that reminded Jed of circuses.

He followed Vasco inside. Mitch was sitting in the back of the store, trying to prise the grease out from under his nails with a key.

Vasco stood in front of Mitch. 'Slow day.'

Mitch winced as he dug too deep. Then he looked up, saw who it was. 'Christ, someone else dead?'

'You shouldn't complain,' Vasco said. 'Someone dies, you get to do another stone. You do another stone, you make money.'

Mitch tossed the key onto the table and stood up. 'Real big shot, aren't you?' He looked at Jed. 'Who's this?'

'This is Jed,' Vasco said. 'He records stuff.'

Mitch left his eyes on Jed, but absent-mindedly, the way you might leave your hand in your pocket. Something Jed learned about Mitch the first time he saw him: Mitch didn't ask many questions; either he knew already, or he didn't want to know. Something he recognised too: the use of silence.

Mitch moved over to the table that held his instruments. He'd worn his jeans so long they looked polished. His hair hung down his back in lank tails, like the seaweed under the pier.

'He's a blackmailer,' Vasco added.

'Only when it's really necessary,' Jed explained.

'Necessary?' Mitch said. 'Jesus, what a pair.'

Vasco grinned at Jed.

Mitch turned round, the needle-gun in one hand, the spray in the other. 'So you want this tombstone or what?'

Vasco sat in a chair, his bare arm braced against the edge of the table. He already had three tombstones. Lucky (obviously he hadn't been, not very), Jack Frost and Motorboy, their names in blue block-capitals, no dates. Now Scraper.

Mitch worked without speaking. There was only the buzz of the needle-gun and the hiss of the disinfectant spray. About halfway through, a guy in a sleeveless leather jacket walked in. He showed Mitch his tattoo: a hooded man with a double-sided axe.

Mitch only took his eyes off Vasco's tombstone for a moment. 'It's shit. Who did it?'

'I got it when I was drunk. Can you fix it?'

'Yeah, I can fix it. For a hundred bucks I'll put in some background too. Make it look real killer.'

'What about tomorrow?'

Mitch nodded. 'Don't come in here drunk.'

The guy grinned foolishly and left.

Mitch looked at Vasco. 'There are too many of those.'

Otherwise it was silence. Homage to Scraper.

Vasco didn't speak to Jed until they left the place. Then he said, 'One day I'll probably be covered with tombstones.' He turned to Jed, laughing. 'One of them'll probably be yours.'

Jed looked at him, just looked at him.

Vasco pushed him in the chest, trying to jog the needle that was saying the same thing over and over. 'No need to get all fucked up about it. It was only a joke.' He ducked into a doorway, lit a cigarette, then stepped out on to the sidewalk again.

Jed watched the wind bend the smoke out of Vasco's mouth and off into nothing. So you're going to wear my tombstone, he thought. So tell me something. Who's going to wear yours? Tell me that. Don't talk to me about I'm fucked up.

He looked through the tattoos the way you might look through church windows, but before he could see Vasco all laid out like some martyr carved in stone he shook the picture loose and hit Vasco on his arm, the arm that wasn't a graveyard, hit Vasco so hard that he fell against a store-front and the glass bulged inwards, creaked and almost gave.

'What's that for?' Vasco said.

Jed grinned. 'Let's go get a beer or something.'

Scraper's funeral was discount. Special offer. Free silver crucifix pendant thrown in. You could always tell. It took place in one of the cemeteries that ringed the northern suburbs. You could see them from the freeway, bare hills covered with a stubble of crosses, bleak places even in the famous Moon Beach sunshine. The poor were buried there. The lost. The forgotten.

The Womb Boys arrived early and sat on stones at the top of the slope. Vasco had taken his bandage off, and his memorial to Scraper looked painful; the new bright blue of the tattoo had raised a raw red welt (though, according to Mitch, this only ever lasted a day or two). They watched the hearse trickle along the gravel avenue. Bald tyres, dented fender. A thin squeal as it braked. Vasco scowled and lit another cigarette.

Two men in moth-eaten black lifted Scraper's coffin on to a stainless-steel trolley and wheeled it across the grass. They looked like waiters in a cheap restaurant. And then the ultimate insult. Scraper was buried at the bottom of a slope. He wouldn't even have a view. There were only two people there who hadn't been paid. A man in a brown suit and a woman in a veil. Scraper's parents. They looked guilty and ashamed, as if death was a crime their son had committed.

'For Christ's sake.' Vasco stood up suddenly. 'This isn't a funeral,' he said, 'this is a charade.'

That night Jed and Vasco sat up late, working on a plan of revenge. It was Jed's first active contribution and he was gratified to find that Vasco backed almost every one of his suggestions. The following evening Vasco called a meeting in the house on Mangrove Heights. The gang assembled in the dining-room at nine o'clock. Tall white candles burned in the two silver candelabras that Tip had stolen from a church the week before. Mario rolled overhead like distant thunder.

Vasco rose to his feet.

'This time we're taking extreme measures. This time,' and he smiled grimly, 'it's Gorilla warfare.'

So he'd heard the whispers with those ears of his. So he knew his name. Laughter shook the room.

'What've you got in mind?' Cramps Crenshaw asked.

Vasco passed his hand across a candle's flame, then looked down at his blackened palm. 'Another fire.'

Two nights later they met outside the construction site of a new funeral complex in Meadowland. It was on the far side of the river, just south of Sweetwater. Standing by the security fence, Jed suddenly remembered this area as fields. When he was young, Pop had taken him for walks here and, together, they'd given names to things. There was an old dead tree that Pop had called Winchester because it was the vague shape of a rifle and because he couldn't be called Winchester himself. Jed peered through the fence at the levelled ground, he peered at the yellow bulldozers, the colour of cowardice, and suddenly he felt the anger Vasco felt. A different root, but just as strong.

After appointing a sentry to keep watch, Vasco scaled the fence. He climbed close to the support stanchion so the wire mesh didn't sag or buckle. The rest of the gang followed, dropping lightly into the weeds on the other side. Dark mounds lay on the ground. Cramps Crenshaw had done a thorough job of poisoning the dogs. Vasco began to hand out pieces of paper. Every piece was printed with the same slogan: DEATH TO THE FUNERAL BUSINESS.

'What are these?' Tip asked.

'They're curses,' Vasco explained. 'Look.' Running into the nearest building, he climbed a series of ladders to the roof. He held up a piece of paper and let it drop into the gap between the still-unfinished walls. 'This building is now damned.'

When the curses had been sealed into the walls of every building on the site, he gathered the gang around him once again. 'Who's got the lighter fluid?'

PS stepped forwards and handed Vasco a small yellow can.

'We're only doing one,' Vasco said.

'One?' PS sounded disappointed.

'One.' Vasco's eyes moved across the faces of his gang. 'The power's in the curses.' he said. 'Burning a house down, that's just our calling card.'

It took PS a moment to see it. The things Vasco came out with, it often took his gang a while to see. Then PS nodded and he fitted his phones over his ears and his music started up.

They watched as Vasco climbed high into the rafters of the main office and sprayed the new blond wood with lighter fuel. He lit the end of the trail of fuel the same way you light a fuse. The central roofbeam was a sudden ribbon of fire. It made the same sound a clean sheet makes when it's snapped out over a bed.

Vasco slid back down the ladders, dropping the last ten feet. He stood in the front entrance, wiping his hands on his coat. Sombre now, he surveyed the faces of his gang.

'This is for Scraper,' he said.

The gang responded, and one word was stamped on the quiet air. 'Scraper!'

Then they were running towards the fence, the rest of the curses spilling from Vasco's hands, streaming out behind him, scattering across the mud. They split into groups, according to plan, just as the sirens started in the distance.

Two hours later each one of the gang-members reported in by phone, as arranged. There'd been no arrests. Lying in bed that night, Jed played the whole thing back. One picture stuck. It was Vasco walking out of the door in his leather coat, the roof on fire above his head.

He woke early the next morning. It was still cool, but he opened the window and, leaning on the ledge, looked down at the river. A ship slid by. Then another. Years later, in exile, he would watch the railway trucks from his hotel, and it would sink a well in him, and he would taste the same calm water.

One night Nathan woke and he was falling. He landed at the bottom of a flight of stairs. It was dark. He reached out, touched a wall. It felt like brick. This was the second time it had happened. The other time he hadn't woken up. He'd just walked round the house turning all the taps on and Dad had walked round after him and turned them off again. He wasn't at home now, though. It didn't feel like home. It was too cold. Too big. He sat still on the cold floor. He tried to work out where he was.

There was a bitter smell. Like metal. No, like oil. And slowly he put it together. Usually he spent at least part of each summer at Aunt Yvonne's house, but this year she was ill and he'd been unable to go.

Dad had sent him on summer camp instead. It was run by people called the Pilgrims. It was a sort of adventure holiday with a bit of God thrown in. They were staying down the coast from Moon Beach in a building that used to be an army barracks, and it still smelt of that thin, dark oil that soldiers rub into guns.

There were three identical dormitories in the barracks, one on top of the other. The stairs that linked the dormitories were also identical. They were strange stairs, wide and deep, their edges sheathed in rubber. His feet didn't know these stairs the way they knew the stairs at home. He must've stumbled almost straight away. This being so, it made sense to think that he'd come from the dormitory directly above. Pleased with this piece of logic, feeling better already despite the bruises on his knee and hip, he climbed back up the stairs and opened the dormitory door. The air churned with the breathing of the other boys. The tall windows were severe with moonlight. He walked to where his bed was, then stopped. He couldn't believe it. There was somebody sleeping in it. Was he in the wrong dormitory after all? No, look. That blanket on the bed, it was his. He could tell by the satiny edge to it. It was his pale-blue blanket from home. Dad had taken it out of the airing cupboard specially.

He went up to the head of the bed and shook the sleeping boy by the shoulder. 'What are you doing in my bed?'

'It's my bed,' came the reply.

'It's *my* bed,' Nathan hissed. 'You're in *my bed*.'

The boy mumbled, shrugged, rolled over.

Nathan checked again, this time by looking out of the window. The view was exactly as it should be. The wide, grey parade ground; the rifle range; four palm trees. It was his bed.

He went round to the other side, shook the boy's shoulder again. 'This is my bed,' he said, 'honestly.'

The boy opened his eyes. There was nothing in his eyes. No sense, no recognition.

'You've got to go back to your own bed,' Nathan explained.

The boy lifted his head off the pillow and stared at Nathan with his dark, blank eyes. He spoke very clearly, as if he was reciting something from memory, something he'd learned but didn't understand. 'It's not your bed,' he said, 'so go away,' and then he lowered his head and closed his eyes. In five seconds he was asleep again. Nathan could tell by the breathing. He knew about breathing. He'd spent whole nights lying awake and listening to it, making sure it didn't stop.

He took one step backwards. He couldn't risk talking any louder. He might wake someone up and then there'd be a scandal. Someone sleeping in your bed, it didn't look good. There'd been a scandal at the camp two years before. Two boys were sent home early. They'd been found in the rifle range after lights out. Everyone knew what that meant.

Miserable now, and cold, he did the only thing he could think of: he began to insert himself into his bed alongside the other boy. They were narrow beds and it took him long minutes, with long minutes of stillness in between, to get into a position where sleep might be possible. He must've fallen asleep in the end, however, because he woke suddenly and it was light. He was a different person to the person he'd been during the night. He looked around and panicked. The blanket on the bed, it wasn't pale-blue like his, it was pale-green. He looked across at the next bed and recognised the face. It belonged to one of the prayer-leaders. It was so obvious this morning. He was in the wrong dormitory. The wrong bed.

Praying nobody had seen him, he eased out of the bed. He tiptoed the fifty yards to the door. Opened it without making one single creak, then closed it again, just as silently. Dad would've been proud of him. Back downstairs he slid into his own cold bed and, closing his eyes, pretended he'd been there all night.

He realised how narrow his escape had been when, less than five minutes later, the rising-bell began to sound. But, as it turned out, somebody must've seen him. Word went round at breakfast that Christie had slept in someone else's bed. Later that day he was summoned to the padre's office.

'So tell me, Christie,' the padre said, resting his chin on one hand and looking steadily into Nathan's soul, 'what exactly happened last night?'

'I was sleepwalking.'

The padre said nothing.

'If you don't believe me, ask my father,' Nathan said. 'He knows I do it.'

'Do you know why you do it?'

Nathan shrugged. 'My father says it started after my mother died.'

No action was taken, but that didn't stop the rumours spreading. Overnight Nathan acquired the reputation for being some kind of prostitute and nothing he said could change anyone's mind. His blond hair and his green eyes were used as evidence against him. The only thing the boys weren't sure of was how much he charged.

Three nights later he walked in his sleep again, but this time he woke up in a field. Once he'd recovered from the terror of not knowing where he was, he felt only relief. There was nothing scandalous about a field. Though, once again, his absence from his own bed was noted and people thought the worst.

He spent the last two weeks of the holidays at home. As the days passed and the new semester loomed, he was overtaken by a sense of dread. He knew that some of the boys at camp went to the same school as he did. What if they remembered? What if word got out? Dad took him into the sitting-room one day and asked him what the matter was. He told Dad that he didn't want to go back to school. Dad wanted to know why. It was a question that he found he couldn't answer. So back he went.

For the first few days he hardly spoke. He tried to will himself into a kind of invisibility. It seemed to be working, because he heard nothing. Then, one evening during the second week, he was leaving the pool with Tip when he noticed a thin figure sitting on the grass bank under the streetlamp. Red baseball cap, acne, spectacles. Something contaminating about him. Like you could get a disease just by looking.

'What's he doing here?' Nathan asked.

Tip looked. 'You know him?'

'I've seen him around. Blackmailed his mother or something, didn't he?'

A grin from Tip. 'You heard about that?'

'It was all over the school.'

'Yeah,' and Tip nodded, 'yeah, I guess it was.' He turned to the thin figure who had uncoiled from the bank and was shambling over. 'Hey, Jed, what's up?'

Jed didn't answer. He was looking at Nathan. 'There's going to be a shark run,' he said.

'Great,' Tip said. 'Who's doing it?'

'I'll give you one guess.' Jed was still looking at Nathan.

Tip understood and looked away. 'How come?'

'There's talk about him. We want to see if he's guilty.'

Nathan's heart sank. So they knew.

'What talk?' Tip asked, but Jed wouldn't say.

Nathan spoke to Tip. 'It's not true,' he said, 'none of it's true,' but nobody was listening.

'He a good swimmer?' Jed was looking at Nathan, but he was talking to Tip.

Tip said he was.

'Oh shit,' and Jed smirked. 'Looks bad.'

Tip scraped at the gravel with his boot.

'He'll do it, won't he?' Jed said.

'I guess.'

'What's wrong?' Jed said. 'He chicken?'

'Ask him,' Tip said.

'What's a shark run?' Nathan said.

Jed took Tip's sleeve. 'It's happening in Blackwater Bay, Saturday night. It's your job to make sure he's there.' Then he turned to leave. Tip turned with him.

'Hey, Tip,' Nathan called out. 'What's all this about?'

Tip spoke over his shoulder. 'I'll tell you Saturday. I've got to go now.'

Nathan was left standing with his bicycle.

He watched Tip and Jed slouch off into the night. As they passed through the streetlamp's pyramid of light, he saw the word WOMB painted across the back of Jed's cheap leather jacket. It was no surprise to learn that Jed was part of the gang.

He watched them move beyond the light and vanish into the darkness where the road was. It was as if they'd both been switched off, as if they'd never been there at all. If only. A fine rain began to fall. He climbed on to his bicycle. He rode fast, but he was still soaked by the time he reached home.

THE SHARK RUN

Summer rose from the river like a sack of dead air. Jed had been living in the house on Mangrove Heights for almost six months now and nobody had even seemed to notice, let alone object. Mario treated him as if he'd always been there. He looked at Jed in the same way that he listened to the money on the far side of the river; Jed was as real as all his other hallucinations. Rita was never in the house long enough to suspect that Jed might actually be living there; she just thought he stayed over a lot. Reg was no problem either. He rarely left his room. You heard him sometimes – a creak on the stairs, the click of a door – but you never saw him. And there hadn't been a sound from Muriel. It was as if Jed had moved from one dimension to another. His original dimension hadn't reported him missing, and his new dimension didn't acknowledge his presence. Maybe what he'd really done was end up somewhere between the two. Some days he almost felt invisible.

One morning in July, while everyone was still asleep, he left the house. The moment he stepped on to the platform in Mangrove East, a train pulled in. It took him across the river to Baker Park. There was a Sweetwater bus waiting at the stop when he walked out of the station. Everything seemed preordained, blessed. If someone had tried to assassinate him that morning, the bullet would've missed his head by a quarter of an inch.

It was still only seven-forty-five when he turned the corner into Mackerel Street. His mother left for work at around nine. Used to, anyway. There'd be enough time; more than enough. He wondered what she'd say when she saw him. He wondered if he'd grown.

He worked his way round to the back of the house. The kitchen door was open, and sunlight spilled into the room. She was standing by the fridge, peeling the silver foil off the top of a yoghurt. Maybe she sensed the light change behind her because she turned suddenly and saw him, and her left hand jerked sideways, knocking a carton of orange juice on to the floor. She fell to her knees with a cloth. One of his hands wandered away from his body, out into the air. It's only juice, he wanted to say. But it was better to say nothing. He knew her. It was already too late. He always seemed to make her break things. He didn't even have to touch anything. It was like those women with high voices, except he didn't even have to sing. He stayed where he was, on the doorstep. The kitchen floor looked dangerous, somehow. He might step on it and fall right through.

She wrung the cloth out in the sink, her face holy and still, as if they were her own tears that she was wringing out of the cloth, her own tears splattering on to the bright metal.

And then, without turning, 'Where've you been, Jed?'

That break in her voice. As if his absence was a hangnail and it had caught on every day that had passed since he had gone. It sounded so convincing that he almost believed her.

'Why?' he said. 'Have you been worried?'

'Worried?' She was facing him now, arms folded. 'Of course I've been worried.'

'Did you think something bad had happened?'

'For Christ's sake, Jed, it's been months. Where've you been?'

'What did you do? Did you call the police?'

'You told me not to.'

He looked at her. That wasn't the reason. 'You didn't call anyone, did you?'

'I called school. I called your friends – '

'I've been staying with a friend. I don't remember you calling.'

'Which friend's that?'

She was sly, but he wasn't falling for her tricks.

'Did you leave a message?' he said. 'If you did, I never got it.'

Of course she hadn't left a message. But he had this knife and he had to twist it. It was the same old duel.

'You don't change,' she said, 'do you?'

He didn't say anything. He tried the floor with one foot, as if it was water. It held.

'You're only thirteen, Jed. I've a right to know where you – '

'Fourteen.'

'What?'

'I'm fourteen now. You didn't even know.'

'It was a mistake.'

'Yes,' he said. 'It was, wasn't it?'

He'd forgotten his birthday too. It had happened a couple of months back, and he'd completely forgotten. It hadn't hurt him to forget. It only hurt him now, now he'd found out that she'd forgotten too. That's what birthdays were. Days when you found out where you stood. Who was on your side and who wasn't. Nothing to do with how old you were.

The sun was in his eyes. He shifted.

'You seen Pop?' he asked.

'Not for a while.'

He nodded. 'Well, anyway,' he said, 'I just thought I'd come and see how you were.'

And now you've seen. And now you've remembered.

'You're not coming in?' Her voice had softened.

He shook his head. 'I should get going.'

'Come and sit down, Jed. I'll make you a cup of coffee.'

'I've got to go.'

'So you're not going to tell me anything.'

He stepped back into the yard.

'I'm your mother, Jed. I'm supposed to know. Legally.'

'Since when did you care about legally?'

'I'll call the police.'

He shrugged. 'Call them.' He had nothing in common with her. It was as if even the blood in their veins had been changed.

He tried to think of something.

'How's Adrian?' he said.

She looked blank. 'Who?'

It was lucky that Dad went to bed so early.

Nathan waited twenty minutes, then he opened the french windows and stepped out into the garden. There was no light showing behind Dad's bedroom curtains. He must be asleep already. Back indoors, Nathan changed into the clothes he'd hidden under the stairs: a black sweater, old jeans, sneakers. He let himself out of the house, leaving the door key on the porch, in the third cactus from the left, then he rode down to the subway station, locked his bicycle to the railings, and caught one of the silver trains that went over the bridge into the city.

He got out at Mangrove Central. Tip was already waiting at the barrier. The clock in the ticket office said ten-thirty.

'You're late,' Tip said.

'Yeah, well,' and Nathan grimaced, 'had to wait for my old man to go to bed, didn't I?'

Blackwater Bay lay at the east end of the harbour, but from Mangrove Central it was inland, due north. It was an area that he'd been taught to avoid, and he moved on light feet, as if the streets could open up and swallow him. He didn't know where he was, and said as much to Tip. Tip just nodded, his eyes swivelling in their swollen lids. He was chewing a huge knot of gum. There was no place left for talk. Nathan felt a tightening in his belly now. He felt he was walking towards his own slaughter. No, not walking towards it. Being led.

'This shark run,' he said, as casually as he could manage, 'anyone done it before?'

'Scraper did it once.'

'He's dead, isn't he?'

Tip nodded. 'PS did it too.'

Great. Just great. Scraper had always been a guinea-pig. If someone had an idea, they always tried it out on old Scraper. He was one of those people who'd do anything. He had a slack smile that covered both pain and pleasure, so you couldn't tell what he was feeling, you couldn't tell the difference. If you'd told him to cut his head off, he would've done it, and that smile'd still be on his face afterwards. As for PS, he was nuts. He'd do it for a dare. Just as long as you didn't make him take those phones off his head. It was no consolation to hear that Scraper and PS had done the shark run, no consolation at all. He wished he'd never asked.

They were walking along Five Dock Road. Trees lined one side, the grey grass of a park between. Dockyards on the other. This was the east end of the harbour, more than a mile from the bridge. The water stopped here. Half a dozen bays of stagnant, black water, the surface smeared with oil slicks, condoms, orange peel, insults hurled at the water by the land.

They passed a row of padlocked gates: ALLIED COAL. PIONEER CEMENT. STERLING SHIP REPAIRS AND ENGINEERING. They paused to watch a crane sink its jaws into the open hold of a ship and rise again with a mouthful of coal, dust spilling from between its teeth, grey against the brown night sky, then Tip nudged Nathan in the ribs, held his watch up, and they hurried on.

They turned down an alley, crossed a narrow iron bridge that spanned a canal. The canal had smooth, concrete banks and held no more than a couple of feet of water, water that was sealed in by a lid of green slime. Metal spars stuck out, like the elbows of people who'd drowned. They climbed over a gate and suddenly they were walking on grass. A breeze clattered in the palm trees that bordered the canal. The grass sloped down to a wall of loose rocks. Beyond the rocks lay the harbour.

'This is the place,' Tip said, and Nathan, who'd been hoping they'd never arrive, began to shiver.

As he looked round he saw several figures moving towards him. They fanned out in an arc, ten-feet gaps between them, like a net trawling for fish. The net closed and suddenly Vasco was standing in front of Tip, black leather coat and a cigarette in the shelter of his palm. He pulled on the cigarette and in the brief red glow Nathan saw the faces of the Womb Boys: José PS Mendoza, Cramps Crenshaw, Slim Jimmy Chung, Jed Morgan, Thomas Baby Vail, two others he didn't know the names of, and the ghost of Scraper O'Malley, half his face caved in, inlaid with silver from that fast car's fender. They were all there, passing a bottle around. Scraper drank too, twisting his mouth away from the wound.

Vasco spoke to Tip. 'It's almost eleven. What kept you?'

'Trains're fucked up.' Tip took the bottle and swallowed a mouthful, then he wiped his lips on his sleeve.

Why had he lied? Maybe, Nathan thought, because you didn't mention things like family to Vasco. He wouldn't've known what you were talking about.

Vasco pulled on his cigarette again, let the breeze haul the smoke across his teeth. He turned to Nathan. 'You've got a pretty bad reputation.'

Nathan looked at his feet.

'That stuff you've been doing, you've been doing it at God camp. God don't like that, Christie. I don't like it either.'

'I got into his bed, that's all. I thought – '

'That's all.' Vasco laughed, and two or three gang members joined in.

'I was sleepwalking,' Nathan said.

Jed stepped forwards. He was wearing a T-shirt that said SUICIDE PACT on the front. On the back it said YOU FIRST. 'You were what?' he said.

'I was sleepwalking.'

'Bullshit.'

'I was. I've been sleepwalking for years. Ever since – '

'Ever since what?' Jed had come a step closer. Nathan could see the dead flakes of skin on his face.

'Nothing.'

'OK, this is the thing,' Vasco said. 'He does the shark run. If he gets taken, he's innocent. If he survives, he's guilty. Right?'

'Right,' shouted the Womb Boys.

'That's not fair,' Nathan said.

Jed stretched his head out on his long, reptile neck and leered into Nathan's face. 'Who the fuck said anything about fair?'

Vasco lifted one arm towards the water. 'See that?' He was pointing at a warehouse that had the words VENUS ISLAND CONTAINER TERMINAL painted across its metal roof.

Nathan nodded.

'What you got to do is, you got to swim to it,' Vasco said. 'That's the shark run.'

'I still don't get it,' Nathan said. 'Why's it called the shark run?'

Sniggers from the gang.

Vasco led him down to the waterline and showed him a sign that was mounted on a metal pole. On the sign was the silhouette of someone swimming freestyle with a red bar drawn through it. Below it were the words DANGER SHARKS.

'That's why,' Vasco said.

Nathan looked round, caught Tip's eye.

'PS did it,' Tip said.

'You told me that,' Nathan said.

'Wore his headphones,' Jed said. 'So he wouldn't hear the sharks coming.'

PS was nodding. Though he might just've been nodding to the imaginary music in his head.

'This is different,' Vasco said. 'This is a trial.'

'If a shark gets you,' Jed said, 'you won't feel anything. Just cold.' He leered. 'Just cold where a piece of you's gone.'

Vasco nodded. 'Yeah, I heard that too.'

Nathan stared out into the bay. A few weeks before they'd found a girl's body floating six miles off the coast. She'd been swimming on Moon Beach and a shark had taken her. Her name, he remembered, was Shelley. According to her mother, Shelley had always been 'real strong in the water'.

Vasco pulled his sleeve up and pointed at the tombstone tattoo on his bicep. The name on the stone was Scraper O'Malley. No dates. 'Just think,' he said. 'You could be next.' His teeth shone in the moonlight. 'That's what you're here for, in this shit-forsaken town. To die. To end up on my arm. I'll carry the lot of you before I'm through,' and he tipped his head back, and his laughter was so dry it was like sticks snapping in his throat, and his shoulders shook under his famous leather coat.

There was a hysteria to Vasco, and it was the first time Nathan had been close enough to notice it. The members of Vasco's gang, they followed him because they couldn't follow him. Nobody could go where he went, but seeing someone do that, it made you want to try. They got as close as they could, and when people did that it looked like some kind of worship. Nathan felt the power of this, the blast, like heat from a furnace, and for a moment he forgot to feel scared.

Tip took the bottle off P S. 'Here,' he said to Nathan. 'Have some, it'll keep you warm.'

'Yeah,' P S said, 'kept me warm,' and he opened his mouth to laugh and left it open, but no laughter came out. So he closed it again and went on listening to music that didn't exist.

Nathan didn't bother looking at the label. He just raised the bottle to his lips and swallowed twice. Handed the bottle back again. Nothing at first, then the whole of his insides lit up. He stripped down to his shorts and felt the breeze move curious fingers across his skin, as if it was blind and trying to work out who he was. He climbed over the cold, slippery rocks, climbed down to the water's edge. So black it looked, just like its name, with bits of smashed gold from the lights on the highway. Feel your way in slow, Tip had told him. There's all kinds of shit in there. The clash and sneeze of a truck as it shifted gears on the causeway. He wasn't thinking of the danger, of the sharks. He was too preoccupied with how strange it felt to be standing at the edge of the harbour in the middle of the night with nothing on. The world had never felt so big.

The water rose past his knees. Another couple of feet and he'd be able to push himself forwards and begin. Over his shoulder he could see the Womb Boys fanned out on the rocks. Silent now, just watching. This was their evening's entertainment. A small red light glowed. Vasco's cigarette. Like the light that shows on a machine when the power's on. No use delaying this. He faced the container terminal again and pushed himself forwards, into the harbour.

He swam breaststroke, that way he could keep his head out of the water. It also meant he couldn't cut through the water as efficiently, it meant he was slower. The waves were small, but they came in quick succession, they kept slapping him in the face, always on the same cheek. He tasted oil on his lips.

Halfway across he heard Dad's voice. Wrap up warm, Dad was saying. Don't forget to wrap up warm.

Nathan began to laugh. He drank the harbour, one mouthful, then another. He was choking now. He had to stop, tread water, he had to fight for breath. And that was when the fear took hold, in that moment, when he was upright in the water, when his legs were dangling, he pictured what might be lying on the bottom, there'd be bodies, there'd be people who'd turned blue with cold down there, and what if one of them reached up and seized him by the ankle, and then he remembered the sharks, their teeth sinking into him, their grip like ice, just cold where a piece of you's gone, and he began to swim as fast as he could, he switched to freestyle, swam the way he swam when he was swimming for the city, he was back in the pool on Sunset Drive, he tasted chlorine now instead of oil, he even heard the cheering, that tinny rushing sound, and the next time he looked up he was only twenty-five yards out, and he still had his legs, and he could see the Womb Boys sitting on a parapet, they must've run round by the highway, or else Vasco had stolen a car again, he was always doing that, apparently, that was why he'd been expelled.

He lowered his legs, but his feet sank into sludge, so he swam as close to the island as he could and then crawled the last few yards on hands and knees, through the shallows, over cans and bottles and plastic bags, and up on to the towpath, and it wasn't until then that he heard the voices:

'Guil-ty, guil-ty, guil-ty.'

Vasco stepped forwards. 'Sharks must be busy someplace else tonight,' he said, and everybody laughed.

Nathan wanted to join in, but it was hard to laugh, his teeth were chattering too much. He was beginning to shiver again, and the wind made his skin feel like metal.

'Where are my clothes?'

Tip threw him his clothes. Nathan wrapped himself in his sweater, and stood hunched, his hands clasped under his chin. Tip handed him the bottle, almost empty now. He took a mouthful, swilled it round, and spat it on the concrete.

'That water,' Vasco said, 'bet that water tastes real bad.'

PS pushed his phones away from his ears. 'Swallowed about half of it myself,' he said. 'Never been the same since.' And slid his phones back over his ears again. Tss-Tss-Tss.

The gang howled. PS and his jokes.

Jed came over. 'Bet you were shit-scared.'

'Anyone would've been,' Nathan said. 'You would've been too.'

Jed pushed his thin lips out and shook his head.

'Yeah, you would,' Nathan said.

'No, I wouldn't,' Jed said and, reaching behind him, he produced the sign that said DANGER SHARKS. 'There's no sharks out there.'

Nathan was staring at the sign.

'Yeah, it's the same sign,' Jed said. 'Vasco got it a few weeks back. Didn't you, Vasco?'

Vasco was smoking a cigarette on the parapet. He seemed bored now, his fires had burned low. He blew a long slow trumpet of smoke into the night. 'Yeah,' he said. 'Ripped it off from some beach. Some beach somewhere.' He eased down off the wall and flicked his stub into the harbour. Tss. 'Let's split.' He had this way of talking to nobody in particular. The sky or something. But everybody listened.

The Womb Boys began to slope off down the causeway. Nathan picked up the rest of his clothes and was about to follow them when Jed barred his way. 'Not you.'

He had to find his own way back. By the time he got home, it was after two. Closing the front door, his hand slipped and the lock snapped shut.

'Shit,' he whispered, and stood in the hallway, listening.

He heard a creak from Dad's bed and a click as Dad's bedroom door opened. Dad's voice, wary and thin, floated down from the landing. 'George?'

Standing at the bottom of the stairs, Nathan saw Dad appear at the top, one hand clutching the banisters.

'It's me, Dad. Nathan. I'm just going to bed.'

'I thought I heard the front door.'

'No, it must've been the kitchen you heard.'

Luckily, Dad's head was blurred with all the pills he took to sleep. The front door and the kitchen door made completely different sounds. Normally he would've realised that.

'Please try and be quiet, Nathan.'

'Sorry, Dad.'

A few minutes later he lay down in bed and stared into the darkness above his head. It hurt to lie to Dad and he wished he didn't have to, but Dad was so fragile and the truth could smash him. He only lied to protect Dad. Isn't that what you did for someone you loved, lied for them? And his lies were soft, like pillows. They were good lies, he told himself. They were white. And, having convinced himself of that, he turned over, and drifted into sleep.

When Vasco went missing, Jed didn't even notice at first. Vasco was always out, doing his rounds or lying low. He always had business to attend to. There was stuff that was hot to be shifted. He was dealing too. Not that Vasco approved of drugs. It was just that he was fighting a war, and drugs were the most efficient way of raising finance. 'After all,' he'd say, 'politicians do it.' Sometimes he'd be gone for twenty-four hours. Then he'd call Jed from some apartment, some bar. Or he'd simply turn up at the house. Not this time. This time Jed didn't hear a thing.

On the third day Jed went upstairs to look for Mario. Maybe Mario would know. Maybe those Gorelli ears had picked something up. He knocked on Mario's door. Wheels trundled over the floor and the door eased open.

Over Mario's head Jed saw dark lounge suits hanging from the picture rail, and sepia photographs of the handkerchief factory in its heyday framed in gold. The light in the room was muted and brown, and the air smelt of Mario's paraffin lamp and the oil that he used to lubricate the moving parts of his two wheelchairs.

'You know where Vasco is?' Jed asked.

Mario seemed irritated. 'How would I know that?'

'I just thought you might've heard something.'

'No.' And then Mario's head tipped cunningly on his neck, and the eye nearest to Jed gleamed, and he lurched forwards, as if he'd been shot in the back, a pearl of spittle on his lower lip. 'I thought I heard a thousand-dollar bill today. Do you think,' and his eye gleamed up at Jed, shiny as glass, and just as dead, 'do you think they make thousand-dollar bills?'

Jed didn't know about thousand-dollar bills, but he knew about Mario. Just then, suddenly. He knew why Mario had never fucked anyone. Mario was too selfish. He wanted to keep all his sperm to himself. Nobody else deserved it. And so he looked like a Roman emperor and rode around in wheelchairs and pretended he could hear money. What a character, people said. Isn't he good for his age? they said. But he wasn't a character and he wasn't good for his age. He was a piece of shit for his age. He was a fraud.

'There's no such thing,' Jed said, 'and you fucking know it.'

He didn't even wait for Mario's reaction. He whirled out on to the landing and stood there, trembling. He'd have to try Reg. As he stamped off down the corridor, his footsteps fascist on the floorboards, it occurred to him that he'd never actually set eyes on Reg. Not ever. Not even once.

He knocked on Reg's door. A silence, then a tiny scraping sound. He could feel Reg staring at him through the Judas eye.

'What do you want?'

'I'm looking for Vasco.'

'He's not here.'

Jed rested his cheek against the door. Like a confessional, only nobody was telling anybody anything. He heard the Judas eye scrape shut, then the creak of floorboards as Reg backed away.

'Reg?' He knocked on the door again. 'Reg!'

But Reg had withdrawn deep into the room. He'd pulled Jesus over his head like a blanket and he wouldn't be coming out for a long time.

The streets seemed empty that morning. Jed scoured the neighbourhood. Somebody had to know something. It was a hot day. Only faded curtains stirring lazily in apartment windows.

At last he found Silence, Tip's ten-year-old brother, standing in a patch of wasteground, throwing stones at a row of tin cans. It was one of Silence's favourite things. He couldn't hear the stone hit the can, or the can hit the ground, but he liked the way it looked.

'You seen Vasco?' Jed said.

Silence picked the words off Jed's lips, neatly, one by one, the way you pick fleas off a dog. He shook his head and began to hunt around in the scrub grass. Eventually he found what looked like a piece of a bicycle. He drew a circle in the mud, a circle with two slit eyes and a downturned mouth.

'A face,' Jed said. 'Vasco?'

Silence nodded.

He sealed the face off with a series of vertical lines and reinforced the downturned mouth.

'Oh no,' Jed said. 'It's jail, right?'

Silence nodded again and touched the lobe of his ear.

Jed translated. 'That's what you heard.'

He watched as Silence scraped his heel across the picture, as if it might be used as evidence. Silence had always been very earnest and very careful. A secret, you always felt, would be safer with him than with anyone.

'You know where?' he asked.

Silence shrugged. He picked up a stone and slung it at the row of tin cans. One dropped. Silence had this way of putting an end to things. That stone, it meant he'd told Jed all he knew. End of conversation.

Jed thanked him. He walked home slowly, the long way round.

That night Rita rang. She was crying.

'Have you heard?' she said.

'Yeah.'

'What's going to happen now?'

'I don't know. What did they pick him up for?'

'Arson.'

That figured. 'Where is he?'

'They're holding him downtown, but they're going to move him soon.'

'Where to?'

'Some detention centre. They won't let you visit, though. You're not old enough. Only people like parents can go.'

'He hasn't got any parents.'

'I know.'

He called the place the following morning, and they confirmed what Rita had told him. Nobody under the age of eighteen. That meant even Rita didn't qualify for a couple of months. He wrote a letter instead, asking Vasco what had happened, and what he should do. It was ten days before he received the reply, and it wrongfooted him when it came.

> Listen, Jed, there is something you can do for me.
> I've got this brother called Francis. He's about nine.
> Lives with some family over in Torch Bay. I go and
> see him, like maybe every couple of weeks, but now
> I can't any more. Maybe you could go and explain
> things to him. He's at 25025 Oakwood Drive. Take
> it easy. Vasco. P.S. The woman who lives there is a
> BITCH.

A brother?

He told Tip, and Tip seemed just as astonished. 'Christ,' Tip said, 'he kept that under his hat, didn't he?'

The next day Jed caught a bus to the harbour. He sat on a green bench at the end of Quay 5, waiting for the Torch Bay ferry. The sky had clouded over, and wind scuffed and pinched the grey water. It was the kind of day that goaded you until you felt like smashing it.

Such anger in him already.

How was he going to, as Vasco put it, explain things? He couldn't even explain things to himself.

The ferry filled with tourists. Their sun-visors, their ice-creams. Their ceaseless, eager babble. Instead of taking a seat, Jed leaned against the metal door that led down to the engines. He read the instructions on what to do if the boat capsized. Half of him wished it would.

When the ferry docked in Torch Bay, he was the first down the gangplank. He pushed through the crush of people on the quay, slipped into the quiet of a sidestreet. Three or four blocks back from the harbour the ground began to slope upwards; boutiques gave way to houses; trees appeared.

Oakwood Drive was a wide residential street, its sidewalks planted with mahogany and wild oak. Houses stood in their own grounds, some Spanish-looking, some ranch-style, all of them the size of palaces. There was no dirt here, no life. The only sound came from a man who was operating a machine that sucked up leaves. It didn't matter where Jed put his eyes, it always looked like a postcard. His mother would've loved it.

25025 Oakwood Drive was a mansion. Red bricks, white shutters. Immaculate green lawns. Even a flagpole. The gravel crunched under Jed's boots as he started up the drive. He felt watched. It was nothing like his experience outside Reg Gorelli's door. No Judas eye here, no lens to draw his nose forwards till he looked like a fish or a rat. No, this watching was far more sophisticated: it was more like a landscape, and he was a speck on the landscape, a dot, something you could swat with ease, and nobody would ever hear, not if you coughed at the same time.

He searched the porch for a bell, but all he could find was a chain of wrought-iron links. He reached up and pulled on it, half expecting a sudden rush of water. Instead he heard two solemn notes that sounded stolen from a church and, before the second of these notes had died away, the door opened and a woman stood in front of him. She had high, horizontal cheekbones, so her eyes seemed to be perching on ledges. Eyes like birds of prey. Any moment one of them might swoop down, snatch at him, and swerve away again, his heart dripping in its beak. Jed heard Vasco's voice: The woman who lives there is a BITCH.

He swallowed. 'I've come to see Francis. I've got a message from his brother.'

'His brother?' Her voice was so cold. She probably kept it in the icebox.

'Yeah, his brother. Vasco.'

'Francis has no brother.'

'But Vasco told me.'

'Who's that?' said another voice, smaller, younger, not cold at all. 'Who's at the door?'

Jed tried to peer round the woman, but she narrowed the gap to six inches and filled it with her buzzard eyes and her rippling turquoise dress.

'Francis has no brother,' she repeated. 'There must be some mistake.'

Strange that she should choose that word.

'Goodbye.' She closed the door.

A gust of air-conditioned air moved past his face and lost itself in the heat of the driveway.

He didn't feel safe until he reached the sidewalk. Then he looked back over his shoulder. The house lay on its lawn, perfectly still, immaculate, blank. He thought of his old tapes, the ones he'd had for years, the ones he'd used over and over again. Their silence was always different to the silence of a new tape: it was loaded, prickly, with things recorded and erased; a silence that was like ghosts. That house was an old tape masquerading as a new one. It had recorded and erased, but it was pretending it had just come out of the cellophane. It had ghosts, but it wasn't owning up to them.

He bought a bag of Hawaiian Teardrops and sat on a wooden bench in the Torch Bay ferry terminal. Hawaiian Teardrops were hard chunks of pineapple candy that were coated with sugar crystals. If you ate too many of them, they took the skin off the inside of your mouth. He ate the whole bag and stared out over the grey water. Rain scratched on the windows, but it was still hot, hard to breathe. He felt the door close again. And that gust of cool air across his face.

He remembered a morning not so long ago. He'd woken to the sound of hammer-blows. He'd reached out, across the gap between the two mattresses, and shoved Vasco in the ribs.

'What's that noise?'

'I don't know,' Vasco mumbled. 'Maybe Reg is crucifying himself again.'

Jed put his glasses on and eased out of bed. He poked his head out of the room. A man in blue dungarees was fitting a lock on Reg's door.

'Morning,' Jed said. 'Nice lock.'

The man patted the lock. 'This is the business, this is. You can't get stronger than this.'

The new lock was just the latest addition to Reg's defence system. They never really found out whether it was to keep Jesus in or the world out. Maybe there was nothing happening behind the door, or maybe there was Reg fastened to a home-made cross, some white cloth draped around his skinny loins, his moustache stained yellow by the vinegar.

Finally it was just another thing you couldn't get at.

He saw that woman's eyes widen like wings and leave her face. He saw the blank sockets, smooth as the inside of nests. He had to go and stand on the deck, both hands fastened to the cold rail. The ferry was rolling now, pitching into the waves. Sometimes it stalled, shuddering. Then it pitched forwards into the waves again. The city see-sawed, rain swarmed out of the sky. The inside of his mouth felt sweet but raw. A woman in a green mackintosh asked him if he was all right, she had to ask him three times before he could answer simply, 'Yes.'

Vasco's case came up the following month. He was sentenced to eighteen months in a corrective institution. The next thing Jed heard, Vasco was somehow involved in the death of another inmate and he was sent to a top-security detention centre in another county.

Jed had always thought of Vasco as high-frequency. He'd always seen Vasco as a kind of radio, picking up stations that no other radio could pick up. Maybe that was true, but maybe it was also true that he was picking up the wrong stations, stations that were dangerous. Jed had read about people hearing voices. He'd seen it in the paper. Some guy kills fourteen people and then he says, It was the voices, the voices told me to do it. That guy, he's picking up the wrong stations. And suddenly he feared for his friend.

It was seven years before he saw him again.

THREE

COLOURS EVERYWHERE

The moment Nathan saw Harriet step out of the taxi, he knew that they'd slipped up somewhere. In the five years since their mother died they'd had nine different au pair girls and every single one of them had been ugly. It was basically Dad's idea. He thought ugly girls were less trouble. Nathan and Georgia would spend entire afternoons sifting through the pictures the agency had sent. It was a game to them, and they often went too far, choosing some girl with a broken nose or a moustache. Even though they were playing by Dad's rules, it'd be Dad, in the end, who'd object. There'd have to be a compromise: they'd settle on some plain girl who'd grown up on a farm.

But there was Harriet, standing on the sidewalk in a pink sleeveless dress and white shoes with straps round the ankles. Her eyes sent out rays like cut glass turning in the sun. Her hair was light-brown, with a fringe that skimmed her eyebrows. Her limbs were slim and tanned. Nathan's first thought on that warm September afternoon, and it may also have been Dad's first thought, judging by the way his voice had lifted an octave in nervousness, was: She's just not ugly enough.

She was smiling as they walked out to the street to greet her, and Nathan recognised the smile from her picture. Her two front teeth overlapped slightly like fingers crossed for good luck. A moment of carelessness in the construction of her face. The slip that made her beautiful. He watched her run a hand through Georgia's hair. He still couldn't understand how they'd come to choose her. It must've been an old picture, taken at an unflattering age. Either that, or she just wasn't photogenic.

He carried her cases upstairs. She followed him. When he reached her room he put the cases down again and held the door open for her. It was a small room, but it faced west, over the garden. The hills rose in the distance, their browns and golds invaded by a wedge of black. There'd been a fire on the ridge that summer.

But she'd stopped inside the doorway. 'Oh,' she said, and turned to him. 'There are bars on the window.'

He smiled. 'There are bars on all the windows. It's just the style of architecture. It's sort of Spanish.'

She reached up, pushed a hand into her fringe. One silver bracelet skittered down her arm.

'It's all right,' he said. 'It's not a prison.'

She sat down on the edge of the bed, tested the mattress with one hand. Then she smiled up at him. A wide, uncomplicated smile. 'I'm glad it's not a prison.'

She was like no au pair girl they'd ever had before. She couldn't cook, she played the radio too loud, she went out dancing at night. The house seemed to be admitting more light than it usually did; it was as if someone had knocked a few new windows in the walls. Nothing out of the ordinary happened, though. Perhaps her beauty was, in itself, disturbance enough. Her six months passed and at the end of that time she did what au pair girls always did: she flew home.

Nathan hardly noticed. Not long after Harriet arrived, Mr Marshal had called Dad and asked him whether he'd thought of putting Nathan forward for the Moon Beach Lifesaving Club. Dad hadn't, but he thoroughly approved of the idea; fitness, a sense of discipline, the ability to set a good example and, if need be, help others, these were all attributes that he held dear. As a result of that phone-call Nathan spent most of the weekday nights that winter training in the outdoor pool on Sunset Drive, and by the time Harriet left in the spring he was ready to apply for membership.

On the first Saturday in April he rode down to the beach to meet with the captain of the Club. It was still early, nobody much about, just a few old people from the hotels; he looked at each of them as a person he might one day save. As he headed across the warm sand towards the look-out tower he passed two lifeguards. He'd met them once, at the pool with Tip. One of them was called Finn, which was a good name for a lifeguard, he thought. The other one was Ade. He told them he was trying out for the Club. They wished him luck.

The captain was waiting by the tower, as arranged. He wore scarlet trunks and every time he moved you saw the muscles shift under his skin. He took one look at Nathan, then he turned his eyes out to the ocean, shook his hands on the end of his wrists. 'You the guy who wants to join the Club?'

Nathan said he was.

'Let's go for a swim.'

They walked down to the waterline. Wave after wave slammed on to the packed sand. A dull hard sound, like a hand brought down on wood. The beach seemed to shudder every time.

'Dumpers,' the captain said. 'Think you can handle it?'

He took a deep breath. 'I'll give it a try.'

The captain nodded. 'You've got to get under the first wave. Then get your head up and grab yourself some air before the next wave hits.'

Easy to say.

Nathan beat the first two waves, and then he had to fight even to stay in the same place. Every time he dived under a wave he felt it haul him back towards the shore. He looked for the captain, but he couldn't see that blond head anywhere. A wave high enough to cut the sun out curled above him. He dived too late. He was sucked down, spun round, the weight of water crushing the breath out of him. Somehow he found the surface for a moment, took in air, then he was rolled again. He fetched up in the shallows, blinded, coughing.

A hand on his shoulder. 'You OK?'

'Yeah.' But the salt burned the back of his throat; he could hardly speak.

'You sure?'

'Yeah.'

'Want to try again?'

'OK.'

And the same thing happened, only this time he almost drowned. He came to the surface, too weak to breathe, and was sinking back again when the captain took hold of him, and it was like some passage from the Bible, he felt as if he'd been raised from the dead, lifted by some divine, invisible hand. He heard a calm voice above the crashing water.

'Relax, just relax.'

And he relaxed. The captain was some kind of prophet.

'You'll be fine. You're going to drink some water, but you'll be fine.'

And he was fine. But it wasn't prophecy. What it was, in fact, as he came to understand later, was knowledge.

Back on the sand he felt limpness and bruising in every part of his body. But even more painful than that was the shame in his head. He hadn't even got past the third wave, he'd failed, they'd never take him now.

'Thanks for getting me out.'

The captain grinned. 'That's what I'm here for.'

'I'm all right in the pool, but this,' and he glanced over his shoulder, 'this is nothing like the pool.'

'No kidding.' The captain turned his grey eyes on the waves. 'The spring tides're on their way.' He looked at Nathan as Nathan got shakily to his feet. 'I like what you did out there. Most guys, they wouldn't've gone in a second time.'

Nathan shrugged.

'Come down tomorrow. We'll see how things work out.'

Nathan heard a chuckle behind him. He turned to see Tip standing on the sand, his feet turned outwards, his arms folded across his chest.

'You must've drunk about half the fucking ocean.'

Nathan just looked at him. 'Yeah, well,' he said, 'I was thirsty, wasn't I?'

He almost died again on the way home. He jinked through the rush-hour traffic on the bridge, skimming down the outside of the fast lane, cutting back inside for the Blenheim exit. He reached the driveway breathless, threw his bicycle down, and ran into the house.

He found Dad sitting in his red chair.

'You remember I had a trial for the lifeguards? Well, I've done it. I'm in.'

Dad was staring into the corner of the room, his spectacles dangling from one finger. 'That's good.'

'For the Lifesaving Club, Dad. Just like you wanted.'

Dad just nodded. 'Excellent.'

'I almost drowned twice doing it.'

'Well done.'

He sat down next to Dad and stared at him. 'What's wrong with you?'

Dad sighed. 'I'm in love with her.'

Nathan looked around the room. 'Who?'

'Harriet.'

'Harriet?'

All his excitement dwindled as his mind whirled back three months to a shopping trip with her. When he climbed into the car, she was smiling at him in that sugary way that used to make his teeth ache. But he'd probably smiled back.

As she shifted into reverse she turned to him again. 'Tell me, Nathan, have you ever made love to a girl?'

He looked at her quickly, then he looked down at his hands. That smile again. There was something greedy under the sugar, something predatory. He felt her words trying to open him up. It was like she had a can-opener and he was just sitting there, a can of something. 'No,' he said.

'Have you ever kissed a girl?'

'Probably.'

'Probably? Can't you remember?'

'Not recently,' he said. 'That's what I meant.'

She gave him a curious look and then smiled to herself. Looking back at the road again, she had to swerve to avoid a man on a bicycle. She was still smiling as she swerved.

'You must tell me about it when you do,' she said. 'When you make love for the first time, I mean. I want to know what you think.'

He glanced away from her, out of the window. An ice-cream parlour, a man with a dog, a tree. How was he going to get out of shopping next week?

'It's so wonderful, it's like,' and she left her mouth open while she thought, and then it came to her, and she smiled, 'it's like colours everywhere.'

Colours everywhere?

'I want to know if you see those colours too.' She was looking at him again. She seemed to have been looking at him practically the whole time. He couldn't understand why they hadn't crashed yet, why they weren't wrapped round a tree or a streetlight, why they weren't, in fact, dead.

Still smiling, Harriet parked the car. She knew she'd embarrassed him. She even seemed to have enjoyed it. He'd thought she was prying at the time, and resented it. But now he saw her questions in a different light. Maybe she'd just been excited that morning, and her excitement had spilled over. Maybe she'd just seen those colours everywhere for the first time. Maybe it'd happened the night before.

He looked across at Dad.

'I didn't want to tell you,' Dad said. 'Not until I was sure.'

'I never realised.'

'You wouldn't have. We were careful. And anyway, you were hardly here.'

'What do you mean, you were careful?'

'We took,' and suddenly Dad looked furtive, almost guilty, 'special precautions.'

'What kind of precautions?'

'We had a piece of string.' Dad explained how he had run the string from under his pillow, across his bedroom, out of his window, along the back wall of the house (where it was lost among the branches of a lilac bush) and in through Harriet's window, ending in a loop that Harriet slipped over her big toe when she went to bed at night. They always waited until Nathan was either out or asleep, then Dad tugged on the string, and Harriet tiptoed across the landing and into his bed.

Dad unlocked his desk and took out a ball of strong brown string. 'There, that's it.' Just looking at the string reminded him of too much. His eyes moved beyond it, out of focus.

'So what are you going to do?'

'I'm going to ask her to come back and marry me.'

But he was more than twice Harriet's age, as Harriet's family pointed out, through Harriet, in her first letter. He wrote back, asking her whether she loved him. Of course she loved him, she said, but she had to think. He said that if she loved him there was nothing to think about. He told her he was going to drive into town and find a piece of string that was six thousand miles long, a piece of string that would reach right across the ocean, from his sad finger to her beautiful big toe. She wrote back saying how much she liked his last letter. She hoped he could find a piece of string like that. But then she said, 'Maybe we need rope now,' which only depressed him.

Towards the end of the summer he began to founder. He was still writing almost every day, but she was writing less. He felt a pain in his right hand that was caused, he said, by the great weight of his love passing from his heart into his pen. He also suspected that it might be arthritis. And then, a few days before his forty-ninth birthday, he received a letter, her first for over a week. She said she had a birthday surprise for him. She was coming back to marry him. He turned pale and almost fainted. Nathan had to reach up under his shirt with a towel and mop the cold sweat off his back.

Three weeks later, the marriage took place. Standing on the steps of City Hall for the wedding photographs in her navy-blue suit and her sheer black stockings, Harriet achieved a temporary sophistication. Dad stood beside her. He looked both proud and guilty of something. As if happiness was a reward and he wasn't sure he'd done enough to deserve it. After the ceremony they celebrated with lunch at the revolving restaurant on Sunset Tower. Forty-two floors up, a 360-degree view. One of the most exclusive restaurants in the city. Harriet ordered a bottle of champagne and four glasses.

'I don't think Georgia should – ' Dad began.

Georgia, nine years old, took out her sulking face.

'Oh, but Jack,' Harriet cried, the fingertips of one hand touching his lips, to silence him, 'it's a special day.'

'Well,' Dad said, 'I suppose so.'

Georgia beamed and swallowed half the contents of the glass in a single gulp.

'That's all you're getting, Georgia,' Dad warned, 'so make it last.'

And Harriet glanced at Nathan, a quick glance, the light in her eyes rocking like buoys in the harbour at night, she was recognising, even gently mocking, her husband's sense of caution, caution on a day that was such a gamble for him. I've thrown it to the winds, her glance seemed to be saying, but look at him. Suddenly he felt as if the marriage was a confidence trick, a joke on someone; he felt as if he was being drawn into some kind of conspiracy. He shifted on his chair and looked away.

He remembered Yvonne's reaction to news of the forthcoming wedding. She'd heard Dad out, then she'd sat back, her eyes focused on the top corner of the room, a cheroot rolling, unlit, between her fingers. 'Just so long as you realise that she'll want to change everything,' she'd said. It was the first time that Dad had seemed worried since the arrival of Harriet's letter. What he looked for in love, what he hoped to extract, was not change but stability.

Nathan let his eyes drift back to the table again. He watched Harriet carefully as, laughing now, she tilted her face towards a waiter. She wasn't beautiful, he decided, that wasn't it, but she seemed to give something off that, like a perfume, excited those around her. The waiters were attentive to the point of subservience. Especially the one with the black hair on the back of his hands, the Italian-looking one, 'The kind of man,' Dad whispered, 'who makes you feel like washing.'

'Like washing?' Harriet didn't follow.

'Didn't you see?' Dad's voice dropped again and they had to lean forwards to hear. 'You could clean shoes with the back of those hands.'

Nathan and Georgia doubled up, but Harriet didn't think it was funny. As for Dad, he'd have preferred not to have had to make the joke in the first place. He'd have preferred less conscientious service. He was the kind of man who was jealous of waiters.

He salvaged the situation by saying, 'Did any of you hear the one about the string?' and soon they were all laughing about the same thing, which was a far better way for a new family to start its life together.

Georgia drank a surreptitious glass of champagne, her second, and began to run round the restaurant with a wide, fixed grin on her face, her arms extended like the wings of a plane. They tried to persuade her to land, but she wouldn't listen, she just went on running, round and round. Just before coffee was served, she threw up on Harriet's new shoes.

'My shoes,' Harriet cried, and a flock of waiters swooped with paper napkins.

Dad mopped Georgia's mouth. 'I told you, George,' he said, 'but you wouldn't listen, would you?' Though, actually, he was talking to Harriet.

Georgia grinned out of her green face. 'I was sick,' she said. 'Sick, sick, sick.'

'She's still drunk,' Nathan said. 'Don't you think we'd better take her home?'

It was shortly after the wedding that he ran into Tip again. The summer holidays had just begun, and he was due back on the beach for his second season as a lifeguard. He was riding the bus down Central Avenue one morning when he saw Tip slouching in a doorway. It was only a split-second, and the windows were tinted green and bleary with diesel, but he was sure. The narrow eyes, the broad sloping shoulders. That white skin, hard as lard. He jumped off the bus at the next stop and ran back.

'Tip,' he said, and when Tip turned round his eyes were shut to slits against the morning glare, you'd have needed a knife to prise them open.

Nathan hadn't seen him for a couple of months and he couldn't believe the transformation. There were shadows the colour of mussel-shells both above and below his eyes. He wore a grey suit that was two or three sizes too big for him. It was a typical thrift-shop suit, it smelt of mothballs and piss, it smelt of death, which was probably its history.

'Christ,' Tip said. 'What're you doing here?'

'I saw you from the bus.'

Tip flicked at a scrap of paper with his shoe. The sole was coming away. The shoe seemed to be grinning. 'So what's up?'

'Nothing much. I'm just going to the beach. You coming?'

Tip shook his head. 'Don't reckon so.'

'How come?'

Tip shrugged. 'Just don't feel like it.'

'They'll miss you, Tip. They'll want to know why.'

'Tell them I'm sick.' Tip looked away into the street. His narrow eyes followed cars as they passed.

'Look, Tip,' Nathan said, 'you're not doing anything. Why don't you just come with me?'

Tip stiffened. 'I've got to be going.' He was looking past Nathan at something. Nathan turned round. Jed was standing right behind him.

Jed wore a cheap leather jacket with round lapels. The sun snagged on his crooked skin. Thumbs in his belt and eyes flickering behind those hostile spectacles.

'Well, well,' he said. 'It's Mr fucking Universe.'

Nathan just looked at him.

Jed held out a soiled bag. 'Like one?'

'What are they?'

'Sugar Babies.' Jed smirked. 'Just about the sweetest thing there is.'

Nathan shook his head.

Jed rattled the bag under Nathan's nose, then he spoke to Tip. 'I've got it. Let's split.'

Tip slowly detached himself from the wall. It was like watching a bandage being peeled off a wound.

'Good to see you, Tip,' Nathan said.

'You want to see us again,' Jed said, 'we live in the Towers of Remembrance. You probably heard of it. Why don't you drop in sometime?'

As they walked away, Nathan saw Jed say something to Tip and then tilt his head back and cackle. He had a pretty good idea what Tip had been waiting for, what Jed had brought. Somebody waiting in a doorway on Central Avenue, it wasn't hard to figure out what they were waiting for.

He was sweeping the clubhouse later that day when the captain walked in. He told the captain that Tip was sick.

The captain gave him a sharp look. 'He knows the rules. He gets sick too much, he gets thrown out of the Club.'

Nathan swam out to the buoys, about a hundred yards offshore. The sky was yellow that afternoon, the sea heavy and grey. He watched the solid waves curl away from him and slam against the land. Looking east he could see four towers rising and falling in the distance, the Towers of Remembrance, and he knew Tip was going under, Tip was drowning.

Two weeks passed and Tip didn't show once. Nathan had the dream about the jets again, only this time it was Tip's hand that he was holding. The next day, after he left the beach, he caught the bus to Mangrove East. It was a long ride through all the bad sections. He picked at his fingers, and didn't look at anyone. Slowly the bus emptied out. He'd only been saving lives for a few months, and wondered if he knew enough.

He was dropped under a streetlamp, the only person left on the bus. A patch of mauled light. Gritty sidewalk, scarred with a million cigarette burns. Weeds and spit and oil. Place like this, the only glitter was the knife just before it sank in. Place like this, there wasn't any gold. He moved quickly, head just ahead of his feet, feet in the shadows. Left down one street, right on the next, left down another, then he could smell the sea. He turned into Ocean Boulevard. Dented cars, flop motels, the Lucky Dip bar. Cars with no aerials, no hubcaps. Neon signs with half their letters missing. People disappeared here too.

The Towers of Remembrance stood back from the road, in a stretch of land that was paved, like a parking-lot, and lit by random floodlights. There were four grim towers set in a loose cross-shaped arrangement and linked by concrete walkways. They used to be cemeteries, high-rise cemeteries, but they'd been derelict for years. To the north and east there were housing projects. To the south, a road that led nowhere and, beyond that, the ocean.

He crossed the asphalt and passed under a walkway. Wind moaned in the passages, stirring bitter smells of urine and fish. He stood in the central area, a kind of concrete garden. A few stone benches, a fountain sprayed with first names, declarations of love, four-letter words. This would once have been a place for contemplation. He looked up at the towers surrounding him. Many of the dead bodies had been removed. Their places had been taken by the living. Squatters, mostly. Of all the towers, the South Tower seemed the brightest, the most inhabited. He would start there. But as he looked into the sky sudden clouds came speeding across the top of the building and the building seemed to be falling on to him. He ran towards the entrance, his insides turning over.

He began to climb the stairs. Six doors on the first floor, all locked. On the fourth floor he found a door that was open. Inside was one bare room. Light filtered through a narrow window. He bent down, felt around. Chips of broken china, plastic flowers, dust. China that might've been an urn. Dust that might've been ashes. Now he had dead people on his fingers. He left the room, climbed quickly to the next floor. Once again, all the doors were locked. He tried to remember what he'd heard. Some of the 'graves' were just cupboards. But others were like apartments. You could sleep there, keep watch over your dead. He shivered.

He climbed again, from the ninth floor to the tenth. He looked up once, and jumped. A man in a shiny suit was standing at the top of the stairs.

Nathan swallowed. 'Do you know where Tip Stubbs lives?'

The man walked right past him.

'What about Jed Morgan?'

The man turned the corner and vanished. Standing there, in the half-light, it suddenly struck Nathan that the man might not have been real.

'Tip,' he yelled into the stairwell. 'Tip? Are you there?'

He ran back down the stairs.

Once outside, he stood in the wind. The desolation crept into his bones and he began to shake. What was he supposed to do now? He looked up at the tower. That vertigo again. He imagined opening a door and finding Tip. His eyes shut to slits. The eyelids burred. Like screws.

'They're going to throw you out.'

'Let them.'

And Jed a shadow by the window, the inside of his jacket lined with needles.

He saw an old man's face. Bald on top, strands of grey hair plastered to his neck. Mouth stretched in the strangest grin. Long teeth stuck into his gums like ice-cream sticks. And, behind him, a curving wall of fast green water. And such noise in his ears, like gravel spilling off a truck. He reached around the man's head, took him by the chin – then he felt the man swerve away from him, and saw him swallowed by the water, swallowed whole. He tried to follow the man, but the wave broke and he was yards away. He swam back to the place. The man had gone.

Back on shore he ran to the captain.

'It was a rip,' the captain said. 'Nothing you could do.'

'One moment he was there and then – ' Nathan couldn't go on.

'Some people get away. It's one of the laws of the ocean.' The captain put a hand on Nathan's shoulder. 'You did your best, that's all that counts.'

But you lost him.

Nathan couldn't eat for days. He kept seeing that man's face against a rising wall of water. It had happened six months ago, but some things stay fresh in your head.

The wind, sticky with salt, clung to his clothes, his skin. He was cold. He walked the half an hour to Mangrove Central thinking of nothing, and caught a train home. The next morning the captain called a meeting in the clubhouse, as Nathan had known he would, and announced that, in view of his recent poor attendance, Tip Stubbs was being expelled from the Club. This came as no surprise to most Club members. Someone who didn't show up, it meant you weren't carrying your weight, it was seen as an act of selfishness, a breach of trust. Tip had stayed away too long; he'd been written off, forgotten. The only surprise was to hear his name again and to think that he'd ever been one of them.

Towards the end of the day Nathan was changing in the locker-room when Finn walked in with Ade and a friend of Ade's called Larry.

'Hey, Nates, I almost forgot,' Finn said. 'Your stepmother was here yesterday.'

Nathan stared up at him. 'When?'

'In the afternoon. She dropped in to see you, but you'd already left.'

'That was his stepmother?' Ade let out a low whistle.

Larry called across the room, 'I could use a stepmother like that.'

'Use,' Ade said, and smirked.

Nathan slammed his locker door back on its hinges. 'For Christ's sake. She's married to my dad.'

'Nates,' Ade said, 'we were just joking.'

'Yeah, it was only a joke,' Larry said. 'What's the matter? Can't you take a joke?'

Nathan sighed. He didn't understand what Harriet was up to. During her time as an au pair, her prying had been innocent, playful. Almost a year had passed since then, and now there was an edge. A persistence. There were some days when he felt as if he was under siege.

'So tell me, Nathan,' she'd asked him only the other day, 'have you done it yet?' They were in the car. On their way back from the supermarket.

'Done what?'

'Made love to a girl.'

He didn't answer her. There was so much sugar in her smile, he felt ill. He thought it might be diabetes.

'How old are you?' she asked him.

'Sixteen.'

'Where I come from, boys've all done it by the time they're sixteen. Where I come from, that's normal.'

He wouldn't look at her. He stared out of the window instead. 'I'm thinking of becoming a monk,' he said.

It was a mild, sunny day and Dad was sitting on the porch, waiting for their return. When he heard the car he stood up, smiling. 'How did it go?' he asked. As if shopping was a polar expedition. As if it could go wrong.

'We had a great time,' Harriet said. Then she turned to Nathan. 'Didn't we?'

But Nathan was already moving past her with the box of groceries. There was a ritual to the unpacking of the groceries. Dad always supervised, making certain things were put where they belonged. 'You know where the tomatoes go?' he'd say. 'Third shelf down.' Everybody knew where the tomatoes went, but Dad was simply expressing his pleasure at the presence of these new tomatoes, at their place in the order of things, at his own tight world. This time, though, Nathan left the groceries on the kitchen table and climbed the stairs to his room. He heard Dad and Harriet discussing him below.

'What's wrong with Nathan?' Dad said.

'Oh, you know,' Harriet said. 'Fifteen, sixteen. It's a difficult time for a boy.'

A shoe bounced off his shoulder, and he looked up. Finn stood ten yards away, poised to throw the other one.

'Lighten up, Nates,' Finn said. 'Lighten up or we'll fucking tie you to a chair and paint you.'

Nathan looked round the room. Finn, Larry, Ade. They were all grinning and shifting from one leg to another. They were always so loose in their heads. If he'd been granted a wish right then, that's what he would've asked for.

It turned into one of those nights. They all tumbled out of the clubhouse at the same time. Finn had someone's black convertible. They drove through a sunset sky to the Vista Room on High Head. Finn knew the girl who worked behind the bar. They drank cold beer and played pool. Out in the parking-lot they smoked a joint that tied the two halves of Nathan's brain together like shoelaces. He tripped and fell into the back of the car. They drove back downtown. Hard lights brushed across his face. They were talking about Tip. Words like loser. Words like sick. Laughter and he opened his eyes. He'd wanted to say something and couldn't remember what. They were crossing the bridge now. Warm air. Arcs of metal dark against the brown sky. That harbour smell of concrete, vodka, seaweed.

Seaweed, concrete. Blenheim Point at midnight.

Sometimes he just had to get out of the house, and Blenheim Point was where he went. It was a floating jetty where you caught the ferry to the city. But at midnight the last ferry would've been and gone. There was never anybody there. He sat on one of the plastic beer crates that the fishermen had left behind and stared into the darkness of the harbour with its lights all prickling gold. Waves came from nowhere suddenly, and rocked the jetty: the tide on the turn. That place. It was his respite, his breathing-space.

And then, one night, a fat man in a dinner jacket and a black bow tie had lurched towards him out of the darkness, his appearance so unheralded, so unlikely, somehow, that Nathan almost laughed. It was like a magician's trick, and he wouldn't have been surprised to find a top hat in the vicinity. He watched the man bounce softly off a pillar; the man's belly, barely restrained by a velvet cummerbund, seemed about to spill. It would have to've been a very large top hat.

'How much?' The man belched rather than spoke, his words reaching Nathan in a blast of alcohol.

'How much what?'

'How much for,' and the man's head swerved on his neck, 'you know.'

'No, I don't know.'

The man leaned one hand on the pillar and swayed like a building in high wind. 'Come on, sonny,' he whispered, and he leaned down, leering, so Nathan could see the copper hairs bristling in his nostrils and the pale bumps on his left cheek, 'don't play games with me.'

Nathan tried to duck under the man's arm, but the man chuckled and took hold of his shoulder carelessly and twirled him closer. Nathan pushed a hand into the man's face. He felt the wetness of the man's mouth, the sharpness of the man's teeth. He pulled his hand back. Suddenly he noticed that the man was only six feet from the edge of the jetty, and he pushed the man again, in the belly this time, as hard as he could. The man staggered backwards, snatched one-handed at the air, as if the air was solid and might save him, and crashed on to his back. One roll sideways and he was in the harbour. It looked so casual, like an afterthought.

Nathan waited to make sure the man wasn't going to drown. Then he bent close to the man's face, but not too close, and said, 'You'd better watch it, there's sharks in there,' and then he turned and ran up the steps to his bicycle and rode home. He hadn't been back to the jetty since.

That fat man, he was like a flash from the past. A hallucination, courtesy of the Womb Boys. Guil-ty, Guil-ty. He could see Harriet smirking, all her suspicions confirmed. It seemed that no matter where he went he encountered the same innuendoes, the same violations. He felt hounded, quarried, cornered. There was nowhere left to go, and it was beginning to exhaust him.

'It was only a joke, Nates,' he murmured. 'Only a joke.'

'Now he's talking to himself,' someone said, and someone else laughed.

But it wasn't a joke, whichever way you looked at it.

They hit the Oasis on C Street. They drank shots. Tequila, vodka, tequila. They met two guys who ran the ice-cream van on the pier. Their names drifted into focus and then out again. Larry and Ade evaporated with two blondes from a basement club called Six Feet Under. Finn was still around, still driving. Nathan took the front seat. A girl was sitting next to him, her eyelids two half-moons. She smelt like cucumber. So fresh and pale-green, so clean. He wondered what to say to her. Bottles knocked against his feet, as if shifting in the currents on the ocean bed. Every time Finn opened his mouth, smoke came out.

Her name, magically, was Lilah.

Have you done it yet?

'Next stop the 22 Club,' Finn screamed into the wind. More lights, Lilah's eyes closed, his thigh against hers. It felt like the only part of him that was alive, that burning piece of skin, the rest of him was cold and nowhere. The 22 Club was a golden doorway framing a flight of stairs that was carpeted in red. Two men stood on either side of the door like pillars, one white, one black, both exactly the same height. Finn knew the black one. They were in free.

He was dancing. Two Oriental girls did delicate things with their feet. Their faces were blank. Like plates. Suddenly he couldn't stand the place. A hand appeared on his shoulder. Ade. He was back. 'Lilah says she likes you.'

He sat down. It was later, but not much. Their table was see-through, surfboard-shaped, its surface littered with ashtrays and drinks.

It's a difficult time for a boy.

He reached out with his right arm and swept the table clean. Bottles and glasses shattered. There were screams. Through the crowd he saw the Oriental girls place their hands over their mouths like fans. Then he was seized by two men, one black, one white.

They dragged him across the Club, down the red stairs and out through the gold doors. They threw him into the gutter. He hit the base of a streetlight with his face and felt his lip split.

'Don't you ever fucking come back here again,' the white man said, 'all right?'

'Don't worry, he won't.' It was Ade. He must've followed them down. 'This whole place stinks of shit.'

The white man turned. 'And you,' he said, levelling a finger. 'I see your face again, I crush it in the ground.'

Nathan laughed.

Finn walked over. 'What's got into you?'

'I never saw anything like that before,' Ade said.

'I saw it in the movies once,' Larry said.

'Where's Lilah?' Nathan asked.

Nobody knew.

Lilah could've saved him, but not any more.

It was time to go home, somebody said.

Colours everywhere. But there was only one colour he could see, and that was red.

KNOW YOUR ENEMY

Jed stood outside the Central Theatre just east of downtown with a can of ice-cold soda. He was on his lunch-hour from the sound studio. He wore a black singlet, boots, fatigues. His baseball cap said AL'S BLANK TAPES. He took a long pull on the soda and sighed as it slid down. Years ago he used to come here with the Womb Boys. 'Let's go down the Central, let's go look at the dead people.' Vasco always went on about how important it was. He called it Know Your Enemy. His eyes would flick across the corpses, across the theatre the corpses were in, out to the street the theatre was on, and he'd say, 'This is what we're up against,' and he'd swing his arm so hard he almost dislocated it, 'all this.'

The Central had pale-blue columns on either side of the entrance and big gilt doors. A white neon strip, like that above a cinema, announced the current attractions. Sometimes it was a famous person. A sports personality, say. Or a movie star. Other times it was an ordinary citizen whose family had paid for the honour. Once he'd imagined that his mother might be displayed here, smothered in make-up and bits of radios. Today it said simply IDENTIFY THE MYSTERY CORPSE. $100 REWARD. Jed peered through the toughened glass. It was a tiny, shrunken old woman. The hill her feet made in the sheet that covered her came only halfway down the coffin. Pathetic, really. Unknown corpses were put on display by the parlours in the hope that someone would recognise them and pay for the funeral. The parlours made a lot of money that way. If a corpse remained unidentified, companies often took pity and stepped in, paying for the funeral themselves. They could call it charity, and charity was tax-deductible. What seemed concerned and altruistic on the surface was in fact exploitative and shabby underneath. This is what we're up against.

Jed tossed his empty can of soda in the bin. What Vasco had been up against, at any rate. After all, it had been Vasco's private war. To the other members of the gang, it had been a flirtation with danger, an excuse for violence; it had given them a cause, the semblance of a purpose. Where were they now? Cramps Crenshaw worked in hotel management. PS had joined a record company. Tip had recovered from his overdose and, the last Jed heard, he'd been taken on as an attendant in the aquarium. The Womb Boys had been aborted long ago. The Womb Boys were dead. Long live Moon Beach.

'Well, well. Ugly as ever.'

The man who'd spoken to Jed had broad shoulders and black, wavy hair. He wore a lightweight camel coat. The face seemed different. Wider. Heavier. The guitar had become a double bass.

The man gestured at the mystery corpse. 'Thought it was going to be me, did you?'

Jed smiled. 'How many tattoos've you got now, Vasco?'

Vasco unfastened his cuff link and pushed the cuff back up his wrist. Jed saw the base of a gravestone just where a watch would normally be.

'All the way up?'

Vasco nodded. 'Both arms.'

'What are you doing here?' Jed asked.

'I'm in the business.'

'That's a bit of a turnaround.'

'Yeah, well. Went to so many funerals, thought I might as well start getting paid for it.'

Jed just stared at him.

Vasco slapped Jed on the shoulder. 'Joke.'

'Ha ha.' But something was making Jed uncomfortable. 'So you're in the business,' he said.

'Everybody who's anybody. What about you?'

Jed shrugged. 'This and that. Bit of work in a sound studio.'

'Still recording people fucking or've you moved on?' Vasco laughed for both of them. 'Listen, you want a real job?'

'What've you got in mind?'

Vasco pointed at the long black car idling by the curb. 'There's a body in there. Right now it's nice and cold, but if I don't get it back to the parlour, it's going to start getting warm again. You like to come along? We can talk.'

'Sure.'

Vasco climbed in. Jed followed. There was enough space for half a dozen people in that car. There was a bar. There was air-conditioning. A whisper up your spine. Give me a job this cold. Give me a job with air-conditioning.

He looked round. There was a man sitting in the corner. The man had a shaved head and the long, pale fingers of a surgeon. He wore mirror shades.

'This is McGowan,' Vasco said. 'A colleague.'

McGowan tipped his head back an inch and bared a set of sharp, uneven teeth.

As they drove through midtown, Vasco described the set-up. He worked for one of the directors of the Paradise Corporation which, as Jed probably knew, was the most prestigious funeral parlour in the city. The director's name was Neville Creed. 'You may've heard of him.'

Jed hadn't.

'He's chief administrator,' Vasco said. 'His field's co-ordination. Efficiency. The way things run.' He stared out of the window, shook his head. 'He's rising so fast, sometimes it seems like there's no oxygen. He's going to be the first man to live for ever.'

Jed remembered the word spelled out in silver studs on Vasco's back: IMMORTAL. 'I thought it was you who was going to live for ever.'

But Vasco didn't seem to have heard. 'He's going to freeze himself,' he said. 'While he's still alive. It's the only way, apparently.'

'You mean, if you want to live for ever, you've got to kill yourself first?'

'You could put it like that.'

'How will he know when to do it?'

Vasco smiled. 'He'll know.'

Jed looked over his shoulder at the rectangular box in the back. 'Shame he didn't think of that.'

'He didn't have time. It all happened a bit too fast – '

'Vasco.' It was McGowan. A warning.

Vasco studied the rings on his left hand. 'Keep your hair on, McGowan.' Then he glanced at the man in the corner. 'Oh sorry. You haven't got any.' Vasco turned to Jed. 'McGowan's so tough he never uses more than two words – '

'Shut up, Gorelli.'

'Well, sometimes,' Vasco said, 'on very special occasions, he uses three.'

A hiss from the corner of the car. The sound of brakes being applied to fury.

Then silence.

Efficiency, Jed thought.

He had questions, but he decided to store them for the time being. Your memory's tape. Record now, play back later.

He stared out of the window. Mangrove West merging with the gritty downtown streets. Pawn shops, sex bars, drugstores. Windows glittering with guns and watches. Cops dressed as dealers. Drunks hardly dressed at all. Kids.

Suddenly he realised what had been making him uncomfortable. He shifted on his seat. 'Vasco,' he said, 'about your brother – '

Vasco cut him off. 'That's all right. I know about that.'

'You know?'

'She didn't let you see him. I know that. I checked it out.' His eyes were soft, a strange contrast with the hand that gripped Jed's shoulder. 'Thanks, anyway.'

Another silence. The car floated across a canal bridge. Its engine sounded like air.

'Can you drive?' Vasco asked Jed finally.

Jed said he could.

'Creed's looking for a chauffeur. I think I could get him to see you. You be interested in that?'

'I'd be interested.'

'You'd be on the outside,' Vasco said, 'but who knows? Maybe you could work your way in. It'd be that kind of job.'

A glimmer from McGowan, a fractional tilt of the head. It was one of those looks. Over my dead body.

'I'll take it,' Jed said.

'You didn't ask about money,' Vasco said.

Jed fingered the sleeve of Vasco's coat. 'You look as if you're doing all right.'

A grin split Vasco's mouth open like water melon. 'Fucking old Jed,' he said. 'Who would've thought it?'

Vasco talked some more about Creed. The facts, the rumours. The future. He gave Jed some advice on how to interview. Then they drew up outside a tall building of black glass. The Paradise Corporation. Vasco said they'd have to drop him here. He told Jed to expect a call. Sometime in the next two days.

'Someone'll be in touch.' Vasco shook Jed's hand through the window and the car moved down a ramp and into the darkness of an underground parking-lot.

From the little he'd heard about Creed and the little he'd seen of Vasco, Jed imagined that the interview would take place on the top floor of some high-rise office block downtown. Instead he was given the address of a funeral parlour in Mortlake, a suburb on the bleak northern edge of the city. When he first saw the place he felt conned. From the street it looked like a fast-food restaurant. White stucco walls, bright red-tile roof. All it needed was a giant Paradise Corporation logo on the sidewalk and a sign underneath that said 63 BILLION BURIED.

He pushed through double doors of glass and into a beige lobby. A rhinestone chandelier chinked and chattered in the draught. Red letters zipped tirelessly across a digital read-out screen above reception: SMOKING IN THE LOBBY AND CAFETERIA ONLY. THANK YOU FOR YOUR CONSIDERATION. Jed scowled. He didn't like being thanked for something before he'd even done it.

His appointment was for nine. It was only quarter to. A girl with ginger hair and a small mouth asked him for his name.

'Take a seat, Mr Morgan.'

There were sofas of brown vinyl, arranged at right-angles to each other. Tall cylindrical ashtrays made of stainless steel stood in between. The place looked like an airport lounge. He counted the sofas. Fourteen. He counted the ashtrays. Twelve. They must do a lot of business, he thought. And the business they do must smoke a lot.

After ten minutes the girl directed him to Mr Creed's office. 'Down the corridor, last door on the right.' It was a plain wood door. All he could think of was the word 'efficiency'. Otherwise he was blank. He looked at his watch. One minute to nine. He waited. Thirty seconds to nine. Twenty seconds. Ten. He tightened his hand into a fist, knocked twice and walked in.

It was a small office. Wood-panelled ceiling, wood-panelled walls. There were no windows. One desk, one framed photograph of head office. One chair, which he sat in while Creed finished his call.

Creed.

Dark suit, white shirt, neat hair. Everything was ordinary, predictable, even slightly disappointing. Until he noticed the gloves.

Nobody had mentioned anything about gloves. They'd told him that Creed was going to live for ever. They'd told him that Creed cast a shadow, even when there wasn't any sun. They'd told him that Creed was Latin for 'I believe'. But they hadn't told him about the gloves.

Bad circulation? A skin disease? Some fingers missing?

Then Jed remembered the advice that Vasco had given him, and he moved his eyes somewhere else. Somewhere safe. The window?

There wasn't one. The photograph would do. You didn't act too curious, and you didn't ask any questions. A driver was deaf and dumb. That's what Vasco had told him. Did he want the job or didn't he?

Creed hung up. He pressed a button and said, 'No more calls for ten minutes.' Then he looked at Jed and said, 'I'm told you're a good driver.'

'I can drive.'

'I need a chauffeur. It's a twenty-four-hour job. Right round the clock. Not many people could do it.' Creed's eyes wandered across Jed's face. 'You can think about it if you like. You can have a couple of days to think about it.'

'I don't need to think about it.'

Creed smiled. 'How do you know you'll like working for me?'

Jed suddenly had the curious feeling that Creed was behind him, even though he could see Creed in front of him. The air in the small office seemed glassy, hallucinogenic. Breathing was like a pill on your tongue. Just breathing.

'Don't you think you should ask around?' Creed was saying. 'Find out what I'm like as an employer?'

Now Jed was looking into Creed's eyes. He noticed how dark they were. You couldn't tell where the pupils ended and the irises began. He stared at Creed, trying for a few long seconds to separate the two, then he became aware that he was staring, and he looked away, looked down.

Creed's voice again. 'You sure you don't want to think about it?'

Jed nodded. 'I'm sure.'

'See my secretary on your way out. She'll take care of the details.'

'Is that it?'

'That's it.'

'When do I start?'

'Monday.'

Jed moved towards the door.

'Before you go,' Creed said.

Jed paused. 'Yes?'

'I expect loyalty from my employees. Do you understand what loyalty means?'

'I think so.'

'Perhaps you'd care to define it for me.'

'Loyalty.' Jed faltered.

His thoughts spilled in all directions like the beads of a necklace when it breaks. For some reason he thought of old Mr Garbett bending to gather the beads and suddenly he had the answer.

'It's silence. That's what loyalty is. Silence.'

And, looking back across the office, he was sure that he was right.

'Monday,' Creed said, and turned back to his papers.

The secretary showed Jed round the office and introduced him to the staff. He was fitted for a chauffeur's uniform: a dark suit, a pair of black shoes, a peaked cap with the Paradise Corporation logo printed on the front in red. He was taken through a familiarisation procedure for the car: the type of performance to expect, the kind of maintenance required. When he returned to the office two hours later he found Vasco lounging in a chair, one leg dangling over the arm.

'Get the job?'

'Looks like it.'

They walked back down the corridor together, Vasco's arm round Jed's shoulder. 'You must come and have dinner sometime,' Vasco said. 'Meet the wife.'

'You're married?'

Vasco laughed. 'Been married three years. Got a kid too.'

They reached reception. 'This is Jed,' Vasco told the girl at the desk. 'He's Creed's new driver.'

'I'm Carol,' the girl said, and her small mouth stretched as wide as it would go.

Vasco showed Jed outside.

'Well,' he said, 'you're one of us now.'

They stood on the neat green lawn in the sunlight.

'Just like old times,' Jed said.

Vasco smiled. 'Just like old times.' The same words, but they seemed spoken from a long way off. The same words, with distance added.

It was nothing like old times. Vasco worked for Creed. That in itself was something new. Creed existed inside a kind of magnetic field. It had a pull that most people, even Vasco, it seemed, found irresistible. But it was hard for Jed to adjust to the idea that Vasco had cut a deal, that he was no longer in control. And if it was hard for Jed, might it not also be hard, at times, for Vasco? Jed wondered.

But he didn't have the time to do much wondering. When Creed said it was a twenty-four-hour job, it had been no exaggeration. He only slept about three hours a night, usually between three and six. He must have some kind of technique, Jed decided. He'd read about it: you dropped down six or seven levels at once, you dropped straight into the deepest sleep, it was pure and concentrated, you didn't need as much of it, and then you rose again, six or seven levels, it was like going up in an elevator, and you stepped out at the top, rested, immaculate, alert. Jed didn't have a technique. He had to learn to sleep in snatches, ten minutes here, forty-five there, often sitting at the wheel of the car. At the same time he was trying to study. He'd bought the most detailed map he could find, and he was learning the city street by street, route by route. He was rewarded during his third week when Creed slid the glass panel open and said, 'You seem to know the city pretty well.' He felt this need to prove himself to Creed. He wanted to become indispensable.

The weeks passed and he began to make the job his own. Not just performing it to the best of his ability, but re-inventing it as well. There was a taxi-driver in Mangrove, Joshua, who'd warned him about piles and haemorrhoids and fissures of the anus. Jed's first purchase was a scarlet velvet cushion. It protected him against dis-comforts of the kind that Joshua had mentioned; it also made him feel like royalty when he lowered himself into position behind the wheel. His eyes would suffer too, Joshua had told him. The constant sunlight, the glare. Jed found a pair of dark lenses in a run-down optician's on Second Avenue. All he had to do was clip them over his glasses and the streets were instantly bathed in a deep and soothing green. It was during this time that he switched to a new brand of candy. He'd discovered Liquorice Whirls. Long-lasting, fresh-tasting, they were the ideal candy for a round-the-clock chauffeur.

Slowly he learned Creed's ways. Slowly the patterns emerged. Creed used the limousine as a mobile office, and he was invariably accompanied by one or other of his personal executives, as they were called, sometimes by all four. These people didn't work for the Paradise Corporation, at least not on paper. They were Creed's inner circle. His bodyguards, his confidants. His eyes and ears. They protected him, they supplied his entertainment, they seemed bound to him, as if by some unpaid debt or hidden leash. Vasco was one. McGowan was another. Fred Trotter and Maxie Carlo made up the number. Trotter had been a docker, a mercenary, a security guard. He had one twisted arm, the result of a fall from the roof of a brothel when he was seventeen. He was fifty now, and hard as marble; his jacket always seemed to stretch too tight across his shoulderblades. Maxie Carlo was a court jester, a vicious clown, the Mortlake mascot.

He wore a silk suit and kept a flick-knife up the sleeve. His small round head sat on his shoulders like a ball that might, at any moment, roll off and bounce around on the floor. He drank from Creed's glass, he sang and danced on restaurant tables, he gave people names. McGowan was Skull. Trotter was Pig. And he'd dug deep into Vasco's past and surfaced with Gorilla. He even had a name for himself. He called himself Meatball, on account of his oily complexion and his no neck. With the possible exception of Vasco, they'd all worked, at one time or another, as vultures. Now they ran teams of vultures, smooth-faced men in grey suits, men who didn't balk at crime, not so long as there was some good commission in it. Jed began to understand the significance of Creed's gloves. Probably he didn't want to get his hands dirty.

For the first few months Jed was ignored. The only words he heard were the names of destinations. He was just 'Morgan' or 'you'. Vasco's words echoed like a sentence: You'll be on the outside, but maybe you'll work your way in.

And the look on McGowan's face. Over my dead body.

And then it was a Saturday morning. Jed had rolled the car out of the garage and into the parking-lot; he was checking the fluids. It was still early, just after eight, and the sun hadn't found its way round the edge of the building. The smell of hot dough and sweet syrup drifted through the wire-mesh fence from the YUM YUM DONUT place on the other side of the street. He heard a door slam and turned to see Creed walking towards him, flanked by all four of his personal executives. Their impeccable dark suits, their circus faces.

'But what about Morgan?' Creed was saying as he walked up. He stopped in front of Jed and stared.

Jed lowered the hood and wiped his hands.

'We need a name for Morgan.' Creed turned to Carlo. 'But remember, no more animals. We've already got two animals.'

'Only two?' Vasco said. 'I thought we had more than two.'

'Jesus,' McGowan said, 'his old woman must've fucking threw his brains out with the garbage this morning.'

'I mean, there's Trotter, there's me,' Vasco said, and he turned to face McGowan, 'and then there's you. Isn't there?'

McGowan took one step forwards. His teeth looked filed down. His eyes were mirrors. Watch yourself. Watch yourself die.

Carlo stepped between them, chuckling. 'Maybe I should think up some new names.' He lifted his dainty hands into the air, palms up. 'Maybe we should all be animals.'

Vasco and McGowan were still staring at each other over Carlo's head.

'Over here, Meatball,' Creed said.

Carlo went and stood beside Creed. They both studied Jed.

'What do you think?' Creed said.

Carlo's head rolled sideways on his shoulders. 'He's so long and thin. Kind of looks like a bit of spaghetti.'

'Spaghetti Morgan.' Creed smiled. 'I like that.' He turned to the others. 'You two. Skull, Gorilla. Spaghetti Morgan. What do you think?'

Vasco and McGowan turned to look at Jed.

'Spaghetti?' Vasco said. 'That's perfect.'

'Goes pretty well with Meatball, anyway,' Jed said in a dry voice.

That joke kept them going all day. They even had it for lunch, at a small Italian place on the east side. They all asked for Spaghetti with Meatball. Jed read their lips through the restaurant window.

'Hey,' Trotter said as they climbed back into the car afterwards, 'that's two foods we got now, isn't it?'

'You only just realised that?' Carlo said. 'You're real quick, aren't you, Pig?'

'Don't call me Pig,' Trotter growled.

'You're growling,' Carlo said. 'Maybe I got the animal wrong.'

Maybe Vasco was right, Jed thought, as he drove them back into town that day. Maybe they were all animals. Trained animals, though. They snarled at each other, they scratched and bit, but one word from Creed and they were back on their tubs and ready to jump through hoops of fire.

Even with his new name Jed was still cut off. He was the driver, sealed behind a sliding sheet of glass. He was deaf and dumb.

But he didn't lose heart. Inside him there was patience like a wide field. Inside him he could feel the slow, green pushing of the future.

The only person he was close to at all was Carol. His clip-on lenses made her laugh. So did his Liquorice Whirls. His scarlet cushion had her in hysterics. He liked to make her laugh because it meant that he could watch her mouth.

The first time he saw her mouth, that morning of the interview, he thought she must've had some kind of operation. It looked as if two people had been sewing it up from either end and then they'd both run out of thread. Every time he made her laugh he thought her mouth was going to tear at the edges. It was almost too painful to watch.

He didn't realise she had a limp until they went out after work one day. Creed was out of town. He'd flown north for an international convention. Jed had a free night and no plans. Carol suggested a walk on the pier.

At first he thought her heel had snapped or something. Then she looked up into his eyes and told him that one of her legs was shorter than the other, and she was sorry if it embarrassed him. She'd had three operations, she said, all without success. Her father had taken her to specialists, physiotherapists, even a hypnotist once, but there was nothing anyone could do. Jed's eyes scanned the faces of passing lovers, scanned the dark ocean beyond, but he was listening. He was definitely listening. It was like hearing a story about himself. Like looking at himself in one of those distorting mirrors. It was like some strange form of vanity. He recognised exactly what she was talking about. She mistook his silence for compassion, and tightened her grip on his upper arm.

They reached the end of the pier. It was a clear night. He could just make out a few faint lights in the distance. Those lights had names: Angel Meadows, Coral Pastures, Heaven Sound. The ocean graveyards, twelve miles out.

Carol shivered. 'How do you like working for Creed?'

'I like it,' Jed said.

'He scares me.' She saw Jed's face. 'I know. I'm stupid.' She shook herself, and turned her back on the ocean. 'What about a drink?'

'Where?'

'Here.' She pointed to the sign they were standing under. 'The Starlite Bar.'

She shifted her weight from one leg to the other, so she was leaning away from him, and her lips tipped upwards, they were so red and stitched in the white light of the naked bulbs that looped above their heads, they were the only colour in her face, but he looked away, it wasn't embarrassment he felt, it was a kind of tortured fascination, but he didn't want to kiss her, or even touch her, it would've felt like incest.

'Let's have two drinks,' she said, 'or maybe three.'

He smiled. She was making light of a moment that had been a risk for her. He took her arm and lowered his voice. 'You forgot. I don't drink.'

'I never knew.'

He told her about the Towers of Remembrance. Thirteen floors up, misty plastic tacked over broken glass. Flap, flap, flap in the wind all night. Dreams where the skin was lifting off your bones. Ghosts above and ghosts below. He told her how he'd lost his seventeenth year completely. How the Towers of Remembrance became the Towers of Oblivion. A mixture of vodka, speed and glue. He'd been down and through and out the other side. He wasn't interested in losing control any more. He wanted a mind that was sharp the way a diamond cuts glass. He drank soda now and ate candy, and that was it.

'I know,' she said. 'Your pockets crackle when you move.'

He laughed.

'Coca-Cola,' she said. 'You can drink Coca-Cola.' There was a power-surge behind her eyes, as if the voltage had increased. 'It's supposed to be very good here.'

They walked into the brash red and chrome of the Starlite Bar. Someone was playing an electric organ, and old couples twirled on a horseshoe of polished wood. He ordered a gin and tonic for her and a Coke for himself. They sat in a booth.

'How come I never noticed before?' he asked her. 'That you've got a limp.'

She grinned. 'Special shoes.'

'So how come you're not wearing them now?'

'I don't know.' She shrugged, sipped at her drink. 'I don't see why I should hide it all the time.'

Halfway through the second drink she said, 'Do you want to look at my leg?'

A wave of heat rose through him. He glanced round.

'You want to, don't you? I can tell.' And, lifting an inch off the seat, she eased her black tights down, so her legs were bare. Her right knee was ringed with scar tissue. It looked like a piece of red barbed wire.

'Can I touch it?'

She nodded, her lips tight.

It felt like dried glue. Taking his finger away again, but still looking, he said, 'They really fucked it up, didn't they?' but the way he said it, he might've been paying the surgeons a compliment.

She looked at it dispassionately, as if it was a ring on her finger, a ring she was trying on, a ring she might or might not buy. 'I think it's because they always cut in the same place.' She emptied her glass. Ice-cubes knocked against her teeth.

'They've tried to fix it three times,' she said, 'but I think they've pretty much given up now.'

'I know,' he said. 'You told me.'

During the third drink she cried.

He dropped her at the taxi-stand outside Belgrano's. She lived on the west shore, over the harbour bridge, and he had to drive east. She stood on the sidewalk, her wrists pressed tight against her thighs. She looked like a child, lost or shy.

He leaned across the passenger seat and looked up at her. 'You going to be all right?'

A sniff, a nod.

'I'll see you tomorrow.' He watched her limp towards a taxi, then he shifted into DRIVE and pulled away.

On his way home he had to stop for gas. As he was paying he noticed someone wheeling a Harley into the yellow light of the pumps. The owner of the bike had a pigtail and a black leather jacket with a death's-head on the back. He couldn't see the face, but he thought he recognised the jacket. He pocketed his change and walked over.

'Mitch. That you?'

Mitch stared at him.

'I came into your tattoo place once. With Vasco. It was years ago.'

Now Mitch's face tipped back. 'Fuck me, the blackmailer.' His eyes travelled the length of Jed. First down, then up. 'What's the fancy dress?'

Jed grinned. 'I'm driving for the Paradise Corporation.'

'Same place Vasco works, isn't it?'

'He got me the job.'

Mitch had this way of squinting at you, as if he was looking directly into bright sunlight, as if he was having his picture taken. It was hard to tell exactly what it meant.

'This is a bit out of your way, isn't it?' Jed said.

Mitch scowled. 'Bike's fucked.'

'What are you going to do?'

'I don't know. Leave it here.'

'You want a ride home?'

Mitch looked at his boots. They were smeared in grease and spilt gas. A breeze shuffled through the nearby palms. 'You could do that?'

'Sure.'

Mitch wheeled his bike to the back of the gas station and chained it to some railings. When he came back, Jed said, 'You still living in the same place?'

'I moved.'

'Where are you now?'

'Rialto.'

Rialto was out by the river. North of Mangrove, west too. It would have taken anyone else half an hour, but Jed knew the shortcuts. He drove it in fifteen minutes. If Mitch was impressed, he didn't let on.

As they turned on to Rialto Parkway, Mitch pointed through the windshield. 'There it is.'

Mitch was still using the sign he'd used on Central Avenue all those years ago, the old gold sign that made Jed think of circuses. He pulled up outside, left the engine running.

Mitch shook his hand and opened the door. 'Come round for a beer sometime. You know where I am.'

When Jed drove into the parking-lot behind the Mortlake office the next morning, Vasco was standing on the asphalt, hands in his pockets, black hair shiny as a polished shoe, the beginning of a wide grin on his face.

Jed leaned out of the window. 'What's so funny, Vasco?'

'I hear you've been out with Carol.'

'So?'

'Cunning son of a bitch.'

Jed stared at him.

'The chairman's daughter,' Vasco said.

'What?'

'Carol. She's the chairman's daughter.'

'The chairman of what?'

'The chairman of what. The chairman of the whole fucking corporation. That's what.'

'I didn't know.'

But Vasco wasn't being taken in so easily. 'Of course you didn't.'

'I didn't.'

Vasco didn't believe him. 'You cunning son of a bitch.'

So he was a cunning son of a bitch. Well, all right. That was what he was then. 'If you know so much,' Jed said, 'maybe you can tell me who else I saw.'

Vasco frowned.

'Come on,' Jed said, 'who else did I see?'

'I don't know.'

'They're not that good then, are they?'

'Who aren't that good?'

'Your spies. Your vultures. Are they?'

Vasco shrugged.

'Mitch,' Jed said. 'You remember Mitch.'

'Mitch?' Vasco looked round. 'Listen, Jed. How about you come for dinner tonight? You could see my house, meet the wife. We could drop in at Mitch's on the way. I haven't seen him for ages.'

'What if Creed flies back early?'

'I'll take responsibility for that.'

It was like the old Vasco talking. Jed agreed, out of a strange sense of nostalgia.

They left the limousine in the parking-lot and took Jed's car. After the Mercedes his Chrysler always felt so sloppy, it was like wearing shoes that were too big for you.

Vasco scanned the worn interior. 'Some car.'

'You don't like it,' Jed said, 'you can always get out.'

'I like it, I like it. I just said some car, that's all. Jesus.' Vasco looked across at Jed. 'You're too sensitive, you know that?'

And you're not, I suppose, Jed thought.

He drove fast. In less than twenty minutes they were in Rialto.

'This is unhealthy, this part of town,' Vasco said. 'This is very unhealthy.'

True enough. Rialto was a no-go area. Half black, half Hispanic. A pattern to the blocks: church club bar; church club bar; church club flophouse bar. A shooting every night. The signs on N.E. 139th Street told you everything: HOUSE OF JOY. Y-TEL MOTEL. LOU'S GUN HUT. EL FLAMBOYAN BAR. JESUS LOVE CHURCH. THE OASIS LIQUOR LOUNGE. BIG MAC'S SHOWGIRL REVIEW – TOTALLY NUDE – PROVOCATIVE. Mitch's sign looked quaint among the stale neon. Jed reached the 11000 block and slowed. He couldn't stop outside the tattoo parlour, so he took the next left, an alleyway, and parked in among a cluster of dustbins. This was where the Chrysler came into its own, in areas like this. Just another piece of scrap metal. Blend.

Vasco was thinking the same thing. 'Good thing we didn't come in the limo. You leave a limo round here, they'd strip it bare in five minutes.'

Jed followed Vasco into Mitch's place. He heard the buzzing of the needle-gun. Mitch was working. A Latin kid sat on Mitch's green chair, his arm braced on a steel table.

Without lifting his eyes, Mitch said, 'Who's dead?'

Vasco grinned. 'Nobody's dead, Mitch. This is just social.'

Mitch tipped his head to the left. 'You want a beer, they're over there, in the corner.'

Vasco opened the fridge and looked inside.

'How's the bike?' Jed asked.

'It's fixed.' Mitch glanced up at Jed. 'It was nothing. Just a plug.'

Jed stopped his smile before it reached his face. Those few extra words, he knew they were the closest Mitch would ever get to thanking him.

Jed and Vasco cracked open a beer each. They sat on a vinyl bench against the wall while Mitch worked on the Latin kid's shoulder. Slowly a skull appeared, slowly a blue snake slithered out through one of the empty eyes and coiled, like a turban, on the crown.

'Haven't lost your touch,' Vasco said.

'Do me a favour, Vasco,' Mitch said. 'Just shut up.'

Vasco glanced at Jed and shrugged. 'Trouble with Mitch is, he works too hard.'

The sun dropped in the sky, gilding the dusty glass of the store-front. The horns of passing cars sounded pinched and distant. Jed opened another beer. He could almost have slept.

'This place,' he said, 'it's just like your other one.'

Mitch grunted. 'Except I live here.'

'Yeah?' Jed looked round. 'Where?'

'Upstairs. Got a yard too. In the back.'

Vasco yawned.

More slow minutes passed.

After Mitch had locked the store for the night, he took Jed and Vasco out the back. They stood on the cracked, tilting concrete, cans of beer in their hands, and let the day go dark. A darkness threaded with the silver of sirens, a darkness heady with alcohol, exhaust fumes, river-silt. Once Jed turned sideways and saw Mitch in profile, the stubborn nose and chippy eyes, the pigtail, like a kind of Chinaman, his fat hand round the can and resting on his belly, he was so firm on his two feet, rooted and content, he had the peacefulness of a tree, the dusty fig tree that splayed above their heads, that rubbed against the windows on the second floor. Then a woman's voice called out, 'You down there?'

Mitch didn't move or speak.

'The guys'll be here soon,' the woman's voice said.

'Who's that?' Jed asked.

'It's his old lady,' Vasco said. 'He got married too, didn't you, Mitch?'

Mitch didn't say anything.

'Well,' Vasco said, 'I guess we'd better be going.'

Driving through Euclid towards Highway 1 and the north-west suburbs, Vasco settled deeper in the seat, his head against the rest. 'Sometimes I don't understand that guy.'

'What's to not understand?'

'All that dirt and grease all over, all that slow time.'

'Maybe he doesn't have any choice.'

Vasco rolled his head on the rest so he was facing Jed. 'You're doing something, it's because you've chosen it.'

They didn't speak again until they reached Vasco's house in West-wood. It was a bungalow, if something that takes up half a block can ever be called a bungalow. Fake chimneys, walls clad in big square slabs of ochre stone. The place looked like it was made of Peanut Brittle. You could've snapped a piece off the porch and eaten it. But it was real estate. No question about that.

Jed peered through the windshield. 'This all yours?'

Vasco sat back with a crooked grin.

'Christ,' Jed said. 'What's your wife like?'

She was like a woman with black hair that curved up and back from her forehead. She wore black high-heels and her tights hissed, but she walked stiffly, as if her hip joints needed oiling. She accepted a kiss from Vasco, and then she took his coat. She seemed too old to be his wife.

'You're Jed?'

'Mrs Gorelli,' he said, 'I'm pleased to meet you.'

'Oh no,' and she waved her hand in the air, backwards and forwards, as if she was polishing it, 'Vasco, he told me so much about you, when you were kids. You must call me Maria.'

They sat down to eat almost immediately. The dining-room was crowded with dark furniture. Sofas of velvet and leather, high-backed chairs of ornate, carved wood. The walls were hung with textiles, nudes in clumsy gilt frames, hand-painted plates. A colour TV stood on the sideboard. Every now and then Vasco reached out and changed channels with the tip of his knife.

'There's a remote,' Maria said.

'I don't like remote.' Vasco looked at Jed. 'You like remote?'

'I haven't got a TV,' Jed said.

'Did you hear that?' Vasco said to Maria. 'He hasn't got a TV.' And changed channels again with his knife.

They talked about old times. Past facts were much easier, it seemed, than the ambiguities of the present. The past, it was so distant, they'd been different people then, they could point at themselves in astonishment, disbelief almost, they could view it all without becoming too involved, like some TV drama. It was clear that Maria knew next to nothing about Vasco's activities. Nor had she any desire to know. So long as the money came in, she was happy. As to where that money came from, it was neither here nor there, it was geography, and geography, that was such a boring subject.

'He was so bad in those days,' she said at one point, lovingly, 'so bad, weren't you?' her hand sliding across the lace tablecloth, covering his.

'The things I did,' and Vasco shook his head. 'Jed too.'

'Yeah,' and Jed, too, shook his head.

After dinner Maria left them alone. Vasco moved to the drinks cabinet and poured himself a tumbler of brandy. He swallowed half of it standing up. Then he sat down in a maroon velvet armchair and began to chew his big square fingernails. He'd been drinking steadily throughout the meal, but he now seemed tenser than ever. Jed waited for Vasco to break out of his silence. He watched as Vasco's rings threw splinters of rich light against the wall.

'You wanted to talk to me,' he said finally.

Vasco almost jumped at the sound of Jed's voice. 'Yeah,' he said. 'Yeah.'

Jed waited.

'It's about the job I got you,' Vasco said. 'I've been thinking. Maybe I shouldn't have done it.'

'I'm glad you did,' Jed said. 'It's a good job.'

'I don't know. I may've got you into something.'

'How do you mean?'

Vasco swirled his brandy around. 'Creed,' he said. 'He's doing some pretty weird stuff.'

'That's nothing new, Vasco. We've always done – '

Vasco cut him off impatiently. 'I'm not talking about that kind of weird stuff.'

'What then?'

'Him and the Skull. They're in it together.'

'What kind of weird stuff, Vasco?'

'It's pretty sick.' Vasco stood up. 'I don't want to talk about it, I just wanted to warn you, you understand?'

'Oh sure,' Jed said, 'sure. I understand.'

But Vasco wasn't listening. He'd gone to the window and parted the curtains with one hand, and now he was staring out, out into the darkness of the garden.

Jed drove home that night feeling like a man who's been told he's going to die but doesn't know when.

HARD WATER

Nathan had only been living in town for a couple of months when he met India-May, but he'd seen her around and he knew what they said. She smoked too much grass, she slept with black men, she wore a silver chain round her ankle that tinkled like the bell-collars you put on cats to stop them catching birds, but it had never stopped her catching anything, that was what they said. The town was called Tomorrow Bay, which was a strange name for a town that didn't seem to have a future. But it was also the reason why Nathan was there; he'd seen the name on a map and liked the sound of it. So one afternoon he walked into a bar on the south side, one of those dive bars where the air smells singed and all the stools are painted black and smoke curls through their legs as if a dragon's just breathed out, and there was India-May with her hand round a double gin and when she lifted the glass to her lips the rim hit her teeth and her bangles spilled down her freckled arm and her pale hair dripped into her eyes. She looked reckless and weary. She looked as if all the stories about her were true.

One of the stories happened to be standing right next to her. An old black man whose name, if Nathan overheard it right, was Twilight. He called himself Twilight, he was saying, because that was about where he was in his life, and she stood up and threw her arms around him and told him he was the fine high sun of noon to her, and he just looked at Nathan over her shoulder and rolled his eyes, much as to say she doesn't know what time of day it is *at all*.

Twilight left soon afterwards, though she didn't seem to want him to, and as she turned back to her gin she caught Nathan watching, and called across to him.

'What's that you're drinking?'

'Coke.'

'You want a real drink?'

He smiled and shook his head. He told her he drank beer now and then, if he was thirsty, but that was about it. Mostly he stayed clean.

She seemed to be gathering him with her eyes, and then she took a spare strand of her pale hair and threw it over her shoulder, like it was salt or something, like it was lucky.

'You're unbelievable. How old are you?'

'Twenty. Almost twenty-one.'

'Most people your age, they haven't even started getting dirty yet,' she said, 'and here *you* are, clean as a goddamn whistle. Unbelievable.'

'I'm not that clean.' He moved up the bar, took Twilight's stool. He told her that he'd been so drunk once that he'd almost lost his teeth. He showed her the scar on his top lip where it hit the streetlight. She bought him another Coke.

India-May wasn't her real name, it turned out. Nobody in that place seemed to have a real name. She'd changed it to India-May when she was seventeen. Just another way of leaving home, she said. Just another line drawn down the past. Talking of lines down the past, he said, he'd drawn his own. He told her about Moon Beach. How he'd left a year ago. How that place was dead for him. How it looked like a heap of rubble to him now.

She watched him with those blurred eyes of hers. 'Where are you living?'

'In town. A few blocks east of here.'

She began to tell him about a house she owned, it was an old farm, out past Modello. She said she had a spare room on the third floor. 'If that's any use to you.'

He hesitated. 'Past Modello?' Modello was north-east of Tomorrow Bay, about twenty miles inland.

'Way past. You interested?'

'Maybe.' He'd been sharing an apartment with a surfer and the surfer's girlfriend. Everything was like, totally intense. He wasn't sure how much more he could take of it.

'That black guy you saw, he stays there sometimes. A lot of people stay there sometimes, I guess.' Then she seemed to tire suddenly, all the light and muscle spilling out of her, and she folded round her drink.

Soon afterwards he said he had to be going. She told him to think about it. Even gave him a number to call. He thanked her and walked out into heat and sunlight and stood laughing on the street. He'd forgotten it would be like this. So hot, so bright. Sometimes one world's so new, it wipes the old one out.

Ten days later he called her and asked if the offer was still good.

'I don't say things I don't mean. When d'you want to come out?'

'As soon as possible.'

She didn't miss a beat. 'OK, this is how you find the house. It's like I told you. It's in the hills, north-east of town. Get on the highway going north, then drop down on to the Modello road. It starts off straight, then it gets to twist a bit, but there's no cars and it's real dreamy on the right, like you're the only one alive. Just real dreamy. How are you coming?'

'Bike.'

'OK. Look for a tight bend about seven miles out of Broken Springs. You'll know it when you see it because there's a white cross there with BABY BOY SOPER painted on it. Some kid blew a tyre on the hill a few years back, the car flipped over, caught on fire, there was only his teeth left and a ring he'd just bought for his girl. So the story goes. Anyway. So right after the cross there's a couple of trees. One of them's deformed because of Baby Boy's car tore a lump out of it on the way down. The track's right there, no sign, just a track looking like it's going nowhere. And it sort of is.' She laughed from deep down in her throat. He thought she was probably stoned. 'Five miles along that track you'll see a grey roof. It's the only house around. Kind of tumbledown. But there'll be smoke in the chimney and beds with springs and dogs to keep the bogeyman away. But look, babe, you sure it's what you want? It's lonely as a grave out here and only the wind moaning and moaning all the time and you look like a city boy to me.'

City boy.

He rode up the next day, salt leaving the air as he climbed into the hills. Once he left the paved road he saw nobody. The track bucked and coiled through a landscape of smooth white boulders, grey pines, and cactus that twisted in the dust like a nest of snakes. After five miles – curiously enough she was accurate where he least expected her to be – he saw the house, crouching at the end of a ridge, just at the point where the track dipped down and hid. All loose tiles and cracked windows and walls patched up with sheets of tin, it used the colours of the land it stood in, grey and brown and yellow, so it had the look of a creature that should've been extinct, a creature that had only survived because it had a good disguise. It used to be a farm, he remembered her saying, and it still breathed like one. When he pulled into the yard, chickens ran off in straight lines through the dirt and dogs began to bounce around his tyres like ping-pong balls and people came round corners and leaned on things.

The place was cut off, true enough, but all that stuff about it being lonely as a grave, that was just her talking. She did a lot of that. She'd talk and talk, and make things bigger than they really were. Or sometimes she'd make them smaller. There was nothing lonely about it, unless you call living with six people lonely. There was Joan, a woman who was recovering from some kind of breakdown. There was an old man by the name of Fisher. There was a young married couple, Pete and Chrissie, and their baby. And there was Twilight, the old black man from the bar. That was six, not counting India-May herself and the family of gypsies who camped among the shredded tyres and blackened car-parts out the back. She surrounded herself with people, all different kinds, sometimes she was lucky, sometimes she wasn't, but it didn't matter to her. In her book the worst people were preferable to no people at all. She was someone who heard each grain in the hour-glass, she felt the passing seconds like sandpaper against her softest skin. Time actually seemed to hurt her, and people helped her get through it. She'd been ripped off more times than she could remember. Jewellery, money, clothes. Even a car once. She was philosophical about it. She believed it evened out, either in this life or the next time round. She was always showing Nathan things that she'd been given. It always seemed to him, as he was asked to examine some painting or basket or packet of seeds, for Christ's sake, that she'd been had, that she'd come off worse. But she'd be smiling, and she'd be tossing her hair over her shoulder like salt, and she'd be saying in that breathless voice of hers, 'See, I told you. Isn't it beautiful?' Sometimes it seemed to Nathan that her life was just that, a feat of held breath, just another ten seconds, just another five, and then death would flood her lungs like water, a string of glass bubbles to the surface and then nothing. She was scared in a way that he could understand. The kind of fear that sends you running across a six-lane highway or jumping into rapids. She was someone who ran towards her fear, screaming. Who tried to frighten it. Who, in another period of history, would've been worshipped as a saint or burned as a witch.

She gave him a room on the third floor. Walls the colour of eggshell, a row of glass bottles on the mantelpiece, and a bed with springs, as promised. It was a spiritual room, she told him, it had been waiting for him, and standing at the window that evening he could almost believe it. He could see right down the valley. Tomorrow Bay glowed beyond the hills, an orange dome in the dark-blue sky, as if a spaceship had just landed. But the town seemed alien to him now, he felt no pull at all. He would be happy where he was. In the morning he sat down at the kitchen table and she explained how the house worked. All her 'guests' paid rent, some in money, some in kind. The old man mended shoes. The woman with the breakdown cooked the meals. And Twilight, well, she'd leave that to his imagination. 'You choose how you want to pay,' she said. 'It doesn't matter to me.'

He chose to pay in money. That year he was working at Seaview Lodge, a mock-Tudor hotel just off the highway as you headed north out of Tomorrow Bay. The people who stayed there were mostly in their sixties, and they preferred the sun-lounge and the tea-room to the beach. Only the fanatics swam, plunging their bald heads and tumbling flesh into the water at dawn. He arranged the deck chairs and parasols in the morning and folded them away at night. He collected litter on a pointed stick. He raked the sand. There was very little actual lifesaving to be done. He saved an heiress once, and almost wished he hadn't. A miracle how her cramp disappeared the moment he took her in his arms. 'He's a hero,' she announced to the small crowd that had gathered on the beach, 'a gen-u-ine hero,' and insisted on inviting him to dinner that night. Over dessert and coffee she told him about the pool she had at home. 'It's inlaid with gold mosaic. You never swam in anything so heavenly.' And then she offered him a position as her own private lifeguard. Position. She actually used that word. 'Money's no object,' she said. But he turned the offer down, making his excuses with a grace and tact that only served to enhance her admiration.

'Do you know what she said?' he told the waitresses later. 'She said, "Money's no object," and do you know what I said?'

They couldn't guess.

'I said, "Nor am I."'

'You didn't,' they said.

He grinned. 'I wanted to.'

For weeks afterwards the waitresses were always sidling up to him and whispering, 'Money's no object.' The chambermaids teased him too. He was, in any case, a mystery to them. He was open and friendly, but he never focused his attentions on any one of them in particular (unlike his predecessor, who had focused his attentions on five of them, one after the other). They decided he must have some violent, jealous woman in the mountains, and he let them believe it.

The ride home took about forty minutes. He headed west on a slim dark road that arrowed across the coastal plain and up into the hills, where it began to come adrift. No cars suddenly. No light. Only thoughts for company, thoughts that jumped like colts from one piece of ground to quite another piece of ground altogether. The whistle of air in his helmet, the smell of the hot dust cooling. If he reached the top before sunset he would stop and watch the last light leave the ocean, the clouds above sweetening in colour, as if they were slowly being dipped in syrup. Real dreamy, just like India-May had said. The landscape was spoiled only by a pyramid of trash that rose into the sky some distance to the north. This was the municipal dump. Though it was situated five miles out of town, its sweet odour would carry along the beaches when the wind blew in the wrong direction, and had even been known, on occasion, to invade the corridors of Seaview Lodge. By the time he reached the farm, the dogs would be chained up for the night. They knew his bike and didn't bark. He'd switch his engine off and listen to the black air buzz.

Once inside he'd climb the stairs to his room and close the door and gaze through the window at the sky. Still as deep water. Only the ripple of a car in the valley, a distant aeroplane. He'd lie on his bed under the roof and turn the leather bracelet on his wrist. He'd been given it by an old woman who played the flute. She sat under a palm tree just beyond the hotel fence. Her skin was olive, the colour of slow rivers, her limbs as thin as wire. She always wore the same red plastic raincoat. Every time it rained, which was most afternoons for about fifteen minutes, she played the flute. She always played the same piece. She seemed to have chosen it specially because it lasted the same length of time as the average shower. Sometimes she finished before the rain did, sometimes afterwards, and he'd never forget one afternoon when her last note coincided with the last drop of rain and he heard her laugh in astonishment. She had sounded, in that moment, like a young girl. He had to speak to her. Though all he could say, when he was standing in front of her, was, 'I'm glad you're here.' She reached into her pocket and handed him the leather bracelet, and he put it on right away. He'd worn it ever since. Sometimes it would seem as if the music rose out of the bracelet and, hands linked behind his head, he'd topple slowly into sleep, only to wake later, his arms numb, the moon caught in the window, and all his clothes still on. And voices drifted up from below, no words, just resonances, it was like the murmur of a plucked string, it was the same hum, like being inside an instrument. And sometimes he'd go downstairs and open the kitchen door, his eyes blinking against the sudden light, and he'd join the others in a cup of India-May's herb tea.

It was on just such a night that he stayed up late and found himself alone with her. She was rolling a joint in her worn fingers.

'So tell me, Nathan,' she said, without looking up, 'what is it you're running from?'

He smiled. It was the kind of cliché you expected from her, but it was also the one question he'd always been asked and never answered. And so he smiled. Because he recognised it. Because he knew that, this time, he was going to answer it.

He began to talk. He didn't know where the talk was taking him, he only felt that it was flowing, and knew that things which flowed were clean. And came quickly to one particular night, a night that had always been a secret.

He was sitting out by the pool at home. It was after eleven, a still, warm night. A tree had blossomed near the water, its white flowers breathing a perfume that was like magnolias. A faint click came from behind him. He looked round. Someone was standing on the terrace, a silhouette against the french windows. It was Harriet. She must've thought she was alone because she stretched in a way that seemed unfettered, private. Then she noticed him, he could tell because she went motionless, then she pushed herself forwards, hips first, into the moonlight.

She came and sat down beside him. 'What are you doing out here, Nathan?'

'Oh, just sitting,' he said, 'thinking.'

'That's the trouble with you. You think too much.'

He laughed softly. Maybe he did. But it was kind of ironic, really. He wouldn't've spent half as much time thinking if she hadn't been around.

'I thought you were in bed,' he said.

'I stayed up to watch a show on TV.'

'Any good?'

'It was just a show. You know, music and dancing.'

She'd thrown the words out lightly into the darkness. But there was a wistfulness, a nostalgia. He remembered a letter that she'd written to Dad. Something about being tired of the bright lights. Even back then he'd thought it sounded strange; she was only twenty-one, after all.

'Where's Dad?' he asked her.

'He went to bed hours ago.'

A bird called from a tree at the end of the garden. A low, brooding murmur. Harriet stood up and began to unzip her skirt.

'I'm going for a swim.' She was laughing at her own impulsiveness.

'Now?'

'Why not?' She looked down at him, the lower half of her face masked by her shoulder. 'Join me?'

He shook his head. 'I don't really feel like it.' But he did. He could already feel that dark water creeping up over his body as he lowered himself in.

Harriet stepped out of her skirt. Then, crossing her arms in front of her, she lifted her blouse over her head and dropped it on top. She'd been lying in the garden all summer, and her skin looked almost black against her white silk underwear. He knew it was silk. She'd told him once in the car; she'd said she couldn't wear anything else. He tried not to look at her. He didn't want her to think he was interested. When he did look at her he concentrated on the flaws, the slightly swollen thighs, the stomach rumpled by childbirth.

Still, he thought she felt his eyes on her, he thought she liked the feeling, because she lingered at the edge of the pool, staring into the darkness, before she moved down the steps and into the water. She waded out of the shallow end, trailing her fingertips across the surface, then she gave herself, the water rustling as it accepted her, like a present being unwrapped. Halfway up the pool she turned and swam back towards him. 'It's so beautiful. Are you sure you won't come in?'

It seemed so intimate, this invitation, with her face tipped up to his and Dad's curtains closed behind her, but it was only a swim, what harm could it do? He stripped down to his shorts and slid over the side. He sighed as the water closed round him like a glove. Floating on his back, he stared up into the sky. The moon was sinking, yellow now. A plane droned overhead, one red light on its wing-tip winking. Trees bloomed dark at the edges of his vision. He'd almost forgotten that he wasn't alone. Then the water rustled and a voice breathed into his ear. 'I told you, didn't I?'

Harriet was standing beside him. He twisted sideways and his feet found the bottom. Now he was standing too. She took her hair in both hands and, looking at him, began to wring it out. Her bra had become transparent, and her breasts showed clearly below her arm, the nipples sharp beneath the wet cloth. She let her arms drop. The insides of her wrists knocked against her hips. She moved a step closer to him and seemed to lose her balance in the water. She put a hand on his chest, as if to steady herself, but then she left it there and reached up with her mouth. He felt his mouth drawn down to hers, he felt one of her thighs edge forwards, wedge between his legs. He pulled away from the kiss. Small waves scuttled to the side of the pool.

She seemed surprised. 'What's wrong?'

What's wrong? He wanted to shout, but couldn't. Those closed curtains. The man sleeping so lightly behind.

'Don't you like it?'

'No,' he hissed.

He could tell she didn't believe him. But maybe when he turned away from her and swam to the edge of the pool and hauled himself out, maybe she believed him then. He didn't bother to look round and find out. Snatching up his clothes, he walked back into the house and up the stairs to his room.

The next day, at breakfast, Dad said, 'There was water all over the floor when I came down this morning.'

Harriet smiled. 'I went swimming with Nathan in the middle of the night. I forgot to tell you.'

'In the middle of the night?'

Harriet smiled. She'd known that Dad would seize on that particular aspect of the story. If something wasn't part of his routine, he found it unimaginable, hugely eccentric, almost humorous. She'd known that. She was much shrewder than Nathan had given her credit for, and he now trusted her even less.

From that time on, she cooled towards him. Those sweet looks she'd always specialised in, they suddenly became barbed, like chocolates injected with poison. She was constantly asking him why he never brought girls home. She began to accuse him of having love-affairs with the other lifeguards. 'I think homosexuality is a disease,' she'd say suddenly, at breakfast. 'What do you think, Nathan?'

He shook his head at the memory, looked across the table at India-May.

'And were you?' she asked him.

'Was I what?'

'Having love-affairs with lifeguards.'

'No.' He smiled. 'She didn't understand the bond. We were close, yes, but it was like brothers.'

India-May nodded slowly, tipped some ash into a saucer. 'So you had to carry all this alone. Couldn't you talk to anyone?'

'There wasn't anyone.'

There was only one person apart from Dad, and that was Georgia. She'd just turned thirteen. She wore her hair greased back and hung out a lot. Espresso bars, mostly. Sometimes he had to go and pick her up. He always rang the place first and told her he was on his way. He didn't want her losing face with her friends just because her old man worried too much, and anyway he liked the air of conspiracy. He'd lean against a wall on the other side of the street and watch her. She'd be sitting at a table, gum tumbling in her open mouth, smoke rising from her hand, as if she was a puppet and that wavering blue thread controlled her every move. In her own time she'd slap some money on the table and then she'd kind of unfold, and the faces of the others would tip to hers. She'd push past some guy and his chin would tilt and his eyes would follow her as she left. She'd stand on the sidewalk, hands stuffed in her jacket pockets, and Nathan would jerk his head, to tell her where the car was, and she'd walk down her side of the street and he'd walk down his, and it was only once they were in the car that anyone would've realised they were connected in any way, and by then it was too late, because nobody could see them. They'd always played games, this was just the latest.

But she was only thirteen. How could he tell her anything? All he could do was sit by and watch as she caught on.

He remembered her first outburst. It was lunchtime. He could still see Harriet putting her fork down and heaving a sigh of relief. 'Well, at least Rona will be normal,' she said, and turned to Rona who was knocking her spoon against her plastic bowl, 'won't you, darling?'

Dad frowned. 'Why do you say that?'

Harriet seemed surprised that he should ask. 'You told me about Kay. You know, the madness in that side of the family. Poor woman,' she said, 'it must've been awful.'

Georgia threw her knife at her plate. A chip of white china hit the wall the same way a reflection does. 'Christ,' she said, 'I'd rather have her blood than yours,' and then, shoving her chair back, she said, 'I'm not hungry any more.' She stamped out of the room, slamming the door behind her.

'Georgia?' Dad's face paled. His hands fastened round the arms of his chair.

Nathan couldn't bear to look at him. Suddenly Dad was stumbling about in a kind of no man's land. In the place where he was he couldn't possibly win. From now on there were only different ways of losing, different kinds of pain.

Without meeting Harriet's eye, and in a low voice, Dad said, 'I think you went a bit far, Harriet.'

Later that afternoon Nathan heard Harriet shouting in the bedroom. 'Why don't you ever stand up for me? You always stand up for them, never for me. Why don't you stand up for me?'

And Dad was shouting too. 'Stop it, Harriet,' he was shouting. 'Stop it, stop it.'

Nathan listened at the foot of the stairs. He was the toy soldier of all those years ago, but he hadn't toppled over, he was marching from room to room, marching from the kitchen to the hall, the hall to the study, the study to the hall again, he didn't know what to do, he couldn't go upstairs and intervene, nor could he leave the scene of what felt like a crime, he was shaking with this terrible indecision. Those jets were flying again, tearing the air inside his head, he could only think one thought: He's going to die. She's going to kill him.

He saw the whole thing as a plot. The clothes Dad liked, the hair Dad liked. It had been so easy. A short skirt, a fringe, no make-up, and she was in. Then she could set to work. Wearing him down, wearing him out. Wearing him away to nothing. She was that dream of his come true, she was the planes made human. He imagined her standing in Dad's bedroom at night, Dad asleep behind her. He watched her looking in the mirror. He saw her face begin to change. The whine of the engines, the slow turning on that one front wheel.

Upstairs Dad was still shouting. 'Stop it, stop it, stop it.' He said it thirteen times, Nathan was counting, and then he couldn't listen any more. He ran into the kitchen and pulled the cupboard open. He was doing everything as loudly as possible. He didn't want to hear anything else from upstairs. Inside the cupboard was a stack of new light bulbs in their cardboard jackets. He stacked them in his arms and took them out into the yard. One by one he stripped their jackets off and hurled them against the outside wall of the house. A flat pop each time one exploded. Then a faint tinkling as the fragments of glass showered to the asphalt. Dad never said anything about the missing light bulbs. He simply put them on the shopping list the next Friday. '8 light bulbs,' he wrote, '40-watt.' Previously he'd always bought 100-watt bulbs, but 40-watt bulbs were cheaper and it didn't matter how bright the bulbs burned if they were just going to be hurled at a wall.

They were still living in a sort of 40-watt half-light when Nathan followed Dad into the sitting-room one day and asked if he could speak to him alone. It was after lunch. He waited while Dad took his usual array of pills: first the flat white ones, then the round bronze ones, then the lozenges, half red, half black.

'Have one of these,' and Dad handed him a dark-green capsule the size of a pea. 'It's good for you.'

Nathan smiled and swallowed it.

'So what is it?' Dad said finally. 'Is something wrong?'

'I'm going to stay with Yvonne for a few weeks.'

'How long will you be gone?'

'I don't know. I think maybe after staying at Yvonne's I'll move on up the coast.'

'Where to?'

'I don't know yet.'

Dad took off his half-moon spectacles. He leaned his head back and stared up into the corner of the room where the two walls joined the ceiling. 'This is your home too, you know. I don't like to think that you're being driven out.'

'I'm not. It's just something I want to do.'

He was lying, of course, and they both knew it. Sometimes he thought of all the lies stored in his head. Or not so much lies, perhaps, as the truth held prisoner.

Dad brought his eyes down from the corner of the room. 'I'll miss you,' he said in a low voice, and quickly looked away.

Nathan broke off. He wasn't crying exactly. It was just that there were tears dropping from his eyes.

India-May put her hand on his. 'It's all right, Nathan,' she said. 'It's all right.' She went to the sideboard and poured a brandy. 'I know you're clean and all that, but I think maybe you could make an exception tonight.'

He drank the brandy down without a word.

Later he said, 'You know, when I worked in Moon Beach, we used to make bets with each other, bets on who could get through the spring tides.' He stared at the glass in his hand. 'Those waves are high, you try and get through, but they're hitting the beach and chewing it up, you dive, you come up, you dive again, you come up again, you're getting nowhere, it's hard water, it keeps knocking you down and pounding on you, but you can't stop, if you stop, you've lost it, it rolls you right back to the shore, it throws you out on the sand like an old tin can, you've got to keep diving, that's where your fitness counts, you dive, you come up, and those waves keep pounding on you, and then, finally, you come to the big one, you get under it, and you're safe, you're on the other side of the water.' He laughed softly and said, 'The other side of the water,' and shook his head. 'Next thing is, you see a nice wave and you think fuck it, I'm going to take that wave, and you take it all the way in, and you get out, and you hold out your hand, someone owes you, and everyone's watching because the red flags are up and there's nobody in that surf, nobody.'

He turned the empty glass in his hands. 'Sometimes you come out of that water and you lie down on the sand and you're so tired you just fall right off to sleep.'

A silence as she imagined it.

'If you won the bet,' she said finally, 'what did you win?'

He laughed. 'Oh, nothing. A hamburger, maybe.'

And they were both laughing. Laughing and laughing. More tears, of a different kind.

Afterwards she said, 'You know, you're lucky having all that. I think it's wonderful.'

'I wish Dad thought so.'

'Doesn't he?'

He shook his head. 'He wants me to do something worthwhile.'

'What could be more worthwhile than saving people's lives?'

'He doesn't see it like that.'

'Well, I think it's wonderful. The ocean, the beach, it's like your own kingdom. Worthwhile,' and she snorted through her nose, 'that Dad of yours, he must be soft in the head.'

It was almost as if he'd had an ear to the ground. As if he'd picked up that tremble in the earth, that hushed drumroll: the hooves of the enemy. Still far away, but moving in his direction. When he came home after work the next day he found a letter waiting just inside the door. It was postmarked Moon Beach, but he didn't recognise the handwriting. He took the letter upstairs and lay down on his bed and tore it open.

'By the time you read this letter,' it began, 'I will have left your father.' There followed three pages of bitterness and accusation, which ended with the words, 'It will be your father who suffers, not me.' Signed simply, 'Harriet Christie.'

His own name thrown in his face like acid.

He let the letter slip to the floor. He tried to laugh, but his laughter sounded forced in that small room.

LOYALTY IS SILENCE

There are times when your life seems to jump tracks. Slow train to fast, local to express. You have the sense that, from now on, you'll be travelling on a different line, you'll be seeing different views through the window.

It was November and Jed had just turned twenty-two. Creed opened the glass panel one morning as they were returning from the airport and said, 'Where do you live, Spaghetti?'

'Mangrove East.'

Creed shook his head. 'I need you closer.'

It was exactly what Jed had been waiting to hear, but he kept his voice level. 'Where've you got in mind, sir?'

'The Palace.'

Jed's heart lifted in his ribs. The Palace was where Creed lived, in a penthouse suite on the fourteenth floor, so the idea made perfect sense. But the Palace was also the most exclusive apartment hotel in the city. It was located on Ocean Drive, between C and D; it took up the entire block. With its two twin towers of baroque grey stone, it was just about the only building in Moon Beach that wasn't either white or pale-blue. Its lobby was the size of a railway station, all peach marble and glass and gilded metal. The central chandelier was gold-plated and weighed, it was rumoured, something in the region of half a ton. Everyone had stayed at the Palace. Heads of state, movie-stars, tycoons. Just to be able to give it as your address!

'You'll be in the basement,' Creed said, 'but it should be adequate.' He allowed himself a smile. 'It can hardly fail to be an improvement on Mangrove East, in any case.'

Jed moved that same week. To reach his new apartment you had to use the old tradesmen's entrance: past the service elevator, down four flights of stairs, along a corridor with a linoleum floor. The basement of the Palace was a lost kingdom of storerooms, washrooms and boiler-rooms. Fat grey pipes hugging the ceilings, dull yellow walls. The air smelt of lagging, paint, damp. And also, ever so faintly, and inexplicably, of marzipan. In the end you came to a door that said (and this was equally inexplicable) 3 D. There was no 3 C and no 3 E. There wasn't even a 3 A. 3 D was unique and without context. It was another dimension. It was Jed's new home.

There were two rooms, both painted a tired pale-green. There was a bed, a TV, a phone. There was air-conditioning. That was about it. If you parted the net curtains and peered sideways and upwards you could see one tiny piece of bright blue sky, but you might pull a muscle doing it. A constant clash and tinkle came from the kitchens across the courtyard, like the percussion section of an orchestra from hell. At night the boiler took over, roaring and trembling until dawn. During his first week in the Palace he hardly slept.

It was during the second week that Carol asked him to dinner at her parents' place. As the taxi moved down off the harbour bridge and into the suburb of Paradise, he remembered what Vasco had said, and turned to her.

'Your father,' he said, 'is he really the chairman?'

Carol looked embarrassed. 'Yes.'

He sat back. Jesus. So her father really was the chairman. Her father was Sir Charles Dobson.

'Why?' Carol said. 'Didn't you know?'

'No, not really. Vasco said something about it, but I didn't believe him.'

'I thought everyone knew.' And she gave him a smile that resembled gratitude. It was as if, in not knowing, he'd paid her a great compliment.

Sir Charles and Lady Dobson lived on Pacific Drive, a road that wound its way through the canyons, then doubled back towards the ocean to link, eventually, with the South Coast Expressway. The house was one of the white, wedding-cake mansions in the 10,000-block, high wrought-iron gates and video security, and just the hills rising in silence behind.

Jed paid the taxi and stood still. You needed millions to breathe this air. This air exactly, right here. Millions. And suddenly he took the rumours and put them on like a coat. Lifted and dropped his shoulders a few times, he'd seen people do it when they tried on clothes in stores. Not a bad fit. Maybe he really was a cunning son of a bitch, just like Vasco said he was. Certainly he was thinking all those thoughts. Jed Morgan, he was thinking. Chairman.

Dinner was plate after plate of food he'd hardly ever set eyes on, let alone eaten: caviar, bortsch, salmon, duck. And then, as if that wasn't indigestible enough, the conversation turned to the subject of advertising. The new Paradise Corporation commercial had just aired the previous night. Jed had seen it. It opened with a black screen and a voice that said, 'This is probably the most frightening place in the world.' It pulled back slowly to reveal a fringe of green around the black. You were looking into an open grave. The voice went on to say that, when you were faced with something as frightening as death, you needed the right people around you, and the right people were the Paradise Corporation etc. etc. One of the papers had attacked the commercial for being too emotive. People at the dinner table were springing to the commercial's defence, using words like 'honest' and 'bold'.

'Well,' Jed said, speaking up for the first time, 'at least there weren't any tolling bells in it.' All the talk around him suddenly subsided; he felt strangely shipwrecked in the silence. 'I used to work on commercials for funeral parlours,' he went on. 'I used to think that if I heard one more tolling bell, I'd go out of my mind.'

After the laughter had died away, he told a story about one particular commercial that he'd worked on. It was a testimonial for a funeral parlour which had dealt with the victims of a forest fire. He needed the sound of a forest fire running under the voice-track, but he couldn't find the effect on file. It was seven at night and the commercial had to be presented at breakfast the next day. In the end he had no choice. He had to create the effect himself.

'How did you do that?' Lady Dobson asked.

'I'll show you,' Jed said, 'but I need absolute silence.'

Out of his left pocket he produced a handful of candy-wrappers and, during the hush that followed, he created a forest fire for the Dobsons and their guests in the Dobson's very own dining-room.

It was a great success.

'And these are only Liquorice Whirls,' he said. 'In those days I was eating Almond Toffee Creams and they came in much cracklier paper.'

Either Sir Charles had forgotten what Jed did, or else nobody had bothered to tell him, because he now leaned forwards and, impressed, it seemed, by Jed's ingenuity and verve, said, 'Perhaps, young man, you should come and work for me.'

All eyes locked on Jed.

He waited three seconds. You have to time things.

'But Sir Charles,' he said, 'I already do.'

He looked round. People were weeping with laughter. He caught Carol's eye, and winked. His skin had picked up a glow from the lilies on the table. The candlelight had taken his cheap suit and made it over in some priceless fabric. The vintage wine had anointed his tongue with new and seductive language. He could do no wrong. When the meal was over, Sir Charles escorted him into the library.

He watched Sir Charles cut the tip off his cigar. Being old had done something to Sir Charles's face, something that being poor sometimes did. It had sucked the colour out. Eyes, hair, skin: all different shades of grey and white. Distinguished, yes. But colourless. And cheeks with folds in them, like old wallets. He wondered how much Sir Charles was worth.

But now the cigar was lit and, turning to Jed, Sir Charles spoke through billowing smoke. 'So who exactly do you work for?'

'I work for Mr Creed. I'm his driver.'

Maybe it was only a coincidence but, as soon as Jed pronounced the name of his employer, the cigar fell from Sir Charles's fingers. It bounced on the carpet, shedding chunks of red-hot ash.

'God-DAMN.' Sir Charles spread his legs and stooped. He flicked the ash towards the fireplace with the back of his hand. Then he stuck the cigar between his teeth and slowly sucked the life back into it.

'Let me ask you something, Jed,' he said, when the smoke was billowing once more. 'Have you ever been to head office?'

'I have, yes.'

'What did you think of it?'

The head office of the Paradise Corporation, as Sir Charles knew perfectly well, was just about the most famous building in the city. Built entirely of black glass, it marked the beginning of what was known as Death Row, a stretch of downtown First Avenue where most of the big funeral parlours had their offices. All night long lights burned in the central elevator shaft and in the windows of the twenty-fifth floor. The result was a white cross that stood out among the familiar neon logos of airlines and oil companies. The cross was a landmark. You could even buy postcards of it. Jed had only been inside the building once, and all he could remember was the angel. She was part sculpture, part fountain. Her head and body were metal and her wings were water, water that was forced through holes in her back and lit from beneath so it looked solid, like glass. He remembered the hiss of those wings, the lick and swish of revolving doors, the warble of phones. All tricks a hypnotist might use. Forget your loss. Forget your grief. He remembered drifting, drifting close to sleep.

'You walk into that building,' Sir Charles said, 'and you know you're in capable hands.' Clouds of smoke trailed over his shoulder as he paced. 'You've got to win people's trust. Trust is very important. Without trust,' and he came to a standstill and tipped his chin into the air, the thought still forming.

'Without trust,' Jed said, 'we wouldn't be standing here now.'

Sir Charles swung round. 'Precisely.' For a moment he was rendered motionless by surprise, a kind of respect. But only for a moment. 'What I'm trying to say to you is, this is a hard business. A cutthroat business at times. But you should always remember one thing. It's people that you're dealing with. People.' He thrust both hands in his pockets and rocked back on his heels. 'I'm sixty-nine and I'm still working. Nobody really retires from this business. It's a way of life.'

He showed Jed to the door of the library. 'Is there anything I can do for you, my boy?'

'Not that I can think of.'

Then his face moved close to Jed's, and he said, 'Are you interested in my daughter?'

'I'll let you into a secret, Sir Charles,' Jed said. 'I'm not interested in your daughter at all. I'm just pretending to be. It's your money I'm really after.'

Sir Charles stared at Jed, and Jed stared back; he wasn't going to help Dobson out with this one. At last a smile began to pull at the folds in Sir Charles's face, as if his cheeks really were wallets and his smile was going through them, looking for cash, then the smile turned to laughter, it pushed between his teeth, it was dry and rhythmic, it sounded uncannily like someone counting a stack of dollar bills. Jed saw Carol at the end of the corridor and began to walk towards her.

'You remember what I said,' Sir Charles called after him.

The next day Creed asked Jed to drive him out to the Crumbles. The Crumbles lay to the east of the city. All the land out there had been under water once. It was flat for miles. There were a few wooden beach huts down by the shoreline. Some old mine buildings in the distance, some gravel pits. Otherwise just shingle, grey and orange, and a soft wind tugging at the heads of weeds.

He followed Creed's directions, leaving the road for an unpaved track that seemed to lead towards the ocean. The track widened and then vanished. Then they were driving over rough ground, loose stones popping under the tyres. He parked close to where the land sloped downwards to a narrow pebble beach, and switched the engine off.

Creed stared out of the window, his chin cushioned on one hand, his eyes doubly concealed, first by the tinted windows of the car, then by his sunglasses. Jed thought he understood. It was like Vasco and the mudbanks of the river. It was where Creed came to do his thinking. Where was Vasco? Jed wondered. He'd scarcely set eyes on him since the night they'd had dinner together at the house in Westwood. Nobody had mentioned him either, and Jed didn't feel he should ask. He poured himself a cup of coffee from his private flask and watched the white gulls lift and scatter against the dull grey sky.

The glass panel slid open behind him.

'I heard you were out at Dobson's place last night.'

'That's right, sir. I was.'

He'd known Creed would find out. He'd even wanted him to. He wanted Creed to be amused, impressed even. A chauffeur at the chairman's dinner table!

'Any particular reason?'

'Carol asked me.'

'Carol?'

'His daughter. The receptionist.'

Creed said nothing.

'The one with the limp,' Jed said.

'I know the one.'

Another silence. Wind pushed at the car.

Then Creed said, 'Dobson's on his way out.'

The chairman? On his way out?

But Creed didn't give Jed time to think. 'When a ship sinks,' he said, 'that's when you see who the rats are. What interests me is, which rats leave which ship.'

The glass panel slid shut.

One week later Sir Charles Dobson resigned as chairman of the Paradise Corporation. The decision had been taken, the statement said, 'for personal reasons'. The new chairman, elected unanimously by the members of the board, was Mr Neville Creed. Jed read the statement three times while he was eating breakfast that morning. It sounded calm and measured, utterly reasonable. But he couldn't make any sense of it. He saw Dobson standing in the library. Nobody really retires from this business. It's a way of life. He couldn't make any sense of it at all. And then he saw Creed sitting in the back of a black car parked on the Crumbles. Dobson's on his way out.

From then on everything that happened seemed to jar. There were minor changes, subtle departures from routine. Creed called at seven. 'Meet me in the parking-lot.' Jed usually waited in the car outside the front of the hotel. Now it was the parking-lot. Underground. When Creed stepped out of the service elevator he wasn't alone. Flack was with him. Flack was one of the corporation lawyers. It looked as if both men had been up all night. Except Flack didn't have a technique. Flack's skin glistened in the white, gritty light, his thin face tight with fatigue.

Jed held out a hand as Creed approached. 'I'd like to congratulate you, sir.'

At close range Creed looked bright, jagged round the edges. As if he'd been cut out of tin. He was staring at Jed. He didn't seem to know what Jed was talking about.

'Your new appointment.'

Oh that. A nod, a quick smile. And then Creed ushered Flack into the car. It was as if Creed had something more important on his mind. But what could be more important than his appointment as chairman of the largest and most prestigious funeral parlour in the city?

Up the ramp and out into the light. That white winter sun, a magnesium flash. At the first intersection Jed snapped his dark lenses over his eyes. A calming green. He glanced at the two men in the back. Flack was crushed into a corner, gesticulating, a beetle turned on to its back. Creed leaned towards him, his hand palm-upwards in the air, the fingers curved and stiff like the setting for a precious stone, but no stone there. They were arguing – but what about? It was a question Jed had never allowed himself before. He saw old Garbett's tape recorder, he saw the wheels turning. If only he could record what they were saying. He began to imagine how he would run the wires under the carpet, and had to stop before it became too real.

Flack was dropped in the city at ten. McGowan and Maxie Carlo took his place. Carlo pared his thumbnails with his knife. McGowan spat bits of words through pointed teeth. Creed stared out of the window, as if it was the Crumbles he could see. The mood was wrong, all wrong. Creed had been appointed chairman, yet there was no sense of celebration. The day was filled with whispers, echoes, nerves.

Towards midday they drove out to Dobson's house on Pacific Drive. Carlo and McGowan waited on the steps while Creed went in. Creed was inside the house for almost an hour and when he emerged on the steps it wasn't Sir Charles who was with him, but Sir Charles's wife. At first Jed thought she was laughing. Maxie Carlo must've cracked a joke. But he saw her hand fly up and hold her mouth, he saw Creed slide an arm round her shoulder. It wasn't laughter. She was crying.

The next stop was Butterfield, where they picked up Morton the embalmer. This, too, was curious: Creed never had anything to do with embalmers. In fact, Jed had only seen Morton once before. He'd spent an afternoon with Morton when he first joined the company, as part of his induction. He remembered the white room. The tinkle of calipers and hacksaws in the sterilising bowl, the naughty smack of rubber gloves. And Morton talking, talking. 'I lie beautifully, that's my job. Or not lie, maybe. Turn the clock back. Tell an old truth.' A hole had opened in the floor and the naked corpse of a white woman rose into view. Later Jed had lost all sense of time as the external heart slowly pumped a solution of formaldehyde into the dead woman's body, as the dead woman's body began to blush. He couldn't help thinking of his radios, the way they warmed up, that slow suffusion of light behind the names. Turn the clock back. Tell an old truth.

The four men had lunch in the Palm Court Motel on Highway 23. Jed waited in the car. Ate half a chicken salad sandwich, threw the rest away. Read the paper and couldn't remember a word of it. He had no appetite. Couldn't concentrate.

At two-forty-seven the four men pushed through the glass doors and out into the motel parking-lot. They stood on the warm asphalt. Creed opened one hand like a fan, words spilling sideways from his lips. Morton dipped his head, his face pulled wide, excited. Carlo and McGowan stood on either side of the embalmer, he might've been in custody. They all wore suits. They all had clean shoes and neat hair. He watched them walk towards the car. They looked like evangelists, or politicians. When they were ten yards away they stopped talking, and they didn't start again till they were safely behind glass.

I need you closer.

That was a laugh. He'd never felt further away.

And then Sir Charles Dobson died. Just ten days after his resignation. Suddenly, at home. The papers bristled with tributes to 'a man who stood for tradition and dignity in a business that has recently been rocked by scandal and corruption'. Creed received a good deal of spin-off publicity. The *Herald* called him 'Dobson's understudy' and 'one of the new entrepreneurs'. The *Tribune* said he exhibited 'the cutting edge and thrust of an aggressive businessman on his way to the top'. It was clear from the cumulative weight of these reports that Creed had already arrived. Many of the papers carried photographs of Dobson and Creed side by side, Dobson's arm around Creed's shoulder, as if Creed was not only heir to the business, but also a son.

On the morning of Dobson's funeral a bellhop knocked on 3D and handed Jed a big square box. There was a card taped to the box: TO 3D. A GIFT FROM 1412. 1412 was Creed's apartment. Jed smiled at the anonymity. All letters and numbers. Like convicts. Inside the box was a black satin top hat. He tried it on. It fitted to perfection, it even seemed to match his scarecrow face. He decided to wear it for the rest of his life.

When he pulled up outside the Palace, Creed was already waiting by the entrance with McGowan, Trotter and Maxie Carlo (still no sign of Vasco). In their black top hats and tailcoats they looked more like vultures than ever. They studied him from their position high on the steps. Creed turned to Maxie Carlo.

'What do you think of Spaghetti, Meatball?'

Carlo scarcely had to look. 'Dressed to kill.'

Laughter jumped from face to face. Creed, Trotter; even McGowan. Then, just as suddenly, they seemed to remember that this was a serious occasion, they were on their way to a funeral, the funeral of a great man, the chairman, their founder and benefactor, and they fell silent again.

The first two cars held the coffin (solid bronze with 24-carat gold-plated hardware) and several close members of the family. Creed rode in the third car, flanked by two of the Corporation's top directors, with Jed at the wheel in his new top hat. The vultures travelled in the fourth car, packed tight into the back, like pieces of a game. Creed had organised the funeral himself. The funeral to end all funerals. A motorcade through downtown Moon Beach, a twenty-one-gun salute, a memorial service in the cathedral. Creed had requisitioned an open car, and he stood for the entire procession, as a mark of his own personal respect for the deceased. From time to time Jed tipped the mirror to the sky to look at him. Hands clasped behind his back, face as grave as stone. Jed could sense a question running like a breeze through the rows of people who lined the streets: *Who's he?* If they didn't know now, Jed thought, they'd know soon enough.

There was a clever piece of stage-management on the steps of the cathedral. The city's funeral barons had turned out in an unprecedented expression of their admiration and their sympathy, and Creed took full advantage of the fact. He engineered it so that he was standing head and shoulders above his rivals when they filed past to shake his hand and offer their condolences. It was a symbolic moment, duly captured and enshrined by the massed bank of press photographers. In the papers the next day it looked as if the funeral parlour heads were sanctioning the transfer of power, as if they were acknowledging Creed's pre-eminence, as if they were paying homage. The funeral had become a coronation.

After the service Jed saw Carol walking across the lawn in front of the cathedral. He hadn't spoken to her since the day before her father resigned. She'd left Mortlake suddenly, without saying goodbye. She wasn't limping today, he noticed; she must be wearing those special shoes of hers. At that moment she caught a glimpse of him through the crowd and came over.

'Jed,' she said, 'how are you?'

He caught Creed looking at him, frowning.

'I can't talk now,' he said.

'Can I call you?'

He gave her the number. 'I'm not there much, though. Pretty busy these days.'

'You're doing well,' she said, 'aren't you?'

He shrugged.

Her face bent close to his. To kiss him, he thought, and he shrank back.

'This whole thing's a sham,' she hissed.

He stared at her, not understanding.

She nodded twice, almost to herself. 'A sham.' Then she was stumbling, legs of china, to her car.

The left side of his head began to beat. What did she mean, a sham? He saw one of her heels sink into the soft grass, she almost fell. She seemed so exposed, so ridiculous, he wanted to point and laugh. What did she know? The loss of her father had opened her up like a can of something and tipped her out. There was nothing holding her together. He couldn't deal with that.

In the event he didn't have to. She never called.

Vasco called instead. At least he thought it was Vasco. The voice just said, 'Watch the papers,' then it hung up.

He forgot about the call until the end of the week when the story broke. It broke in the tabloids first, where it would do the most damage. The *Mirror*'s headline was a classic:

FUNERAL BOSS DIED TWICE

According to sources that couldn't be revealed, the Paradise Corporation had pretended that Sir Charles Dobson was alive for ten days after his death so that the leadership of the company could be handed over without shaking public confidence. In a move variously described as 'ghoulish', 'Machiavellian' and 'sick', Mr Creed, it was alleged, had orchestrated this posthumous resignation, instructing expert embalmers to preserve the corpse and even arranging a photo session two days after Sir Charles's death (Sir Charles's lifeless arm around Mr Creed's shoulders) so a picture could be released to the press along with a transcript of the letter of resignation. Only once the transfer of power had been smoothly effected and accepted by the general public, the paper claimed, had Sir Charles Dobson been allowed to die.

These were extraordinary allegations and they turned the city upside down. For the first few days after the story broke Creed lived in the car. He banished his vultures. In the present climate of opinion they could only damage him. Flack was his adviser now. As they drove from press conferences to radio stations, from radio stations to television studios, Creed and Flack huddled in the back of the car hatching strategies. Creed's statement seldom varied: 'This entire story is a monstrous fabrication, an attempt to smear the good name of the Paradise Corporation.' In between the public appearances, they were hounded by the press. There were two or three car-chases a day, with Jed using every hidden fold and secret pocket of the city to lose some persistent journalist or camera crew. They ate in the outskirts, obscure highway diners, and cafés in bleak residential suburbs. They hid in the city's petticoats. They stayed awake. One night they almost snapped an axle when Jed's eyes fell shut and the car left the highway and began to lurch across dry yellow grass. A strange closeness developed, a shorthand, a kind of telepathy. Jed began to know where Creed wanted to go without a word being uttered. There was the afternoon when he drove out to the Crumbles and they slept for three hours, the wind pushing at the side of the car like a crowd. He woke suddenly and turned. Creed was sleeping with his eyes wide open. Jed saw Creed wake. The only difference was a subtle shift in breathing.

'I dreamt we were made of gold,' Creed said, 'and there were people trying to melt us down.' One of his eyebrows arched ironically. As if anyone could melt them down.

Jed knew the story in the papers was true. He only had to remember the day after Dobson's resignation. Creed's distracted blankness in the parking-lot. Flack's anxiety. The tension on the faces of McGowan and Carlo. Mrs Dobson's tears. Morton's jittery elation. I lie beautifully. All those ambiguous, jarring pieces fell into place. He remembered the picture in the paper. He remembered thinking that the smile on Dobson's face looked false. And it had been, of course. Dead men didn't smile. Not unless they fell into Morton's hands. Turn the clock back. Tell an old truth. No, he didn't believe in Creed's innocence, not for a moment, but then innocence and guilt had never been the parameters, had they? There was only one question in his mind when he read the papers: had they taken the story far enough? It occurred to him as a possibility, for instance, that, prior to being 'kept alive' for ten days, Dobson might first have been murdered. Was that what Carol had been trying to tell him?

The days passed. Jed ate Liquorice Whirls, and virtually nothing else. He hardly slept. At times he felt himself departing into hallucination. The rumours were still flying, but the proof was lying low. Creed's vultures were out there, Jed was sure of it, sealing lips and twisting thumbs. Sometimes Creed would turn his face to the window and smile. Just the flicker of a smile when he thought that nobody was looking (but Jed had practised the deft glance in the mirror and he didn't miss much). Creed was like a gambler. Spin the wheel. If you lose, just spin again. There were always more chips. It was down to nerve. Who got chicken first. Which rats left which ship.

Silence was descending all over the city. The hollow roar of nothing being said. The Dobson story had yet to be substantiated, and the family were still unavailable for comment. The Paradise Corporation was suing three of the city's leading newspapers. Creed met McGowan and Trotter at Papa Jim's Bone-A-Fide Rib Place on the South Coast Expressway. A chequered tablecloth and lighting like melted butter. Jed could see them from the car, drinking beers and swapping jokes. It was real mood-swing. They looked like three guys relaxing after a ball game. Once again he wished he could've listened in.

Then, nine days after the story broke, the *Tribune* published a cartoon. It showed a coffin with the lid nailed down and two candles burning at the head. A voice-bubble rose from the inside of the coffin. It said, simply, 'I resign.'

The morning that the cartoon appeared, Jed overheard Creed talking to Maxie Carlo. He had the paper in his hand. 'The press are beginning to have fun,' he was saying. 'The worst is over.'

There was a new confidence. An air of leisure, recklessness, infallibility. McGowan was seen smiling. Maxie Carlo came to work in a yellow plaid suit. Creed gave Jed two nights off.

Jed drove down to Rialto to see Mitch.

'Ask him,' Mitch said as Jed walked in. 'He works there.'

Some friends of Mitch's had come round. A couple of them had ridden in the Moon Beach chapter together. There was a black girl there too. Her name was Sharon. She wanted to know what Jed thought about the Dobson affair.

Jed cracked a beer. 'It's all true,' he said, 'every word of it,' and he sent Mitch a wink.

'No, really.'

And suddenly he felt a slippage, a letting go. His nerves had been on hold for days. No sleep and all that road unwinding before his eyes, inside his head. It only took this one slight pressure when he was least expecting it and he came loose.

'How am I supposed to know?' he snapped. 'I'm only a fucking driver, all right?'

The black girl shrank. 'Christ. Sorry I asked.'

Jed drank two more beers and a couple of shots of tequila. Suddenly the room smelt of dead flowers and stale smoke, and it was loud, even during silences, with the ticking of Mitch's clocks. He went to the bathroom, hung his head over the toilet bowl. The ammonia helped. This hunchback darkness on his shoulder and the room behind him, high and narrow. It was all the liquor, he wasn't used to it any more. In the old days he could've swallowed a six-pack in half an hour and then gone out and walked a tightrope. Not any more. He shut his mouth and hung his head. Waited for the darkness to lift.

'How did you get to be a driver, Jed?'

He slowly looked up. It was much later. He was back in the lounge. Mitch was rolling a cigarette, running the tip of his tongue along the shiny edge. 'Somebody say something?'

'How did you get to be a driver?'

Jed shrugged. 'I'm pretty good mechanically. I don't mind working long hours – '

The black girl cut in. 'It's his eyes.'

'His eyes?' one of the bikers said. 'What d'you mean?'

She leaned forwards. 'I've seen eyes like his in jails. Eyes that've killed. Or look as if they could.' And she shuddered.

Jed stood up. He stared into the mirror that hung above the mantelpiece. He'd often asked himself the same queston. What had

Creed seen in him? He thought he had it now. It was what that girl had said. It was what he looked like.

'He never blinks,' he heard her say. 'It's like those lizards.'

He was still looking at himself. His qualifications, so to speak. They were all there, in the mirror. A tall thin body built almost entirely out of angles. A body which, cramped in the black livery he wore, became still thinner, still more angular. His face was flaky in some places, the texture of dried glue, while in others it bore the pin-prick traces of acne. His glasses with their steel frames made his eyes look chilly, merciless. He was ugly, there was no denying it. He was verging on the grotesque. And yet, looking at himself now, he couldn't help taking a kind of pride in his appearance. For as long as he could remember, people had stared at him. His ugliness set him apart; his ugliness had made him vain. He was smiling now. His lips didn't curve or pucker when he smiled. They just lengthened. His smile seemed to prove the point.

Later the black girl came and sat beside him on the sofa.

'I want to apologise,' she said. 'I didn't mean to be personal or anything.'

'What's your name?' he said. 'I've forgotten.'

'Sharon.'

'I'm Jed.'

'I know.' She was staring at him intently. 'Tell me something. Are you a virgin?'

She was close to him now. Her pink shirt blurred. Her breath smelt of damp hay, hay that had been stored too long.

'You are, aren't you?'

He admitted it.

'You want to do something about it?'

He began to shiver.

'What's wrong?' she said. 'You cold?'

'Yes.'

Her voice softened. 'Well, you're the driver. Why don't you drive me home?'

They left in his Chrysler. At the first stoplight she leaned over and kissed him. Something flashed pale-mauve in the side of her teeth.

'It's amethyst,' she said. 'It's my lucky stone.'

He was too drunk to be driving, he thought, angling a glance at her wide, sloping thighs on the seat beside him. Her breasts slopped like water under that pink shirt of hers. Like the bags of water you buy goldfish in.

Then a room with blue lights, the whining of a child. A swirl of orange as he lurched to the window.

'Baker Park,' she said.

Her voice, the room, tonight. All gritty and distant now. Dregs in the bottom of a bottle. One week when he was fifteen he'd slept under the pier. Seaweed dangling from the metal struts like matted hair, wind so rough against his skin. You could've used that wind to scour pans. And the dragging of the waves all night. Water like slurred words. The bottom of the bottle.

And then marooned on her black flesh, two circles round her throat, and her chin pointing at the ceiling like the toe of a boot on a corpse, one arm bent backwards, nothing on except the slacks around her ankles, but no way in, at least none that he could find, and the cheap carpet burning his elbows and his knees, and sleep beginning to ooze from her ridged lips.

He woke on top of her, she might've been a beach, he might've been abandoned there by waves. He rolled away from her and she woke too. One absent-minded hand moved up to scratch a breast.

'Did we do it?'

'I don't know,' he said. 'I don't think so.'

She yawned. A mouth like ice-cream. Strawberry and chocolate. 'Want to try again?'

'When?'

'How about now? Morning after's always good.' She reached for him with one blind hand.

He moved away, sat up. 'Not now. Maybe tonight.'

Her eyes opened. She looked at him across her cheeks. 'What's wrong? Don't you like me?'

'It's not that.'

'You don't like my body.' She handled one of her breasts sorrow-fully, the way you might handle a bird with a broken wing. 'It doesn't do anything for you.'

'It's not that. It's just I've got things to do.'

It wasn't true. He had the whole day off. It was just that everything seemed too close, like staring at a light bulb. He was looking down at her, and seeing green and purple on her skin.

'I can't figure you out.'

He buttoned his pants. 'Where did I leave my car?'

She was lying on the carpet, the lips of her cunt, soft and blunt, pushing up through a mound of black curls. She shrugged at him, and he looked away. She was still lying on the carpet five minutes later when he left the apartment. He saw her knees and calves through the half-open door.

'Well?' she asked him, when he showed up again that night. 'Did you find it?'

He scowled. 'In the end.'

It had taken half an hour, the inside of his head fitting loosely, like a drawer in an old chest. He'd searched the streets around her house that morning. Streets scratchy with children, broken glass and weeds. He'd even searched the vacant lots. A trunk with burst locks. A drunk in a yellow armchair. Those things shouldn't've been there, for some reason they'd infuriated him. The night before he'd driven drunk. OK, so he'd lost his virginity (well, almost). But he'd risked losing everything else too. His licence, his job. His entire future. When he found his car he sat behind the wheel, gripping it so tight he could've snapped it.

'I can't stay long,' he told her.

'You better get those pants off then.'

'What's that round your neck?' He'd noticed it the night before. A small leather pouch on a string. It was the only thing she'd been wearing that hadn't come away when they undressed.

'It's nothing you need know about.'

His anger was still there, and he used it to break into her. He liked the way her eyes widened in alarm, as if he was forcing a lock, as if he was breaking and entering. It was the first time he'd ever slept with a woman and it felt like burglary.

That night, back in the Palace, the phone rang. He switched the light on. It was after two. He thought it must be Creed and said, 'Yes, sir?'

'Christ, you even crawl in your sleep.'

'Who's this?'

'Who do you think?'

'Vasco. Where are you?'

'I don't think I should tell you that.'

'Creed's been looking for you.'

'How about that.' Vasco's laughter sounded tight. 'Listen, you've got to meet me tomorrow.'

'I can't do that. You know what my schedule's like.'

'Do this for me, Jed.'

'I can't.'

Vasco hung up.

Towards morning Jed dreamed he was waiting at a bus-stop. When the bus pulled in, hundreds of people pushed towards the door. He managed to force his way on. As the bus pulled away, he saw Vasco through the window. Vasco was trapped on the sidewalk. Vasco had been left behind.

That night the phone rang again. He didn't want to answer it, thinking that it might be Vasco again, but he couldn't afford not to. So he picked up the receiver and waited.

'Spaghetti?'

It was Creed.

'Yes, sir?'

'I want you to pick me up.'

'Where are you?'

'A place called the Box. It's a club. You know it?'

The line was cluttered with background noise, and Jed had to ask Creed to repeat the address several times. At last he had it. 75 V Street. 'I'll be outside in half an hour.'

'Don't wait outside. Park the car and come in.'

'Half an hour,' Jed said, and hung up.

Ever since that story broke in the papers, Creed seemed to be testing loyalties. Pushing those around him to the brink and saying jump. Jed thought he understood. It was like when his radios were thrown away. You could shrug your shoulders, put on a face that said you didn't care, but you did and nothing could ever be secure again. The next time security appeared as a possibility, you smashed it yourself. And went on smashing it. That, he was sure, was how Creed felt. And the people round him weren't jumping. Trotter had been away for two weeks. Something to do with that twisted arm of his. Meatball's sense of humour was fraying. He still told jokes, but they were the jokes of a man who couldn't see anything funny any more, the jokes of a man with one eye on the door. Vasco was nowhere. A voice on the phone at three in the morning. A dream in your head. Only McGowan had lasted. If Jed waited long enough, surely his moment would come. The days of liquorice were over. He'd started buying Iceberg Mints. They were clear and cool. They were how his thinking had to be.

He switched the light on and looked at the clock. Two-twenty. The smell of sex rose in a gust as he left the bed. Sharon didn't wake. He thought he'd heard of the Box. It was down by the old meat-packing warehouses. It was one of the hard-core gay clubs.

75 V Street was a black door with a small glass panel at head height where you could see your own face reflected. A two-way mirror,

presumably. The knocker was a nude male torso in brass. Jed took hold of the cold metal and knocked twice. The buttocks hammered at the door as if they were fucking it.

The door opened about six inches. A strong man with a beard stared down at him.

'I'm with Mr Creed,' Jed said.

The gap widened and he passed through. He paused inside, adjusted his top hat.

The strong man was still staring. 'Like the outfit.'

Jed stared back. One thing he'd learned how to do. Learned early on and never forgotten. 'I'm a chauffeur.'

'That's what they all say.' The strong man lit a cigarette. It looked too frail for his hand. They looked like King Kong and Fay Wray, that hand, that cigarette. There was a movie going on right under his nose and he didn't even know. The guy had about one brain cell and he was doing time in it.

'Where is he?' Jed said.

'In the back.'

Creed was sitting in a booth. McGowan on one side of him, a young blond guy with cheekbones on the other. Creed told Jed to sit down. 'This is Ollie.' He meant the blond guy. 'He's a tourist. You know McGowan, of course.'

Jed looked at the tourist.

'I'm pleased,' the tourist said, 'wery pleased.'

Jed was still looking. Weird stuff.

'Sit down,' McGowan said. 'Have a drink.'

'I'm driving,' Jed said, 'remember?'

'Have some of this instead,' and McGowan passed Jed a brown vial. 'We'll get home quicker.'

Jed took the bottle. 'What is it?' Though he already knew, of course. That little bottle with the plastic spoon attached, it had just taken him back about five years.

'It's powder,' McGowan said, 'for your nose.'

The tourist laughed.

Jed felt Creed's eyes on him. He had two spoons, one for each nostril, and handed the vial back.

'Good boy,' Creed said.

'You know Gorilla pretty well,' McGowan said, 'don't you?'

'Kind of.'

'You're a friend of his,' Creed said.

'I used to be. It was years ago. We were kids.' It was so strange talking to Creed like this. They never talked like this. He felt as if all his teeth were stones.

'You been seeing much of him recently?' McGowan said.

'Only in dreams.'

'Only in dreams,' Creed said, and laughed.

'I'd keep it that way, if I was you,' McGowan said.

'Why?'

'He's been a bad gorilla.' McGowan swallowed the rest of his drink. 'He got a bit greedy. Too many bananas.'

'That's right,' Creed said. 'He's been a bad gorilla.' And he stared at Jed for a moment, then he smiled slowly.

Jed looked at McGowan, but McGowan was looking somewhere else. Riddles.

The tourist wanted to go to another club, but Creed insisted on a drink in his apartment. 'You're on vacation. Relax.'

At last the tourist gave in. Maybe he thought he was on to a good thing.

They took the scenic route back to the Palace. Down through the old meat-market streets, into the tunnel with its rows of lights like neon stitching and its shiny cream tiles, up into Venus, then round the western edge of the harbour and back over the bridge to C Street. The sliding glass panel was open for the first time ever.

'He's a romantic,' Creed said. 'He wants to see the sights.'

'We'll show him the sights,' McGowan said, and he leaned back and laughed, and the city lights on his mirror shades looked like gold zips that had come undone.

The tourist laughed along with them. In his rear-view mirror Jed saw the vial being passed round. The tourist was sitting in the middle. He was getting twice as much as anyone else. No wonder he was laughing.

Slipping down into the parking-lot under the hotel was like being swallowed, the entrance a dark throat with the tongue cut out. Loyalty is silence. The tyres squealed as they braked, the concrete smooth as skin and slick with fluids that had bled from other cars. Jed parked next to the service elevator. He opened the doors.

And then Creed's voice soft against his back. 'Why don't you come on up with us?'

Jed turned. 'I ought to get some sleep,' he said, but the coke had taken hold, it was lifting him, and he had such a good seat at the circus, he didn't really want to leave.

'Come on up,' Creed said. 'We should get to know each other better.'

The wallpaper in Creed's lounge looked like zebra skin. The curtains, so blue that they were almost black, were drawn against the view. Creed gave Jed a drink. 'After all, you don't have to drive to get home any more, do you?' and then he went and sat down next to the tourist. The tourist was talking about his homeland.

'It's not, you know, it's not like here,' and he waved a hand around to include the zebra-skin wallpaper, his new friends, the small brown vial on the coffee table. 'It's more like,' and his face lit up as he remembered the word, 'like a willage.'

Jed turned to McGowan. 'Willage,' he said.

McGowan tipped his head back. 'He's a long way from home.'

'Maybe too far.'

Now McGowan turned to look at Jed and Jed saw his own face twice. 'You don't know how right you are.'

'Don't I?'

They stared at each other for another ten seconds, then McGowan smiled. There was nothing humorous or well-meaning about the smile. McGowan had simply chosen it from among a number of possible reactions.

'You know something?' Jed said. 'I've never seen you without those glasses on.'

With one swift motion McGowan reached up, took the glasses off and tucked them in his pocket. His eyes seemed pinned wide open. Too much white. The irises looked oddly suspended.

Jed nodded. 'Now I know why you wear those glasses.'

'Oh yeah?'

'You'd frighten too many people with them off.'

McGowan liked that. He liked it so much that he decided to laugh. Jed laughed with him. He looked at Creed. Creed had just produced a pile of leather stuff and dumped it on the coffee table. Handcuffs, harnesses, ankle-holsters, studded chokers, and a mask with no eyes and a zip for a mouth.

'Uh-oh,' McGowan said.

Reaching forwards, Jed picked up a see-through zip-lock bag. Inside was an assembly of metal rings and leather straps. The label said THE FIVE GATES OF HELL. Five? Why five? he wondered. Wasn't one enough? And then he put the bag back on the table.

Creed was showing some of the pieces to the tourist and explaining how they worked. His tone of voice objective, dispassionate, as if they were kitchen implements or gardening devices. Then, without altering his voice, he picked the handcuffs up, snapped them on the tourist's wrists, and flipped the key through the air to McGowan.

'Uh-oh,' McGowan said again.

'Hey,' the tourist said, 'you guys are choking, right?'

Creed didn't appear to have heard. He was looking at McGowan.

'Choking,' McGowan said. 'We're choking.'

'Hey, come on, you guys,' the tourist said. 'Get me out of this, OK?'

McGowan reached out and picked up the mask. He dangled it from one finger, swung it slowly backwards and forwards in front of the tourist's eyes. 'Only if you put this on.'

Creed was nodding.

The tourist was well built, stronger possibly than either Creed or McGowan, but there was a pleading look in his eyes now, like a dog that knows it's going to be kicked. 'OK,' he said. 'I put this on.'

Jed left the room to go to the bathroom.

When he returned, the lounge was empty. He walked down the hall and stopped by a door. Through the crack he saw McGowan holding the tourist down on a bed. The tourist was lying on his stomach, his face twisted to one side. He was naked, except for the mask. McGowan had a gun in his hand and he was pushing the muzzle through the zipper and into the tourist's mouth. Creed sat on a chair by the window, gloved hands in his lap, one wrist resting on the other. His face had switched to automatic. He looked up and saw Jed standing in the doorway.

'Want some?'

The tourist might've been cake. Jed shook his head.

Creed smiled. Not so much a smile, perhaps, as a slackening around his mouth.

'That guy,' and Jed nodded at McGowan, 'he's a psychopath.'

'But he's loyal,' Creed said. 'He's very loyal.'

Jed turned. 'I'll see you tomorrow.'

Suddenly Creed was standing next to him. So suddenly that Jed jumped. He wasn't sure how Creed had covered the distance between the window and the door.

Creed slapped Jed on the shoulder, a gesture straight out of the boardroom. 'Get some sleep. I don't need you till eleven.'

It was seven-thirty when Jed climbed back into bed. Sharon was still asleep. There was shine in the wings of her nose. Her breath came in puffs, ruffling her top lip. He lay down under the single sheet and closed his eyes. Sleep slipped through his fingers. His body itched where the cotton touched it. He had to keep scratching. Always a different place.

'Where've you been?'

His cock tightened at the sound of her voice. 'I had to drive somewhere.'

'What time is it?'

'I don't know. Eight.'

'Christ.' Both her eyes were still shut. One dark breast spilled sideways across the sheet.

He bent down. Bit the wide nipple. Tugged on that glossy skin until her eyes stretched wide and her chin tipped back. He slid between her legs.

She pushed a hand down. 'I've got my period.'

'That doesn't matter.'

But she twisted round and took him in her dusty hands, he felt the blood pump past her fingers. He heard a clock strike eight. And closed his eyes. Soft shapes colliding, exploding. One colour bled into another. Like bacteria. Her mouth round him now, her teeth grazing that tight skin. Her back so hot, and slick as ice. Their sweat pooling on the sheet. And then the slow ink spreading outwards and the wheels turning and a voice, it was Vasco's, warning him. He must record. He must record again. To protect himself. To lay himself open. To what? From what? Which rat leaves which ship. That slow ink again. His vision flickering, black round the edges, gaps in the tape. Loyalty and silence. Two wheels, round and round, he couldn't take his eyes away, and this time it'd be like worship, I dreamed that we were made of gold, he'd seen too much, his eyes were gold, they'd have to melt them down. Turn the clock back. Tell an old truth. Lie. Truth. Maybe it had been like worship then, worship that begins in love and dovetails neatly into hate. Bacteria and radios. Zebra walls. Leather masks and foreign names. Moscow. Brussels. Ollie. Vasco. Vasco? He called out, but the bus had gone. He was alone. Those five gates of hell, he'd be put through every single one of them. Would he? He couldn't see round the next bend, he must record, tapes were periscopes, his only chance, and the slow ink stolen and the wheels turning, and everything remembered, everything proved, he was whispering now, 'Why five,' he was whispering, 'isn't one enough?' and a voice came back, a woman's, Sharon's, 'One what?'

TEETHMARKS

Nathan called Dad long-distance from Seaview Lodge. He didn't say anything about the letter that Harriet had written him. In fact, he didn't mention Harriet at all. He just said he was thinking of coming home for a couple of days, if that was all right.

'Is that all you can manage?' Dad said. 'A couple of days?'

'I'm working, Dad.'

'Well, try and get here early. I go to bed at nine.'

He took the train down, even though it was twenty-six hours. He wanted to know exactly how far he'd come. He wanted the distance to count. They were held up just north of the city, repairs on the line, and by the time he reached the house on Mahogany Drive it wasn't early any more, it was after midnight. He tried the front door. It was locked. He tried the french windows. They were locked too. He checked the other windows, knowing at the same time that it was pointless. Dad had always been fanatical about security at night; he even bolted the inside doors. Three years away, all those miles, and now he couldn't get in. He had to laugh. But it wasn't funny, not really.

When his laughter had gone, he realised that something was different: lights were showing in the windows. In any other house this would've been normal, but in theirs it was eerie, unnatural. Dad worried about electricity, how dangerous it was. He never went to bed without making sure that every single appliance had been switched off. He couldn't sleep if he thought there might be a plug in a socket somewhere. He was always having visions of the house catching fire at night. All this light spilling on to the driveway, it just wasn't like him. It was asking for it. Nathan's heart began to jump. Suppose something had happened. Maybe that was why Dad wasn't answering. He knocked on the door, but much harder now. And he was calling too. 'Dad? Dad?'

Nobody came.

He ran round to the back of the house for the second time. He stood in the garden, at the edge of the pool, and looked up at Dad's window. The curtains drawn, no light. Cupping his hands round his mouth, he called again. 'Dad?'

He went over to a flowerbed and felt around in the mud. He came back with a handful of pebbles. He missed with the first. The second just touched the glass and fell away. The third almost shattered it. He waited. Nothing happened.

Moonlight lay on the glass roof of the sun-lounge, blue sheets of it, like lightning paralysed. The rain, still fresh on the grass, began to seep through the soles of his boots. He turned and stared at the pool. Those black patches on the surface, they'd be dead leaves. Every time he came home he had to scoop them off the surface. It was one of his jobs. But now the anger rose in him again. All this way and fuck it, I can't even get in.

He ran round to the front door. This could go on till morning, it was ridiculous. He pushed the mailbox open, pressed his cheek against the metal, and yelled. 'Dad? Dad? DAD!'

This time he heard a click and knew instantly what it was. That click was printed on his memory. It was the sound of Dad's bedroom door. He took his mouth away from the mailbox, and put an ear there instead. He could hear Dad's voice, distant, shaky.

'Nathan? Is that you?'

'Yes, it's me, Dad. It's only me.'

He saw Dad feeling his way down the last flight of stairs, the pyjamas, the slippers, the blue cardigan cut off just above the elbows, feeling his way through some kind of thick barbiturate mist. He heard keys turning in the locks, bolts being drawn. The door opened, and he moved past Dad, into the hall.

'Sorry if I look odd, but I was dead out.' Dad was bent over, locking the door again. 'Sorry if I look strange.'

And he turned, shy, somehow, and they held each other. Nathan smelt warm sleep, clean skin. If someone had told him that he'd been angry a moment before, he would've denied it. 'You go back to bed now,' he said gently. 'I'll see you tomorrow.'

Next morning, after breakfast, Dad said, 'It was that calling, that word "Dad" in the middle of the night. It took me back all those years. You never forget it.'

They were sitting in the room that overlooked the pool. Dad had taken his pills, and now he was relaxing. Nathan sat next to him. He could hear the au pair girl washing dishes, the mutter of Dad's radio. It was all so familiar and yet, at the same time, it was utterly remote.

'When I arrived last night,' he said, 'all the lights were on.'

'Were they?' Dad was staring at the blank wall above the TV. 'It must've been Helga. She's new, you see. I haven't trained her yet.' He looked at Nathan. 'Have you been eating properly?' And then, before Nathan could answer, 'You look thin to me.'

It was always the same when he went home: Dad didn't stop talking until his voice hurt.

That morning Dad told his favourite story again, the story of his drive along the coast with Kay, only this time he took it one stage further, down from the cliffs and into the house. It had been lying empty for months, he said. It was almost derelict. A leaking roof, cobwebs slung across the rooms like hammocks, moss growing on the walls. People had broken in too. The downstairs was inches deep in sherry bottles, newspapers, strange men's shoes, and someone must've lit a fire in the kitchen because there was a big black patch on the floor, as if a rocket had taken off. Later that day he found a letter for Kay's mother lying in the hall. The address on the envelope was 'Viviente', 7729 Mahogany Drive, Moon Beach. 'Viviente' used to be the name of the house, Kay told him. It meant 'full of life'.

'And you know what?' Dad turned to Nathan. 'It was almost a miracle, really. The week after we moved in, we discovered she was pregnant. With you.'

'I never knew that,' Nathan said.

'Well, there you are. You learned something.' Dad sat back, looking pleased with himself.

Nathan smiled. It was no wonder that Dad went back over that day so often, especially in the light of present circumstances. He was returning to a world that had been kind to him, a past he could be sure of. His love for Kay was one love that had never spoiled. It was over, yes, but it would never end.

In the afternoon Nathan drove to Georgia's. She had two rooms above a hardware store in Venus. The place was littered, as Georgia's places always were, with science fiction, jewellery, sunglasses, invitations, tapes. From the window you could see one thin strip of blue between the houses opposite; her view of the harbour. She made coffee in a dented silver pot and served it in dark-green cups with gold rims and gold handles, cups she'd stolen from home. 'They were Grandma's, I think,' she said. 'You know, before she went mad.' She was so jittery at seeing him, she couldn't keep still. Everything he said, she talked over the end of it. 'I think I'll roll a joint,' she said. 'Might slow me down.' She spread her materials on the floor, her legs tucked under her, her tongue stuck to the centre of her top lip. He remembered her painting on brown paper when it rained. It was the same look. It took her so long to roll the joint, she'd slowed down before she even put a match to it.

There was some party they had to go to. As the taxi jolted through the streets of Butterfield, she linked her arm through his and kissed him. 'You've been away so long, I almost forgot what you smelt like.'

'Don't tell me,' he said. 'I don't want to know.'

'No, it's good. It's like,' and she had to smell him again, to remind herself, 'it's like fruit.'

Smiling, he stroked her hair. In the three years since he'd last seen her she'd grown it halfway down her back.

'Do you think Dad's all right?' he asked her.

She frowned. 'It's hard to tell. All he ever says when I go and see him is, why do have to wear all that stuff on your face, why can't you be natural?'

He laughed.

She rested her cheek against his shoulder. 'You know what I'd like?'

'What?'

'I'd like to be your brother.'

He smiled. 'Sister isn't enough?'

'That's different.'

'What's different about it?'

'Brothers tell each other everything.' She nodded to herself. 'Everything.' And her dark eyes glittered and she ran her tongue over her lips, and then she said, 'How about it?'

'Nobody'll understand.'

'They never do, do they?' She smiled up at him. 'Give me something.'

He stared at her. They ran on parallel tracks, he knew that, but some nights, especially nights like this, she drew ahead of him.

'You have to give me something,' she explained. 'To make it official.'

He unfastened the woven leather bracelet from around his wrist. She watched, eyes wide, as if he was performing magic. He reached into his pocket and took out a pen. On the inside of the bracelet he wrote, 'To George, my brother for forty years.'

'Here,' he said. 'Put it on.'

She looked at it. 'Is it special?'

'It's very special.' He told her about the woman with the flute. He told her what he'd said to the woman and how stupid he'd felt. He told her that the bracelet had the woman's music in it, and sometimes, if you waited for rain and then listened very carefully, you could just hear it, very faintly, like someone playing in the distance.

'I don't know.' Georgia was looking at the bracelet the same way she used to look at the hill when she was five, she was in awe of it, it might be too strong for her. 'Maybe it's too special.'

'Some things there comes a time when they have to go to someone else.' It sounded exactly like something that India-May might have said. She must be rubbing off on him.

'You wrote something on it, didn't you?'

He nodded.

She read the words, then looked at him. 'Why forty?'

'It was the most I could imagine.' He fastened the bracelet on for her. She sat back, looking down at it. Then, suddenly, she leaned forwards again and asked the driver to stop. 'I've just got to get something,' she told him. 'I won't be long.'

Nathan watched her run into a supermarket. Moments later she was out again. She didn't seem to be carrying anything. She slid into the car and slammed the door. 'OK, go,' she said to the driver. 'Go.'

When they'd turned the corner, she pulled out a bottle of champagne from under her coat. 'I stole it,' she said. She took off the wire that held the cork in position and put the bottle beside her, then she set to work. In five minutes she'd fashioned a ring out of the wire. She slipped it over his finger. 'There,' she said. 'Now we're brothers.' She glanced at the bottle thoughtfully. 'I only stole it for the wire,' she said, 'but now we've got it I suppose we might as well drink it.'

They'd almost reached the place where the party was, but she told the driver to keep going. 'Just drive around,' she said. 'Take us back in twenty minutes.'

They didn't arrive at the party until they'd finished the bottle. They were both drunker than they'd been for years. She had a bracelet and he had a ring. They'd missed each other so much. The cab fare was thirty-three dollars.

The next morning Dad woke him at eight. 'You were naughty last night,' he said. 'You woke me up.'

'Did I?' Nathan said. 'I didn't mean to.'

'It was your door. It made a noise.'

'Sorry, Dad.'

'You were very late.'

'I know. I went to a party with Georgia.'

Dad sighed. He couldn't understand why anyone went to parties. He even hated the *word* 'party'. It was almost as bad as the word 'hospital'. In his head you probably went straight from one to the other.

'Don't worry,' Nathan said. 'I'm staying in tonight.'

That evening Dad opened a bottle of wine. As a rule he only drank one glass, but that night he drank three, and when he noticed the full moon in the window he became excited, almost too much white in his eyes and a bulb of spit shining on his front teeth. He watched the moon rise through his binoculars. After a while he offered them to Nathan. 'Do you want a look?'

Nathan shook his head. 'Maybe later. When it's higher.'

'It's so clear. You can even see the holes.'

The holes. It was the kind of thing a child might say. Rona, for instance. Yes, Rona might easily have said something like that. He looked at Dad, but Dad was unaware. Under the moon's influence his mind had flown giddily on, like a witch straddling a broomstick. Here. He was turning again. With something else.

'Did I ever tell you about Harriet and the spaceship? No? It was the strangest thing.'

Nathan could only stare. He hadn't expected to hear her name mentioned at all. It had to be the wine. The wine and the excitement of having someone in the house to talk to.

'I was down here one night, it was about nine, and there was a knock at the door. It was Harriet. She was wearing a dressing-gown, but it was hanging open, and underneath she only had a négligé on, one of those flimsy things, I could see everything. She said she was frightened. I asked her why. She said she'd seen a spaceship and it had frightened her.'

'A spaceship?' Nathan said.

'That's what I said. "A spaceship?" I said. "Where?" She said she'd seen it in her window. Her curtains were open and it went across her window in the sky. "Did it go fast or slow?" I said. "Slow," she said. I asked her to show me where she'd seen it. She went to the window, that window,' and he pointed to the french windows that led out on to the terrace. 'We stood over there and looked for it. Of course there was nothing. We were standing very close, and I got the feeling that if I opened my arms she'd come inside. I didn't know what she wanted. Me to kiss her or what. Anyway I put my arm round her. After a while I asked her whether she was all right and she said yes. Then she went back to bed.' He sipped at his wine again, then put it down on the arm of his chair and, keeping a finger and thumb on the stem, twisted it one way, then the other. 'At the time I thought it was so, I don't know, romantic. Now, well. It seems so obvious.' His excitement had gone. Now there was only bitterness. His binoculars lay abandoned on the floor.

Two nights later, on the train, Nathan remembered the last fragments of that conversation. His vain attempt to win Dad's mood back.

'It sounds romantic to me.'

Dad shook his head so violently, he might almost have been in pain. 'I should never have trusted her.'

Like the hospital, Harriet had cut something out of him. He'd been exploited, hoodwinked, lied to. The whole thing had been an elaborate deception. He'd trusted for the last time. There'd be nobody else now. Nobody. He'd gathered his life around him like a cloak in which there was only room enough for one.

On Nathan's last morning they'd driven down to the supermarket together. When they returned, there was the usual ritual of putting the shopping away. Dad squatted on the pantry floor and Nathan stood behind him, handing him the groceries.

'You won't be able to help me again,' Dad said. 'Not till the next time you come, anyway, and that might not be for ages.'

Nathan felt the guilt rise into his throat, bitter as some half-digested thing.

'Hold on,' came Dad's voice from inside the pantry, 'I've just got to clear a space.' The shifting of packets and tins, and then a silence. Then a soft sound, like a gasp or a sigh.

'What is it, Dad?'

Still squatting, Dad turned round. There was a block of raw jelly lying in the palm of his hand. The packet had been ripped open and a small bite was missing from one corner. You could see the teethmarks.

'Rona,' Nathan said, and Dad nodded.

She must've sneaked into the pantry one day when nobody was looking and taken a bite out of that jelly. Orange flavour had always been her favourite. Nathan looked from the jelly on Dad's hand to Dad's face, and saw the tears in his eyes.

Now, as the train swayed up the coast, there were tears in his own eyes too. He didn't want anyone to see so he cupped his hand to the window and looked out. The tracks ran alongside the ocean here. He saw a pale strip of sand. The ocean heaving, unlit. No moon tonight.

Tight in his hand he held the silver coin that Dad had given him at the front door. It was the same coin that Dad always gave him, every time he went away. It was just a small coin, worth practically nothing.

   Worth everything.

YOU, ME, AND THE
CHAIRMAN

It had been a normal day. In the morning Creed had a meeting with a city bank. He lunched with the police commissioner at a fish restaurant in Torch Bay. After lunch he spent half an hour with McGowan in an outdoor café by the river. Then, during the afternoon he put in a personal appearance at three of the funeral parlours that he'd recently acquired for the company as part of his new expansion programme. By late afternoon the sky was grey and the air seemed hard to breathe. As they left the northern suburbs, the car began to tremble in Jed's hands. He touched his foot to the brake and slowed to about thirty.

Creed slid the window open. 'Something wrong?'

'I don't know,' Jed said.

Then the streetlights began to sway. Dreamily, like charmed snakes.

'Earthquake,' Creed said.

They were on a raised section of the Ring, the road that acted as the circumference of downtown, and all Jed could see was freeway, sky, and rows of swaying grey poles. He wanted to get back down to ground-level.

Then it was over. Less than six on the Richter scale, he found out later, only a tremor, really, but it was enough to change Creed's mind about returning to the office. He asked to be driven home instead.

Creed stood on the sidewalk outside the Palace Hotel. Jed watched him in the wing mirror, watched him without seeming to. Creed was looking into the sky as if scanning for omens.

Jed shivered. He couldn't get that earthquake out of his blood. He kept seeing the streetlights again, those streetlights trembling, as if the whole world was scared. 'Do you need me again today?' he said. He hoped the answer was no. He wanted to go home and lie down.

Creed's head turned slowly on his neck. Every movement seemed to be performed in a trance that day. Death had been and gone, but it was still in the air, like static. 'I want you back here at ten. There's something we've got to discuss.'

McGowan opened the apartment door that night when Jed buzzed. 'Weird day,' he said. He was gloating. It was going to get weirder, that was what he meant.

Jed's eyes flicked round the lounge. He half expected to see some naked tourist in the corner, bound and gagged. McGowan closed the door and slipped a small glass vial into Jed's hand. 'It's going to be a long night,' he said, and he turned to Creed, who had just walked into the room, and smiled.

Jed glanced round the room again. Zebra walls, curtains drawn across the windows like a second night sky, carpet the colour of fresh blood. None of this was strange to him, and yet he sensed something different. A heightened atmosphere, an air of ceremony. The skin seemed looser on Creed's face. Some kind of decision had been reached.

He'd known he was going to be tested, and he'd prepared himself. Mitch had given him the number of a guy called Turner. Turner worked in a security systems retail outlet on Rocket Boulevard. Jed had dropped into the store late one Saturday afternoon.

'I'm doing a bit of surveillance,' he told Turner. 'Mitch said you might be able to help.'

Turner listened to Jed's requirements, then he led Jed to a glass display case. 'This is what you need.' He unlocked the case and lifted out what looked like a Walkman with a small black box attached. A ballpoint pen slid into a hole in the box. 'We call it the pen recorder,' Turner said. 'You take the pen out and it automatically activates the recording mechanism.' He demonstrated. 'Put it back again, and it deactivates the mechanism. It's simple.'

'How much?' Jed asked.

'Fifteen hundred,' Turner said, 'but since you're a friend of Mitch's.' He scratched the back of his neck. 'I could do it for thirteen.'

Jed nodded. It was still expensive, but he couldn't afford not to take it. Turner showed him how to wire himself up. The recorder slotted neatly into his jacket pocket. The mike clipped to the inside of his cuff. When Jed walked into Creed's apartment that night he was, in Turner's language, 'live'.

He wanted to stay straight, but that small glass vial was always being pressed into his hand, it seemed bottomless, the hours passed and they never reached the end. They were everywhere that night. The

Bar Necropolis. The Jupiter casino. A private party in some high-rise apartment block; looking down into the city from the forty-second floor, it was like being inside a radio, one of those old valve radios, and Jed almost told Creed what he thought, he almost blurted something Creed wouldn't even have understood, You must've had radios thrown away some time, didn't you? but the rush blew over and he was still staring down into the forest of lit buildings and he still hadn't spoken. Another bar, further west, in Omega. It was like that game where you were blindfolded and spun round, and then you had to try and touch someone, Creed and the Skull, they were close one moment, then they were dancing out of reach, and nothing would sound like anything when he played it back, it would sound like interference, nonsense, silence, but he stayed with it, trips to the bathroom to sluice his nose and throat, more trips to replace the tapes, because he sensed they were leading up to something, there was something at the end of this rainbow of places, not gold but something.

At three in the morning everything suddenly moved back. A clearing in his head, a sudden loss of sound. It was a club. They were sitting at a round table. A candle in a red glass. Drinks. The faces of devils, all empty eyes and bright teeth. Creed was drinking water. He always drank the same brand. Drained from a glacier. Sodium-free. McGowan was talking. His words emerged from silence, as if they were the first words of the evening. Jed stared at McGowan's face as it tilted and leered, all blocks of colour and deep shadows. Jed listened hard.

'We pick them up,' the Skull was saying, 'they're guys with no links, like on the pier or down in the meat streets, they're always suckers for a few lines and a limousine. We pick them up, we take them somewhere, then we turn them blue. There's a guy we know, works in the morgue, he gets the delivery. Few hours later he calls, we're the funeral parlour, right? He's recommended us, we do the honours, bury them,' and his mouth opened like a grave, you could fall into that mouth for ever and ever, amen, and all those crooked grey teeth of his, no names that you could see, no names or dates, just blank, so nobody could find you, nobody could visit, nobody could leave flowers. 'I mean, if you're going to die you want a decent burial, stands to reason, doesn't it, and who better to give you a decent burial,' he said, 'than the Paradise Corporation. You, me,' and he levelled a hand at Creed, 'and the chairman.'

Creed put his glass of water down. 'Skull,' he said, 'just shut up, will you?'

That vial again. Some amyl too, which blew Jed's head up like a mushroom cloud. In the distance, in a big gilt cage, he could see nude bodies gluing and ungluing, the sticky rhythmic contact of flesh. Male or female, he couldn't tell. Did it matter? Flesh of some kind. Tourists, maybe. Kill them later. His vision shrank. Their table again. McGowan was running on about his gun collection.

It was after four when they reached the Palace. McGowan vanished with a couple they'd brought home in the car. A buzzing started up. Some kind of aid. That psychopath. Jed looked across at Creed and saw that Creed was already staring at him. Jed didn't flinch. He remembered what Sharon had said about him, remembered the chill in his eyes. Eyes that've killed. He never blinks. It's like those lizards.

'You remember what you said about loyalty?'

Jed snapped back at the sound of Creed's voice. 'About it being silence?'

Creed nodded.

'I remember.'

'It's kind of passive, silence,' Creed said, 'isn't it?'

'Well,' Jed said, 'you don't do anything.'

'That's what I mean. So would you go further? Do something?'

There could be no hesitation here. 'Yes.'

'Make yourself comfortable, Jed. Take your jacket off.'

Jed's stomach lurched. Had Creed suspected? 'No, it's all right. I think I'll keep it on.'

'What's wrong? You cold?'

Sharon's words. In Creed's mouth. Did he have another virginity to lose? 'Yes,' he said. 'Just a bit.'

Imagine if he had to take his jacket off. All his insurance would be gone. But Creed had turned away and Jed breathed easier.

'Do you know who talked to the papers?' Creed said.

Jed shook his head. 'I've no idea.'

'It was your friend,' Creed said. 'Your old buddy.'

Jed felt a trap closing. 'I don't understand.'

'Vasco Gorelli,' Creed said. 'It was Vasco Gorelli talked to the papers.'

'How do you know?'

Creed traced the outline of his drink with one finger. 'I put a couple of new vultures on it. You know what those new vultures are like. Keen isn't the word. They get right down to the bones of things. They tear out the truth. Blood, guts, organs, the lot.' He paused. 'Gorelli said he was loyal,' and he looked across at Jed and his eyes glittered.

Curiously it was Vasco's advice that Jed remembered now. Be single-pointed. No grey areas. 'He sold you out.'

'He lost his nerve,' Creed said. 'But you,' again that glitter in his eyes, 'you'd do anything for me.'

'That's what I said.'

'You'd lie.'

Jed thought of that night at Mitch's and what he'd said to Sharon. 'I already have.'

'You'd steal.'

'No problem.' He knew what was coming now. It was like counting down to an explosion. He waited for the blast. He braced himself.

Creed's hand reached carelessly for his glass of water. 'You'd kill someone.'

This had to sound right. First a chuckle, then the words, 'Why? You got someone in mind?'

Creed didn't lift his eyes from his drink. He was watching that pure water the way you'd watch a fire.

The dread rose through Jed's body. He had to speak before he drowned in it. But he remembered to use names. He was taping this. He needed names. 'It's Vasco,' he said, 'isn't it?'

Still Creed watched his drink. 'Too obvious.'

Jed tried to think. His mind kept curving away, the way a golf ball curves when it's sliced or hooked. That beautiful, lazy parabola into somewhere you don't want to be.

'Think sideways,' Creed said. 'I don't want to kill Vasco, I just want him,' and finally he raised his eyes and smiled, and the smile was almost benign. 'I just want him to pay.'

Jed got it. 'Vasco's brother.'

Creed lifted his glass. 'Congratulations.'

But Jed had to make sure. 'You want me to kill Vasco's brother?'

'That's right.'

'How?'

'Don't you worry about that. It's taken care of. It's nice. Yes,' and Creed leaned back in his chair, 'we're going to send Gorilla a little Christmas present.'

'You're going to send him his brother,' Jed said, 'dead.'

Creed smirked. 'Something like that.'

Jed left the apartment at ten to six, the wheels still turning next to his heart. He couldn't sleep now. He took the service elevator down to the parking-lot and got into his car. As he drove across Moon River Bridge, the day rose over the estuary, the colours you find in the skin of fish: brown and pink and palest blue. He stopped the car at the Baker Park end. Leaving the engine running, he went and leaned on the railings. The metal cool against his palms, his heart still pummelling, he drew the fresh dawn air into his lungs. The wind had blown the surface of the river into streaky lines, stretchmarks on the water's tired skin. Gulls picked at the mudbanks where once he'd searched for jewellery. He heard a voice call Vasco's name. It was Vasco's brother, Francis. The boy behind the door. He turned to face the ocean.

Just before he left, Creed had given him the date. Next Wednesday. Exactly a week from now. And as he leaned against the railings he suddenly tasted it, the moment Creed had planned for him, the moment he'd always longed for, dreaded now, still longed for, and it was burnt sugar, sweet and caustic, on his tongue, it was like the flight of a bird across a window, it was there and it was gone, he couldn't dwell on it, he couldn't let the terror in, all he knew was what it would do for him, he knew that it would give him membership, he'd be past the sliding sheet of glass, he'd finally belong.

During the next week he concentrated on his job to the exclusion of all else. He was silent, deferential, precise – the perfect chauffeur. He didn't need to wire himself. There was nothing being said, nothing to record. This was empty time. He felt close to Creed. Superimposed on him, somehow. Bound. He thought he recognised in Creed qualities that he had himself: the ability to wait and to charge the act of waiting with the current of anticipation, to check and double-check, so that when the waiting was over everything would go like clockwork. He knew that, if he ever told Creed the story of the radios, Creed would understand. It might even be something that Creed already understood, that he'd divined on their first meeting in the Mortlake office. It was something they recognised in each other and shared. It made them, Jed thought with satisfaction, extremely dangerous enemies.

Wednesday came around. When Creed called, Jed was watching a news report about a vulture who'd just been arrested on a murder charge. Apparently he'd brought the corpse in and then tried to claim commission on it.

'It's the big night,' Creed said.

Jed waited.

'There's a warehouse in Mangrove. United Paper Products.' He gave Jed the address. 'Leave the limousine there. Be back here at nine-thirty. Under the building. We'll be using your car.'

Jed wondered why Creed was dispensing with the limousine. Too conspicuous, he supposed. And, now he thought about it, he was glad. Using the Chrysler would be to his advantage. No glass partition, much less chance of Creed noticing anything unusual. Jed spent most of the afternoon in the parking-lot, wiring up the back seat.

At nine o'clock he drove to the gas station two blocks south of the hotel. He checked the tyres and the oil, and filled the tank. When he returned to the parking-lot, it was nine-twenty-five. Creed and McGowan were already waiting in front of the elevator doors. McGowan wore the faded blue overalls of a city sanitation man. He was holding a long canvas bag and a cardboard box.

Jed opened the door as usual, even though it was his own car. Habit. He watched McGowan lay the bag flat on the floor.

'What's in there?' he asked.

McGowan grinned. 'Tools.'

In the car Creed leaned forwards. 'Gorelli's brother lives in Los Ilusiones. Housing project on North East 27th. Lives with his girl-friend. You're going to knock on his door and you're going to bring him outside and you're going to put him in the car.'

McGowan handed him a gun. 'You might need this,' he said, 'to persuade him with.'

Jed put the gun in his jacket pocket. Though he hadn't really looked at it, he was sure it was the same one that had been forced into the tourist's mouth.

'Then what happens?' he said.

'Then what happens is, we take him for a little ride out to the Crumbles.' Creed paused. 'You got that?'

Jed nodded.

He moved off. Past the security guard, up the ramp, out on to the dim street. It was 89 degrees. Clouds hung over the city. There were more of them than there used to be, he was sure of it. It was all the burning that was going on. Sea burials were as popular as ever, but they weren't cheap. The poor were still being burned. And some of the crematoria were cutting corners. There'd been a thing about it in the paper. They were burning at temperatures of less than 1300 degrees, which meant that dioxins were being released into the air. Sometimes he looked at the clouds and wondered what percentage ashes they were. Sometimes he wondered how many dead people there were to a cloud. How many dead people came down with the rain.

He was driving at a steady thirty-five. Down First, left along G, right into Central. They passed the viewing theatre. Another mystery corpse: YOUR LAST CHANCE TO IDENTIFY! $100 COULD BE YOURS! Someone's forgotten Grandma. Some runaway. Some drunk. More smoke for the chimneys. More clouds for the sky.

His throat was dry and he'd forgotten to buy any candy.

It was the big night.

They reached Los Ilusiones in less than half an hour. Creed directed him to a narrow sidestreet. He killed the engine and the lights. Latin music took over. Somebody's radio.

Los Ilusiones was 99 per cent ghetto. It was bounded by Moon River in the east, and the suburbs of Mortlake and Rialto in the west and south respectively. It had pretty much the same kind of reputation as Rialto, only more so. A high-octane mix of racial minorities, a flair for riots and looting. Taxi-drivers wouldn't take you there. The only whites in the area were winos and dealers, and they mostly ended up in the river. Jed wanted this part over with, and quick.

Creed leaned forwards and pointed through the windshield. 'That's the building.'

It was a five-storey apartment block built in a C-shape. The gap in the C faced the street. Concrete balconies ran the length of each floor. There was a courtyard below, lit by spotlights.

'Looks like a fucking jail,' came McGowan's voice from the back.

'It's number 22,' Creed said. 'Second floor.'

'You know which side?' Jed asked him.

'Take the stairs on the left.'

Jed stepped out of the car. He was only aware of two things now. The weight of the gun in his jacket pocket and the night air, thicker here than in the city centre, it was further from the ocean, you sometimes felt you couldn't breathe until you found your way to the end of the land. He crossed the street. It was bright in the courtyard. Five cars. A burned-out motorbike. A drain. He turned left, walked close to the edge of the building. He sensed he was being watched, one of the balconies above, but he didn't look up. He noticed the cars. A Mercedes. A Cadillac. This was cheap city housing, and cars like that could only mean one thing. Two things. Armed robbery and drugs. He suddenly felt he was facing impossible odds.

Once he reached the stairs he felt safer. The walls were brick low down, then pale-blue and scarred with graffiti: SEX and a phone number. He smelt meat frying, then urine, then washing powder. On the second floor he turned left. The first door he came to had lost its number. He swore under his breath. The second door said 20. That was good. It meant that number 22 would be close to the stairs. He could still feel eyes on him, they were like fingers, they poked him in the ribs, the shoulderblades, the neck, it was hard not looking round. He reached number 22 and knocked with the flap of the mailbox. He took the gun out of his pocket and held it at waist-level. That way it would be invisible to anyone watching from the other side of the building. The door opened. A man in a white vest, grey flannel pants. Ears like Vasco's. Less fat on him, though. No rings.

Jed moved the gun one inch to the left and back again. 'Out,' he said. 'Right now.'

Gorelli blinked. 'What?'

'You're leaving.' Jed grabbed Gorelli by the upper arm and spun him on to the balcony.

Out of the corner of his eye he saw a face appear in the corridor. A girl in a yellow dress. Hands in the air beside her ears. Lives with his girlfriend. Girlfriend was about to scream. He slammed the door shut and shoved Gorelli along the balcony towards the stairs.

Gorelli turned. 'What about my shoes?'

Jed shoved him again. 'Keep moving,' he said, 'or I'll blow your fucking kidneys out.'

They reached the ground and the screaming began.

'Francisco! Francisco!'

The girl was swaying on the balcony above. Her yellow dress, her hands searching her black hair. For lice, Jed thought. Lice like Gorelli. His loyalty had come in a rush, like a drug, he had no doubts about which side he was on. They were all playing by the same rules. Gorelli, he'd won for a while, but now he was losing, and he was losing big. Jed had to hate him. It was the only way.

When Gorelli turned his face up to the balcony, Jed hit him on the shoulder with the gun. Gorelli yelped. His arm shrank, hung against his ribs. The girl on the balcony was still swaying, screaming. You want to do something about it, Jed thought, why don't you jump?

He shoved Gorelli against the Chrysler with his gun and pulled the rear door open. He pushed Gorelli in. McGowan was still sitting in the back, Creed had moved into the front. Jed handed the gun to McGowan and climbed into the driver's seat.

'Nice work,' Creed said. 'Now drive.'

Jed let the clutch out and the Chrysler took off. He swung right and took a bite out of the kerb. The car rocked, straightened up. He beat a red light and turned right again, on to the parkway that led along the river to the bridge.

'The Crumbles, right?' he said.

'Yeah, and slow down,' Creed said. 'We don't want people smelling something funny.'

Jed slowed to thirty. The lights of Rialto slid by on the right. On the left: the boatyards, wire-mesh fences, metal gates. Then a stone parapet and bright white globes on poles like giant pearl hat-pins. The oily swell of the river beyond.

'Who are you?' Gorelli said.

'You don't know who we are?' McGowan said. And then to Creed and Jed, 'He doesn't know who we are.'

'He doesn't need to know,' Creed said. 'Where he's going he doesn't need to know anything.'

'Nothing,' McGowan said, 'nothing at all,' and Jed could hear the cocaine in his laughter.

Jed glanced at Gorelli's face in the mirror. It was grey, and strangely motionless, as if there'd been a sudden rush of concrete to his head.

'I don't understand,' Gorelli said.

'Ah,' Jed said, 'he doesn't understand.'

'I think he's going to start crying,' McGowan said. 'Anyone got a Kleenex?'

Jed laughed.

'Look,' Gorelli said, 'I'm sure we can come to some arrangement here.'

'Arrangement?' McGowan said. 'What arrangement?'

'We've already made all the arrangements,' Creed said. 'We're funeral directors.'

Gorelli lunged for the door, but it was locked. McGowan clubbed him with the butt of the gun. Blood bloomed on Gorelli's head, a dark rose appearing from nowhere, a magician's trick. He slumped back in the seat.

'Any time you want a headache,' McGowan said, 'Doctor.'

Creed turned to Jed. 'Take the old coast road. Less traffic out there.'

Jed left the expressway at the Baker Park exit and cut down through houses of clapperboard and dull red brick. The old coast road ran parallel to the shoreline. All shale and weeds and winds that picked up speed as they swooped in off the ocean, this strip of barren land prepared you for the final desolation of the Crumbles. Baker Park faded. They passed a used-car lot, a twenty-four-hour café, a gas station, then darkness closed round the Chrysler like a fist.

After driving for about ten minutes Jed looked away to the right. The old gravel mine crouched against the sky. So still, so derelict, yet it looked capable of sudden movement. All those metal limbs and struts, all those tense right-angles. It could jump, land up fifteen miles away. It could carry fear with it, like disease. Some dead things seem more horribly alive.

Creed told him to take a right turn, down a narrow track that led towards the ocean. A gate barred the way. A notice hung on the gate and he read the words in the beam of the headlamps: DANGER. NO ENTRY WITHOUT AUTHORISATION.

'Don't worry,' Creed said. 'It isn't locked.'

Jed got out of the car and opened the gate. He thought of the children buried alive at the bottom of the mineshafts. He heard the click of small bones.

The track beyond the gate was all potholes and ruts. He nursed the car along in low gear. After half a mile Creed told him to stop. He switched the lights and engine off. Wind pushed at the car with spread fingers, whispered across the hood.

Creed inserted his voice gently into the silence. 'Get him out of the car.'

They walked Gorelli across the stones to the edge of a gravel pit. The moon dipped out of a cloud, and Jed shuddered. The walls of the pit were almost sheer, falling fifty feet to smooth, dull water that was jagged at the edges, like the top of a tin can. He looked into Gorelli's face, the face he'd never seen, the face he'd only heard, and so many years ago. Gorelli was standing with his arms by his sides. He was looking at the ground, he seemed to be concentrating; he might've been trying to remember something. Then the moon went and Jed's vision shut down. Then Creed's voice:

'Give him the gun.'

McGowan handed the gun to Jed. A sliver of white that must've been teeth. McGowan grinning.

'I can't see,' Jed said.

Creed's voice again: 'Wait for the moon.'

He waited. The night slowed down. Time like a clock with its hands tied. He felt the water in the pit rise up to meet him. Rise up all silver, spill across the land. Into the hands of the dead, the clawing hands and shifting bones. Into their hands and never to return. The moon came on. He raised the gun and fired twice. So loud suddenly, so bright. A choir in his ears, a furnace in his eyes. When he looked again he saw a black shape on the ground, another black shape crouching over it.

He heard McGowan's voice: 'He's dead.' Then Creed's: 'Get the stuff.'

Jed lowered his arm.

McGowan walked to the car and returned with the long canvas bag and the cardboard box. He unzipped the bag and lifted out a chainsaw. A glimmer of silver as moonlight snagged on the serrated blade. Like holly, Jed thought. In two weeks it'd be Christmas.

When the motor started, distant and ragged, Jed looked away. The wind blew soft across his face. He was shivering. He'd never in his life felt colder. It wasn't until Creed took his arm and he looked into those black eyes that he remembered where he was.

'Throw the gun,' Creed said.

He stared into those eyes.

'The gun,' Creed said. 'Throw it.'

He pulled his arm back and hurled the gun towards the pit. He saw it drop out of sight below the lip. He didn't hear it land. Creed held a tiny bottle under his nose and the world turned white. He gasped and shook his head.

'Can you drive?' Creed asked him.

Jed nodded. 'I think so.'

When he climbed into the driver's seat he saw that McGowan was already sitting in the back. The cardboard box sat next to him. Everything seemed so bland and ordinary now.

'Where's the rest?' Jed said.

'In the gravel pit,' McGowan said. 'With stones to hold it down.'

The clawing hands, the shifting bones.

Jed turned to Creed for solid ground. 'Where now?'

'The paper warehouse. Change cars.'

When they reached the warehouse, he opened the door for Creed and McGowan as usual. They climbed out and stood still. He moved towards the Mercedes, and then stopped and looked round. Creed and McGowan hadn't moved. The canvas bag and the cardboard box stood on the concrete by their feet. He could see the blood on McGowan's clothes.

'What's going on?' he said.

'You're not coming with us,' Creed said.

'I don't understand.' The words echoed. He wished he hadn't said that. But it was too late.

'You killed someone,' McGowan said. 'You best leave town.'

Creed walked towards him and handed him an envelope. 'It's the going rate.'

The going rate. Jed stared at the envelope.

'But,' how could he put this? 'I thought we – '

'We did,' Creed said, 'but it's over.'

McGowan was smirking.

Jed walked to the door of the warehouse. He stared up into the sky, his vision pulsing. The stars floated free like buoys cut loose on a dark sea. No markings any more, no guidelines. Adrift.

He saw the streetlights again. It seemed as if they were laughing now. Rows and rows of streetlights shaking with laughter. It's funny, he thought, it's just funny, and he thought it hard to keep the fear and rage away.

A hand on his shoulder. A glove. 'I'm asking you to do something for me. It's the hardest thing I could ask you to do.' A slight pressure from the hand. 'I think you can do it.'

McGowan still smirking.

Lies. Not even clever. Not even beautiful. He felt the veins swell in his head. And cried, 'Why me?'

That soothing voice again. 'There was nobody else. Nobody we could trust. Nobody,' a pause, 'close enough.'

'What about,' and Jed turned and pointed at McGowan, 'what about him?'

A sad smile on Creed's face.

'You used me,' Jed said.

The same sad smile. 'You'd better leave now.'

'You, me, and the chairman.' Jed's lip curled. 'Like fuck.'

McGowan took a step forwards.

'You do this all the time, don't you?' Jed said. 'Pick people up and throw them away.'

He drew his arm back and hurled the envelope at Creed. Money showered through the yellow air. One note paused on Creed's shoulder, then launched itself again, one long swoop sideways, a flip, and it was lying on the ground.

McGowan positioned himself between Jed and Creed. 'You better get going.'

Creed stood with his gloved hands clasped behind his back. There was no warmth left in his face. He could switch it on and off like central heating.

'And don't come back,' McGowan said, 'not ever.'

'What if I do?'

McGowan took Jed by the arm and led him over to the cardboard box. He opened the flaps and reached inside. He pulled out a transparent bag and held it up in front of Jed's eyes. Gorelli's face stared at Jed through the bloodstained plastic.

Jed pushed past him. He got into his car and switched the ignition on. Without glancing at the two men, he drove out of the warehouse, through the metal gates and back on to the street. He drove very calmly, the way he drove when he was working. He even indicated. He stopped at the Palace to collect a few things. It took about twenty minutes. By the time he left the apartment, it was raining. That soft sound on the rooftops and the grass, someone putting a finger to their lips.

Instead of driving west, towards the expressway, he doubled back, crossed the bridge again, and cut down into Baker Park. He passed a police car on the bridge. It was parked in the safety zone with its headlamps off. His heart surged. The murder was still so fresh in his head, he felt that anyone could smell it. Some cop's lucky night. But the police car shrank in his rear-view mirror, and the lights stayed off.

He reached Sharon's house and then he wasn't sure. He drove past once, then he drove past again, going the other way. The last time he'd seen her she'd been drunk, they'd had a fight, he'd left her sprawling on the carpet. There was too much to explain to her, and nothing he could say. As he pulled away, the leaves on the trees shuddered and the rain began to fall so hard that it jumped back off the tarmac, turned to mist. He had to hunch over the wheel to see anything. It was almost three. He felt he had to speak to someone before he left for good. He thought of Mitch. Mitch was often awake till dawn. Mending his clocks and drinking beer. He couldn't sleep when it was dark. Something to do with what he'd been through in some war.

When Jed drew up in the alley behind Mitch's place, he saw an oil-lamp glowing in the kitchen window. He parked his car and walked in through the yard. He knocked on the back door. Then waited, shivering, as the rain tipped off the brim of his top hat and spattered on the ground. He had to knock twice more before Mitch heard and opened up.

Mitch stood under the light in a tartan shirt and jeans that hung off his buttocks. Jed had turned up without knowing what he was going to say, but now he knew.

'I know it's late, Mitch,' he said, 'but could you do me a tattoo?'

'What's wrong with tomorrow?'

'I won't be here.' He saw Mitch hesitating. 'It's a pretty simple job,' he said. 'No dragons or anything. No fish.'

Mitch stepped back from the door. 'You better come in.'

Jed followed him into the kitchen. He was still shivering.

'Go sit by the fire,' Mitch said. 'I'll get the stuff ready.'

Jed took off his hat and sat down by the fire.

Taped to the wall above the mantelpiece was a large-scale map of Moon Beach. Mitch knew the city better than anyone. Jed had seen a street in Westwood that was called Success Avenue, and he'd told Mitch about it. Mitch said there was a street called Failure running parallel. The next time Jed drove through Westwood he looked for Failure, but he couldn't find it. He reported back to Mitch. 'There's no such street,' he said. Mitch just looked at him. 'Of course there isn't,' he said. 'Who'd live on a street called Failure?'

Mitch returned. 'So what do you want done?'

'You got a pen and paper?'

'Hold on.' Mitch rummaged in a drawer. 'Here.'

Jed scribbled seven numbers on the piece of paper. 'I want these seven numbers,' he told Mitch. 'I want a gap between the second number and the third, and another gap between the third number and the other four.'

'What's it supposed to be?'

'It's my birthday.'

'Today's your birthday?'

Jed nodded.

'Happy birthday.'

'Thanks.'

Mitch didn't ask any more questions. They moved to the tattoo parlour. Jed sat on the green plastic chair while Mitch selected the needles.

'Blue all right?'

'Blue's fine.'

'Where do you want it?'

'Here.' Jed pointed at the inside of his right wrist.

'It's more painful.'

'That's the idea.' One small pain to hide the larger one.

Mitch switched on the needle-gun. A buzzing. McGowan and his tools. Zebra walls and all that talk of loyalty. Why hadn't he seen through it? But then, how could he have seen through it? There hadn't been any cracks.

Mitch began to talk. About his time with the Angels, about the day he met his old lady, about tattoos. This was unusual, he almost never talked while he was working, but maybe he sensed that Jed wanted the silence filled and knew that Jed couldn't do it on his own. Jed wasn't really listening. Odd words and phrases came to him but, like sticks dropped into rapids, they were quickly whisked away. Sometimes he felt himself wince and it was strange because he couldn't tell whether it was the needle or his memory. In his head he was already driving through heavy rain to a life he couldn't imagine.

CATS FOR DROWNING

Nathan had been living at India-May's for almost three years when Donald moved in. Donald was about forty-five, with short hairless arms and a belly that looked hard. His face had an unpleasant shine to it, the kind of shine you get on the walls of places where they've been cooking in cheap fat since for ever. He just showed up out of the blue one day while Nathan was working. He'd taken a taxi out to Baby Boy's grave, and then he'd walked the rest of the way. 'Five miles along a dirt track in his city shoes, can you imagine?' India-May had that glazed look, as if she was describing a miracle, a miracle that she'd witnessed with her own eyes. The arrival of somebody new, perhaps it was always a miracle to her. Donald sat beside her, listening with a modesty that seemed sly. A bandage round his head, a cup of tea in his blunt hands, he looked like the only survivor of some great catastrophe, and Nathan could understand exactly why he'd been able to move India-May to tears and why he'd been given a room on the first floor, one of the large ones, for nothing.

Donald came from an industrial town about fifty miles down the coast. It was a town of factories and bars, its streets laid out on a grid pattern, its air a crude blend of oil, salt and gas. (Nathan had passed it once, and remembered a sky lit by ragged flames, torches held aloft by the refineries.) He'd been some kind of engineer. Fifteen years working for the same company. Then a merger, cutbacks at the plant, and he was out of a job. When he walked through the factory gates that afternoon he'd walked away from everything. The wife and kids, the mortgage loan, the car payments. Down the chute with the lot of it. He bought a bottle of brandy at the first liquor store he found and he began to drink. Those bottles, strange how they multiply. He'd drunk his way right from the north end of town to the south, one night in some woman's house, one night in jail, one night on the porch of a church in the rain. Then he remembered a woman he'd met once on a train, she was singing hymns to the window, he'd been embarrassed at first, half her fringe was missing as if someone had taken a bite out of it, only he knew she'd done it because she caught him staring and laughed and said, 'I always cut it when I'm loaded,' and he remembered something about a house, and because there was nothing left to cling to, because it was the only piece of wreckage left afloat, he remembered how to get there too, it was either remember or die.

'You don't want to think about that now,' India-May told him. 'It was bad, but it's over.' She patted his hand. 'It's cats for drowning, Donald. Just cats for drowning.'

Donald nodded.

He was quiet to begin with, he just stayed in his room. For days this hush lay on the house like dust. But a change was in the air, a season was drawing to a close. Twilight left, as if he could smell the storm coming. Pete and Chrissie's baby couldn't keep its food down. Joan, the mad woman, stopped cooking.

The first time Nathan knew for certain that something wasn't right was when Donald smashed him over the head with a can of beans. He'd come in after work and found two cans of baked beans in the cupboard. He hadn't eaten all day, so he opened one of them and cooked it up. He didn't think twice about it. One of the house rules was, nothing belongs to anyone. That was why India-May could handle being ripped off all the time. So he was sitting at the kitchen table eating his plate of beans when Donald walked in. Donald stood just behind him, that place where you can't see someone unless you actually turn round, that place where it feels as if someone's going to sink a pickaxe into the soft part of your skull, Donald stood behind him and took a deep breath, as if he was about to dive under a wave, and said, 'Those are my beans.'

Nathan stopped eating and thought about it. But there was really nothing to say. Donald knew the rules, same as everyone else. As he began to eat again he heard Donald move towards the cupboard. The next thing he knew he was lying on the floor, half stunned, beans everywhere. It's not stars you see. You're too close to them to call them stars. It's more like planets.

His head buzzed and sang as if power was being fed into it. He saw Donald standing over him, a can of beans in his hand. Those cans of beans, he thought, they're not safe. Then he thought he could smell Donald's feet. He wasn't particularly surprised. Some people, all you need is one look at them and you just know their feet are going to smell.

'Don't ever,' and Donald took another breath, through his mouth this time, as if he'd only surfaced for a moment, 'don't EVER eat my beans again.'

That was the first time Nathan knew that something wasn't right.

He spoke to India-May about it. She explained that Donald was going through a difficult time, 'We all have our difficult times, right?' and Nathan would have to be patient with him. Patient? He couldn't believe it. How many times can you sit in your chair and let someone smash you over the head with a can of beans? Nathan reckoned about once. Definitely about once was the limit. But he gave Donald another chance. And wished he hadn't because, two weeks later, Donald was holding him up with a sawn-off shotgun for an hour and a half. Nobody had called Donald down to supper, that was the reason, and he was holding Nathan responsible.

'Why me?' Nathan asked.

'There's no one else here.' Which may have been the reason, but also sounded like a threat.

'What about India-May? It's her house.'

Donald jammed the shotgun into the crook of bone under Nathan's jaw. 'Shut up.'

Nathan wondered if the gun was loaded. No way of telling. But even if it wasn't, Donald could still hit him with it. He hoped Donald wasn't going to do that. He still had the bruise from that can of beans.

'Next time,' Donald said, 'you CALL me, you understand?'

Nathan didn't want to move his chin. But it's hard to say something without moving your chin.

'YOU UNDERSTAND?'

'Yes.' Nathan managed to squeeze that one word through his clenched teeth.

He went to India-May again, and told her of his fears. Donald was trying to take over. Donald wanted an empire of his own, like some kind of Napoleon or something. Donald would use force. India-May was stoned that night. She thought Nathan was making it up. 'Napoleon?' she said, and laughed until she couldn't see. She said she was glad Nathan had moved in. She said it made a real change to have a bit of humour round the place.

'He held me up,' Nathan said, 'with a shotgun.'

'A shotgun? Napoleon?' And she was off again, tears pouring from her eyes.

He could get no sense out of her.

Donald's son came to stay at weekends sometimes. The boy was ten, and slight for his age. Shy too. He'd stand in the doorway and watch Nathan tinkering with his bike and then, when Nathan looked round, he'd step back into the shadows. One Sunday afternoon, as Nathan was leaving the house, he came across Donald and the boy in the yard. Donald had one hand in the boy's hair, and he was whipping the boy with a leather belt. There was blood on the back of the boy's legs. Nathan stopped ten yards away. Suddenly the sun felt raw against his neck.

'What's going on, Donald?'

Donald didn't even break his rhythm. 'Little bastard,' he said, 'he deserves it.' The sweat evenly distributed on his face, as if he'd been greased.

'What did he do?'

Donald's mouth swerved in his direction. 'Is it time to eat?'

'No.'

'Then fuck off.'

That night Nathan went to India-May for the third time. 'You've got to throw him out,' he said. 'You've simply got to.'

'I can't,' she said. 'Imagine what it'd do to him.'

Nathan tried to hold his anger down. 'What it'd do to him?' he said. 'For Christ's sake, India-May. What about what he's doing to everybody else?'

Her mouth tightened. 'I think you're over-reacting.'

He walked out of the room and slammed the door. He imagined Donald listening at the top of the stairs. He saw the smirk on Donald's glassy face. He walked until the farm was two small lights in the darkness. Somewhere down the hill Lumberjack began to bark. India-May had called him Lumberjack because his bark sounded just like someone sawing wood. She called him Jack for short. Suddenly his frustration with her turned to pain. She was putting her trust in the wrong people again. Her trusting Donald like this, it was lessening the value of her trust in him. It made it so much cheaper, worthless even. He wanted her to know the difference.

Out on the ridge that night he decided there was nothing for it. He'd have to take the matter into his own hands. He went and knocked on the door of Pete and Chrissie's room. Pete opened the door. Chrissie was sitting on the bed, the baby's head resting sideways on her shoulder, a bottle of Infant Suspension beside her. The baby was whimpering. The room smelt chalky and damp. Sour milk. Vomit.

'How is he?' Nathan asked.

Chrissie sighed. 'The same.'

They talked about the baby's health for a while.

'It's weird,' Chrissie said, 'but the moment that guy showed up, she got sick.'

'Which guy?' Nathan asked, though he knew. He just wanted everything to be clear, like in a court of law. This was, after all, the judgement of Donald.

'You know,' she said, 'Donald.'

'Yeah,' he said, 'and Joan suddenly stopped cooking.'

Chrissie's eyes opened wide. 'That's right.' She turned to Pete. 'You remember, Pete?'

Pete nodded slowly. He adored her. He'd remember anything if she asked him to.

Nathan told them about the can of beans, the shotgun hold-up, the brutal thrashing in the back yard.

'We didn't know,' Chrissie said.

'I did,' Pete said. 'I saw him beating one of the dogs.'

That clinched it. They sat up late, trying to work out how to get rid of Donald. He wasn't going to go peacefully, that was for sure.

One evening a friend of Pete's called Tommy came round with a bottle of something. Tommy had been a marine. Pete told him about Donald. Tommy listened, nodding, as if it was a story he'd heard before. When Pete had finished, Tommy said, 'There's only one way to do it, and that's kill him.'

Silence in the room except for the bottle emptying into Tommy's throat. It was strange but, since they'd started talking about getting rid of Donald, the baby had quietened down. Now it was sleeping on the bed. Tommy wiped his mouth and handed the bottle to Nathan, who passed it straight to Pete. Tommy bared his teeth. 'I'll do it.'

'Listen,' Nathan said, 'maybe we can do this without making any mess. Maybe we can do it clean.' Though he hadn't sampled the contents of Tommy's bottle, he felt drunk.

'What the fuck you talking about, clean?' Tommy said.

So Nathan told him.

One night they were all sitting round the same as usual, in the kitchen this time, Pete and Tommy and a friend of Tommy's, they were sitting round drinking the whisky Tommy's friend had brought over when they heard footsteps in the yard. They all watched the door as it opened and Donald's face poked round the edge, and then they all looked at each other and they all thought the same thought: Now?

There was a moment of absolute stillness. Nathan thought of the shotgun locked under his chin; he'd held himself so rigid that night that he'd ached for three days afterwards. Only Donald was moving in the room – lighting his pipe, shaking a paper open.

That was when they jumped him.

Suddenly Donald was tied to his chair with the flex from the lamp, the plug still attached. Pete gagged Donald with an apron that had a picture of a spaniel on it. Tommy set fire to some of Donald's hair by mistake. It must've been the pipe. They spent some time telling him what they thought of him. Tommy had to make it up, because he'd never met Donald before. It's strange to see someone crying without using their mouth. It's hard to watch. They turn red and the tears fall out. There's hardly any noise. It's like those dolls.

They stood Donald in the back of Tommy's pick-up truck, then they climbed into the cab. It was a thirty-mile drive. They took the side roads. They didn't want any cops pulling them over and asking them what they were doing with a man tied to a chair in the back of their truck. Once they had to stop at a red light, and they heard Donald whimpering. 'They're all cowards,' Tommy said. 'Deep down they're all fucking cowards.' Most of the time they couldn't hear anything because of the engine.

Then it began to rain.

It was after midnight when they reached the place. The gates were open so they just drove right in. They got out of the truck. That smell of rotten meat, and the warm rain running over their heads and hands. Tommy shot the bolts on the tailgate and let it drop. The chair had toppled over with Donald still attached. His cheek pressed against the studded metal. One eye blinked as the rain splashed into it. He must've thought they were going to kill him, but that was why they didn't have to. The fear was the same. Tommy peered upwards, through the darkness. The pyramid loomed above.

'On top, you said.'

Nathan nodded. 'I think so.'

'Right.'

A dead dog lay close by. Three of its legs had been sawn off. Tommy's friend stood over it. 'Who'd do that to a dog?' he said. 'Who'd do that to a poor, defenceless dog?'

Tommy took him by the arm and led him to the chair. 'Get the front.' He turned to Pete. 'You help him.'

Tommy and Nathan lifted the back and, between the four of them, they half-dragged, half-carried Donald to the top. Once there, they set him upright. Stood back, breathing hard. There was a curious silence, a moment when it seemed that something might be said. But nobody spoke. The wind moved the hair on Donald's head.

They ran back down, huge crunching strides. Tried not to think what they were treading on. When they reached the bottom they automatically looked back. Donald was an inch high. Nathan nodded to himself. It was right. Donald had wanted to rule. Well, he could rule that pile of trash. He could be Pharaoh of that pyramid, a Pharaoh with a crown of flies.

Tommy's friend shuffled in the dirt. 'Think the rats'll get him?'

Tommy laughed.

'What about the gag?' Tommy's friend said. 'Think we should've taken the gag off?'

'They'll find him tomorrow,' Nathan said. But it was hours till tomorrow. There was plenty of time for Donald to think things over. Smell the smell of his own foul behaviour.

Tommy looked up at the pyramid, then out towards the ocean. 'Some view he'll have,' he said.

Then they drove home.

The next morning India-May wanted to know where Donald had got to.

Nathan looked her in the eye. 'He left.'

'He left late last night,' Pete said. 'He didn't want to disturb you.'

India-May looked from one to the other, colour creeping up her neck. 'Where's my chair?'

'What chair?' Pete said.

'You know what chair.'

'I'll get you another one,' Nathan said.

'I didn't ask you to get me another one, did I? I said, where is it?'

Nathan shrugged.

India-May turned and whirled across the kitchen. Her dress shrieked as it caught on the corner of the table and tore. 'Whose house is this,' she said, 'that's what I'd like to know,' and slammed the door behind her.

But they did get her another chair, and put it in the old chair's place. She didn't thank them, but she did start using it, and perhaps that was all the thanks they could expect. She was using it a week later when Nathan walked in through the kitchen door. It was close to midnight and India-May was the only one up. She was making necklaces, which was a form of meditation for her, a method of forgetting. Coloured beads mingled with flecks of tobacco and grass on the surface of the table, and the air was draped with smoke that smelt as sweet as creosote. Lumberjack sprawled on the tiles at her feet, whining softly in his sleep like a damp log on a fire.

Nathan sat down.

She looked at him, her fingers threading the beads blind. She might've been calculating something. The amount of trust she had left, the days till the end of the world.

'What's new?'

'I've come to tell you that I'm leaving.'

She nodded. 'I had a feeling you were going to say that.'

He told her it was like the moment when the tide stops coming in and starts going out again. It seems like nothing, but suddenly everything's different. And the longer you wait, the clearer it becomes. It was a pretty lie.

But she was nodding. She understood this kind of talk. He'd almost learned it from her.

'Where will you go?' she asked.

'I don't know. Somewhere further up the coast.'

'You going to work on the beaches?'

'I think so.' He pushed a bead around on the end of his finger. 'What could be better than saving people's lives?'

She recognised her own line and smiled.

He knew how their voices would sound from above. The hum of a plucked string. Like warmth, if you could hear such a thing.

'I wish – '

'What?'

He wished he could explain about Donald. But he knew she'd cut him off. That's old history, she'd say. That's cats for drowning. In any case, at some deeper level, perhaps she already understood. And in the future would remember.

He shook his head. 'Nothing.'

Lumberjack's paw tapped the floor. Lumberjack was dreaming. Once, last fall, he'd walked Lumberjack to the pine forest in the next valley. Lumberjack had started barking and then, just as abruptly, stopped again, and in the silence he'd heard a tree come down. Lumberjack had looked up at him, as if for approval, his tongue dangling from his jaws. No wonder there were no trees left standing round the farm. Lumberjack had sawed them all down with his voice. And now he was dreaming, dreaming of some great forest stretching out in front of him . . .

India-May lit a joint. 'When I first met you, in that bar, you were all cut out round the edges, like something out of a cereal packet that doesn't stand up when you've made it.' She touched the tip of her joint to the ashtray and smiled. 'You seemed, I don't know, kind of brave, somehow.'

This woman, she was so vague, so blind. But she could surprise you with moments of sharpness. She was like a needle in long grass, a knife in fog.

The next morning he wheeled his bike out of the barn and into the winter sunshine. Lumberjack lay panting in the dirt beside him while he changed the oil, checked the tyre-pressures, adjusted the tension of the chain. In an hour he was ready, his map taped to the gas tank, his few possessions strapped on the seat behind him. India-May came outside to wave goodbye. She seemed to be frowning, but it was probably just a bad hangover and the white sun in her eyes. His rear wheel spun on the loose stones, searching for grip, then he pulled away. Lumberjack came leaping around his front wheel, and he had to go slow. As he topped the rise he let out the throttle. But Lumberjack was running alongside him now, a serious expression on his face, as if he saw this as a real test of stamina.

'Go back,' Nathan shouted, 'go back,' and he pointed behind him. But Lumberjack just leapt at his outstretched hand. It was part of the game.

After three miles Nathan had to turn round and ride all the way home again. India-May locked Lumberjack inside the house. As Nathan pulled away for the second time he could hear Lumberjack in the kitchen, frantically sawing the legs off tables and chairs. Somehow that was worse than anything.

But he rode hard to the end of the track and when he reached Baby Boy's white cross he hesitated, then he turned right, into the mountains, something that he'd never done before.

FOUR

THE FIRST DROP OF RAIN

Jed drove north to begin with, his wrist a rectangle of heat and all that numbness just behind his eyes, but after two days the roads drew him inland, over high mountains, and soon he was heading due west. The mountains lay down, sprawled on the land like tired dogs. Then there were no mountains at all. Sometimes he saw a row of trees on the horizon. In the heat-haze they were saints walking on water, they didn't seem to touch the ground at all. Towards nightfall the sun balanced on the end of the road and then not even his special lenses helped. He'd be half blind by the time he stopped for sleep, his vision clunking with green and purple balls. In the mornings, standing in some motel parking-lot, the air scorched his lungs, it was like breathing the air above a fire. He drove with the windows shut. It was cooler. Skulls and dust outside. Tornadoes that spun across the blue sky like vases thrown on some mad potter's wheel. The weather was like a scourge, the land could kill you. Out here, on the desert's edge, penance could be done. Out here he could spend his years of exile.

The first time he drove into Adam's Creek he saw a picture of Creed in a store window and he stabbed the brake. The car slewed. A truck filled his mirror and overflowed. A sneezing of brakes, a clash of gears, and it lumbered past, the driver glaring down, fingers twitching and a black hole for a mouth. It wasn't Creed in the window, after all, it was just some advert for brilliantine, but his heart didn't know the difference and he sat there until it slowed.

Two miles out of town he pulled into a shallow ditch and switched the engine off. Looking around, he saw that he'd parked outside a graveyard. There was no church. Only a tin shelter with three walls and a bench. A few gaunt trees. Some rocks. It was the kind of place where you waited for a bus that never came.

He left his car and moved through the yellow grass, his arms clutched across his chest. He felt the inch of bare skin above his socks as two cold metal bands. He'd never thought that you could shiver in a desert, but it was late afternoon and the sun had fallen behind the hills and a chill wind cut across the graves. The wind dropped once, and he watched in astonishment as flies landed on his face and hands in clots. Then the wind rose again and plucked his top hat off his head and sent it bowling among the stones. He'd been sitting in the car so long, it was hard for him to run. His ankles clicked, his knees snapped, but he was after it, past crosses, round tombs, over mounds. Families passed beneath his feet, and he caught glimpses of their tragedies: TREASURED DAUGHTER. OUR DEAR BABIES. BELOVED WIFE. Only two days before he'd called his mother from a pay-phone on the highway. When she answered, he just listened.

'Hello?' she said. 'Who's this?'

He waited.

'That you, Henry?' she said.

So. It was Henry now.

'Henry?' she said, raising her voice now. 'Is that you?'

He put the phone down. He didn't exist for her. Henry existed (whoever Henry was). But he didn't. That was the truth.

His BELOVED MOTHER.

'Stop,' he shouted at his hat. 'Stop,' he shouted. 'Wait for me.'

All the biggest words rose off the stones towards him: mother, love, father, memory, son, heaven. He felt nothing. He was nobody his mother knew, and there were no beloveds. He caught his hat and put it on.

He was so cold when he climbed back into the car, his lips mauve in the mirror, his teeth drumming in his head. All week he'd been trying not to think. He'd wanted to drive until anything he remembered would seem as if it had happened to someone else. A movie, another person's memory, the words of a song. And finally, that afternoon in the graveyard, he knew the door had slammed on his life and the door was one of those big silver refrigerator doors and he saw his life hanging behind that door like meat. It no longer felt like a life. His or anyone else's.

He fumbled the key into the ignition with numb fingers. Once the engine caught, he turned the car round and drove back into Adam's Creek, population 2,200, elevation 21 metres.

When he arrived he found that he'd already become something of a legend. The landlord of the Commercial Hotel gave him a nod as he walked through the door. 'How are you doing?'

Jed nodded. 'Not bad. You?'

The landlord nodded. 'Saw you earlier.'

'Yeah?'

'Yeah. You were the one who braked on Main Street. Denny Butler nearly crushed you flat.' The landlord was smiling, his face broad and red and open.

Strange to be seeing still things, Jed thought. He was used to white lines, asphalt, trees. All moving. Towards and past. Faces didn't do that. They just hung in front of you, like lamps.

He blinked. 'You got a room?'

'We got single rooms. Seven dollars a night.' The landlord licked his thumb and flicked the register open. 'You going to be staying long?'

'I don't know yet. A couple of nights, maybe.'

'Names's Wayne,' the landlord said.

Jed stuck a hand out. 'Jed,' he said. 'Jed Morgan.'

He paid cash for the room.

'Yeah,' Wayne said, 'just about everyone must've saw you this morning. Not often you get someone braking like that on Main Street. And wearing a hat like that and all. Thought you were selling bibles, some of them did.'

When Jed said nothing, Wayne said, 'You don't sell bibles, do you?'

Jed shook his head slowly. 'No, I don't.'

'So what do you do then?'

Jed couldn't figure out why, but he didn't mind the landlord's curiosity. In other towns he'd left way before the question mark, his Coke still fizzing at the top of the glass. Now it seemed like a relief to be talking, a novelty, a test of wit.

'I used to work back east,' he said. 'Got laid off. Thought I'd take a trip.'

'You got here a week ago, you'd've cooked.'

'Still pretty hot.'

'You did right coming through Adam's Creek,' Wayne said. 'It gets a bit rough round here from time to time, there's a power station out past the ridge and the boys do their drinking here, but mostly we're pretty friendly.'

Rough. Jed smiled. They didn't know what rough was.

Wayne showed him to a room on the first floor, at the front of the building. A cracked sink, an iron bed. When Jed opened the wardrobe, the empty hangers jangled like wind-chimes. It was a nice illusion. Not even the faintest of breezes here. The window looked out on to a wide wooden verandah with a few deadbeat chairs and a metal table that took one leg off the ground when you leaned on it.

'Bibles,' he muttered.

From the verandah you looked down on Main Street, with its asphalt all cracked and splintered by the heat. A high wire-mesh fence divided the street from the railway tracks beyond. The line wasn't used much any more, Wayne had told him. Only for taking coal from the hills in the south to the power station just over the ridge. The yard was a desert of flint chips and rolling stock that was almost extinct. The signal box had shed its paint. Weeds grew, mauve and yellow, between the rails.

He lay down on his bed that first night, his hands folded on his chest, his boots still on. He'd been driving for days, he'd forgotten how many, and he was tired of the white lines painted down the middle of the highway, he was tired to the centre of his bones. The trouble was, once you'd been driving for that long, you drove right through your tiredness and out into a dreamland where only the road was moving. He'd driven into Adam's Creek the same way he'd driven into a hundred other small towns. But he'd braked suddenly, and broken the momentum. He'd looked round and it had seemed like just about the first place he'd seen, and some part of him deep down had said: It's got to be somewhere, why not here? After all, he couldn't go on driving for ever, he'd just drive straight into another ocean, and that was what he was trying to get away from, wasn't it, the ocean?

At nine o'clock he left his room and went down to the bar. Wayne drew him a beer. 'Welcome to Adam's Creek.' Wayne turned to the two men at the bar. 'One creek that never runs dry, eh, boys?' The laughter that followed was routine. The echo of a million other nights.

Jed hadn't drunk beer since the night he met Sharon, but he didn't flinch. He raised his glass. 'It's good to be here, Wayne,' he said, and swallowed half of it before he put it down. He made that noise that men who drink beer make, and wiped his mouth on the back of his wrist.

One of the two men leaned over. 'So where's all the bibles then?'
'Bibles?' Jed said. 'What bibles?'
'Ain't you selling bibles?' The man had slack cheeks that shook like jelly when he spoke.
Jed smiled and took a risk. 'I'd sell my sister first.'
Wayne spluttered. He turned and yelled to the woman who was polishing a glass at the other end of the bar. 'Did you hear that, Linda? He'd sell his sister first.'
Linda took one look at Jed and went on polishing the glass. 'Wouldn't fetch much by the look of it.'

Jed raised a grin. 'What are you drinking, Linda?'

'I'll have a beer,' she said.

He got drunk that night, though not as drunk as he pretended to be. He was a man drowning his sorrows, he'd decided. He was a man drinking to forget. And slowly he let his sorrows spill. He'd seen a hundred funerals. He knew how it was done. Six or seven drinks inside him, he leaned on the bar. 'I just want to forget her, Wayne.'

'Who's that, Jed?'

'My wife.'

You couldn't show up in a place like Adam's Creek without a few questions being asked, Jed knew that, so he'd dreamed up a story. He'd got the idea from a song he'd heard on the radio while he was driving. It was about a wife who'd cheated on her husband, she'd left him for his best friend, and now the man was on the road trying to mend his broken heart. To him it sounded ridiculous, but he thought it was the kind of lie that people might believe. People like feeling pity for people, it makes them feel lucky. Well, he was going to give them the chance, wasn't he? After being the man who'd sell his sister, he was about to become the man who'd lost his wife.

'She made a fool of me, Wayne,' he said. 'I just want to forget the whole damn thing.'

'You go ahead,' Wayne said. 'She wasn't worth it. You just go right ahead and forget her.'

And because Jed couldn't picture the wife who was supposed to have left him, because he had no idea what she looked like, he found himself believing that he was doing a pretty good job.

When, just before closing, Wayne said, 'So what's with the top hat, Jed?' Jed knew what the answer was, and he was drunk enough to carry it off.

Slowly he removed the hat and slowly he looked down at it, his vision blurred by alcohol, but for all anyone knew it could have been tears. 'This hat?' he said. 'This is the hat I wore to my wedding.'

He looked up. There was a big rear-view mirror over the bar so he could see the glances being exchanged behind his back. He could see the pity surfacing.

'You know, it's strange, Wayne, but I've completely forgotten what she looks like.' He smiled bravely. 'It's almost like she never existed.' And, looking down again, he felt the weight of Wayne's hand on his shoulder.

*

A couple of days, he'd said, but he ended up staying in the Commercial Hotel for almost a year. During the first few months he worked with a gang of local road-menders, filling pot-holes on the highway, smoothing cambers, paving the dirt tracks that led to ranches. He spent most of his daylight hours outside. His lean pocked body tightened, turned brown, found a different shape. In that clear air he felt himself settling into his new skin. Some days he didn't say a word. He just didn't have any. Words would take longer. Not that anyone noticed. The road-menders were a sullen bunch. Then, towards Christmas, the work dwindled and he was laid off. He took the first job he could find, washing dishes at the Wang Garden, a Chinese restaurant two blocks down the street from the hotel. Lunchtimes and evenings, $4.50 an hour. Shortly after he started at the restaurant he told Wayne that he was moving to Mrs O'Neill's boarding house on the corner of Main Street and Railway Avenue.

'How long are you going to stay there?' Wayne said. 'A couple of days?' He laughed so hard, he almost pulled a muscle.

Mrs O'Neill had startled red hair and a face that was like a dried-up river bed. She sat in her front room with the curtains drawn and the TV on and the door ajar. All you could see through the gap was a strip of wall and half a fridge. There were two pictures taped to the side of the fridge: Jesus and Donald Duck. Mrs O'Neill had the sweetest tooth in Adam's Creek, and Jed won a place in her affections on his very first day by buying her a Rocky Road on his way back from work. He'd just discovered Rocky Roads. Made from peanuts, nougat, and chunks of glacé cherry, and covered in a thick coating of milk chocolate, it was the best candy bar that he'd ever come across. Whenever he passed Mrs O'Neill's room after that, it was always, 'Bring me a Rocky Road, would you, Matt, there's a dear.' That was the other thing about Mrs O'Neill. She thought his name was Matt. 'My name's Jed,' he'd told her, more times than he could remember, but every time he passed her door she called out, 'Matt, honey, is that you?' Maybe it was her way of telling him that she knew he was lying. Not about his name, but about everything else. But then, how could she know that? he thought. How the fuck could she know anything with Jesus and Donald Duck taped to the side of her fridge and her brain blended to mush by all that TV? She didn't know. Nobody knew.

He had a large room on the second floor, with bright-green walls and a tangerine bedspread. The curtains looked like spring, but a spring that had happened somewhere else: all green shoots and rainfall and blossom. There was a plug-in kettle, an electric ring for cooking on, and a Gideon's bible, for solace. It was from this room that he wrote his first and only communications with the outside world. One weekend he bought two postcards of the Adam's Creek power station at night (they were the only postcards there were) and sat down at his rickety table by the window with a pen. He wrote the first card to Mitch. He thanked Mitch again for the tattoo and said it was lasting pretty well, considering. He told Mitch to say hello to his old lady. He said the clock in the local post office was busted and maybe Mitch would drop by and fix it sometime. Then he put, 'But your bike probably wouldn't make it, would it? Yours, Jed.' Grinning, he turned to the second card. This would be for Sharon. There were times when he missed her; hers was the only woman's body that he'd ever known. He remembered surprising her once at work. She'd just got a job at Simon Peter's, a twenty-four-hour supermarket chain that catered for all funeral needs. Their logo was a yawning grave (a black triangle with the top cut off). Their slogan? OUR PRICES ARE SIX FEET UNDER EVERYBODY ELSE'S. His eyes lifted to the window, but they didn't see the telegraph wires or the railway tracks or the range of dusty yellow hills beyond. They saw Sharon standing in the plastic-flowers aisle. She was wearing a black nylon coat and a badge that said SHARON LACEY. SECTION MANAGER. Her eyes widened at the sight of him. 'What are you doing here?'

'Make like I'm a customer,' he whispered. 'Show me where something is.'

She took him to the far aisle and showed him the salt tablets. They were called Weepies. You took them to replace the salt your tears had bereaved you of. Or so the packet said.

He noticed a door that said STAFF ONLY. 'What's in there?'

'Nothing,' she said. 'Just stock.'

He led her through the door. She was right. Boxes stacked in piles, nobody around. He sat her down and began to unfasten her coat. She smelt of ammonia, violets, sweat. 'It must be hot wearing all this nylon,' he said. In the distance he could hear the requiem mass that was being piped at a discreet volume throughout the store.

'You can't,' she whispered. 'I've got my period.'

'I don't mind about that.'

'It's not safe.'

'Of course it's safe. You just said. You've got your period.'

'It's not safe *here*,' Sharon hissed. 'My job. They'll kill – '

He was inside her before she could finish the sentence.

'They won't kill you,' he said after a while. 'You're too important.' He tapped her badge. 'You're Section Manager.'

'That's the whole point,' she said, but she was laughing by then. 'I'm supposed to set an example.'

Afterwards Jed tore open the cardboard box they'd done it on. Inside, conveniently, were hundreds of packets of black-edged tissues. As he crouched behind her, mopping the blood off the back of her thighs, he could feel his erection returning. It was the first time he'd realised that a woman's blood had the power to excite him.

'You're crazy,' Sharon said, 'you know that?'

But he'd stopped now, he was staring at the tissue.

'I know who invented these.' He smiled up at her. 'I lived in the same house as him once. He thought walking was old-fashioned, so he used to go round in a wheelchair.'

Sharon was shaking her head. 'Crazy.'

Smiling, he lowered his pen to the paper. He told her he was very far away. He was working in a Chinese restaurant, he said. He hoped she was all right. He hesitated, then he wrote, 'Remember that time in the storeroom?'

He never really expected to hear back from either of them. He didn't know why he'd written, except maybe to let people know that he was alive. If you could call working in the kitchens of a Chinese restaurant being alive.

The Wang Garden was like no Chinese restaurant he had ever seen. From the outside it looked like a bank (and with good reason, if Wayne was to be believed: 'That guy,' Wayne said, 'he's raking it in'). It had a façade of brand-new brick, a solid wooden door, and no windows. But walking inside was like walking into some hijacked piece of a South Sea island. Fake sunbeams played on tables of polished black wood. Guitars crooned softly against a rustling of surf. The real highlight, though, was the grotto, which took up most of one wall. If you looked past the rock pools and the exotic plants, past the miniature waterfall, you could see blue sky, a stand of coconut palms, and even, in the distance, a lagoon. Through hidden speakers came the rhythmic itch of cicadas. And, every twenty minutes or so, a storm broke: thunder rumbled, lightning flickered, and tropical rain came crashing down from the showerheads fitted in the ceiling. The man responsible for all this, the 'guy' who was 'raking it in', was Mr Zervos. Zervos had a huge dense beard that might have been a cutting from the grotto's undergrowth. He stamped through the restaurant beating the pineapple air with his short muscular arms.

Zervos was the only Greek in town. Everybody called him Adam's Greek.

The Wang Garden was the only restaurant in that part of the country, unless you counted the Paragon Café, which served pizza and eggs and didn't seem to know the meaning of its name. At weekends people came from up to fifty miles around. On busy nights like these Zervos paid Jed an extra $1.25 an hour to pack take-outs. He made it sound like a fortune, this extra $1.25, it was only because he liked Jed so much, he didn't know what had come over him, maybe he had a fever, an extra $1.25, it was madness. And Jed would be smiling, not at Zervos and his torrent of language, but at the memory of the $10,000, the *eight thousand* $1.25s, that he had thrown in Creed's face.

He spent most of his time in the kitchens, among blue neon flytraps and steaming silver vats. There was no door between the kitchens and the alley at the back, only a curtain of brown and yellow beads that clicked when there was a breeze, which was just about never because it was summer and the only time the air moved was when Zervos waved his short arms or a truck went past outside. It was one of the busy nights, a Friday, most likely, and he was just spooning some number 42 into a white take-out carton when a voice from behind him whispered, 'Give me a bit of chicken, mister. I'm going to die of hunger otherwise.'

He looked up and caught his first glimpse of Celia through the beads. He saw some tangled blonde hair, he saw the white light of the kitchen catch on the rough edge of a broken tooth.

'Go on, one of those little boxes, that'll do.'

The curtain parted, clicking, and now he saw her hair all coarse and fraying like rope coming undone and her breasts pushing against an old green cardigan, and he knew who she was. He'd heard men in the bar talking about her. Men with nothing in their heads always filled them up with bits of women's bodies.

'You can't come in here,' he hissed.

She flinched, stepped back. The bead curtain closed behind her, closed over her like water. It was so sudden, so complete, that it unnerved him. He went to the curtain and peered out. She'd flattened herself against the outside wall like someone in a spy movie. She was facing away from him, down the alley.

'Why don't you go home to eat like everyone else?' he said.

She kept her face turned away. 'It's my mum and dad. They locked me out while they throw stuff at each other. And I can't buy anything because I haven't got any money.' Now she looked at him. 'What's wrong with you?'

He stared at her. 'What do you mean?'

'Your eyes, they're pinned wide open.' She grinned. 'You look like an astronaut. You look like you just landed back on earth or something and it's a real shock.'

He said nothing.

'Where did you come from anyway?'

'From the coast.'

'I know who you are. You're the strange one who turned up in a top hat. I heard you shouting at it. In the cemetery.'

He handed her the carton of chicken. 'Here.'

'Thanks.' When she smiled her two front teeth stuck out. One of them was chipped. She caught him looking. 'My brother hit me with a stone.'

'I'd better go back in,' he said.

She nodded. 'I'll see you around.'

When he turned back into the kitchen, Zervos was scowling at him. 'Where's the take-out?'

'Problem with the chicken.'

'Problem with the chicken? What problem?'

'It was bad, Zervos. Bad chicken. I had to throw it out.'

'You throw out my chicken?'

'It was bad, Zervos. You can't give people bad chicken. People die of bad chicken.'

'My chicken, my chicken.' Zervos was dancing on the tiled floor and beating at the air.

'Chicken's a weapon, Zervos. You can murder people with chicken.'

'Just fix me some more, OK? Good chicken, bad chicken, any fucking chicken. Just chicken. And fix it real quick, OK? I don't pay you extra one twenty-five to throw my chickens in the garbage. Jesus God. I could get someone they do that for nothing.'

Jed didn't know it, but Celia was listening on the other side of the curtain, her laughter stifled by a mouthful of number 42. The next time she said, 'Give me some chicken,' she said it in the vacant lot behind the Commercial Hotel, and it was a different kind of chicken altogether.

That first time, he couldn't be sure, it was after midnight, too dark to tell, her belly and her legs lay like patches of moonlight on the ground, he couldn't be sure, but as he lifted away from her he thought he smelt that rich, metallic smell. It was like scrapyards, old boats, money. He had to check. He jumped to his feet and pulled his pants up over his knees.

'What are you doing?' she hissed.

'I'll be right back.'

He scrambled across the lot to a lit window, the men's room at the back of the hotel. In the yellow light that fell all bleary through the frosted glass the blood showed up brown. It excited him so much, he had to fuck her again. He didn't tell her it was the blood, though. Not then.

After the second time she stared up at him, her eyes wide.

'Now who's the astronaut?' he said.

'You remember everything,' she whispered.

'No, I don't,' he said. 'Most things I forget.'

'What about me?' she asked him. 'Will you remember me?'

He didn't say anything.

One frog croaked, and then another, and then they couldn't hear each other speak. That was why she'd chosen the place. It was dark, and there were two kinds of frogs, one fast, pitched high, the other deep and slow. Nobody would hear them fucking with all those frogs croaking, that was the idea. Nobody would know.

'Why?' he said. 'You done this before?'

She grinned up at him. 'Maybe.'

The next month they drove up to Blood Rock. It was a place that Jed had found by chance during his first few weeks in Adam's Creek. You drove east, up into the hills. About ten miles out of town there was a turning on the right. The track was two miles long and ended in a precipice. It was a vantage point, marked on the map. The Adam's Creek power station sprawled in the dust-bowl valley below, its chimneys lit as green as Mars. Smoke poured upwards, pale-grey and blurred, like make-up smudged by tears. Away to the east lay the cooling-water lake, known by local people as the Blue Lagoon. To the west you could see a sprinkling of town lights and, further west, the hills where the coal came from. West of the hills was the highway, a finger dipped in the dust of the mines and run all the way across the land to the horizon.

He parked two hundred yards from the precipice and let her walk the rest. She reached the edge and stood still for a long time, only her skirt fluttering, and the ends of her hair. It was obvious she'd never been before. Later she told him that she was surprised he'd found the place, grateful that he'd taken her. It said something about what he felt for her. It said something that she knew he'd never put in words.

The sun set in front of her. It seemed too bright that evening, almost chemical. A sulphurous yellow, the blue of gas. He went and opened the trunk. Lifted a sheet out and sent it billowing through the air. Watched it drift down, settle on the ground. Dusk made the white cotton glow.

'What's that for?' She stood ten yards away, her chin tucked into her shoulder.

He knelt down on the sheet. 'I thought we could fuck on it.'

'But it's my time.'

He liked the way she said that. 'I know it's your time. That's why I brought the sheet.'

'Don't you mind?'

'Why should I mind?'

'Some people think it's disgusting.'

'Whose blood is it?'

Her forehead puckered. One finger curled into her broken tooth. It was as if she really didn't know the answer.

'It's your blood,' he said, 'isn't it?'

She was grinning now, and once she'd grinned, of course, she had to let him. She was too intrigued not to.

It wasn't actually called Blood Rock, that was just their private name for it, because it was there that Jed made his confession. About what excited him most. He'd timed that first drive with such care. It occurred exactly four weeks after the frogs. He'd been counting the days.

The summer passed. Every month they drove up into the hills, their sheet folded neatly in the trunk, their lust, by contrast, scarcely containable. One evening in August – it was their fourth night in a row; her blood kept flowing that month – he turned to her and saw an expression on her face that he didn't recognise. It was like wonder, and he couldn't guess the root of it.

'You know the weird thing?' she said. 'The weird thing is, you take my pain away.'

She told him how she used to dread her time. There'd be one night every month when somebody took a knife to the softest part of her. She'd twist and turn, she'd fold herself double, she'd cry out. Nothing helped, not even aspirins. It just had to be gone through. Since she'd met him, though, it didn't happen any more. It was because he fucked her at the beginning of her blood, she said. It was like he loosened her inside. Her look of wonder deepened. It was like they were made for each other, she said, wasn't it?

He was sitting on the edge of the sheet now. In the valley below the power station was lit up like a tangle of pearls, like some romantic gift.

'I wish I could give you that,' he said.

She saw where he was looking, and laughed and kissed his face.

Soon afterwards he left the Wang (though Zervos tried to tempt him to stay by offering him an extra, wait for it, *thirty-five* cents an hour!) and started working days at the ice-cream parlour on Main Street which belonged, coincidentally, to Celia's uncle (or maybe not so coincidentally since, in a town like Adam's Creek, population 2,200, most people ended up being related sooner or later). It was a move that sealed him in Mrs O'Neill's affections: he now brought her free ice-cream as well as the traditional Rocky Road.

One morning in October he was wiping the counter down when he heard a motorbike approaching. He thought nothing of it at the time. Two of the power-station boys had bikes. They held races out by the railway tracks on Saturdays. But he looked up all the same and saw the bike pass by, the rider wearing an unfamiliar black helmet and black leathers, the motorbike low-slung, bulging, making a noise that made him think of someone beating cream in a bowl with a wooden spoon.

Five minutes later the door jangled and the man in the helmet and the leathers walked in. He looked at the card on the counter. It said WELCOME TO THE WORLD OF 45 FLAVOURS.

'Give me all forty-five,' he said. 'Large cone.'

Jed smiled. Mitch took off his helmet. There were streaks of vanilla in his hair.

'You're getting old, Mitch,' Jed said.

'Is that a nice way to greet someone who's ridden three thousand miles to see you?'

'You wouldn't ride three thousand miles to see anyone,' Jed said. 'That's what I always liked about you.' He vaulted over the counter and wrapped his arms round Mitch. They didn't reach. He smelled the dust and oil of three thousand miles on Mitch's jacket. He spoke into the smell. 'It's good to see you.'

Mitch sat down on one of the fancy white chairs with the scrolls on the back and the dainty feet. 'I was doing a trip, coast to coast. Thought I'd call in.'

After work Jed took Mitch to the hotel for a drink. He introduced
Mitch to Wayne and Linda. 'He's an old friend of mine,' Jed said.
'Haven't seen him for years.'

'I heard you come in,' Wayne said. 'Sounded like a jet plane'd
landed on the street.'

Mitch nodded. 'It's not built to go that slow. Place to hear it is on
the highway. Sounds real sweet out there. Sounds like sugar being
poured in a dish.'

The door slammed open and Celia walked in. She was wearing her
short fluttery pink skirt with the flowers on and her denim jacket and
a pair of pink hightops.

'Hey, missie,' Wayne said. 'Why don't you bust right through the
wall next time.' He looked at Mitch and Jed, and shrugged.

Celia walked right over. She gave Jed a slow wink and then leaned
back against the bar, the points of her elbows resting on the old brass
rail. 'Who's this, Jed?'

'This is Mitch,' he told her. 'He's an old friend.' He turned to
Mitch. 'This here's Celia.'

Mitch's chin dipped an inch and then lifted again. 'Pleased to meet
you, Celia. How would you like to come for a ride?'

Celia just looked at him, running her tongue back and forward
through that chip in her teeth, then she looked at Jed. 'You say he's
a friend of yours?'

'Yes, he is.'

Celia looked at Mitch again. 'What kind of bike've you got?'

Mitch smiled. 'Harley.'

'What the hell.' She pushed away from the bar and linked her arm
through Mitch's. 'Let's see what it does.'

Jed played pool in the back with one of the power-station boys. He
was just losing for the third time when Celia walked back in, Mitch
behind her. She looked as if the wind had blown everything except
sheer joy clean out of her head.

'Oh Jed.' She was still breathless and there was air in her words.
'We went right out to the Blue Lagoon. We did a century on the
power-station road.' She put an arm round him and kissed his neck.
The buttons on her denim jacket were cold. She smelt of speed, cool
dust, high blood. She broke away from him again. 'Can I get you a
drink, Mitch?'

Mitch smiled. 'Beer.'

'You, Jed?'

'The same.'

Mitch sat down at the small round table in the corner. Jed leaned his cue against the wall and joined him.

'You better get a bike, Jed.'

'Looks that way.'

'So how long you been here now? Five years?'

'Close enough.'

'How much've you told them?'

'Nothing.'

'They don't know anything about you?'

'All they know is stuff I made up.'

Celia was returning with the beer, three glasses in between her hands, her tongue wedged in that chip in her teeth.

Mitch watched her. 'Not even her?'

Celia put two of the beers on the table, then she stood back, knuckles of her right hand on her hip, and said she had to go and talk to someone.

Jed waited until she'd left and then he said, 'Not even her.' He swallowed some beer. 'You seen Sharon?'

'I seen her.'

'How is she?'

'She's fine. She married some guy.'

Jed nodded. 'I sent two cards, one to you and one to her. That's all the remembering I've done. And telling, even less than that.'

Mitch turned his beer can on the table, made a few new rings. Then he said, 'I heard a story that might interest you.'

Jed lifted his head.

'You remember Vasco?'

'Of course,' Jed said. Fear suddenly. It had come from nowhere, out of a long silence, like something fired from a gun.

'I did a tattoo for him. One of those tombstones he always has, you know. Only this time it covered half his back.'

'What was the name on it?'

'Francis.'

Jed looked down into his drink. 'Where is he now?'

'Two days after I did the tattoo they found him on a street in Los Ilusiones. It was sometime after midnight. He was all curled up in the gutter, naked. No sign of his clothes. It was in the papers. They took him to that private clinic, the one in the hills. Far as I know, he's still there.'

Jed sipped his beer. It tasted sharp and frothy. He could see Vasco on the street, fourteen years old, face like a guitar. It's not my time.

'Seems a parcel was delivered to his house on Christmas Eve. To be more specific, a box was delivered. Seems his brother's head was inside it.' Mitch glanced at Jed. 'Kind of an interesting Christmas present.'

When Jed didn't say anything, Mitch went on. 'And here's the really interesting part. Seems the box was delivered by none other than Mr Neville Creed. In person.'

Jed could see it. A ring on the doorbell and Maria's tights hiss their way across the hall. A postman's standing on the doorstep. 'Special delivery, ma'am.' Maria's never seen this postman before, but it's not so strange, they always take new people on at Christmas. She signs for the parcel. 'Happy Christmas, ma'am,' the postman says and, as he steps back into the darkness, she notices he's wearing gloves. If anything's strange, that is. Because it isn't cold. Not cold at all.

Jed shivered. He was imagining what happened next. Christmas morning. The tree's all lit up. It's the moment everyone's been waiting for. It's time to open the presents –

A sudden explosion of glass made him jump. One of the power-station boys had knocked a table over on his way to the bathroom. Drinks everywhere.

'Creed had Vasco's brother killed,' Mitch said, 'and then he delivered the head himself. What do you think?'

Jed picked up his glass and swirled the last inch of beer around. 'I wouldn't say anything about it if I was you.'

'I'm not saying anything about it. I'm just telling you.'

'How did you hear?'

'I've got a couple of friends from the old days, they're vultures now. One night I was down in a bar on V Street and their tongues got loose.' Mitch looked up at Jed. 'Why? You think it's just talk?'

'No,' Jed said, 'I think it's true.'

Mitch said nothing.

'I worked for Creed,' Jed went on. 'I watched him. Driving someone, you get to do a lot of that. Stuff like what you're talking about, it's a game for him. It's entertainment.' He saw that face again, he heard the voice. 'You know what he told me once? He told me there are no borders.'

'If you knew all that,' Mitch said, 'how come you worked for him?'

Jed just stared at him across the top of his glass.

'Yeah, I know,' Mitch said. 'Stupid question.'

Wayne came over. 'You boys are getting mighty serious.'

Mitch laughed and drained his glass. 'Give me another beer, Wayne. Then we'll see who's serious.'

Mitch left the next morning at dawn. They walked to the edge of town and shook hands. The sun lifted over the hills and threw their shadows across the road.

Mitch took a last look round. 'You know what I like about out here? The air's clean.'

Jed didn't say anything.

Mitch swung his leg across the bike, braced his foot on the kickstart, and pushed down hard. The engine fired.

Jed squinted into the low yellow sun. 'Safe trip, Mitch.'

Mitch nodded. 'Be well.' He fitted his goggles over his eyes. 'Sell lots of ice-cream.'

The back tyre mimed a shallow S, then the bike straightened up, began to shrink. The rasp and snap of the engine bounced against the walls of the houses behind him, tumbled over the rocks and dust beyond. There were gaps as Mitch eased his wrist back on the throttle. Then one long hum that slowly faded, became part of the silence.

When Jed turned round, he saw Celia standing on the road. She was dressed in nothing but her cotton nightgown and her cardigan. Her feet were bare. He knew what she'd done. She'd crept out through her bedroom window, but she'd left half a dozen coarse blonde hairs behind her, flickering on the damaged flyscreen wire, like evidence.

'He's gone,' she said.

He nodded.

'I liked him.' She tipped one ear to the road, listening to the last of Mitch. The hem of her nightgown stirred. 'Now he's really gone.' She moved her toes in the orange dust at the edge of the road. 'He didn't stay long, did he?'

'Why would he stay?'

'I don't know.' She scratched her ribs through a tear in the cotton. 'Why did you?'

He stuck his hands in his pockets. Then took one hand out again and picked at his neck. The sun prickled on his skin. Those early rays could feel like insect legs.

After Mitch came through, things were never quite the same. It was as if Mitch had left the freezer door ajar. There was the distant drone of an alarm and things began to thaw.

Celia stole into his room one day while he was out at work. When he came home he found her peering into the well of his top hat. He took it away from her.

'Moon Beach,' she said. Her eyes were wide as new horizons.

He heard the voices of the power-station boys on the street below. They always got drunk at the Commercial Hotel when their shift was over. He wanted Celia to leave. She pulled the blankets back instead and took off all her clothes.

'What about Mrs O'Neill?' he said.

Celia laughed. 'If it's not on TV, she's not interested.'

But he wouldn't fuck her, so she went to sleep. He paced round the bed. Felt invaded, nervous.

'You're not ugly,' she said later, though nobody had mentioned ugliness, not even once. 'You're more sort of, I don't know, hurt.' She was lying on her back, pulling lazily at one of her nipples, watching it stretch. 'Your skin,' she said, 'it shows it. Like you had boiling water on you or something. Like you were scalded. Did that happen, Jed? Did you have boiling water on you?'

Her voice had brightened suddenly. She thought she was on to something. She thought she could know him as well as he knew himself. Maybe she thought she could know him better.

He turned away from her. He didn't want to look at her. He knew what the expression would be. All blown-up with sleeping. Fat with trust. People were always telling you things. What did they think they were, mirrors? Did they think that was the only way you could find out who you were, by listening to them?

He went and stood by the window.

Adam's Creek, midnight. View from the second floor of Mrs O'Neill's boarding house. A yellow light in the street, the yellow smudged with coal or dust. One telegraph pole, with a metal sign attached: MAIN STREET. A railway line.

Just then a row of trucks rattled from right to left. They looked like giant soft-drink cans on wheels. They always passed at about the same time, right after midnight, and it was something he liked to watch, the way other people watch sunsets or the ocean. It was like letting your breath out slowly, it took him far away from himself.

A man moved in front of the silver trucks, moved in the opposite direction. Shoulders pulled back, fists knocking against his thighs.

'He's late tonight.'

Celia shifted in the bed. 'Who is?'

'Wayne.'

A silence.

'You're all locked up,' she said. 'I wouldn't be surprised if you were all rotten in there.'

He turned again, surprised. He saw her breasts spilling across her ribs and that chip missing from her tooth where her brother hit her with a stone. She didn't know she was right. She was just saying stuff. He saw her breasts and her broken tooth, and he moved towards the bed, seconds away from fucking her. It was best when it felt like you were fighting gravity, fighting the pull of forces greater than yourselves. Just now they were in the same place, like Wayne and the trucks, but sometime soon they'd be miles apart.

Still. He'd allowed her closer than anyone else, and when his clothes were off and he was tired she read him the way she read the weather or the mountains or the dust, she ran her fingers over his pale, scarred body and she guessed close to the truth.

They were still driving up to Blood Rock. Sometimes they'd fuck right away, or sometimes they'd wait till they were about to leave, but they'd always do it on the sheet, the same sheet he'd brought that first time, as if, without it, some spell might be broken and everything would fall apart. By now it was stained with blood, but Celia liked that, she thought it was romantic. 'It looks like flowers,' she said, 'like roses.' The sheet was a diary of their meetings, a history of their love. She suspected it might have special powers. If you wrapped it round you, for instance, it'd keep you from feeling any pain. Or if you spread it on the ground you could study it like tea-leaves and read the future there. Jed wasn't so sure, he didn't like the idea that the future was all decided already and he didn't know anything about it, but he indulged her, and the bloodstains remained, and grew. He couldn't have got rid of them anyway, even if he'd wanted to. He'd tried once, secretly, in Mrs O'Neill's washing machine, but the powder wouldn't shift them. It just wasn't true what they said in those commercials.

The last time they went to the rock, everything began the same way as usual. The sun was going down, the power station laid a creased white sleeve of smoke against the darkening sky. She sat and stared at the view, while he opened the trunk and lifted out the sheet, complete with its light-brown rose of blood.

When she turned and saw the sheet spread out on the ground she smiled and scuttled through the dust on her heels till she was next to him. He put a hand on her shoulder. Reached into her mouth with his tongue and moved it across her uneven teeth. Felt that tiny missing triangle. A murmur lifted in her throat like the sound of the wind blowing. His hand dipped through the buttons on her dress, grazed her nearest breast, felt the nipple gather.

They fucked and fucked, and the flower on the sheet blushed red and grew new petals. A slow breeze moved across his naked back. She smiled at him with her mouth, her eyes wide and still.

'Where's your wedding ring?'

He wasn't quick enough. 'What wedding ring?'

'You've never been married,' she said, 'have you?'

And, to his surprise, he said, 'No.'

He pulled out of her and lay down. His face seemed pressed against the sky. There was a long silence. Then an aeroplane flew by. It was so high up, it whined like a fly.

'You've been lying all along,' she said.

Sooner or later he'd known that he would tell the truth. You can lie and lie beautifully, but sooner or later the truth comes back like a wave and sweeps everything before it. The people of Adam's Creek had accepted him. People like Celia. People like Wayne and Zervos. They thought he was a bit peculiar, maybe, but they'd accepted him all the same. Peculiar, but not a liar. Well, they were fools. They were all fools. He'd been like that once, he'd trusted and believed, and look what had happened to him. He'd been thrown away. Thrown away like a candy wrapper, thrown away like trash. In his head they were trash too, for trusting and believing him. Part of him didn't want to get away with it. Part of him wanted to be found out and punished. And so he'd told Celia the truth. And now there was nothing else he could say.

There was one thing he hadn't lied about, and that was her blood, how much he'd loved and honoured it, that wasn't a lie. But it wasn't enough to save them either. And she wouldn't listen now. She turned her face away. He could only see one ear, some damp hair. When he leaned over her, tried to bring her face back, she tucked her lips inside her mouth and wouldn't speak.

It wouldn't have been enough, though. It really wouldn't. She belonged in this stage set, among these lies. She belonged here, where things weren't real. It was a warp in time, a secret crease in space. This precipice, this sheet. She was here, but he wasn't. Not really. It wasn't really him.

After he dropped her outside her house that evening he never saw her again. He woke up every day and went to work at the ice-cream parlour, but he began to hate the taste, the sight, the very thought of it. It was his life, all that frozen mess. His fury when the doorbell jangled and a family of tourists in shorts and visors came babbling in. His fury while they scanned the world of forty-five flavours.

'Fudgana?' They'd be blinking, their heads tilted at him, all at different angles. 'What's Fudgana?'

'It's our special,' he'd hiss. 'Four scoops of vanilla with hot fudge, banana wheels and whipped cream. It's two-fifty.'

They often had Fudgana and they were often, he hoped, violently sick in the car about half an hour later.

His fury, his revulsion.

One day he took the afternoon off without telling anyone. He drove out past the graveyard where he'd stood alone in the wind and hurt. He drove out of town and just kept going. There was nothing west of Adam's Creek, nothing for miles. A low range of hills lifted in the north, yellow, rumpled, threadbare, as if someone had been carrying a lionskin and had grown tired of it and had thrown it down. Otherwise the land was flat and hot, studded with dull stones. Shreds of rubber twisted and coiled at the edge of the highway. Just tyres that had burst. When he first set foot in Adam's Creek he used to think they were snakes or lizards, some kind of reptile anyway. It was that kind of country, somehow, safe things looked dangerous, specially in the corner of your eye. Or maybe the landscape was his mirror, and he was just seeing himself. In any case, he was still deceived sometimes, even after six years.

He drove further than he meant to. The road was so straight, it was hard to stop. Stopping would've been like looking away from a hypnotist's swinging silver watch. His long spine ached, and his eyes felt hot and flat against the windshield, like eggs broken on to a rock. The dense grey sky seemed denser than before, so grey in places that it seemed almost green. Then he saw the sign. A wooden sign stuck at the beginning of a red dirt track. LAKE QUIRINDI, it said. 24 MILES.

He took the turning without knowing why. Thinking, maybe, that it would break the monotony, the tedious spell of the highway. He had to drive now, where before he had merely steered. There were pot-holes to avoid, riverbeds to cross. It seemed to give him a purpose which, up until he saw the sign, he hadn't had. Though he couldn't have said what that purpose might be.

Soon there was nothing except the laboured surging of the engine and his head jolting on his spindly neck and a swarm of red dust in the rear window. He seemed to have been driving for ever. He'd be reaching the lake soon, and then what? A sudden vision of Celia, and the blood rushed to that part of him. He took one hand off the wheel and tried to push it down. He couldn't leave it there for long. He was driving fast and the road kept surprising him. Those riverbeds could snap an axle as crisply as the way that Zervos snapped his fingers when he danced. One of those deep troughs of dust could suck his wheels down, and there'd be nobody passing on this road, not for days, maybe, maybe not even then, and he hadn't thought to bring water along or tell anybody where he'd gone, it had all happened too fast, there hadn't been a moment. He sat up straighter and locked both hands on the wheel. He could die out here, and he wasn't ready. It wasn't his time.

The loud engine, the road slippery with dust. And then he came over a rise and saw the lake below. He stabbed the brake, stabbed too hard, and his back wheels slurred in the dirt.

There was no water.

Now he remembered someone telling him about this place. The lake itself had dried up thousands of years ago. It was some kind of ancient burial site. Relics had been unearthed. Pots, charms, bones. There were sand dunes here, he remembered. They'd been given names by the local people – the Grand Canyon, the Great Wall of China – on account of the strangeness of their formations. He could just make out the sand dunes now, a blond strip on the far side of the lake, a good ten miles away.

He let the car forwards, down the hill, and on to the white road that led across the lake bed. Halfway across he imagined the water there again, he saw the lake fill up, some ghost of the ocean haunting him, and shuddered at the thought of drowning in such loneliness, in such heat. There were no animals here. Only a twitching at the edges of his vision. Snakes, he thought. And then he thought: Tyres. Just tyres.

He stopped the car where the road lost itself in sand and got out. He stood still and listened. Heard one bird. It sounded like a tap dripping. Give it time and it would fill the lake all by itself, just with its song.

The air was thick. So thick that the oxygen seemed buried in it, hard to extract. Breathing like mining. He looked up at the sky. Clouds on the boil, the whole sky simmering. White cracks showed in the grey, white cracks fanning out like the bones in the wings of birds. He looked down again and the sand seemed pink in this storm light. He began to walk, his eyes still on the ground. He passed scattered jawbones, pale twists of wood. He stopped and picked one up, and was surprised by how light it was. Everything had been sucked out of it. All the wood's blood gone.

He was climbing now. The sand under his feet had been crusty at first, ribbed, but now it was turning smooth, soft, unmarked. He'd left the castles and the monuments behind, he was climbing a dune that was featureless, untouched. Another footprint would've been a shock, a threat. The wind had risen. His ear to a seashell. There was only that now, the hollow roar and scrape of the wind and the scuffing of his feet in the sand. He lifted his eyes and saw that he was almost at the top. He was about to move on when something tapped him on the shoulder. Someone. He jumped, spun round. Nobody there. And yet he could have sworn that someone had tapped him on the shoulder.

And then raindrops began to fall in the sand all around him. Fat drops of rain placed in the sand, almost one by one, like counters on a board game. But there was no board. Or was there?

And then, just as suddenly as they'd started, they stopped. It was the shortest rainstorm he'd ever seen. He could count the drops. There were thirty-six of them.

And then he knew what it was that had tapped him on the shoulder. It was the first drop of rain.

And he knew what it meant too. He'd been singled out. He'd been anointed. He was special. Places like this, they knew.

He moved past the collection of dark holes in the sand and, with half a dozen steps, he'd reached the top of the rise. He half expected ocean, the white towers of Moon Beach, but there was only land, land that looked infinite, land without end, and he stood still and stared, as if by staring he could make something happen, the first drop of rain already drying on his shoulder.

HEAVEN IS A REAL PLACE

The phone woke Nathan out of a deep sleep. He reached out and picked up the receiver. 'Yes?'

'Nathan?'

He could tell it was long-distance, the line was so gravelly and hollow, but he didn't recognise the voice. 'Who's this?'

'It's Georgia.'

Georgia? His eyes opened. This was unheard of, Georgia never called. He was about to make a joke about it when she said, 'I don't know how to say this.' She sounded strict, almost officious. It took any jokes he might've made and threw them away.

'I've never said it before.' She paused. 'My dad's dead.' She paused again. 'Sorry, I don't know why I said that. He's your dad too.'

They were on the phone for an hour, not really speaking, a few words scattered among the silence. They were linked, that was the important thing. It was as if they were clinging to each other, and they couldn't let go. If one of them hung up they'd be torn apart again, three thousand miles.

Afterwards he couldn't move. Something lowered over him like glass, something seemed to be positioned between him and the world. He could see his room – the white walls, the shelf of shells, the ocean in the window – but they could've belonged to anyone, they meant nothing.

Then the crying came, surprising him. Came like a sudden gust of wind, banging doors in him, shaking him to his foundations. Later, he sat on the bed, his insides chilled, his throat raw. He tried to sleep, but sleep hid somewhere else. He switched the radio on, just for the company of voices. He thought maybe he'd make some soup. It seemed absurd, everything ordinary did, but he made it anyway. In the afternoon he ran through light rain to buy a plane ticket home.

An hour into the flight he noticed a woman in a black dress sitting across the aisle from him. She clutched a bouquet of flowers in both hands, and her lips moved constantly, as if in prayer. Then, as the plane began to circle above Moon Beach, her head drooped and tears fell into her lap. The stewardess tried to comfort her, but the woman waved her away without looking up. Nathan turned to the window. He had a curious feeling of release; other people had taken portions of his grief upon themselves, and they were expressing it on his behalf. He was feeling lighter and lighter with every second that passed. There was helium in his blood. He could've floated clean away. Was this how you were supposed to feel? Dad's dead, he told himself, dead. The way you might pinch yourself to see if you were dreaming. But he felt nothing. Nothing except this lightness, this elation.

The plane banked, and he pressed his face against the cold window. The ocean tilted up to meet him, its dark surface studded with points of light that looked like constellations, fallen stars. The tourist sitting next to him asked him what they were. Nathan explained that the bright lights marked the boundaries of the ocean cemeteries. The lights that were fainter were memory buoys. They were the equivalent of tombstones on land: they marked the actual graves. While he was talking he noticed scratch-marks on the water, hundreds of white gashes, and suddenly the captain's voice, crackling over the intercom, interrupted him. The ships they could see on the right side of the aircraft were returning from a rehearsal for the service of remembrance that was held on the ocean every year. Towards the end of the week, in case they hadn't realised, a unique festival was due to take place in Moon Beach. It was known as the Day of the Dead.

Nathan leaned back in his seat. He *hadn't* realised.

Of all the weeks to be flying into Moon Beach, he thought. Of all the times for Dad to die.

When he was young, it had been one of the days he most looked forward to. Yvonne would come and stay, and she'd always bring a fish with her, a huge fish freshly caught from the ocean, and she'd gut it on the kitchen table. Fish should be eaten, she said, because fish were the guardians of the soul, and she was so powerful in her belief that nobody dared to disagree. He remembered how the fish lay gaping on its bed of newspaper, the flesh dark-red and subtly ribbed where it was split in half, and Yvonne with her sleeves rolled back and her wrists dipped in blood that smelt of tin.

It was a day that abounded in peculiar traditions. Pass any candy store in the city and there'd be marzipan skulls and sugar fish and little white chocolate bones for 5 cents each. Pass any bakery and you'd see cakes slathered in blue icing, cakes sprinkled with sea-salt.

If you made a Day of the Dead cake at home you always hid a coin in it, and the person who found it was supposed to live for ever. Once, when she was four, Georgia had swallowed the coin and almost choked. It was still one of her favourite stories about herself. In the afternoon there'd be costume parties. You dressed up as Lazarus or Frankenstein, or you went as one of your dead relations. Or, if you couldn't think of anything else, you just wore something blue because that was the colour you went when you were buried at the bottom of the ocean. And everywhere there were bowls of candy and slices of special home-made Day of the Dead cake. He could still remember the taste of that blue icing. Nobody's mother ever got it right. You always had to spit it out and shove it down the back of some chair.

Later, when it grew dark, a fleet of ships would set sail for the ocean cemeteries, and the remembrance service would be held. Lying awake in his room, he'd imagine the boats rocking and the priest's voice pushed and pulled by the wind. And then, later still, after the boats had gone, the dead would rise from the ocean bed and walk on the water. They gathered the flowers that had been left as offerings, they blew the floating candles out. Smoke that smelt of churches poured from the wicks, drifted over the slowly heaving ocean, hid their feet. It was a night of strange occurrences. It was the night that everyone was Jesus.

The plane landed. He said goodbye to the tourist and wished him a pleasant stay. From the airport he took a train into the city. He travelled in the buffet car, leaning against the window with a drink. The track ran parallel to the South Coast Expressway, through land that was flat, a wasteground of weeds and shale. It was almost ten now, long after rush-hour, but the road was bright with cars. Southbound there were tailbacks for miles. Thousands drove in for the celebrations. All Friday night the streets would be packed with people dressed from head to toe in blue. Sometimes they painted their hands and faces too. Sometimes they dyed their hair. That was what you did in Moon Beach. Turned blue once a year. And then, sooner or later, you turned blue for ever.

Now they were racing through the inner-city suburbs on slick rails. Rialto, Euclid, Mangrove West. The eastbound helix coiled against the sky like a giant concrete snail. Beyond the tenement blocks and the shopping malls lay the ocean, a black cloak spread on the ground, a hem of white foam where the waves broke. The train pulled into Central Station and Nathan stepped down on to the platform with his case. Moon Beach Central had been built in the style of a temple. A floor of polished marble, a domed ceiling of gold mosaic. Footsteps merged with voices, merged and echoed, the air seemed to be filled with whispering, the sound of prayer. Nathan walked swiftly to the exit. He passed posters for funeral parlours and women shaking tins for God. Heat, such heat, even at ten o'clock at night. There was an old man from one of the doom societies. He was raving about Armageddon and the fires of hell. He had to keep breaking off so he could mop the sweat from his face and neck.

Nathan hailed a taxi on the front steps of the station. 'The west shore,' he told the driver. 'Blenheim.'

The driver eyed his case. 'You on vacation?'

'I live here,' Nathan said, then he corrected himself. 'I grew up here.'

The driver was searching for a gap in the traffic. 'It's like a fucking circus tonight.'

Nathan grinned. Moon Beach taxi-drivers were famous for their pessimism, their own vicious brand of gloom.

'The paper the other day,' the driver was saying now, 'you know what it said? It said people aren't dying fast enough.' He put a finger to his temple like a pistol. 'Is that crazy or what?'

Nathan agreed that it was crazy.

'The funeral parlours, that's a business, they got to expand, but people're living longer than before, advances in medicine, right? So there's all this advertising to get people to move here. Suntrap of the south, the gold coast, shit like that. They're giving people tax breaks, casino vouchers, free cars. You name it. You know why? They've got to feed the funeral parlours, that's why. You listen to those buildings sometime. You can almost hear them chewing, man.'

They passed the Moon Beach Hilton. This was the traditional venue of the Annual Day of the Dead Ball. Blue tie and tails, of course. They passed the Paradise Corporation building. That famous cross of white neon would soon be glowing blue. You can almost hear them chewing.

'Maybe you're right,' Nathan said.

'Sure I'm right. You been away too long is all.' The driver tipped his head back, without taking his eyes off the road. 'How long you been away?'

'About four years.'

'What did I tell you?'

Nathan conceded the point. 'And I wouldn't be back here now if my dad hadn't died.'

'Your father died, you say?'

'Yeah.'

'I'm sorry, man.'

'It's all right.'

'No, really, I'm sorry. I wouldn't've talked that way if I knew that.'

They were in Blenheim now. Nathan leaned forwards, stared at scenery that, even in the dark, he knew off by heart and could recite. That tree, that store, that view. And there was the gatepost Dad had driven into because he'd been eyeing some young girl instead of looking where he was going. Nathan smiled. Then they were turning into Mahogany Drive and something lurched inside him, as if it was love he was meeting, not death.

They pulled up outside the house. He put his case on the sidewalk and paid the driver, then he looked over his shoulder.

Viviente.

The name had taken on an ironic, almost malicious air. The whitewashed walls were stained with mould. The windows skulked behind their black wrought-iron grilles. The paint had chipped off the gate. The house must have looked like this, he thought, when his parents first arrived, more than thirty years ago. It had come full circle. Now he could imagine children being frightened of it. Only the bravest would break in, light fires on the tile floors.

He turned to thank the driver, but the taxi had gone. He looked up just in time to see the two red tail-lights drop behind the hill. He shrugged and, picking his case up, walked towards the house.

He rang the bell. The door opened and Harriet stood in front of him. He thought for a moment that time had been operated on. A nip here, a tuck there, and it was seven years ago. But then he noticed her hair, she'd dyed it black, it curved round and down, into her jawbones, and the skin above and below her eyes looked shiny and hard. She'd aged. This realisation touched him, took the shock of seeing her and softened it.

'I tried to call you this morning,' she said, 'but you'd already left.'

'That's all right,' he said and, stepping forwards, he kissed her on the cheek.

As he moved past her, into the hallway, she took his arm.

'About Yvonne,' she said.

'What about her?'

'It's been very hard on her.'

'Is she here too?'

Harriet nodded. 'I just wanted to warn you.'

He walked down the tile hallway and into the kitchen. It was a big room with a polished oak table and a door that opened to the garden. Yvonne was sitting at the table with a cheroot and a tall glass of wine. Veiled in smoke, only dimly visible, she looked like the result of a magic trick.

'Yvonne,' he said.

'Oh Nathan,' she cried out, 'thank God you're here.'

They embraced. He could smell jasmine, garlic, turpentine, and, closing his eyes, he could cling to the illusion that nothing had changed.

But she was talking into his shoulder. 'You're so late. We were worried about you.'

Smiling, he pulled away from her. Her hair was the same bright copper glow, and yet, below it, her face had collapsed in heavy folds, like cloth.

'I know,' she said, 'I look dreadful.' She shrugged and reached for her cheroot. 'I supppose it's the grief.'

'You look like nobody else,' he said, 'same as always.' He held her again, then he looked round. 'Where's George?'

'She's going to be late,' Yvonne said.

Harriet handed him a glass of wine. 'She said she'd come and wake you up when she got back.'

'You must be hungry,' Yvonne said. She made him a sandwich and brought it to the table. He looked down at it, smiling.

'What's so funny?' she said.

He held the sandwich up. 'It's the first sandwich you've ever made me that hasn't got any paint on it.'

They opened another bottle of wine and sat round the table. He told them about the journey down, the woman in black, the taxi-driver. Yvonne lit another cheroot, filled the room with the smell of the inside of cupboards. Harriet washed the dishes. The TV muttered in the background. It all seemed quite familiar, ordinary, relaxed. That, in itself, was strange. He felt snapped back into a past that had never happened.

At midnight Yvonne went to bed. There was still some wine left in the bottle, so he stayed up with Harriet to finish it off. Harriet seemed to have forgotten the grievances she'd had against him. It was as if that letter had never been written. He remembered something Georgia had said about her once. 'The fights we had, they blew away like bad weather. Mostly I got on with her.'

He looked up again just as Harriet spoke. 'You must've been surprised when I answered the door.'

He smiled. 'Yes, I was.'

'You weren't angry?'

He shook his head. 'No.' Anger wasn't something he'd felt even a flicker of.

Her eyes lingered on him, then believed him. 'You see, I had to come.'

'Why?'

She tapped her cigarette against the edge of the ashtray. 'It was like an instinct. I loved him. When you love someone like that you want to say goodbye.'

'I thought you said goodbye seven years ago.'

Her face hardened. She crushed her cigarette against the side of the ashtray.

'I'm sorry,' he said. 'I didn't mean it to sound like that.'

She stared down into her drink. 'Just because I left him,' she said, 'it doesn't mean I stopped loving him. I just couldn't live with him any more. I couldn't breathe.' She lifted her drink and swirled it around. 'I just had to get away, that's all.'

He could imagine the suffocation, he really could. The string that had once been fastened lightly round her toe had tightened during the years of marriage, slowly tightened into a leash. And she'd strained at it, strained at it until it snapped. But, looking into her face, it didn't seem as if her years of freedom had been particularly kind to her. There were those, of course, who'd say that she'd only herself to blame. She shouldn't have left, should she?

He turned his glass on its base. 'What does Yvonne think about you coming back?'

'I don't think she minds.'

'I was going to say. You seem to be getting on pretty well.'

She fastened on to his meaning. 'Yes, that's funny, isn't it? She never had much time for me before.'

'She thought you were too young,' he said. 'She thought you were going to change everything.'

Harriet shook her head. 'That wasn't the reason. I think she was in love with him. She wanted to look after him.'

He thought of those months after their mother died when Yvonne had come to stay. He could still see her painting in the garden. 'It would never've worked,' he said. 'Dad couldn't stand the smell of her cigars.'

They both laughed for a while and then fell silent.

'Isn't it strange,' she said, 'how death can bring a family together?'

That night he decided to sleep in Dad's room. When he opened the door and turned on the light, everything was exactly as he remembered it. The smell of vanilla and talcum in the air. The glint of the green bottle on the glass shelf above the basin. The seven pillows.

He thought of the last time he'd seen Dad. When they said goodbye they'd embraced by the front door, a taxi waiting on the road outside. He'd caught a glimpse of the two of them reflected in the hall mirror and his heart had lurched because it looked as if he was propping up a corpse. Dad's body seemed to sag, as if his bones had turned to mush, and his breath, usually so fresh, smelled sweet, the sweetness of rotting plants or compost. That sweet smell, it was strange how he'd recognised it. That sweet smell was death's footman. It was the announcement you heard just before death made its entrance.

Back on India-May's farm he'd hung that picture in his head. He'd carried it around with him, framed by the mirror's gilt, like some kind of talisman. So long as he remembered the frailty of Dad's grip on life, Dad's fingers would never loosen and let go. That was how the superstition worked. But time passed; the picture faded, moved him less. He began to take Dad's life for granted again. He forgot to remember. Dad had lasted so long, it was tempting to believe that he would last for ever. And that was fatal, of course.

He got into bed and lay down. He thought he heard the foghorn once, off High Head. Ten minutes passed, or maybe half an hour, it was hard to tell. Then a voice rose out of the darkness, hovered in the air, almost visible, like a hallucination.

'Nathan? You awake?'

At first he didn't know where he was, whose voice it was. He must have been asleep. And waking suddenly like that, you woke in a thousand different places at once, all the places that you'd ever been. It took him a moment.

'Georgia?'

She was standing at the end of the bed with a candle. The room bucked and tilted in the unsteady yellow light. He watched her place the candle on the windowsill.

She came over and sat down and held him. 'I didn't want to sleep in my old bed,' she whispered. 'I wanted to sleep here, with you.'

'What time is it?'

'I don't know. It must be about one.' The bed listed, creaked, as she climbed in.

'Are you all right?' he asked her.

'I think so. How about you?'

'I'm fine,' he said. 'Just tired.'

'Do you want me to blow the candle out?'

He shook his head. 'I had a friend who used to say that if you burned a candle in your window and it burned all night, then the world wouldn't end while you were sleeping.'

Georgia smiled. 'Who was that?'

'She was called India-May.'

'Funny name.'

'She made it up. It was the name she started using when she left home.'

'Where is she now?'

'I don't know. I haven't seen her for ages.'

He'd called the farm about a year after he left. He'd wanted to see how everybody was. Pete had answered. Pete was the one who'd told him.

'She died, didn't she?' Georgia said.

He looked at her across the pillows. 'I didn't want to tell you.'

'You did tell me. You're my brother. You tell me everything.'

He was silent.

'How did it happen?' she asked.

'It was funny, people were always saying things about her, about how she'd come to no good – ' He stopped again.

'Tell me.'

'There was a bar in town, it was down at the end of the main street, right where the buildings ended and the scrub began. There was a hill there, pretty steep, and the bar was at the bottom of it. She went in for a drink one time, she liked a few drinks around midday, she used to say it helped the long hot afternoons slide by,' and Nathan smiled to himself, because he could hear her saying it. 'She met some guy in there that day, some guy she used to go with, and he must've said something because the next thing anyone knew, she was screaming at him, Pete was in the bar the morning after, he said the window was all over the floor, apparently she'd thrown an ashtray at the guy and it had missed and taken the whole window out instead, and when he took her by the arm and tried to calm her down, she shook him off and ran out of the bar, right out in the street, and like I said, it was the bottom of a hill and there was a truck coming – '

He could see that part of Broken Springs so clearly, almost as if he was standing there. There was a wall on the far side of the street which was always being knocked over. Trucks would come hurtling down the hill, their brakes would fail, and they'd plough right through the wall and on into the field beyond. As soon as the wall was mended, another truck's brakes would fail.

He could see the bar opposite too. The road dipping down into town and the bar with its brown tin roof and its dusty verandah, and a woman running out into the street, hair horizontal in the air behind her, strings of wooden beads swinging in a loop around her neck like a cow's jaw chewing, her mouth wide open, a wedge hewn out of her face, as if someone had taken an axe to her, as if her mouth was a wound and her screaming the bleeding.

He looked across at Georgia. Her head on the pillow. Her face still, as it sometimes was before she began to cry. He felt for her hand and held it tight.

'I didn't want to tell you,' he said.

He watched their candle moving the shadows around, keeping the end of the world at bay, keeping the two of them alive.

'I had to go to the hospital,' she said eventually. 'I had to collect his things.'

'Did you see him?'

'They asked me if I wanted to. I said no. I just wanted to get out of there.'

'I think I've got to see him. I haven't seen him for so long.'

'You'll have to call them.'

'I'll call tomorrow.'

'Maybe I'll come too,' she said, though her voice had shrunk at the thought.

'My brother still,' he said after a while, 'aren't you?' And he waited, and then he heard one word come back, spoken in a whisper, she must have been close to sleep.

'Yes.'

The hospital lay in the hills, about an hour away. Yvonne drove. Georgia and Harriet sat in the back. It was a bright day. White, blinding clouds and a breeze in the treetops like hands in hair. But Nathan felt a sickness rise in him at the thought of arriving, he didn't want the journey to end. The sickness rose into his throat, and he had to keep swallowing. He was glad that they'd all decided to come. He wouldn't have liked to be doing this alone.

Nobody talked much on the way out. As they climbed into the hills, the sky lowered over the car. A light rain began to fall.

The road that led to the hospital sloped upwards through a forest of pine trees. It was a straight road, the kind of road that leads to a temple or a sacred monument. Nathan looked out of the window. Once he saw a glade, a secret place with a floor of pale, sandy soil. Then the pines closed ranks again, their tall red trunks glowing softly in the gloom of the afternoon.

When they reported to the hospital reception, the nurse on duty showed them into a waiting-room. They sat on orange plastic chairs. There was a fish tank and a heap of magazines. There were paintings of flowers on the walls. A man in a white coat limped past the open doorway, pushing a trolley piled high with linen, a cigarette between his fingers. Nathan stood by the window, and looked out into the gardens.

That morning he'd revived an old custom. Leaving Georgia sleeping, he'd knocked on Yvonne's door and asked her if she wanted to go swimming. They drove to a quiet beach west of High Head. It was still early. The sand took the glittery morning light and threw it back into his eyes like a mirror. One wooden jetty crept out over the water on brittle insect legs. And the waves, pale pale green and mauve between.

When he was tired of swimming he climbed a ladder to the jetty. The wooden slats had bleached grey. A creaking like old doors opening and closing. The same rhythm as breathing. He walked down to the end. An old man was sitting on an upturned beer crate, a plastic bag for bait and a bucket of fish beside him. He wore great clothes. A maroon jacket and a panama hat with a shiny black ribbon. White bristles stood out on his cheeks. Nathan sat down. The wooden slats were already warm from the sun. He dangled his legs over the edge and let his body dry. He could see Yvonne, she was floating on her back. Beyond her, further out, a motor launch cut through the water. Not long afterwards he felt the wash slopping against the jetty. The jetty moved lazily, like someone in their sleep. He watched the old man fit another piece of bait on his line and flick the hook backhanded through the air. A prim plop as it landed, sank. The old man tugged gently on the line.

'What kind of fish are you catching?' Nathan asked.

Smiling, the old man shrugged. 'I don't know the name of it.'

It seemed right, what the old man said. You sat in the sun, the hours passed. In the end, sooner or later, something happened. You didn't need to know the name of it.

After their swim, Nathan and Yvonne stopped for coffee and doughnuts in a diner on the highway. They sat at a small table by the window. Sunlight on formica, salt on skin. Yvonne began to talk about Dad.

'I hardly ever saw him,' she said, 'but we used to talk on the phone for hours. We used to send each other pictures. Look,' and she opened her handbag and reached inside, 'this was one I'd been saving for him – ' Her voice cracked and she began to cry.

He put his hand over hers. 'It's all right.'

'I'm stupid,' she said.

'No, you're not.'

'All these people,' she said. 'I'm embarrassing you.'

He wanted to cheer her up. 'Do you remember the time I was staying with you and that couple came round?'

'Couple?' She looked up, her eyes swollen.

'That nervous couple,' he said. 'Their car broke down. You let them use the phone.'

After they'd used the phone, Yvonne said they could wait in the lounge. She sat them down on the sofa. She gave them brandy. The wife didn't know what to make of Yvonne at all. Her eyes kept alighting on Yvonne and taking off again. They tried the walls instead, but there were forty-six paintings on the walls. Every colour moon you could imagine (and some you couldn't). Nowhere to land, not unless you had a spaceship.

Her husband was braver. He rose from the sofa and placed himself in front of a picture. Green moon, yellow universe. 'Very good,' he said, 'really very good.'

Yvonne was standing at the far end of the room in her red tent dress, her arms extended, a glass of brandy glimmering in one hand. She looked like a sort of fierce lamp. She took one step forwards and shouted, 'Yes, I'm in the middle of my ball period, if you want to know,' and the brandy slopped out of her glass and dropped into the part of the carpet that was orange and was never seen again.

'I think they're moons,' Nathan said. Then he turned to the couple. 'What do you think they are?'

But Yvonne couldn't wait. 'Balls,' she shouted. 'They're balls.'

Yvonne was smiling down into her coffee. 'Those were good times,' she said, 'weren't they?'

He pressed her hand. They weren't good times, of course, they were terrible, but he knew what she meant.

'I'm so sorry to keep you waiting.' It was the sister. She was standing in the doorway with a tight smile on her face. 'We had an emergency.'

She ushered them down a long corridor through countless swing doors. The temperature dropped. A morgue appeared on the left like a reason.

She talked to fill the silence. 'Mr Christie was known here,' she said. 'He was very well liked.'

These were dead sentences. She might have been reading from a tombstone.

There was nothing you could say.

They passed through another set of doors and out into the open air. It seemed cold up here in the hills. Mist had collected in the trees. There was a sense of abandonment and neglect. A tap dripping endlessly.

They followed the sister across a lawn and into a small chapel built, like the rest of the hospital, out of crumbling red brick. She vanished behind a velvet curtain. They waited, not speaking. A few moments later she appeared again and told them they could go in. She warned them about the steep steps. She said she'd be outside if they needed her.

Nathan passed through the curtain and stopped at the top of the steps. Georgia stopped behind him. She was peering over his shoulder, he could feel her breath on his neck, warm and then nothing, warm and then nothing. Dad lay below, stretched out under a heavy cloth of blue and gold. Two candles flickered at his head. Nathan walked towards him, down the steps, across the stone floor.

They'd covered his face with a square of gauze. It looked as if it had landed there by chance, like a piece of paper or a leaf. The next gust of wind would blow it away. Except there wasn't any wind. The air was still, chilling.

His face was curiously smooth and youthful. His mouth had fallen open in a kind of sigh. There were no signs of violence, nothing to suggest that his death had not been peaceful. He looked like a pope, Nathan thought, or a saint. A holy man who'd prepared for his death, who might even, perhaps, have welcomed it.

It was only when he moved round to the side that he saw the blue, chapped ears and the hair, frozen and brittle, as if you could snap it off. It was only then that he noticed how raw and scalded the neck looked, how it bulged. Now that the death looked painful, now that he could see traces of a struggle, he began, in a kind of panic, to say things in his head, he began to talk to the dead man. He said he was sorry for not visiting more often, sorry for not being there, for not, for not, for not, these omissions of his, these confessions, they rose into his closed mouth until it seemed that he might choke, they were jumbled up, dislocated, like old bones in a crypt, but he knew they fitted together, he knew they would form a skeleton where he could hang the flesh and muscle of his guilt.

He looked at Georgia. She tried to smile, but her smile wavered, didn't hold. He remembered taking her to school, it was after their mother died, Georgia would've been seven, she didn't want to go, there were girls who tied her to trees, it was her accent or her looks, he couldn't remember now, but he had to take her because he'd promised Dad, Dad who didn't know anything, the scratches on her legs were brambles, the bruises on her wrists were something else, he couldn't remember now, how could they tell him the truth, how could they tell him anything when all he did was sit in dark rooms with his head in his hands, his head haunted by her ghost, and each dawn broke like the slow blow of a hammer. It was a nice road, the road that led to the school. High grass banks and trees for carving your initials on and ditches trickling with water. One morning he saw a clock lying under a bush. 'Look at that,' he said, and crouched and peered, drawing her in, 'a clock, how strange,' strange because it was an antique clock with inlaid wood and round brass knobs for legs, it should have been softly ticking away on someone wealthy's mantel-piece, a china shepherdess on either side, a marble fireplace below, and yet here it was, lying under a bush, and tilted at a curious angle as if it was drunk, and not ticking at all. That morning they parted under the trees, he never took her all the way to the gates, that would only have made things worse, that morning she looked the way she always looked, rings under her eyes and her whole body braced for the ordeal that lay ahead, how hard it was to leave her always, maybe that was why they always drew the parting out, sometimes it took minutes, just the saying goodbye, they backed away from each other, then stopped and called something out, then backed away again, they called out special words that they'd made up, words to fill the distance between them, words for the things they couldn't say, they backed away till he was under the trees or she was through the gates, whichever happened first, she looked the same way she always looked that morning, except for one thing, she had a clock tucked under her arm, the clock they'd found together, the clock that didn't tick, the lonely clock. It was the same thing, his sister then, his father now, Georgia walking towards a beating in the school yard, Dad fighting for breath in his red chair, he wanted to save them, only he could do it, who else was there, but he hadn't, he couldn't, not really, but the wanting to, the failure to, you couldn't get away from that.

Harriet climbed back up the steps. Yvonne followed her.

He wanted to leave now too, but he had to make some kind of contact with the dead man first. Touching the face through that gauze would have seemed like sacrilege, so he chose the hair instead. He reached out cautiously. It was stiff, chilled. It was both wet and dry at the same time. Like ice. He shivered, turned away. Georgia had been watching him.

'What did it feel like?' she whispered.

'Cold,' he whispered. 'Not like hair at all.'

She came closer, reached out, touched. Then drew back quickly, as if she'd just been burned.

After leaving the chapel, they went walking in the gardens. They set off from the same place but, like pieces of something that had just exploded, they each took a different course across the lawn. Though later, driving home, Nathan saw it another way. It wasn't like an explosion. They were separate, there was space between them, but, like flowers in a vase, they were all standing in the same water.

The next morning Nathan and Georgia were required, as executors of the will, to meet with Dad's lawyer. He was a dull man with bad teeth. His jacket was ripped at the armpit. They sat obediently in leather chairs while he read the document out loud. A massive, antiquated fan whirred and clattered in the corner of the office, turning on its metal stem, examining them one by one. The will was straightforward enough. Dad had left slightly more money than expected, and that money was to be divided equally between Nathan, Georgia and Rona, Rona's share to be held in trust until she attained the age of eighteen. The lawyer reminded Nathan and Georgia that the house on Mahogany Drive already belonged to them since, as they doubtless knew, their mother had died intestate and, when their mother's mother died some years later, the house, deemed to be two-thirds of her estate, became legally theirs. (Yvonne, the other beneficiary, had received a cash settlement.) Now their father was dead, the house was theirs to do with as they wished.

'As for the manner of burial,' the lawyer said, 'it appears that your father wishes to be buried in the same place as his first wife. In other words, a sea burial in Coral Pastures. Just in case there's any confusion,' and he smiled, 'he's written down the exact co-ordinates.'

'Harriet's not going to like that,' Georgia said.

'Harriet?' The lawyer's eyebrows lifted.

'Our father's second wife,' Nathan explained. 'Our stepmother.'

'Of course,' the lawyer said. 'I met her once.' And then he drew his eyebrows down again. 'Is she,' and he hesitated, looking for the most delicate statement of his question, 'involved in the proceedings?'

'She's staying with us,' Georgia said. 'In the house.'

'Ah,' the lawyer said. 'Yes, I can see how that might be awkward.' He leaned forwards. 'It will require,' and he paused, 'a certain amount of tact.'

On the way home Nathan turned to Georgia in the car and said, 'It will require,' and he paused, and then they both shouted, 'a certain amount of tact.'

They laughed so hard that Nathan had to pull off the road. Later, when they were over it, Georgia said, 'I never knew death would be so funny.'

It was the morning of the funeral. Almost twelve o'clock. From where Nathan was sitting, in a chapel adjacent to the altar, he could hear the cathedral filling up. Looking along the pew, he saw Georgia, Harriet, Yvonne, all three in profile, stern as the heads on coins.

He realised suddenly that he had to go to the bathroom. He checked the watch on Georgia's wrist. Five minutes till the service began. There was still time. Just.

He slipped out of the pew and hurried back down the aisle. He was surprised at how crowded the cathedral was. He hadn't realised that Dad knew so many people.

Once outside he paused. He was standing in a square paved with dark-grey stone. There were statues on pedestals, angels or statesmen, he couldn't tell. A great many people sat at the feet of the statues or stood about in groups near by. They were all dressed in black. They were all crying. Some dabbed at their eyes with handkerchiefs, others covered their faces and wept into their hands. One man stood alone, his breeches held up with string, his arms pinned to his sides. He shed tears the way a flower sheds petals, they fell to the ground, lay scattered round his feet. It struck Nathan that these were all people who had been unable to get in.

But the pressure in his bladder was growing, and he set off across the square in search of a public toilet. He turned down the first street he came to, turned left, right, left again, he walked down a hill, along an alley, through a deserted square, but still he couldn't find one anywhere. He noticed a clock on the top of a building. The two gold hands were almost one. He had to get back. And then, looking around him, he realised that he no longer knew where he was. He began to run in what he thought was the right direction, but he didn't recognise any of the buildings. I was born here, he thought. Surely I'll see something familiar soon. He could hardly hear his thoughts above the rasping of his breath.

He saw an elderly couple approaching.

'The cathedral?' They consulted each other, they disagreed, they changed their minds. At last they pointed back up the street, nodding and smiling.

'Are you sure?' he asked.

'Yes,' they chorused gaily. 'Yes, we're sure.'

He ran off up the street, turned a corner, then another, and stopped. Still no sign of the cathedral. The elderly couple must have been mistaken.

He teetered on the brink of panic now. One step forwards and he would fall headlong. He looked one way, then he looked the other. Sweat seeped into his eyes. Thoughts came from all directions and collided. He felt he might be going mad.

A car came towards him. He stepped out into the road and waved his arms. The man behind the wheel was only too willing to oblige. 'Of course, of course,' he said. 'Jump in.' He seemed to think that Nathan was new to the city. Every now and then he lifted a finger off the wheel and pointed out some famous bridge or statue or museum. Nathan was about to free the man from his illusion when the man braked and, leaning across Nathan, opened the door for him.

'There you are,' he said.

Nathan got out and looked around. 'But the cathedral.'

'You're welcome,' the man said. And, shifting into gear, he drove away.

Nathan looked round. Scrapyards, jetties, railway tracks. The sun was setting. He felt no sense of urgency now. Waves were pages turning. Railway trucks were edged in gold.

When he woke he was lying in Dad's bed. Georgia was bent over the basin, throwing up. It was the morning of the funeral.

The day proved awkward from the beginning, like a knife you can't pick up without cutting yourself. Harriet slipped on the stairs and twisted her ankle. Yvonne couldn't find the fish brooch that she always wore for funerals. She lit a cheroot to calm herself, and promptly burned a hole in her dress. Georgia had taken pills to settle her stomach, but she was still throwing up every hour.

The car arrived at two. The funeral director had a cold; he had to keep reaching into the back for tissues. 'Usually, of course, these are for clients,' he said, 'but in this case, if you don't mind,' and he blew his nose again, and sighed.

Nathan glanced at Georgia.

She summoned up the makings of a smile. 'I think the pills are beginning to work,' she said.

He pushed the hair back from her forehead. 'One thing about a sea burial,' he said. 'If you want to throw up, at least you can just do it over the side.'

They arrived at the Y Street wharf. The chartered boat was already moored by the quay. The traditional awning, white canvas with black edges, fluttered in the breeze. A modest congregation sat underneath on benches.

As they waited for the casket to be hoisted on to the boat, Nathan noticed a preacher on the other side of the quay. You could tell he was a preacher. He had a microphone in his hand and his eyes were set way back in his head, as if he'd seen the Lord once too often. Nathan watched him step on to a crate. There was a crackle and a whine from the microphone.

'This is God's distant early-warning system.'

A drunk lay slumped against an oil drum, a bottle wrapped in a brown paper bag beside him. At the sound of the preacher's voice he twitched, wiped one eye with the back of his hand, and looked up, moistening his lips.

'Heaven is a real place,' the preacher said. 'There are people up there right now, enjoying themselves.'

The drunk lifted his bottle and shook the last few drops into his throat. 'Well, how about that,' he said and, turning his head in the direction of the preacher, he shouted, 'Hallelujah,' then he winked at Nathan, as if they were in this together, and fell back in a heap and shut his eyes.

The preacher turned his volume up. His voice now carried across the quay to the boat, interfering with the sombre piped music. Several members of the congregation looked round.

'Seven years ago,' the preacher informed them, 'I was a useless person.' He pointed at the drunk. 'Seven years ago I was like him, but then Jesus,' and his voice rose and wavered, and his eyes lifted to the sky, 'yes, Jesus, he came to me and he planted the seeds of truth in me – '

A black woman stood below the preacher. She tilted her head on one side as if she was trying very hard to understand.

Then she must've said something.

The preacher levelled a finger at her. 'You've got a filthy mouth.'
His eyes scoured the small audience for support. 'You see? This here's
what – '

Suddenly Yvonne was standing below him. She reached up,
snatched the microphone out of his hands. With two brisk movements
she wrenched the wire loose and tossed the microphone into the
water. It was so brutal, and yet so matter of fact. It was like watching
somebody wring a chicken's neck.

'Someone had to do it,' she hissed through her black veil as she
passed Nathan on the way back.

They followed the coffin on to the boat and took their seats in the
front row. The engines shuddered, the ropes were loosed; the quay
slid backwards like a piece of moving scenery. Nathan could still see
the preacher standing, shocked and speechless, on his box. The
earthquakes in people's heads, half the city's population was cracked,
a rabble of doom-merchants, psychos, ghouls. They could smell a
funeral a mile off, and out they crawled, out of the woodwork. A
funeral lit them up, it was like fuel, it kept them burning for days. It
wasn't just the old and the rich who moved to Moon Beach. The city
was like a dangerous bend in a road. If you sat on that bend for long
enough you'd be sure to see something.

A shadow passed the length of the boat and Nathan looked up.
The bridge arched high above. This was where the harbour ended
and the ocean began. The boat lurched as the first real waves lifted
the bow and dropped it again. He glanced at Georgia. Though pale,
she seemed to be holding up.

She put her head close to his. 'Everything's going wrong.'

He squeezed her hand.

'It's so quiet,' she whispered. 'I hate it.'

He nodded. Then he nudged her. 'Dad would've liked it.'

She smiled at that.

It was quieter still when they reached the place. They passed
between two floating pedestals, the gateway to the cemetery.

YOU ARE NOW ENTERING CORAL PASTURES.

The engines cut out, some kind of anchor dropped. Then only the
slapping of waves against the hull, the creak and whine of timbers
straining, the screech of gulls.

The priest rose to his feet and began to speak. He talked of Dad's
faith. His courage and resilience in the face of adversity. His sense of
humour.

Nathan's mind wandered. His mood seemed like a distillation of his dream. The panic, then the calm. His eyes drifted over the side. They were such queer, still patches of water, the ocean cemeteries. The sites had been chosen carefully, between the main shipping lanes and north of the gulfstream, so they were free of disturbance, both from boats and from currents. The ocean bed was a maze of fissures and ravines. Nobody knew how deep they went. There was a story about an oil tanker that had veered off course and steamed right through Heaven Sound. That was the last anyone heard of it. Helicopters were sent out, teams of divers too, but the water yielded nothing, not a single body, not a trace of oil.

There was a crash. He turned just in time to see the coffin sink below the surface of the waves. The engines spluttered, churned. The congregation shifted on their benches, moved their feet. Somebody coughed. The boat swung round, cutting a neat sickle of white water on the ocean, and Nathan saw the city on the horizon, twelve miles away. It must be a long time, he thought, since Dad had travelled this far.

The wake took place at the house on Mahogany Drive. No more than a dozen people came. Nathan moved among the guests, offering drinks, accepting condolences. His dream came to him in flashes. The packed cathedral. All those people weeping. How sarcastic that now seemed.

After an hour most people had left. Yvonne looked round, assembling a courageous smile. 'Well,' she said, 'at least they're together now.'

Harriet was standing right behind her. 'Who's together?'

And suddenly the air seemed deadened, as if there'd been an explosion. The few guests that remained stood about in small, shocked groups.

It will require, Nathan thought, a certain amount of tact.

'Who's together?' Harriet asked again.

Nathan spoke gently. 'Dad asked to be buried with our mother. It was in the will.'

Harriet put her glass on the table and left the room. In the hush that followed they heard the back door slam. Through the window Nathan saw Harriet stumbling down the garden.

'I didn't mean – ' Yvonne began.

Nathan put an arm around her. 'I know you didn't.'

'Go after her,' Yvonne said. 'Make sure she's all right.' She turned away. 'I just wasn't thinking.'

Nathan left the house by the french windows. He crossed the lawn

and passed through a covered archway. The vegetable garden beyond
had been allowed to run wild. He walked between rows of fruit trees.
The fruit lay rotting, unwanted, in the long grass. He passed through
a second archway. The wooden hoop supporting the foliage had
almost collapsed beneath its weight. He had to bend double to get
through. Once on the other side he stood still and looked around.
This was the part of the garden they used to call the Jungle. There
was something about the Jungle. It wasn't big enough to get lost in,
but almost. When you stood in the Jungle, the house seemed dimen-
sions away, as if, in order to get back indoors, you had to alter the
way your mind worked, you had to think your way back in. How
foreign their names sounded when they heard them called. How eerie.
And suddenly he remembered standing here, it was dark-green all
around him, but the sky above was blue, the sun must've been setting,
it was quiet, just the creak of a tree, the whir of an insect's wing, he'd
been standing motionless, as if in a trance, and then he heard a voice,
his mother's voice. 'Nathan?' she called, and he called back, 'Yes?' but
there was no second call, and he turned round, and there was nobody
there, not a sound, and he felt strange then, he felt as if he'd been visited.
It couldn't have been far from where he was standing now, though he
wouldn't have been able to say where exactly.

'Harriet?'

He'd almost forgotten that he was looking for her. If she was still
in the garden, there was only one place she could be, and that was
the summerhouse. As he bent down and began to force his way
through the undergrowth he could taste alcohol in his mouth. It was
a stale taste, musty, pale-grey.

'Harriet?'

His voice only seemed to travel a few feet, then it stopped dead.
As if it had been swallowed up. That was how that voice had sounded
to him all those years ago. Dead. But near. Against his ear. That was
why he'd turned round. And then, when he saw there was nothing
there, he ran. He burst over the threshold and into the house, his
right arm ripped open from the wrist to the elbow. It must've caught
on something, a thorn, a bramble, a sharp branch. He hadn't noticed.
The blood ran down the inside of his arm, where the skin was pale,
and collected in the palm of his hand as he held the wound out for
Dad to look at. He still had the scar now, twenty years later, a long
thin groove down the inside of his right forearm, as if he was made
of candlewax and someone had run their fingernail the length of it.

'Harriet?'

He saw her as he called her name for the third time. She was sitting on the steps of the summerhouse. He was seeing small things with such clarity now. A green leaf in her hair. Part of a spider's web. The whites of her eyes clouded with red. She'd been crying, but she wasn't crying now.

When she saw him she attempted a smile. It didn't quite work. Her face was like a plate on a stick. Spinning. Balanced. But only for so long. The edges of her mouth were flickering, as if miniature hearts beat there. He sat down beside her, put an arm round her shoulders. He wanted to comfort her. She turned and pressed her face against his chest. She cried into the air below his chin.

He felt her shaking all the way through her bones and into his. He looked up through the branches into the sky, waiting for her tears to pass. The sun coloured the high branches a deep burnt orange. Down below, where they were sitting, the air softened, became almost visible, as if shaded in with charcoal, closer to smoke than air. A bird sang four notes and stopped. The first three notes were identical. The fourth started out the same way, then it stretched and lifted an octave. It was as if the bird had asked a question in whatever language it spoke.

She looked up at him and her mouth, already close to his, moved closer, seemed to falter, then moved closer and they kissed. He kept his mind completely still, it was like something preserved, like something in a jar in a laboratory, but his body came undone and shook, there was a sound inside him like the sound tracks make when a train's coming, that hiss and crack the length of his veins, that shudder in his blood.

He couldn't speak. He knew this was something that had been happening slowly for a long time, something that had to happen or he was lost, but it was such a brittle structure they were building, one word would topple it, shatter it, one word would be enough to jerk them back into that ordinary daylight where nothing could be changed or righted, nothing could unravel.

He took her hand and led her up the steps. It was the past inside, it was long ago. A tennis racket, a pair of flippers, a garden hose. The window with its barricade of foliage. The light barely filtered through. The smell of old dry rubber and dead grass. The smell of the wooden handles of spades. Two buttons of her blouse had come unfastened. He could see her breasts tilting against the black silk. She was sitting on his lap. They kissed again. He didn't need to see her face. It was printed in his head, his memory. His knees between the insides of her thighs, she drew him sliding into her. He bit her neck, that muscle at the back. A gasp. Her hair swung against his face, and something metal fell. He heard himself, it sounded like a door opening somewhere inside him, it was an old door, it had been stuck for years, you had to heave on it, you needed all your strength, and then it gave a few inches, and cried out as it gave.

He felt silence descend and press on him. He looked at her. She was squatting on the floor, some distance from him.

'Colours everywhere,' he said.

She found a tissue, wiped between her legs.

'You said that was what it was like,' he said, 'remember?'

She straightened her skirt. 'We should go back.'

He watched her merge with the undergrowth until only her calves showed, pale as milk in the shadows.

It was done, she was gone; he was alone.

SKULL CANDY

Now that Jed was driving, and the lines were feeding into the front of his car like white candy, piece after piece after piece, he thought of himself as others thought of him. He thought of himself as a parasite, a leech. No sense pretending otherwise. He knew whose blood he wanted too. Though he'd known that for six years.

It had happened soon after his drive out to to the lake. One night he was standing outside the back of the ice-cream parlour, washing the stainless-steel vats, when he heard voices coming from the manager's office across the yard. It was so quiet out there. Turn around and there was desert clear to the horizon. Just wind plucking at the scrub and the soft electrical humming of the stars. He had no trouble picking up the conversation.

'That guy Jed,' Celia's uncle said, his voice sloppy with alcohol, 'you know the guy I mean?'

'Yeah, I seen him.' The second man had his back turned. Jed could only see a piece of blue shirt and one thick forearm. He didn't recognise the voice.

'That guy, there's something about him – '

'Makes your skin go cold just looking at him.'

'Yeah. I don't know why I hired him. Stranger like that, shit. There's something about him, that's for sure.'

One of the two men crushed a beer can.

'It's like you look at him and he's sucking you dry,' the second man said. 'It's like he's a leech or something.'

Celia's uncle let out a high cackling laugh. 'You hit it there. We oughter call him that. We oughter call him the leech.'

When Jed heard that cackling laugh again, the stars went out. There was just the night and that lit window and his white fury. He wanted to kill them both.

Then later, stretched out on his bed at Mrs O'Neill's, he let the name sink down through him like a stone, he watched it go, and by the time he saw it settle on the bottom he decided he liked it. The name began to grow on him, he began to feel it in his fingertips and in his blood, and in his love of blood, he began to see it as his power, his future.

A road sign loomed, snapped by. Four hundred miles to go. If he drove all night he might make Moon Beach by morning. He reached into his pocket, pulled out a cream toffee, stuck it in his mouth. The wrapper joined a heap of identical wrappers on the seat beside him. Your pockets crackle when you move. That was Carol's voice in the car with him. He saw her standing outside the Starlite Bar, her mouth tilted upwards, stitched. He saw her stumble down the steps of the cathedral. He saw the barbed wire of her scar. You take kindness where you find it, she'd said to him once, because most of this world's cruelty. We know that, Jed, don't we? We know that. Some nights he'd felt such scorn for her, Don't put me in the same coffin as you, it may be your time, but it isn't mine. Other nights he'd almost cried. Most of this world's cruelty.

They'd come for him. He'd known they were going to come, it was part of his initiation, he couldn't leave until it happened. He heard their boots in the hall and up the stairs. He heard their voices pushing at the flimsy, chipboard walls. Celia's uncle, that man in the blue shirt, a couple of the power-station boys. No shortage of men for the job. He waited on the edge of his bed. He watched their boots trample across his orange carpet. Steel toecaps, steel heels. Cracks in the leather red with dust.

'Pack his stuff.'

The important packing was already done. It had been done for days. The sheet, the hat, the tape. They were all locked in the car. The rest didn't matter.

They threw his clothes into a case and wedged it shut. Part of a shirt poked out of the side. It was like a sandwich. The lettuce leaves never quite fit. Celia would've liked that. She always liked it when he brought food into it. Ever since their first night. The night of the chicken. But there was nobody here who'd understand.

They pinned his arms behind his back and hauled him down the stairs. It was difficult. The landing was narrow, and the stairs were steep. The men were wide, they didn't fit. For the first time he really liked the place. For the first time he felt as if he belonged.

'You going out, Matt?' Mrs O'Neill called out. 'Bring me a Rocky Road, would you?' Until one of the men pulled the door shut in her face. Goodbye, Jesus. Goodbye, Donald Duck.

He was going out. Out into the dark. But still orange. The streetlamps. Hotel windows. A passing truck. They pushed him up against a fence. It was someplace near the railway tracks. He could smell that corroded metal on the wind.

'Celia says you been bothering her.'

She'd said something. Good. He supposed he must've been relying on her. If she hadn't said something, none of this would be happening. And it had to happen.

'Celia says you been,' a pause, 'messing with her.'

They were obedient men. They had their orders, they were only doing what they were told. The rain, his christening, and now these men. It was right. Thinking about it, you might almost say that he had given the orders. He nodded. Yes, the orders had originally sprung from him.

The first blows didn't hurt. They were just surprises, even though he'd been expecting them. The streetlamp leaned over, then it blew, a yellow flower with long tapering petals, petals snapping off and dropping through the gloom, dropping on his body, on his eyes. Then a sudden white flash of pain in his ribs and his own voice crying out.

And then another voice: 'Don't break anything. He's got to drive out of here.'

Still following orders. That was good.

They must've put him in his car. He woke at nine minutes past one. He pushed the door open and was sick.

Afterwards he sat with his head against the window. At ten to two he was sick again. Initiation always hurt, it had to.

When he looked out through the windshield he couldn't see anything at all. He glanced in the mirror. A few scattered lights, the slant of a roof, a gas pump. They'd driven him to the edge of town. They'd pointed him in the right direction. The rest was up to him.

He drove all night. It wasn't fear, it was completion. As the light spilled back over the hills, as the sun came up in a strange place, he pulled over to the side of the road and cried. That was normal, he supposed.

Now it was three days later, and the bruises were sunset colours: yellow, purple, brown. He'd been beaten like metal, like the edge of a scythe. He was sharp. All doubts, all fears, all hesitation, beaten out of him. He'd left them behind, along with that job in the ice-cream parlour and that rented room with its bright-green walls and its bedbugs and its carpet tangled with other people's hair and nails. They were outlived, redundant. More dead skin for the carpet, more ghosts for the cemetery. He coasted down the centre lane, and the darkness seemed to cushion him. He felt as if he was tunnelling, as if he was going to strike it rich. The lights of other cars swung across his face, glinted on his glasses' steel frames, glinted on the battered satin of his black top hat. He was smiling.

In two hours he'd be switching to Highway 12 because he wanted to enter the city from the west. It would be about five in the morning by then. At that time, just minutes before dawn, the tall buildings looked like piles of ashes. The place would feel like his then, his for the taking. He squeezed the gas pedal and reached into his pocket for another piece of candy. These were new ones. He'd found them earlier that day. They were called Peppermint Surprises and they were very good. He wondered how he could've stood that ice-cream parlour for so long. He'd always had a sweet tooth. Maybe it was something to do with that.

In the end he timed it all wrong. It was after sunrise when he passed the famous billboard that marked the city limits. A girl in a bikini about to lob a multicoloured beach ball. The ocean, palm trees, white hotels. WELCOME TO MOON BEACH, it said. SUNTRAP OF THE SOUTH. He shook his head. There were more doctors in Moon Beach than anywhere else. More lawyers. More grief therapists. More rest homes. More obituaries. It was a place where people went to die. And yet, year after year, it went on pretending to be a beach resort. He remembered the time someone climbed the billboard scaffolding. They sprayed a line through the word SUN and sprayed the word DEATH above it in black: WELCOME TO MOON BEACH. DEATHTRAP OF THE SOUTH. For several days the famous billboard actually told the truth. It was after Vasco's time, but it was exactly the kind of action he would've taken.

He sensed the first stirrings of rush-hour, bright cars speeding past, as if by starting early and driving fast they could reach the weekend quicker. The wheel gripped tight between his fists, he released a few sarcastic words. He wanted candy now, he wanted to feel it splinter against his teeth, but when he checked his pockets he found nothing. He must've eaten them all. He glanced in anger at the empty wrappers piled on the seat beside him. They shifted, hissed. They looked like scales, he thought. As if, somewhere in the car, there had to be a naked fish.

CITY CENTRE 8.

Steam was lifting from the waterways. The moored launches glared in the early sun. He waited for a stoplight, then he pushed his glasses up and rolled the bones in the back of his wrists against his eyes.

He stopped at Diana's Gourmet Diner. The air outside the car smelt hot and damp, as if the world was sweating. He clipped his sun lenses over his glasses, sighed as he descended into cool, deep green. He took one step and his leg buckled. Maybe those power-station bastards hadn't broken anything, but Christ, they'd certainly come close.

He pushed through the door and took a stool at the counter. The waitress set a cup of coffee in front of him. He drank it right down. He asked her for a second cup, then he ordered eggs, wheat toast, and orange juice. A rustle next to him and an old guy in baby clothes sat down. Yellow towel shirt with blue stripes. Pale-blue shorts. A gurgle every now and then. These old Moon Beach guys, they were all the same. They'd lost their wives, they drove big cars too slowly, they talked about gambling and operations. His focus shifted from the old guy to the old guy's morning paper: WIDOW SUES FUNERAL PARLOUR. GANG-SLAYING IN RIALTO. HYDRO-CARBONS POLLUTING CITY AIR. It didn't seem like much had changed.

The old guy snapped him a look. Pretty fast, considering. 'You got a problem?'

'Just tired, that's all. Been driving all night.'

The old guy looked Jed over. His head flicked up and down a couple of times. It was like someone painting a wall. 'You're one of them funeral guys,' the old guy said, 'ent yer?'

'Used to be.'

'You ent gonna get me, young fella.'

Jed smiled. 'I wouldn't count on it.'

'Oh no, you ent gonna get me. I'm gonna live for ever, I am.'

Jed eyed the old guy carefully. 'I'd say you've got about another eighteen months.'

It would've been hard to say which way the old guy was going to tip. At last his mouth cracked open and all this dry laughter came rustling past his teeth. Old newspaper, the shed skin of snakes, fallen leaves.

'Another eighteen months,' the old guy said, 'I like that. Hey,' and he flapped a hand at the waitress. 'What's yer name?'

'Alice.'

'Alice?'

'Alice. Like in Wonderland.'

'You hear what he said, Alice? He said I've got another eighteen months.'

Alice eyed him. 'I'd say he was being kinda generous.'

The old guy had so much laughter in him, he couldn't get it out. He was looking at Jed and tilting a thumb at Alice and making a noise like a needle stuck at the end of a record.

You ought to be careful, Jed thought, or you're going to do something in those baby clothes of yours.

Turning back to his coffee, he dipped his long neck down to the cup and sipped. He traced the veins on the formica, the dents in the silver sugar bowl. He studied their flaws with silent ferocity. He could feel a smile spreading through his insides. OK, OK, so maybe he was crazy to come back. But being here was such defiance. Just being here.

'Hey,' the old guy said, 'you know what day it is today?'

Jed had to think. 'It's Thursday.'

The old guy shook his head like a rattle. 'Today is the Day of the Dead.'

Jed glanced at the calendar. Christ, the old guy wasn't kidding. He thought of Celia and her omens. If this wasn't an omen, nothing was. The smile reached his face and spread.

He turned and saw the old guy standing at the cash desk with his check. The woman gave the old guy the wrong change and the old guy noticed. The woman had to apologise.

'That's quite all right,' the old guy said. 'I'm glad you make mistakes. Know why?'

The woman didn't have a clue.

'Dead people don't make them.'

The woman just stared at the old guy.

'Mistakes,' the old guy said. 'Dead people don't make them. See?' And he turned to Jed and opened hs mouth. And there it was, the needle at the end of the record again. And the woman with a smile like a swallowed yawn.

Jed tipped the rest of his coffee down his throat. He paid up and left. No time for jokes. Leave that to the old guys in baby clothes.

At the first set of lights a black woman pulled alongside him in a yellow Plymouth. A holy bible sat on the dash. A twist of black lace hung from the mirror. She beat him away from the green light, and he saw the sticker on her bumper: BEAM ME UP, JESUS. He'd driven all night, mile after mile sliding beneath his wheels, and now he was back in the place where death was part of the scenery, as much as houses were, or trees. They spoke a different language in Moon Beach, and he'd forgotten that. It had been six years. He'd have to learn it all over again. Though there'd be some, he was sure, who'd tell him he'd been gone too long.

He thought of driving to his mother's house, but then he decided against it. She was like static. She would fuzz his signals. He drove south instead, over the old swing bridge and down into Rialto. There were more bars open than there used to be, there were more closed churches. He slowed as he passed Mitch's tattoo parlour. It looked closed too. He parked further up the street and walked back. The door was locked. He hoped Mitch hadn't taken off on another trip. He'd kind of been relying on Mitch.

He thought of Sharon next. It was a holiday. She ought to be home. As he drove across the Moon River bridge he couldn't help remembering that night. The cop car in the safety zone. The rain bouncing two feet off the road. Rising back into the air, thick as mist and full of shapes, like raw material for ghosts. Some nights all the bad things networked. Though it was 85 degrees and six years later, he found that he was shivering.

He took the first exit after the bridge. It swept him round in a long curve, then he was under the expressway, heading south. The tenement blocks of Baker Park held the sun on their scarred red-brick façades, their windows dark as blind men's glasses. He'd had this feeling all day. He was doing the rounds, but nobody could see. He was here, but he wasn't here. It was partly the city itself. It seemed to face the ocean, face away from the land. Driving in from the west, you felt as if you were doing something behind its back, as if you were creeping up on it. He'd had the same feeling all day: the city's blind.

He reached the street where Sharon lived. The washeteria on the corner, caged in wire-mesh. The stunted dusty trees. He rang the doorbell. A shadow moved behind the panes of frosted glass. The door opened six inches, shackled by a chain. Sharon eyed him through the gap.

She'd put on weight. He could tell just from the thin slice of her that he could see. Her skin looked drier, dustier than he remembered. The years; but also, he suspected, kids. She'd told him once that she'd had five abortions. You couldn't keep that up. Sooner or later a child would slip through. One that really wanted to.

'Sharon,' he said. 'How've you been?'

She was still staring, she was like those windows up the street. 'My

Christ,' she said. 'Jed.' Her surprise quickly turned to wariness. 'You can't stay here.'

'Who said anything about staying?'

'It's just it's lunchtime. Max'll be back soon. What are you doing here, anyway?'

'Max?' he said. 'That the guy you married?'

'How do you know that?'

He shrugged.

She unhitched the security chain. The house smelt of pepper and sweat. He remembered her sweet nothings, her sour breath. He remembered her flesh, blue at the edges and flickering, like gas.

She saw him looking beyond her. 'Don't even think about it.'

'It's all right,' he said. 'I just came back to see the place, that's all. Memories, you know. To see you too.' Not the truth, maybe, but lies never hurt.

'Bullshit. Not a word out of you for six years.'

He smiled. 'Didn't you get my card?'

'One card. Right. That made all the difference.'

'I had to leave town.'

'Sure.' She fitted one hand on her hip. Copied his smile, made it sarcastic. 'Sure you did.'

He said nothing.

'So where've you been?' The way she said it, she was getting ready for a tall story. It didn't matter what he said.

'In the desert.'

'Which one?'

He told her. She'd never heard of it.

'Not a word for six years,' she said. 'And what about the last time you were here?'

He hadn't seen her for weeks and then he'd gone round at one in the morning. It was only a day or two after Creed had told him what he had to do. He had to take a break from that. He wanted to see her and forget the rest. But she'd been drinking, rye straight up and sweet white wine, and she had started right in on him. He was never around, he lied to her, he didn't care. It was true, most of it, but he hadn't come to her for that. She began to push him in the chest. He had to shove her away. She fell and hit her head. It didn't knock her out, it just slowed her down a bit. He left soon afterwards. That was the last time.

'I was edgy that night,' he told her.

'Edgy?' She looked at him. He'd have to do better than that. But he couldn't. 'Yeah, well.' He took a step backwards. 'Max'll be back soon. I'd better get going.'

She seemed to be about to say something, but he didn't wait. He reached the gate and she still hadn't said it.

'See you around,' he said.

He saw her in the mirror as he pulled away. She was standing on her doorstep, one hand still welded to her hip.

Driving back across the bridge, he smiled. The way he'd cut that meeting short. He was on the edge now, and when you were on the edge, you had to sharpen up. His thoughts were sparks leaping off a blade.

He drove to a diner on V Street. A waitress flipped him a menu. 'Coffee?'

He remembered her from six years ago, but she didn't remember him. She didn't even give him a second glance. The city was blind.

He looked out of the window. V Street. The wrong end of the alphabet. To the west lay downtown: hotels, banks, the crescent of white sand that was Moon Beach. East of here were the grit and cigarette-butt streets of Mangrove, and then Moon River, wider than a mile, its waters laced with oil and chemicals.

He knew these streets, knew every crack. He'd grown up watching cars cruise the promenade, skulls dangling from their mirrors, numberplates like 998 DIE and a bumper sticker to match: ROOM FOR ONE MORE. (He'd bought his first plate three blocks south of here: CREAM 8. He still had it now. In Moon Beach people understood it right away. Drive somewhere else, they thought you were in the dairy business.) Then, when he worked for the Paradise Corporation, he drove V Street almost every day. The city morgue was two blocks away, Central Avenue and X Street (X marks the spot, as Maxie Carlo used to say). The most respected coffin-maker had set up in a warehouse just round the corner. People who worked in the business were everywhere, and people who didn't looked as if they did. Down on V Street even the bums wore dark suits. He wouldn't have been surprised to see himself through the glass. He'd passed this way so many times, surely he must've left his echo on the street. After all, if ever there was a city of ghosts, this was it. No, he wouldn't have been at all surprised to see himself walk by. He might even have waved.

'You stay here any longer, sir,' the waitress said, 'I'll have to charge you lunch.'

'All right,' he said, 'I'll have lunch.'

'What can I get you?'

'Spaghetti,' he said. 'With Meatball.'

He was going to eat the past.

After lunch he felt tired. He drove south to the ocean and parked on Pier 22. He leaned his head back, closed his eyes. The sun landed on the windshield in dusty yellow blocks. Hundreds of people were out strolling. Their footsteps jumbled up, made a curiously wooden sound. He could hear the car's engine cooling, ticking, like a dog's paws on the sidewalk.

A loose rumble and he saw a plane lift above the rooftops. The car shook. The ignition key chinked once. He blinked, stretched. His teeth felt numb and fat in his head. He slowly pulled himself upright, found his face in the mirror. His eyes were pinned wide open, they'd seen everything and it had been too much, Now who's the astronaut? He had stomachache. The past obviously hadn't agreed with him. He checked the clock. It was five. He'd been asleep for almost three hours. In another three it would be dark.

He drove into Mangrove South and stopped at the first bar he saw. Polystyrene skulls hung from the ceiling. The Day of the Dead ceremony was being broadcast on TV. There was a phone in the back. He called Mitch. No answer. He drank a beer, watched TV.

Half an hour later he called Mitch again. Still no answer. He tried Carol instead. Lady Dobson answered. Carol had moved out, she said. She gave him Carol's new number. He called the new number and Carol was home. Well, kind of home anyway. She used his name, but it didn't seem to mean anything to her. He imagined her surrounded by hundreds of special shoes. None of the shoes made pairs.

'This weekend's no good,' she was saying. 'Can you do Monday?'

Monday? Every day was so big at the moment, Monday seemed like someone else's life.

'Sure,' he said. 'OK.'

She gave him a time and place, but he was still thinking about Monday. He just couldn't picture it.

At last she realised. 'Are you OK, Jed? Where are you?'

But it was too late, he was already hanging up.

Back in his car, he began to drive. He was only one of thousands who'd arrived in the city during the last twenty-four hours, and people were beginning to mass in the streets, some in blue body-paint, some in skull masks, some in luminous skeleton suits. There was a man lying on the bottom of a glass tank that was filled with water. A placard

above him read PLAY DEAD! ONLY $1.25!. As he passed Jed by he
opened one eye and winked. It was the Day of the Dead all right. Part
fairground, part nightmare. Jed took comfort in the thought that he
could hide in all this chaos and hysteria, that he could wear the
carnival like a disguise. There was no way he'd be able to stay
downtown, though. He'd passed a few hotels, and it was the same
story all over: SORRY WE'RE FULL. He'd have to resort to the
perimeters. Newtown, Austin, Normandy. No SORRY WE'RE FULL
signs out there. It didn't matter how eager tourism was, it never quite
reached that far.

Then, as he crossed the bridge for the third time that day, he saw
lights on the west bank, high above the river. That row of grey houses.
He had lived there once. With Vasco and his uncles. Last time he'd
seen the uncles (though he'd never actually *seen* Reg, of course) was
fifteen years ago. They'd been senile then. They could be dead by
now. The house might be standing empty . . .

In five minutes he was pulling up outside. Though the sun had
almost set, no lights showed in the windows. That didn't prove
anything, of course. The uncles had always been tight. He climbed
the steps to the verandah. Two punctured flyscreens lay on the
bleached wooden boards. He thought of afternoons spent here with
Vasco. Tins of beer and talk of war. He looked back down the garden.
From here you could see clear across the river to the Crumbles in the
distance. He turned away from the memory, the view. He pushed on
the front door and it swung open.

It was dark inside except for one thin bar of orange light that had
found its way into the hall and now stood propped against the wall.
Dust dropped slowly through the air, as if settling in water. He began
to move towards the stairs then, noticing the door to the elevator,
hesitated. He punched the button, thinking nothing would happen.
There was a clunk from somewhere up above. A snap as metal gates
slid shut. Through a glass panel he watched the thick black cables
loop in the empty shaft as the car dropped down.

The gates slid apart. Jed opened the door and then let out a gasp.
In the elevator was Mario, sitting in his wheelchair. His head had
fallen sideways, so he appeared to be listening to his shoulder.

'Mario?'

Jed took one step forwards. Large black flies rose from Mario's
eyes and lips.

When Jed could look again, it was the wheelchair he noticed. The
leather upholstery had started to decay. In some places it had lost its

lustre and worn thin. In other places it had torn. Underneath the leather Jed could see bright paper. He moved closer, trying not to breathe. He reached into a gash behind the dead man's back. His hand closed round several hundred-dollar bills.

Listen. Hear that? Money.

Jed felt a queer, crooked smile appear on his face. Everybody used to think that Mario was senile. Everybody used to wonder what he'd done with all his millions.

Listen. Hear that?

Every time he moved he must've heard it. He'd been sitting on it. He'd been wheeling himself around in his own mobile bank.

Jed was still smiling when he parked outside the Lucky Strike Motel an hour later. He'd chosen the Lucky Strike because it was in Newtown. The bleak north-western edge of the city. Even so, he knew he was running a risk. Vultures had always favoured motels. Motels were low-life information banks. They were ideal places to hold meetings, do deals. Skull McGowan used to run a team of vultures out of the Ocean Bed Motel on Highway 12. One night, Jed decided. Then he'd move on. He hid his car in the darkest corner of the parking-lot, and checked in under the name Matt Leech.

It was still early, just after eight. There was a liquor lounge next to the motel. He walked in, sat down at the bar. There were only two other guys in there. Just old guys from the neighbourhood, drinking beer and shots, watching the service of remembrance on TV. Jed said it was his first day back in the city after being away. He said he'd like to buy them both a drink. The barman too.

Jed turned his eyes to the TV. The first boats were just reaching Angel Meadows. He raised his glass.

'One day it'll be us,' he said, 'but not yet.'

'I'll drink to that,' one of the guys said.

They all drank to it.

'So here we are,' the TV presenter said, the sun setting behind him, the breeze toying with his fringe, 'coming to you live from Moon Beach – '

'Live,' the barman said. 'That's a joke.'

They all chuckled.

The boats were dropping anchor. They'd reached the Angels of Memory, the most famous of the cemetery gateways. Two white angels watched over the cemetery. They were both standing on pedestals, their wings spread wide against the sky, their hands folded modestly in prayer.

An aerial view.

From the helicopter the fleet of boats was a loose collection of lights on a great dark surface. They had gathered round the two floodlit angels. The service was about to begin.

Then the cameras swooped down. Closed in on the bridge of one of the larger boats. Froze on a man in a dark suit. Still face, still hair.

' – Mr Neville Creed,' the presenter's voice was hushed and reverential, 'chairman of the Paradise Corporation – '

Jed's hand jerked and his whisky spilled.

'Something wrong?' the barman asked.

Jed shook his head.

Later that night he lay on his back in bed and watched small blocks of light move along the top of the wall above the window. It worried him and then he worked it out: it was just cars passing. It was late now, past midnight, but there was a highway outside. Those small blocks of light would cross the wall all night.

He closed his eyes, but couldn't stop the image forming. That still face on the boat. That still face slowly turned towards him. Those still lips began to speak.

Here I am.

It was as if Creed had known that he'd be watching. As if Creed knew everything. As if Creed was some kind of god.

Jed switched the light on. He hauled himself upright, leaned against the headboard. Remember what you came here for. He lifted his wrist and checked his tattoo, the way you might check a watch, and it reminded him, as time does, that he was locked in a process that was irreversible, inescapable. He wouldn't be used again. He wouldn't be outwitted, or double-crossed. This time the boot was on the other foot. He had the power now. He had the initiative, the surprise. And there were people who would help him, people who knew. Carol. Mitch. Even Vasco, maybe, when he learned the truth. The boot was on the other foot and, when he kicked with it, it was going to hurt.

The truth.

He reached into his jacket pocket and took out the tape. He didn't need to play it. He knew it word for word.

His own voice first: 'You want me to kill Vasco's brother?'

And then Creed's: 'That's right.'

His own voice again: 'How?'

Then Creed's: 'Don't worry about that – it's taken care of – it's nice – '

Jed lay back down again. Blackmail would be his instrument. He would make a demand. For money. But this wasn't about money. He knew that for certain now. Mario had appeared in his wheelchair. Mario had frightened the fucking daylights out of him. Mario had made things clear. He saw the brown envelope of bills bounce off Creed's chest and flutter to the ground. This had never been about money. Remember what you came here for. That face on the boat, it was just skin and bone. It could wear fear on it, it could die. It was just skull candy for his sweet tooth.

His eyes drifted shut.

Towards three, it began to rain. And suddenly he was back in Adam's Creek. Waiting in the alley behind the restaurant. Celia was late. A sound that could've been paper in the wind and he looked round. She was standing next to him. Her face lit up as if the sun was setting on it. Her blonde hair hung against her collarbone like frayed rope.

He took the key out of his pocket, unlocked the back door. Through the kitchens, out into the restaurant. It was dark, but he knew the layout blindfold. She followed, one hand on his belt.

'It smells in here,' she whispered.

'It's chicken,' he whispered back. 'It's a number 42.'

When he switched on the lights in the grotto, she was already sitting on a rock with her head thrown back and her arms behind her, supporting her. Her long, coarse hair just touched the backs of her elbows. She was naked from the waist up.

'Hey, Jed,' she whispered across the restaurant. 'Do I look like one of those kind of mermaids?'

He smiled and flicked another switch. There was a distant rumble of thunder. He made his way through the empty tables towards her. When he reached her, it was just beginning to rain for the first time.

'We're going to get soaked,' he said.

'Yeah,' and she tipped her head back, 'yeah, I know.'

Each storm lasted five minutes, then the coloured lights came on. Cicadas chattered in the palm trees, wet leaves dripped. After Celia had come for the first time she turned her head and looked out into the restaurant. 'I've sat out there so many times,' she said, 'eating that shitty Chinese food.'

One of her breasts was red, the other one green. Her nipples had darkened, tightened. Her wet hair straggled across a bed of plastic lilies.

She turned to him. 'I never thought I'd be lying here like this.'

'Yes, you did,' he said.

'I wanted to, but I never thought it would happen.'

Then it began to rain again and she bit her bottom lip and reached for him and whispered, 'Put it inside me again and let's pretend we're somewhere like a desert island.'

The drizzle on his back as he moved in and out of her. A shiver of lightning against the sky. Her long ribbony cries were lost as thunder unloaded on the roof like rocks. They fucked until they were cold.

The next evening she waited for him in the alley.

'You know last night?' she said.

He grinned at her. 'I know last night.'

'You know how long we fucked?'

He shrugged.

'Three thunderstorms,' she said.

The storm had moved away. He turned in his motel bed and pulled the cover over him.

He could hear cars on the highway, like someone sweeping floors. One small block of light edged along the top of the wall and stopped halfway, but he was already sinking back, sinking into sleep.

FIVE

OLD FRIENDS

It was the Friday after the funeral, the day after the Day of the Dead. Nathan was sitting in Tin Pan Alley, an Irish bar downtown. He was waiting for Georgia.

He had spent most of the past forty-eight hours at Georgia's apartment. Every time he thought of returning to the house on Mahogany Drive he thought of Harriet, and every time he thought of Harriet he saw her crouching on the floor in the summerhouse, dark eyes drifting in their sockets, a tissue in between her legs. If he was away for long enough, she might just leave, go home. After all, the funeral was over. There was no reason for her to stay.

He finished his second drink, bought a third.

Tin Pan Alley. Back of the bar the street sloped down to the harbour. The heart of the old meat-packing district. Cold storage, wasteground, stolen cars. Through the window he could hear the hiss of truck brakes on the hill.

Georgia had said ten, but he knew it wouldn't be ten. She was out scoring something fast for them. He let her take care of that end of things. She knew the city better than he did, she knew the routines. No, it wouldn't be ten. Nowhere near. She'd float in, midnight at the earliest. Flat eyes, numb lips. Head dipping left and right. What had she said once? 'I'm like a chicken when I go in places.' He smiled. There was no shortcut through this stretch of time and he wasn't looking for one. He could wait for days, if need be. Mind on a slow burn, fingers cooled by the sweat of a glass.

He'd been there an hour when this guy pushed through the door. Tall, thin figure in black. Limbs you could fold away. Sort of creaky-looking. Just this one glance at him and something happened in Nathan's mind, it was the same as when you put money in a pool table and all the balls come tumbling into the lip.

Nathan stared, but he couldn't be sure. Someone he knew, or someone who looked like someone he knew? The tight black pants; the black jacket, too short in the arms; the black top hat. Like a drainpipe and a chimney-stack combined. The guy had Moon Beach tattooed all over him. Wrong end of the alphabet. Nathan watched as he ordered a beer, pushed small money around on his palm, lifted one curling finger to his ear and scratched. When the beer was set down in front of him, his lips reached out greedily for the rim of the glass. He gulped, sighed, wiped his mouth on his wrist. He'd been dying for that beer. Fingering those tiny coins all day. But then he must have sensed somebody watching him. His head veered round, he swivelled. Cold eyes, glasses, face as pale as ice. Now Nathan knew. And couldn't believe it. All those years. Even the name came back to him. Jed Morgan.

'Been a while,' Jed said, 'hasn't it?'

'I didn't recognise you,' Nathan said.

'Maybe I changed or something.' Jed sipped his beer. 'You still swimming?'

Nathan smiled. The reference wasn't lost on him. 'I've been working up and down the coast. As a lifeguard, mostly.'

'So what brings you back?'

'Somebody died.'

Jed's head reared and twisted on his stringy neck. 'You shouldn't joke about that.'

'I'm not joking.'

'Who was it?'

'My father.'

'Sorry to hear it.' Jed wasn't sorry, not even remotely.

'The number of times I've heard that recently,' Nathan said.

Jed shrugged. 'Somebody dies, that's what happens.'

'What about you?' Nathan asked.

'What about me?'

'You been away too?'

'You could say that.' Jed's lips seemed to be travelling towards a grin, but they never got there. His eyes were motionless, behind glass, like something in the reptile house. 'It's a long story, you know?'

'Not yet I don't.'

Jed jerked a thumb in Nathan's direction and told the barman, 'We've got a sense of humour here.'

The barman was grinning. Nathan was grinning.

Grins all round.

Nathan thought it strange that he was talking to Jed like this. He'd never liked Jed in the past, and he wasn't sure he liked him now. Those eyes, that skin. Other times it would've put him off, but right now he was in too big a mood. It was going to be a long night. He was waiting for Georgia. The moment she pushed through those swing doors he'd lift like a jet at the end of a runway.

And so he could turn to Jed and look him right in the face and say, 'You going to tell me or what?'

Jed reached a finger down, scratched the inch of white skin between his sock and the leg of his pants. It was his way of cocking the trigger on his story. Then he eased off his stool and used the same finger to point at the bench opposite Nathan.

'Sure,' Nathan said. 'Sit down.'

Jed leaned both arms on the table and his eyes moved out into the bar. 'I used to work for one of the parlours.' His eyes flicked back, checking Nathan for a reaction. There wasn't one. 'I used to work for a guy called Creed. Maybe you heard of him.'

Nathan shook his head.

'It was Vasco got me the job. Remember Vasco?'

'What happened to him?'

'Some guy killed his brother.' Jed sucked down some more beer. 'Last I heard, he went nuts.'

'Christ.'

'He was kind of nuts already. That family, they were all nuts. His uncles. One of them, he used to lock himself in his room all day. I lived there more than a year, never saw him once. The other one – ' and Jed stopped suddenly. He dropped his head down to his beer and gulped.

'This guy Creed, though,' and he leaned closer, lowered his voice as if it was suddenly a church they were in. 'It was six, seven years ago. Back in those days there was this loyalty thing. We were all locked into it, it made us feel valuable. It was like being gold. Everyone wanted a piece of us. We used to cruise the city in a stretch hearse, the ones where the front goes round a corner and the back goes round about five minutes later. I was the driver. Black top hat, red velvet cushion to sit on like a king, pair of dark-green lenses for the glare. We cruised the city, this whole gang of us. We put the fear of Christ Jesus into people.'

He was talking from the deep past now, his voice rose up from the quarry of his memories. It felt much later than it was.

'One time we're driving along the promenade and these kids start giving us shit. McGowan, he rolls the window down and leans out, with his head all shaved and mirrors on his eyes, and he says, "You're going to die," he says, real quiet but so they can hear. "You're going

to die and we're going to bury you."' Jed grinned and drained his
glass.

'Nice guy,' Nathan said.

'McGowan,' Jed said, and shook his head. 'We used to call him
the Skull.'

'How come?'

'It was just the look of him. We all had names. There was the Skull,
there was Pig, and Vasco was called Gorilla, just like in the old days.
Then there was Meatball – '

'Meatball? Why Meatball?'

'No neck. His head just kind of sat on his shoulders. So we called
him Meatball. He was there for entertainment.'

I was your entertainment once, Nathan thought. But he pushed the
memory back.

'What about you, then?' he said. 'What were you called?'

'Spaghetti.'

Nathan laughed. 'This guy, sounds like he could've opened a
restaurant.' He held up his glass. 'Want another?'

Jed nodded. Nathan went up to the bar and came back with two
more beers.

'It was real power.' Jed scraped at his cheek with one long fingernail.
'The things we did then, they were on a different level.'

'So I don't get it. Why did you leave?'

'I did a job for Creed. Job like that, you get your hands dirty. I had
to leave.'

Nathan nodded as if he understood.

'I ended up in a small town in the desert, you wouldn't've heard of
it. I worked in an ice-cream parlour. I sold ice-cream.' Jed's face
opened like a cave, and Nathan felt a chill pass through. Old bones
and spiders, centuries of damp. 'Fudge Ripple, Swiss Chocolate
Almond, Pecan Buttercrunch,' Jed said, 'you name it. I sold them
all.'

Nathan couldn't see it, somehow. 'You like ice-cream?'

'I fucking hate the stuff.'

They laughed over that for a while.

'And now you're back,' Nathan said.

'That's right.'

'Got anything planned?'

'Yeah,' and Jed leered, 'I got something planned.'

But when he asked Jed about it Jed just shook his head and, lifting
his glass again, tipped his chin into the air and slid the beer down his

throat, it lay straight and gold along the side of the glass, it looked as if he was swallowing a sword. Then he put his hands flat on the table, stood up, walked over to the jukebox. -

Nathan checked his watch. Almost twelve-thirty. When he looked up again, Georgia was sitting next to him. She was dressed for business. All in black except for a denim jacket and an amber necklace.

'That guy you're with,' she said, 'he's really ugly.'

Nathan smiled. 'I know.'

'You been waiting long?'

'About two hours.'

'That's not bad for me. I'm practically early.' She sounded breathless, as if she'd been whirled round and round and bits of her were coming loose.

It was still the funeral, he thought. That was what a funeral did. It climbed down into your bones and hid. And every now and then it jumped back out again, took hold of you, and shook you till you rattled.

Jed slid back into his seat. 'Well, well,' he said, 'new blood.'

'Who's this?' Georgia asked.

'We used to know each other,' Nathan said. 'Years ago.'

'Old friends,' Jed said.

Nathan turned to Georgia. 'Did you get it?'

She lit a cigarette. 'In the end. I had to go out to Sweetwater. Great name for nowhere, that. Hasn't even got any water at all, let alone sweet. Who names these places? Jesus.' She blew smoke across the room and shook her head. Then she seemed to realise it was over with, she'd got where she was going to. She slumped back in the seat, let her head slip sideways till it was resting against Nathan's shoulder. 'Sorry I was so long.'

He smiled. 'Like you said, you're practically early.'

'Sweetwater,' Jed said. 'That's a real dump.'

'You know it?' Georgia asked him.

'Used to live there. Every time a plane went over, you had to shout. If you had a bath, you got waves in it.'

Georgia looked at him. 'What did you say your name was?'

'They call him Spaghetti,' Nathan said.

'They used to call me that,' Jed said, 'but it's not my real name.'

'What's your real name?' Georgia said. 'Lasagne?'

Jed's smile was a thin flexing of the lips. You're on the border, it said. Don't step over it.

'His real name's Jed,' Nathan said.

Georgia was frowning. 'That's not very Italian.'

'Who said anything about Italian?' Jed said.

'So why Spaghetti?' But her interest was fading, she was looking round. 'I think it's time for the bathroom.'

In two minutes she was back again.

'So what are we doing?' Nathan said.

'Let's go back to the house,' she said. 'There's a pool. There's videos.' She took hold of Nathan's arm. 'We won't have it for ever.'

'What about Harriet?' he said. 'And Yvonne.'

'They'll be asleep, dummy.'

'It's a long way.'

'We'll get a taxi.'

'We don't need a taxi,' Jed said. 'I've got a car.'

Nathan turned to him. 'You don't mind?'

'No, I don't mind,' Jed said. 'I kind of like driving.'

They left the bar. Nathan waited on the sidewalk while Georgia bought a couple of six-packs from the all-night liquor store next door. He watched her gesturing under the harsh fluorescent lights. She was making the old man behind the counter laugh. He looked round. Jed was ten yards away, chin tipped in the air, fingers at his throat. Nathan could hear the scratching. Could almost see the dry skin floating to the ground. He walked over to the gutter. It was choked with debris from the day before: flowers, fireworks, skulls. 'They'll be asleep,' he muttered, 'dummy.' He must be drunk, he thought, to be talking to himself like this.

Then Jed was standing next to him. 'This house we're going to,' he said, 'whose is it?'

'It's ours,' Nathan said. 'We're selling it. It's going on the market sometime next week.'

'You got any spare room?'

Nathan looked up. 'Why?'

'Well, like I said. I only just got back. I haven't found a place yet.'

Nathan nudged a skull with the toe of his shoe. 'Shouldn't be a problem.'

The door of the liquor store swung shut on muscular spring hinges. They looked up. Georgia was walking towards them with the beer. They crossed the street to Jed's car. It was an old Chrysler with steel radials. Mud had dried in streaks behind the wheel arches. Jed must have been driving across country.

'It's beat up,' Jed said, 'but it goes.'

It looked like it went. The sprawling hood hinted at a powerful engine. The radiator grille had caught flies in its fierce, bared teeth. The numberplate said CREAM 8.

'Nice plate,' Georgia said.

'Some people don't get it,' Jed said. 'They think I'm in the dairy business. A milkman or something.'

Laughing, they climbed into the car. They sat in the front, all three of them, with Nathan in the middle. Jed turned the key in the ignition. The engine rumbled.

He seemed to know the city well. He took shortcuts all the way across town, streets that Nathan had never even heard of. He drove methodically, seldom raising his speed above thirty-five. Nathan smiled. He could feel Georgia shifting next to him, and knew it was only a matter of time. Sure enough, as they crossed the bridge, she leaned forward.

'You drive very slow,' she said.

'It's habit,' Jed said.

She didn't understand. 'What do you mean?'

Nathan turned to her, smiling. 'He used to drive hearses.'

There were no further questions.

When they reached Mahogany Drive, Jed didn't want to leave his car on the street. He asked if there was anywhere more private. Nathan showed him the small courtyard behind the house.

'It'll be safe there,' he said.

Jed gave him a smile that he couldn't read.

They settled in the lounge. It had always been their favourite room. The french windows opening on to the terrace, the pool glittering beyond. Georgia cut some lines. Jed sat in Dad's red chair and watched TV. He found the cartoon channel, said it was just the right speed. Georgia thought so too.

'How did you two meet?' she asked.

'Mutual friend,' Jed said. 'When we were about twelve.'

'You seen anything of Tip?' Nathan asked.

'I haven't seen anything of anyone,' Jed said. 'I told you, I've been away.' He smiled. 'I'm not even back yet, not officially.'

'What do you mean?'

'Nobody knows I'm here.'

'You on the run or something?' And Nathan couldn't help laughing.

Jed took the question seriously. He pulled his sleeve up. 'You see this tattoo?' he said.

Nathan leaned forwards. He saw a series of blue numbers on the inside of Jed's wrist. 'What's that?' he said. 'Your phone number?'

'That's a good one,' Jed said. 'That's the first time I've heard that one.' And his top teeth glistened and his mouth turned down at the corners. While the smile lasted, he looked exactly like his car. Nathan pictured dead flies spattered on his teeth.

'So what is it?' he asked.

'It's a date,' Jed said.

'The date of what?'

Jed leaned back in Dad's red chair. He made them wait. 'The date I killed someone,' he said.

'Yeah?' Nathan didn't believe it. But then he thought back, all the way back to the shark run, the SUICIDE/YOU FIRST T-shirt, that sense of contamination, and then later, Central Avenue, his vision of the jacket lined with needles, and suddenly he did believe it.

'Anyone we know?' Georgia asked.

Jed ignored her. 'You remember I told you I did a job for a guy called Creed?'

Nathan nodded.

'Well, that was the job.' Jed reached for another beer. A snap, a hiss. 'All that stuff with the Womb Boys, that was just practice for the real thing. I didn't know it at the time, but it was.' He stared at the can and then put it down. 'I had to do things working for Creed, anyone who got close to him, they had to do things, that's what Creed was like. I had to do things and then,' and he looked up and suddenly his eyes looked too pale, almost blind, 'and then,' he said, 'I had to leave.' He took his hat off, turned it in his hands.

Nathan glanced at Georgia. Georgia shrugged. Nathan looked at Jed again.

Without his hat on, Jed looked curiously mutilated, raw, no longer whole. The hat seemed such a part of him, almost like a hand or a smile. His pale-brown hair lay flat and lifeless against his skull. A red line crossed his forehead horizontally as if the removal of the hat had been an operation and had left a scar.

For a while nobody spoke.

It was during this silence that Nathan heard a creak. He thought he recognised the sound. It had come from the hallway, it was one of the last six stairs. He looked round and saw the tail of the door handle begin to lift. The door had always been hard to open, ever since Dad had painted the leading edge. Even now, years afterwards, it often stuck. The crack it made as it was pushed from the other side made everybody jump.

The door opened and Yvonne stood in the gap. She had thrown a coat over her nightgown. Her copper hair lifted away from her head on one side where she had slept on it. She clutched her metal box of garlic in her hand. To keep the devils on their toes.

'I heard a voice.'

She was staring at the red chair, and at Jed, because he was sitting in it.

'I thought it was him. I thought he was calling me.'

Nathan stood up and walked towards her. 'Sorry if we woke you, Yvonne.'

Yvonne looked at him. 'What time is it?'

'Four-thirty,' Georgia said.

Yvonne nodded to herself.

Nathan put his hand on her elbow. 'Come on, Yvonne,' he said. 'I'll take you back to bed.'

At the top of the stairs she stopped and turned to him. 'It wasn't him,' she said.

'No.'

She gripped his arm. 'But who was it?'

'Just a friend.'

He helped her back into bed and drew the covers over her. She lay on her back, her eyes wide as a child's.

'I painted him a picture,' she whispered.

'I know.'

'You think he would've liked it?'

'Of course he would.' He kissed her on the cheek. 'Now you go to sleep.'

Back in the lounge Jed was still sitting in front of the TV. Nathan sat down next to Jed, but found he couldn't concentrate. Jed kept scratching himself. First the side of his neck, then an ankle, then his stomach. It was as if his whole body itched, but not all at the same time. Nathan couldn't help watching. And as he watched he began to imagine the tiny flakes of dead skin building up around the legs of Dad's chair. He stared at the piece of floor where the chair stood and saw the flakes of skin piling up like snow, and then drifting.

And suddenly he couldn't watch any more. He had to say something. 'Jed?' he said. 'You seen Georgia?'

Jed didn't look away from the TV. 'I think she went outside.'

Out on the terrace birds were beginning to call from the trees, hinges on the door that would soon let morning in. Georgia was sitting on the steps, one leg drawn up against her chest, her cheek resting sideways on her knee. Only the fingers of her right hand moved, twisting the chunks of her amber necklace. The pool trickled and dripped behind her.

'How's Yvonne?' she asked.

'She's all right.'

'Her hearing his voice like that,' and she shuddered.

He sat down beside her. 'It was only us. She was half asleep and all mixed up. She'll have forgotten by morning.'

It was still dark in the garden, but dawn had spilled across the sky like acid. It dripped down into the trees, eating night from between the branches. The hedge was no longer the silhouette it had been an hour before; hundreds of individual leaves stood out. When you had been up all night, dawn was like a magic trick: even though you knew what was coming, it still managed to surprise you. It was sinister too: you realised just how slowly the world turned, how slowly and relentlessly; you realised there was no escaping it.

Georgia broke the pool's dark surface with a racing dive. He saw her rise again, her black hair shining, tight against her skull. He looked back towards the house. There was a white face framed in the lounge window. It was Jed, he realised. But not before he'd gone cold. Dad used to stand like that. Stand at the window, looking out into the garden. Then he used to tap on the glass. He couldn't shout. He had to save his voice, his breath. He couldn't open the door either and come out. The air itself was dangerous. Too humid, too moist. It collected in his windpipe like moss, it blocked his narrow lungs. Nathan always thought it looked as if Dad was trapped, as if he wanted to get out, but couldn't. Or he was dead already, under glass. Once, when Dad tapped on the window, Nathan had shouted, 'Do you HAVE to do that?' And then, when Dad had looked at him, wounded, he hadn't been able to explain why he was angry.

The sudden sound of flung beads. But it was just the water spilling off Georgia's body as she climbed out of the pool. She stood beside him, wrapped in a thick towel, her hands bunched under her chin. 'I just remembered. He said he killed someone.'

Nathan smiled up at her. 'It was probably just the coke talking.'

Jed was folded up in the red chair when they went in. One hand supporting his cheek, asleep. The TV was still on. A cartoon chipmunk danced across the lenses of his glasses.

Georgia tilted her head sideways, read the numbers on his wrist. 'You're probably right. It's probably just some phone number.' She yawned. 'I'm going to bed.' She kissed Nathan on the cheek. 'I'll see you in the morning.' She laughed. 'I mean, afternoon.'

He waited till she'd left the room, then he looked down at Jed again. The early morning light caught on Jed's skin like torn fingernails on wool. He touched Jed on the shoulder.

Jed's eyes slid open. 'What's up?'

'You did kill someone,' Nathan said, 'didn't you?'

The laughter sifted out of Jed's nostrils. 'Where am I sleeping?' he said.

AND SPRING CAME FOR EVER

He shouldn't have talked so much.

The lights turned red and Jed was so angry, he stamped on the brake much harder than he needed to. His bald tyres screeched on the hot asphalt. A woman almost toppled off her gold high-heeled sandals. She was wearing a T-shirt that said I CAME TO MOON BEACH AND LIVED.

BUT ONLY JUST, Jed thought, through gritted teeth. BUT ONLY JUST.

It was Monday morning. The sun cut down through the sky like a guillotine. He could still feel all that beer and cocaine behind his eyes, he could still feel them in his blood, like grit. His skin didn't seem to fit this morning. He should've known better. He had to keep his eyes clear, his blood pure.

He drove down the promenade and parked close to the Ocean Café. This was where he was supposed to be meeting Carol. He was early. He sat behind the wheel, the radio murmuring. He watched people in bright clothes flash by like parts of a headache. Friday night. OK, so he'd talked too much. But really, who was going to remember? Nathan and that sister of his, they were both so trashed, he doubted they'd remember anything. And even if they did, what of it? Stories about murder and tattoos and gangs, who'd believe stories like that, specially in cold daylight.

He leaned back in his seat, tucked a piece of candy into his cheek, sucked on it thoughtfully. Stories were his ticket to places, they always had been. Now they'd taken him to Blenheim. The word brought a smile to his face. Say there actually were vultures on his tail. They'd never dream of looking in Blenheim. It just wasn't him. It wasn't anything like him. He'd really landed on his feet this time.

He celebrated by putting 50 cents in the parking meter when he got out of the car. It always amused him to obey small laws.

Nathan slept badly. All night the sheets felt rough against his body, and when morning came the glare seemed to reach through his eyelids with metal instruments. In a dream he saw Jed at the bottom of the garden, a wheelbarrow beside him. He was shovelling his dead skin on to the bonfire. He was burning the dead parts of himself.

When Nathan woke he went straight to the window, expecting Jed to be standing below, a spade in his hands. But there was only bright sunlight and green grass. He rubbed his eyes. His skin stretched taut and thin across his face, the tail-end of all that cocaine rattling like a ghost train through his blood. It was Monday. He looked at the clock. It was almost eleven.

In the kitchen he found the one person he had been trying to avoid: Harriet. She was sitting at the table with a cup of coffee and a cigarette.

'There you are,' she said.

She had the face of a witch that morning. A shield of black hair and skin like candlewax. Her two front teeth were crossed swords in her mouth. He could no longer believe what had happened on the day of the funeral.

'I'd like a word with you,' she said.

He poured himself some coffee. 'What about?' He kept his hand steady, his voice even.

She glanced at the ceiling. Yvonne was moving about upstairs. 'In the dining-room,' she said. 'I don't want us to be disturbed.'

In the dining-room she lit another cigarette and stood by the fireplace. All the furniture had been sold. There was nowhere to sit.

'That person who's staying,' she said, 'who is he?'

'He's a friend.'

'A friend.' She gave the word some extra weight.

He knew what she was implying, but he didn't rise to it.

'This,' and she paused, 'friend, how long is he staying?'

'I don't know.'

'I want him out of here.' She held her right elbow in the palm of her left hand and stared at him, her lit cigarette aimed at him and burning, like a third eye.

He looked at his feet. 'This isn't your house, you know.'

'It isn't yours either.'

'You're wrong. It's mine and Georgia's – '

'And Rona's.'

She didn't know, he realised. She really didn't know.

'No,' he said. 'It's not Rona's.' He told her the story. He explained why the house had never actually, legally, belonged to Dad. 'I'm sorry, Harriet,' he said, 'but that's how it is.'

She walked to the window, stared out into the driveway. 'Tell me something. Do you like this city?'

Her voice was thin now, a voice you could cut with. It would cut the way grass cut. First the pain and nothing to see, then the blood welling seemingly from nowhere.

'Why?' he said.

'I could make things difficult if I wanted to.'

'In what way?'

'I could contest the will. It might take six months to sort out.' She faced into the room again and smiled at him. 'Maybe longer.'

'I thought you said you were leaving after the funeral.'

'I've decided not to.' She walked to the fireplace and tapped half an inch of ash into the grate. 'I've got my daughter's interests to take care of. You see,' and she looked up at him, 'I'm not sure I trust you.'

It was so absurd, he had to laugh. But his laughter sounded false in the hollow room. 'What about Yvonne?' he said. 'What's she going to think about all this?'

'Oh, hasn't she told you? She's leaving today. She's driving back to Hosannah Beach. She said she had some things to do. You know,' and Harriet sneered, 'paint.' She picked up her pack of cigarettes and her lighter from the mantelpiece, and moved towards the door. 'In the meantime,' she said, 'I'm sure your friend can find somewhere else to stay.' She gave him a mocking smile. 'There are plenty of those men's hostels on the west side.'

Nathan stood in the middle of the room. A thin spiral of smoke rose from the grate. It was Harriet's cigarette. He went over and crushed it out under his heel.

From his table in the corner of the Ocean Café Jed watched Carol walk down a flight of steps, across the terrace, and through the glass doors. She was wearing a yellow shirt and black slacks. Her limp had got worse. She clung to the strap of her shoulder-bag with both hands, as if for support.

She stood beside the table, smiling uncertainly.

'I'm late,' she said, 'aren't I?'

She sat down. She unhitched her bag from her shoulder and put it in her lap. Her mouth seemed even smaller than he remembered. As if they'd stitched her up some more. As if they were trying to stop her talking altogether.

'I've just been to the doctor,' she said.

'Is it your leg?'

'Not my leg,' she said, and she was still smiling, 'no.'

A waiter arrived to take their orders. She looked up at the waiter, then she moved her head back down, moved it so fast that the smile flew off.

'A tea,' she said.

Jed ordered the same.

When the waiter had gone, Jed leaned forwards. 'What's wrong with you?'

She turned away from him.

'You're taking pills, aren't you?' He paused. 'Aren't you?' He'd raised his voice. He didn't know why he suddenly felt so angry.

She was staring out to sea. His anger didn't touch her.

He was reminded of the old people who sat in rows behind the plate-glass fronts of their hotels. Vasco used to call them pawns. They sat in rows all day, they watched the waves wrinkling in the distance like their own skin, and when they died it was as if death had come in from the ocean, come in on a surprising diagonal like a bishop, and suddenly there was a gap, someone had been taken, one of the pawns had gone.

'What are you so scared of?' he asked her.

'The sun's too bright. There are too many colours. Noises scrape at me.' She turned to him. 'I'm scared of feeling like me. Really like me, with no layers of anything over it.'

He didn't want to hear this. This wasn't what he'd come to hear.

She saw the look on his face. 'You asked,' she said.

He sipped his tea. It was cold already.

'Aren't you scared?' she asked him.

'What of?'

She shrugged. 'They say people who aren't scared, either they're brave or they're very stupid.'

'That's like saying nothing, isn't it?' he snapped. 'That's like saying precisely fucking nothing.'

She looked down at her hands. 'Why did you want to see me, Jed? What do you want?'

'I need your help.'

'I don't see how I can help you.'

'I want to know what you meant that day.'

She frowned. 'What day?'

'The day of your father's funeral. You came up to me and you said, "This whole thing's a sham." I want to know what you meant by that.'

She turned her cup on its saucer. Noises scrape at me.

'Carol?'

She lifted the cup and sipped. 'Why do you have to open all that up again?' she said. 'It's over.'

'Not for me it isn't.'

'It was years ago.'

'I want to know, Carol. I need to know. It might help.'

She brought her cup down so hard, the saucer fell into two neat pieces. 'You're so selfish, Jed. You only want to listen now it suits you. You wouldn't listen back then. Back then you were having too good a time, weren't you?'

Too good a time. That was a joke. But he didn't say anything. He just drank some more cold tea.

'All right,' he said, 'suppose I tell you what I think you meant.'

She shrugged.

'I think Creed was responsible for your father's death,' he said. 'I don't know what he did exactly. But he played a part in it, didn't he, him and his people?'

'You were one of his people.'

'I was his driver. They never told me what was going on.' He leaned forwards on the table. 'I think maybe,' and he paused, and lowered his voice, 'I think maybe he was even murdered.'

Her face hardened. The bones showed white in the bridge of her nose.

'You can think what you like,' she said. 'It doesn't make any difference now.'

'It might make a difference,' he said. 'It could.'

She shook her head.

'You're not listening to me, Carol. You used to listen to me.'

'You used to be funny. You're not funny any more.'

He sat back.

'I think I'd better go now,' she said. 'I only get an hour for lunch.'

'Yeah,' he said, 'you'd better go. You'd better go because it takes you longer than most people.'

She took her bag and put it over her shoulder, then she rose to her feet. She stood beside the table, looking at the ground. 'It's not good for me to see you,' she said. 'Don't call me again.' She moved away across the terrace. He wasn't the only person who watched her go. It was the limp. It had definitely got worse.

He pushed back from the table suddenly, his chair shrieking on the tile floor, and she was standing in front of him, naked, her arms weighed down with fish. There were fish lying at her feet, some still twitching, some already dead. She looked different, her face seemed rounder and calmer, but he could tell it was her: her right leg was strapped into a metal contraption. He turned away, he looked at the ocean for a while, and when he turned back again, she had gone.

He returned to his car. He was just opening the door when the phone began to ring. He picked up the receiver. 'Yes?'

'Jed, it's Nathan.'

'What's up?'

'We've got a problem.'

'What is it?'

'Can I meet you somewhere?'

'At the house?'

'No.' Nathan was silent, thinking. 'Where are you?'

'Outside the aquarium.'

'I'll meet you there. Say in about ten minutes.'

'Meet me inside.'

'Where?'

'In front of the sharks.' Jed switched his phone off and put it back on its cradle.

In front of the sharks.

His mouth widened an inch. That was a nice touch, that was.

Nathan saw Jed first.

Jed was staring up into the Deep Reef tank, his face close to the glass. It was a vast tank. A pillar of seaweed and kelp grew in the centre, twenty feet high and encircled, near the top, by fish of such untarnished silver that they might have been made of aluminium.

Sunlight spilled from somewhere above, turning blond then green as it filtered down through the water.

Nathan moved closer. A shark approached. Swayed past. It moved the way some women moved. Almost as if it had hips.

Jed turned. 'Leopard shark,' he said. Then he read from the information panel at the base of the tank. 'Electro-receptors in their snouts help them to home in on buried prey.' His teeth glistened. He seemed to relish this notion of homing in.

The shark passed again, its skin a camouflage of beige and grey, its eye slit, bevelled, like the head of a screw. It was strange how the body seemed to move around the eye: the eye seemed fixed, the body seemed to swivel and rotate.

Nathan suddenly felt as if his throat was swelling. It was dark in the aquarium; the only light was the light shed by the tanks. There were so many people, there was nothing to breathe. His hearing began to swirl.

'Not much air in here,' Jed said, 'is there?'

Nathan took a few steps back. He went and stood in front of another, smaller tank. It contained something called Moon Jelly. He heard a woman's voice. 'Make a pretty lampshade, wouldn't it?' He heard somebody laugh. He was finding air now, close to the glass, a down-draught. He was breathing slowly, cautiously. Soon he felt well enough to return to where Jed was standing. He couldn't watch the sharks, though; the way they moved was a trigger for nausea.

'What's wrong?' Jed said. 'Don't you like sharks?'

'Tell me something,' Nathan said. 'If they'd asked you to do the shark run, would you have done it?' He paused. 'Or would you have chickened out?'

Jed smiled that even, unnerving smile of his. 'I can't swim,' he said. 'Now you tell me something. This problem we've got, what is it?'

'It's my stepmother. Harriet.'

'What about her?'

'She doesn't want any strangers in the house.'

Jed opened his mouth to speak and then closed it again. 'She doesn't want any strangers in the house.' The way he said it, it sounded like a riddle.

'That's it.'

'You want me to leave. Is that what you're trying to say?'

'There's nothing I can do. I'm sorry.'

'What about tonight?'

'I'm sorry.'

Jed turned round. For a while he just looked at Nathan. Then he reached into his pocket and took out a piece of candy and put it in his mouth. Nathan heard the candy shatter between his teeth.

'Like one?' Jed said.

Nathan shook his head.

Jed seemed to lose interest in him. He stood close to the glass, his pale eyes tracking fish.

'Where will you go?' Nathan asked him.

'I don't know,' Jed said. 'Worst comes to the worst, I can always sleep in the car.'

Nathan nodded.

'Can you lend me some money?' Jed said.

'How much?'

A shrug. 'Ten dollars?'

Nathan felt in his pocket, pulled out a few squashed bills. He flattened them out, and counted them. 'I've only got eight,' he said. 'Here.'

Jed took the bills and slid them into his back pocket. They walked to the exit. Jed got into his car and rolled the window down. He leaned his elbow on the window. One hand picked at the side of his neck, the other fitted a key into the ignition. A slow drumroll from the engine. 'See you around,' he said.

'See you, Jed.'

Nathan sat on the pale-blue railings that ran along the promenade and watched the Chrysler pull out into the traffic. Though he felt guilty about throwing Jed out, he also felt a sense of relief. It was pretty ironic to think that he had Harriet to thank for this.

As he shifted his position on the railings he saw a man walking across the grass towards him. The man was wearing a dark suit and a white shirt. A tie that had loosened slightly. Dark glasses. He was late thirties, early forties. Maybe it was his faintness earlier on, but Nathan seemed to be breathing pure oxygen now. He couldn't account for this sudden alertness of his; it seemed to have no origin.

He expected the man to take the steps down to the aquarium, but the man stopped by the railings instead, a few feet away, and stared at the ocean. The man was wearing gloves on his hands. Fawn leather gloves with holes for his hands to breathe through. They must be for driving, Nathan thought. Driving gloves.

The man took a deep breath and then let the air out slowly. 'You know, when my father died, he asked for the words AND SPRING CAME FOR EVER on his gravestone.' He smiled faintly, sadly. 'Maybe

I'm sentimental, but I've always liked the words. They seem to be saying that death's just a beginning. That there's something fresh and new about it.' He breathed in again, filled his lungs. 'Days like today, with spring on the way, I can't help thinking of him.'

A plane slid through the bright air, a finger tracing skin. The same care, the same slow pleasure.

'Do I know you?' Nathan said.

'No.' The man took off his dark glasses. He was smiling. There were traces of amusement, faint embarrassment. 'I saw you from my window.'

'What window?'

'I live up there.' The man pointed at the two towers of baroque grey stone that rose above the palm trees at the end of the promenade.

'The Palace Hotel?' Nathan said.

The man nodded. 'You know it?'

Nathan had to smile. Everybody knew it. It was the most exclusive apartment hotel in the city. 'Do you live there?'

The man glanced at his shoes. 'I saw you from my balcony. I thought I'd come down and speak to you. If you were still here, that is.' He looked up again. 'I thought we could drink a cup of coffee together.'

It was Nathan's turn to look away. 'I don't know.'

'I know what you're thinking,' the man said. 'A complete stranger asking you for coffee. But I meant what I said. A cup of coffee. No strings attached.'

'No strings attached?' Nathan said.

'No strings attached,' the man said, and lifted his gloved hands away from his sides, as if he might've been concealing the strings about his person. 'What's your name?'

'Nathan.'

'My name's Reid.'

Nathan looked at him. 'Strange name. Sounds kind of made up.'

'Does it?' Reid laughed.

They walked to the Ocean Café. They both ordered black coffee and sat facing the marina. Reid leaned back in his chair, right ankle on his left knee, hands folded in his lap. He seemed very calm and sure. The masts of yachts clicked in the wind.

'You don't seem very happy,' Reid said.

'Well, it's strange what you were saying about your father,' Nathan said. 'Mine just died.' He paused and then added, 'Just when I least expected it.'

'Isn't death always unexpected?'

Nathan shook his head. 'You don't understand,' he said, and found himself talking, though he hadn't intended to.

Reid was the first person who hadn't said how sorry he was. They'd moved on, beyond the conventional responses, and Nathan was grateful for that. No, more than grateful: refreshed. He felt Reid's silence stretching under him like a kind of safety net, he felt he could say anything and not be hurt. That was how confession worked, he realised. We're not important to many people. We rarely feel safe. He thought of India-May. She'd listened to him. The only difference was one of gravity: this man seemed more earnest, more concerned. Something struck him suddenly and he stopped in the middle of a sentence. 'You're not a priest, are you?'

'No, I'm not a priest.' Reid smiled. 'But tell me, what is it that I don't understand?'

Nathan began to explain how he'd grown up with the conviction that his father was about to die, that it could happen any moment. Some nights he'd lie in bed and imagine that it had already happened. It was practising. He'd see his father on the ocean bed. His father would be wearing the same cardigan he always wore, the one with holes in the elbows. His hair would be standing up on end. There'd be fish swimming in and out of his clothes.

Some nights they'd have conversations.

'Dad?' he'd whisper.

And Dad would whisper back, 'Yes. I'm here.' His voice sounded the same, even though he was underwater.

'Can I come and visit you?'

There'd be a silence, and there'd be something sad about the silence, and then Dad would whisper, 'No, I don't think so.'

'Why not? We could just sit and drink a beer together and then I could rub your back. Does your back still ache?'

Another silence. Longer, sadder, then the last. 'It's better you don't, Nathan.'

'Just a beer, Dad. Just one.'

'I'm sorry.'

When Nathan thought about it now, it seemed to him that he'd been practising for his own death, as well as for Dad's. If Dad had really been dead, and Nathan had gone and had a beer with him under the sea, it would've meant that Nathan would've died too. That was why Dad had to say no.

'Does that make any sense?' Nathan looked at the man on the other side of the table, the man who wasn't a priest but listened like one, the man with the gloves.

Reid tasted his coffee. 'Yes,' he said, 'it makes sense.'

'It wasn't always sad,' Nathan said. 'Sometimes he'd produce a fish from his breast pocket like a magician. Or he'd do a trick with beer. Tip the glass upside down and nothing would come out. Other times he'd crack a joke. "The air's much better down here." Things like that.' Nathan smiled. 'In the mornings I'd always be surprised to see him sitting at the breakfast table with his hair all flat and not a fish in sight. He used to wonder why I was staring at him. I couldn't tell him, of course.' He looked up and his vision blurred. 'Now he's really there I can't imagine it at all,' he said. 'Isn't that funny?'

Reid leaned forwards. 'If you need any help,' he said, 'any money.'

Nathan shook his head.

He let Reid pay the bill. They rose from their chairs.

'Can I drop you somewhere?' Reid said. 'My car's just over there.'

'I've got a car too,' Nathan said.

'Oh yes.' Reid smiled. 'I forgot.'

They stood for a moment, looking in different directions.

'I'd like it if we could see each other again,' Reid said.

'Maybe.'

'There's a bar called Necropolis.'

Nathan nodded. 'I've heard of it.'

'I'll be there on Wednesday night.' Reid smiled again and walked away across the grass.

Wednesday night, Nathan thought.

What was today? Monday?

THE OCTOPUS MANOEUVRE

It was no skin off his nose, being thrown out like that. After all, it wasn't exactly the first time. He didn't even need the $10 he'd asked for. He'd just asked for it on the spur of the moment, to see what he could get away with, to make Nathan feel guilty. And Nathan had given him all he had. Jed took his eyes off the road and glanced down at the crumpled money in his hand. $8. He tossed it over his shoulder into the back of the car. He didn't need $8. He thought of the money he'd thrown in Creed's face. He thought of Mario's wheelchair stuffed with bills. $8. His laughter hammered at the roof like fists.

In half an hour he was in Rialto. He steered his car into the narrow, unpaved alley that ran behind Mitch's place. The rumble of the engine seemed louder between these two high walls; the tyres munched on loose dirt and gravel. He parked up against Mitch's garage. He switched the engine off and opened the door. Nothing moved in the alley. A tree reached its dusty branches over the red-brick wall opposite, as if it had died trying to climb out. Such heat. The sky was almost white. Telegraph poles wavered in the air like ribbon.

He walked up to Mitch's back door and knocked twice. Some blue paint flaked away under his knuckles. The door opened inwards and Mitch stood in the gap. He had a can of beer in his hand.

'Surprise, surprise,' Jed said.

Mitch stared at him. He was wearing the same clothes he always wore: the faded tartan shirt, the jeans that hung off his buttocks. 'Christ,' he said. 'The ice-cream man.'

'I've been trying to get hold of you,' Jed said.

'I've been busy.' Mitch turned round, shambled back up the passage. 'Want a beer?' he called out, over his shoulder.

Jed followed him into the house.

They sat on two wooden chairs on the back verandah, their feet propped on the railing. Jed cracked his can open, tipped some beer down his throat and sighed. Mitch's back yard was small. It didn't see much sun. Just shadow and cracked concrete and truck tyres stacked against the wall. The fig tree had dropped its fruit all over the ground. Ripe figs lay in the dust, exploded, bloody, as if the sky had rained organs.

Mitch looked at him. 'When did you get back?'

'Few days ago.'

'You staying long?'

'I don't know. Depends how long it takes.'

Mitch was still looking at him. 'I hope you know what you're doing.'

Jed drank from his can instead of answering. Sure he knew.

'Because it seems to me,' Mitch went on, 'that you've lost touch.'

Jed rested his can on his belly and scratched his ribs with his free hand. 'What are you talking about, Mitch?'

'I'm talking about maybe you've forgotten how this city works.'

'I know how this city works. I was born here.'

'I said maybe you forgot. You've been living out in the middle of nowhere selling ice-cream, for Christ's sake.' Mitch took a deep breath, let it out again. 'When did you get back?'

'I told you. A few days ago.'

'How many?'

'Four.'

'Four days.' Mitch nodded to himself. 'They'll know you're back by now.'

Jed's body seemed to freeze up. He stared into Mitch's face and only his heart was moving. 'What do you know about it?'

'Don't look at me like that,' Mitch said. 'You know what they're like. They've got eyes in the back of their heads. You've been here four days and you've been walking round in that fucking hat and you think they haven't noticed.' He crumpled his can and threw it in the yard. 'Shit. You want another beer?'

'Sure.'

While Mitch was indoors, Jed thought back.

His first night. Thousands of tourists in town for the celebrations, the streets jumping with firecrackers, blue suits, the dance of death. Chaos: surely that was the best disguise there was.

Then three nights in Blenheim. There was nothing to connect him to that section of the city. Nathan was from the deep past. They were linked by the finest thread. Go back fifteen years and walk into a field and turn over the right square-inch of ground. It was that fine. No chance.

He'd talked, sure he'd talked, but he hadn't given anything away, not really. He hadn't told anyone his name, though he'd been tempted to. The more people who knew it, the less power it had. He'd remembered that. Ideally nobody should know. And, at the moment, nobody did.

He thought of Sharon and the pouch of soft leather she used to wear on a string around her neck. He'd asked her what it was for. He remembered how her eyes widened with suspicion and her hand moved instinctively to her neck. She wouldn't tell him. He used the kind of arguments that other people used. Blackmail in its most trivial and vulgar form.

'You're holding out on me,' he said once.

'It's like there's something between us,' he said some other time.

He kept on and on at her, and in the end, of course, she succumbed. She called it her magic bag, she said. She claimed it protected her. She made the mistake of telling him that nobody, *nobody*, had ever looked inside.

One night they were lying in bed. It was late, they were drowsy, it was after love. Light came from somewhere, blue neon light, the washeteria across the street? It switched parts of their bodies on and off.

'That bag you've got,' he said, 'it's shit.'

She rose out of the bed, the sheet clutched against her chest. 'What did you say?'

'I looked in that bag of yours when you were asleep. A few fish bones and some dust. What's that going to do?' He chuckled, leaned up on one elbow.

One of her breasts pushed past the sheet, the nipple wide and glossy, the blue light teased him with glimpses, he felt a shifting against the inside of his thigh, he wanted to take that nipple between his teeth, to run his lips across the soft, slack skin of her belly, to put his tongue between her legs and watch her eyes roll back, he'd lost all contact with what he'd said, the blue light, her body, now you see it, now you don't, so when her fist sent flame through his head, it was as if she'd struck a match, it was suddenly too bright, then, just as suddenly, dark again, and he was on the floor, the force of the blow had lifted him right off the bed, tumbled him across the room.

She leaned over him, her breath stale with grass and cheap white wine. 'I could kill you.'

He opened one hand, a feeble appeal. 'A few fish bones,' he muttered.

The breath gushed out of her. She wrenched at the bag. The string bit into her skin, drew sudden blood. She heaved the window open, flung the bag into the street below.

He understood it now, that rage of hers. He should have understood it then. When your magic was stolen from you, it left you open and alone, you were skin against knives and knives against stone. It blew air into the lungs of your nightmares so they grew tall and straight and walked through the dawn with you and on into the day. There was nothing between you and all the bad things. Maybe, in a way, he'd known what he was doing. Maybe he'd been trying to tell her something, trying to teach her a lesson. You can't wear your magic on the outside. That's just asking for it. You've got to keep it somewhere deep down and secret. He knew because it had happened to him. The radios. All those years ago, but still. He had new magic now – a name, that drop of rain, some bruises – and he wore it out of sight, under his skin, inside his head. It was safer there. Nobody could take it away from him because nobody could see it, nobody knew it was there.

Mitch came back with two beers. 'You been thinking about what I said?' He stood against the light, one hand tucked into the back of his jeans, feet spread wide on the warped boards of the verandah.

'Yeah.' Jed opened the can, swallowed a mouthful. The chill slid into him and spread.

But he was still thinking about the night Sharon threw her magic bag out of the window. They couldn't have been in her apartment in Baker Park, he was thinking. There was a washeteria across the street from the apartment, but it didn't have a neon sign. It had never had one. He thought hard. There had been storm-force winds that night. He could remember Sharon crouching on the bed. The building was swaying, she said. She had vertigo.

He swallowed another mouthful of beer. He had it now. That blue light wasn't the washeteria. It was a strobe-light in the East Tower. The light wasn't usually there, but there'd been a party going on that night.

It wasn't Baker Park. It was the Towers of Remembrance. *The Towers of Remembrance.*

When he left that place on the thirteenth floor he'd given it to Tip's brother, Silence. He wondered if Silence was still living there. Silence. The youngest member of the Womb Boys. A deaf mute.

He was grinning now. It was so obvious. Why hadn't he thought of it before?

He looked up and saw that Mitch had been watching him. 'I've got one piece of advice for you,' Mitch said.

Jed took the grin off his face. 'I'm listening.'

'Leave town.'

'You know I can't do that.'

'Well,' Mitch said, 'don't say I didn't warn you.'

Instead of driving south from Mitch's place, towards the Towers, Jed drove west, into the setting sun. He might have been followed to Mitch's and, if that was the case, then the trail had to end, and end suddenly.

As he drove he remembered the video he'd watched while he was waiting for Nathan in the aquarium. It was about an octopus that could take on the precise colour and texture of its surroundings. It could also move between its various disguises with extraordinary speed and guile. There was one sequence in the video when the camera found the octopus lodged in a bed of weeds. The octopus was almost invisible; its body had turned a dark-green, its tentacles drifted, blending with the strands of plant life. But as soon as it sensed the presence of the camera it reacted. One twitch and it was hurtling along the ocean bed. It seemed almost jet-propelled. Abrupt changes of direction. Sudden clouds of ink. Then it vanished. When the camera found it again, it was fifty yards away, masquerading as a piece of rock. This was pretty much the kind of manoeuvre that Jed had in mind.

He drove at a steady thirty-five; if anyone was following him, he would lull them into a false sense of security. When he reached Highway 1 he turned north. It was rush-hour. The air was fogged and glittery with exhaust. As he passed the Butterfield turn-off, the traffic slowed to a standstill and, just for a moment, Jed felt alone; just for a moment he wished that he too was leaving work after a hard day, that he too was heading for a cocktail and dinner in some comfortable house in the northern suburbs.

Then, as the traffic picked up speed and distances began to open between the cars, the sign appeared. Not green like the highway signs, but black and white. Discreet. Innocuous. STATE ABATTOIRS 1 MILE. Jed stamped on the gas and cut into the exit lane, his speed close to fifty now. This was the moment of acceleration, this was the cloud of ink. Down off the highway, round in a circle, under an overpass, and then he was slamming down the narrow road that led to the abattoirs: fifty, sixty, sixty-five. The mirror was empty. Two clangs as he cleared the metal cattle grilles. He swung left into an alley. Pipes coiled overhead, white steam gushed from vents. A sweet smell like beaten egg. A smell that sweetened and decayed. He saw row after row of animal hides slung over rails in an open barn.

The alley fed into a concrete yard. His wheel slithered on mud and straw. This must be where the animals were unloaded. He took a wood ramp that led down past a slaughterhouse and sent his car twisting and rocking along a dirt track. The buildings were behind him now. There were ditches on either side and stands of yellow weeds. Ahead of him, through the windshield, he could see a thin blue strip, a forgotten piece of the harbour. He gunned the car up a steep bank and on to a disused railway. His tyres crackled on chips of stone. In front of him was an old iron swing-bridge. A sign whispered DANGER in small red letters. The sign amused him. Danger was relative.

Not many people knew about the railway. If you didn't know, and you consulted a map of the city, you could be forgiven for thinking that the line was still being used. On the map, the abattoirs looked like a dead end. To anyone following him, this detour of his would seem like a serious mistake – the result, possibly, of panic. That was the beauty of the manoeuvre. By the time they realised that the mistake was theirs, it would be too late.

He drove slowly over the bridge, the metal wincing under the weight of the car. Then down off the bridge, over wasteland, through the switchback streets of Venus. Down again, into the darkness of the harbour tunnel. In twenty minutes the Towers of Remembrance rose in his windshield. He checked his mirror. Still empty. He was seaweed in seaweed, rock on rock. They'd never find him now.

THE SUIT OF BONES

Nathan heard the stairs creak, the front door slam. He reached the window in time to see Harriet climb into her car. She was wearing a dark coat, the same coat she wore to the funeral. Her face showed nothing. A sealed envelope. Her scarlet lips set hard, like wax.

It was Wednesday morning. He sat at the kitchen table drinking coffee. Tell me something. Do you like this city? Her threats stood around in his head like jailers with bunches of keys. I could make things difficult. The day before he'd asked Dad's lawyer if it was possible to speed up the handling of the probate. Dad's lawyer had given him a glance that barely cleared the rims of his spectacles. 'There are very good reasons,' he said, 'why the law moves as slowly as it does.' The fan turning on its long neck. The wall the colour of soiled shirt collars.

Nathan lifted his eyes from the table. Clouds gathered above the hills and the garden darkened. He saw the rain come swirling out of the sky. He watched the drops crawl down the window. Another six weeks, the lawyer had said. Minimum.

Morning tipped over into afternoon and still he'd done nothing. He moved to the lounge and stood with the french windows open and listened to the rain on the surface of the pool. He remembered days like this when he was young. They used to sit at the kitchen table and paint on sheets of shiny brown paper. Though he tried to paint blue skies, they always came out muddy. When he complained, Dad said, 'Look at George, it doesn't bother her.' Of course it didn't bother her. She never put any sky in her pictures, did she? She just left big patches of brown everywhere. If you asked her what the patches were, she'd say, It's brown things. Brown things? It's earth, she'd say. It's a table. I don't know. It's dogs. She would always have an answer. She could always find a way round things.

He closed the french windows and turned back into the room. There was something he'd been meaning to do and he should do it now, while he was alone, with no excuses. He climbed the stairs and walked into the bedroom that had once been Dad's and was now his. He took a key out of the bedside-table drawer and unlocked the closet. Inside were two rows of clothes. Old suits, mostly. Blazers, coats. Frayed at the cuffs and buttons gone. Epaulettes of dust. This part would be all right, he realised. If Dad had worn these clothes at all, he'd worn them before Nathan's memory began; they preceded him and wouldn't hurt. He emptied the closet of everything except the wire hangers and the sheets of Christmas paper. All he kept back were two suits and a jacket. The suits were for him. The jacket was for Georgia. He thought she might like it. It was brown.

The airing cupboard next. Here were the familiar parts of Dad's wardrobe. Here, for instance, was the blue cardigan. Nathan lifted it out and touched it to his nose. It smelt so clean and warm, of talcum and vanilla, of his father. This was the cardigan Dad used to wear in bed. This was the cardigan he'd worn when he drank beer on the bottom of the sea. His face buried in the blue wool, Nathan thought of the nights he'd rubbed Dad's back for him, that peculiar blend of smells, skin and eucalyptus oil, he could hear Dad's voice rising drowsy from the pillows: 'A bit further down, a bit further, yes, that's it, that's perfect.'

He looked at the clothes arranged in such neat piles in the cupboard, then he looked down at the clothes already packed into boxes at his feet, already creased and growing cold. He had to look away, through air that seemed warped. He folded the blue cardigan, put it back in the cupboard. He put the heels of his hands in his eyes and pressed. The rest of the clothes he sorted briskly, mechanically, as if they belonged to a stranger. He left no room for thoughts to start.

When the airing cupboard was empty, he dragged the boxes to the top of the stairs. He looked out of the landing window. Brown-paper skies and big silver raindrops sliding down the telegraph wires. No view of the harbour or the city, no sense of the time of day.

He reversed the car out of the garage and round to the front door, then he carried the boxes down the stairs and out to the porch, and loaded them into the trunk. At the gate he had to brake and wait for a car to pass. It was then that he noticed the man standing outside their house. The man was wearing a grey suit and holding a large black umbrella. Something told Nathan that the man had been standing there for quite a while. He couldn't be sure, the rain was falling harder now, jumping back off the sidewalk, it was like looking through smoke, but he thought he recognised the man. In that same moment the man realised that Nathan had seen him. One of his shoulders twitched. He spun round and hurried away. It must be someone who's heard about the death, Nathan thought. Another coffin chaser.

In ten minutes he was parking outside the local charity store. A sign hung in the window: CLOSED. He took his hands off the wheel, leaned his head back against the seat. He hadn't expected this. It was more than dismay that he felt now. It was some slow disintegration; he felt as if he was gradually being crushed in someone's fist. He couldn't face taking the clothes back home again. He'd have to leave them on the doorstep and hope they were still there in the morning. He hated doing it, but he could think of no alternative.

He stacked the boxes against the door in two piles and ran back to the car. He sent swift glances left and right. Nobody had seen him. The rain was still coming down and the streets were empty.

Back inside the car he couldn't move. He couldn't even turn the key in the ignition. He could picture the clothes inside the boxes: how they were slowly losing their warmth, how they were slowly growing cold. Somehow it was worse than seeing Dad in that chapel. It was worse than seeing him dead. He reached up, touched his face. It was wet. He couldn't tell where the rain ended and his tears began.

He didn't know what to do next. A drink, maybe. Wasn't that what people did? He drove south through Blenheim. The main street widened into highway; water jolted in the harbour, the masts of boats duelled against a low grey sky. When the arrow showed overhead, left lane for HARBOUR BRIDGE and DOWNTOWN, he thought of Georgia and took it. On the city side he dipped into the shadow of the bridge and stopped outside the first bar he saw. He walked to the back and found a phone. He dialled Georgia's number, waited. The window next to the phone was open. Some gutter must've snapped and rain was splashing down into the dark yard. It sounded like a massage parlour. Hands on fat.

Georgia wasn't answering. He walked back through the bar. He wanted a drink, but not here. In the car he remembered the man on the promenade. What was his name? Reid. He looked at his watch. It was just after six. He could drive to Necropolis and have a drink. If Reid turned up, then he'd have someone to talk to. If Reid didn't turn up, he could try Georgia again.

Necropolis was a blood-and-sawdust bar on the waterfront. High ceiling, low lights. Tables the shape of tombstones. Famous names cut into the marble. Nathan ordered brandy, a large one. He sat on a stool and looked around. Always a real mix in here, everything from whores to millionaires, but no sign of Reid. In a way, he was glad.

He'd wanted the advantage of arriving first. This time, perhaps, he could do some watching of his own. Those few seconds before someone sees you, they can give you leverage, they can let you into secrets.

He was halfway through his third drink when the door opened and Reid walked in. There was a glimmer of gold as, pausing just inside the doorway, he placed a cigarette in his mouth and lit it. It would have been hard to mistake him for a priest again, and yet he had this presence, he shone around the edges, it was as if he'd been standing at God's right hand on high and some of that power and glory had rubbed off. When he walked towards the bar he seemed to occupy the air above his head, you might almost have said that he owned it. He passed close to Nathan, brushing Nathan's left thigh with the tail of his jacket. He ordered bourbon on the rocks. Then, on second thoughts, a double bourbon, no ice. He skimmed a hand across his short black hair. He was still wearing those gloves of his. Nathan felt a slow fizzing begin inside him, as if he'd swallowed sherbet: an effervescence.

'I didn't frighten you off then.'

Nathan finished his drink. 'Did you think you might?'

Reid ordered him another. There are people who know exactly what you want, and when. There are also people who time their evasions perfectly.

'You must've used binoculars,' Nathan said. Then, when Reid didn't seem to understand, he said, 'To see me from your window.'

Reid smiled.

'Do you make a habit of watching people like that?'

'Habit? No.' But the word prolonged Reid's amusement. 'Sometimes there's distance, that's all,' he said. 'Sometimes that's as close as you can get.'

'Not much distance any more.'

Reid was still looking at Nathan, still amused. He lifted his glass to his lips and drank. He set his glass down again. 'Why did you come?'

Nathan shrugged and looked away. 'I don't know. I haven't been here for ages.' He looked at Reid again. 'I suppose I felt like a drink.'

'What else did you feel like?'

Nathan smiled to himself. He didn't need to answer that. It wasn't the kind of question you answered.

'I mean, do,' Reid said. 'Do you feel like.'

Nathan's smile lasted, but he was thinking now. This was a risk he was taking. Out on a limb and what if it was amputated? The future? It could be reward, it could be punishment. He no longer knew what he deserved.

Afterwards he couldn't remember how Reid achieved it – a jerk of the head? a gloved hand on his forearm? – but suddenly they were leaving together. Outside the bar the night felt padded. Air so rich and dark, you could've cut it into slices like a cake. He felt his veins swell. A limousine slid past. The lick of tyres. Through open windows came staccato laughter, music, smoke.

He was steered towards a low car. Black or blue, he couldn't tell. It looked fast. It could split the air in two.

'Get in.'

He obeyed. The perfume of new leather. And, faintly, cigarettes. Reid lit one, switched the engine on. The car hissed like a jet. Turbo. Money. Death.

They were heading west on Paradise Drive. They took the long curve inland at the Delta, the knitting-needle click as the gear stick shifted in its metal gate, the engine spitting, fighting the drop in speed. They approached the Palace Hotel from the rear, dipped down a ramp, it was like being swallowed by an open throat, they were underground.

They crossed the parking-lot, footsteps echoing on concrete. They reached an elevator. Reid turned a key in a silver panel. The doors slid open.

'My back door,' he explained.

Once inside, he pressed 14. They didn't talk in the elevator. Nathan tried to see his reflection in the scratched stainless steel of the walls. All he could see was a blur. The doors lurched open on the fourteenth floor and Reid stepped out. Nathan followed. He stopped just outside, looked round.

Such quiet corridors. The carpet was a burgundy red, interrupted every ten feet or so by a black oval containing the letters P H in ornate red script. All the doors were black. Glass globes fizzed overhead, leaking a low-voltage yellow glow. In the distance, the word EXIT in weak red neon. He'd always wondered what the inside of the Palace looked like, but something seemed held back: it was as if, in the act of revealing itself, it had become still more mysterious.

'Is something wrong?'

Nathan had almost forgotten he wasn't alone. He turned, saw Reid standing ten yards away, one hand fitted casually into his jacket pocket, a man in a clothing catalogue. 'No,' and he smiled, 'nothing's wrong.'

It was a long walk to Reid's apartment. Every time they turned a corner they were faced with the same view, the same silence; each new length of corridor was like an echo of the last. They stopped outside apartment 1412. He waited as Reid unlocked the door. Inside, the air smelt warm, slightly acrid, a smell that was like new dollar bills. Lamps bloomed in the corners, showed him the room. Sofas of dark velvet and walls papered to resemble marble and mirrors with no frames. There were windows on two sides. One looked down on the promenade: car headlamps, lights looping through the palms, a white line where the waves broke. The other faced west: the harbour bridge spanning the narrow stretch of water that separated the western suburbs from the city; a golden clasp on a head of smooth black hair.

'Some champagne?'

Nathan took the offered glass. 'Thanks.' He moved back to the centre of the room. It seemed to contain nothing that was personal. No books, no pictures, no flowers. It was an expensive hotel suite, somewhere you passed through, somewhere you never actually changed or even touched. It went with the gloves. This man leaves no trace of himself behind, he thought, not even fingerprints. If he was a criminal, he'd never be caught.

Reid leaned over and placed a white capsule beside Nathan's champagne glass. 'That's for you.'

'What is it?' Nathan asked.

'It'll make you feel good.'

Nathan hesitated.

'What's the matter?' Reid said. 'Don't you trust me?'

Nathan smiled. 'I don't know you. Why should I trust you?'

'You're here. You might as well.' Reid leaned forwards, opened his capsule and tipped the contents into his champagne. He raised his glass to Nathan and drank the champagne down. He poured a little more champagne into his glass, swirled it round. He drank that too.

Nathan nodded. 'You're right.' He did exactly what Reid had done. 'Where's the bathroom?'

Reid showed him.

When he switched the light on, it multiplied. There were mirrors everywhere. He could see himself from every side at once. If he stood in a certain position he could see clones of himself vanishing into misty green infinity. He felt an excitement building in him now. He'd been in this situation before, in the water. Sometimes you got taken by a current, a rip that ran at an angle to the beach. You didn't fight the current, you went with it. You went with it, waited for a wave and then, when the wave came, you took it. You rode that wave right out. Out of the current, back to the shore. He'd done this kind of thing before. He could relax.

When he walked back into the room he was smiling. Reid was smiling too, his head resting against the back of the sofa, his face almost parallel with the ceiling. Smiling with lips that even now, somehow, Nathan knew he'd kiss. He sat down. The champagne had risen in his glass. He drank some.

'You all right?' Reid asked him.

Nathan sat down. 'I'm better than all right.'

'Is there anything you want to know?'

It was a strange question. Nathan couldn't think. He looked at the man on the sofa instead. His hair, his tie, his smile, his suit, his gloves. 'Those gloves,' he said. 'Are you trying to hide something?'

'Not hide,' Reid said, 'protect.'

'Protect?'

Reid rose to his feet, moved towards the drinks cabinet. 'I'm a hand model. I have to protect my hands. And also,' and he smiled, 'I like the way things feel when they're on.'

'Things?'

'Yes,' Reid said, 'things.'

He opened another bottle of champagne and brought it to the table. 'You've probably seen my hands a hundred times without even knowing it. Holding an electric razor, lighting a cigarette, slipping a diamond ring on to a woman's finger.' His smile widened. 'Nobody sees my hands,' he said, 'except the general public.'

Nathan was about to return the smile when something happened to the wall. It bulged as if it was only paper-thin and there was a great weight of water behind it. Or not water, maybe, but a heart. Because the wall was moving in and out. Some kind of massive heart sluggishly beating. Then darkness poured inwards from the corners of the room, until only he was lit, nothing else. 'It's dark,' he said, 'it's getting dark.'

'Don't worry,' came a voice, 'it'll soon be light again.'

And instantly the darkness began to lift. He could see the sofa again, his glass on the table, the man across the room. It was as if the voice had worked a miracle.

'That was really strange,' he said.

'What was?'

'The way you said that, and then it happened. That's what I do when I save lives. Someone's drowning and I swim out to them and

I say, "Don't worry, I'm here, you might drink a bit of water, but you're going to be all right." That's sort of what you just did to me.'

'I'm surprised the parlours haven't made that illegal,' Reid said.

'What, lifesaving?'

Reid smiled. 'It's not exactly in their interests, is it?'

'That's one way of looking at it,' Nathan said.

'The last time I saw you down there, on the beach,' Reid said, 'you were with a guy in a top hat.'

Nathan laughed. 'Oh, that's Jed.'

'Kind of strange-looking.'

'Yeah.' Nathan had a sudden vision of Jed driving over the bridge at night. A dark-purple car, its pale driver wearing a top hat and a radiator smile, its back seat heaped with dead skin.

'He a friend of yours?'

'No, not exactly. I knew him years ago, when I was about twelve. I didn't see him again till last week. Ran into him in a bar on Second Avenue.'

'Small world.'

'He acted so weird that night. He kept saying he'd got plans.'

'To do what?'

Nathan shrugged. 'He's after someone's blood or something. He came out with all kinds of stuff. Seemed like most of it was bullshit.'

'He sounds like a pretty desperate character.'

'You should've heard him. He stayed over last weekend. Told some big story about how he'd killed someone. He had this tattoo on his wrist. Said it was the date he did it. The hand he did it with.'

'He's not still staying, I hope?'

Nathan smiled at Reid's concern. 'No. We threw him out. Same day I met you. I expect he'll be in touch, though. He owes me eight dollars.'

'Maybe he won't be in touch,' Reid said.

Nathan grinned. 'Maybe you're right.'

'It's strange,' Reid said, 'some people just fasten on and you don't feel a thing.'

Nathan leaned forwards, reaching for his drink. That feeling had returned. His head moving much slower than his body. He sat back again, without his drink. He felt dizzy, as if he'd stood up too suddenly. It was just another rush, he told himself. It would pass. He stared at the sofa. It was some dark colour, there were no patterns, it couldn't play any tricks on him.

'You know something else I noticed when I looked through the binoculars?' came Reid's voice.

He couldn't look. He could manage only one word. 'No.'

'I noticed how beautiful you were – '

He could look away from the sofa now, back into the room. The blood was sprinting through his veins, it was like a relay race, he saw a runner kick off a curve, hand the baton to another runner, who kicked again, a relay race all round the tight circuit of his blood.

'Your body – '

The room ballooned away from him, the walls were sails filled with wind.

' – and your face – '

His skin beneath his clothes, so comfortable. And Reid standing over him. Hair like a cloud. Dark like a storm coming. The ceiling above him concave, domed, and one gloved hand reaching down.

And down again, on to a bed. He lay back, passive. Cool sheets under him. A gloved hand moved to his fly, he felt the metal button give, he heard the rasp as the zipper threads split open. He held his breath. Felt his cock lift and the caress of leather. And then, almost as if he had passed out, maybe he had, he was naked. He shut his eyes and listened to the passage of those gloves across his skin. It was so hot. He looked down. The gloves, their palms were dark, it must be the sweat from his body. He whispered it, and Reid said he'd never noticed that before; he liked it. Nathan lay back again, saw an open window with a surf beach beyond, it was somewhere that he'd been, it was the same sound. He saw the tops of trees hurled by the wind and didn't remember this. And now Reid's mouth closed over him, a tightness, slow and tight. A flickering, like leaves, on the soles of his feet.

Reid rolled him gently over, on to his belly, and he felt Reid slide between his buttocks.

He lifted his head, said, 'No,' and then louder, 'No.'

Reid murmured something.

He turned on to his side, moved down the bed. He thought he heard music somewhere, asked what it was, but Reid said it was nothing. He took Reid between his fingers, between his lips, he did what he liked people doing to him. It was so strange being on the other side of things, he'd forgotten the salty taste of it, the power of those final moments just before it came, when the muscles arched and sang, the lick and snap of railway tracks when a train's approaching.

Then only the darkness pressing against his ears and the pumping of his heart.

Later he woke, it was still dark, he saw his dreams. His dreams were red and gold. He lay without moving, almost without breathing. The milky oblong of a window. And light from the window catching something that was hanging on the door. A silk gown, a kind of kimono. A vulture embroidered on the back. Feathers of metal, breath flaring from its open beak, breath that was red like fire or blood. Eyes like stones in the white bowls of their sockets, dead grey stones. He lay without moving, almost without breathing.

This was the wave he had to take. This wave.

He slid out of bed and tiptoed to the window. He stared out at the black uneven trees and the dark grey sky. Was that the ocean, between the two, a shiver of silver, the blade of a knife seen sideways on?

It must be. Hundreds of miles of darkness and one pale strip where the moonlight fell. He turned back into the room, felt around the bed for his clothes. Reid's breathing surfaced, sank again. He had to be so quiet. Or Reid would wake. Or the vulture would come screeching off the back of that kimono. Red Indian feet. Now more than ever. Now.

He couldn't find his socks. His feet still bare, his arms stretched in front of him, he felt his way through the apartment. It was bigger than he remembered, but then he didn't really remember, did he? Or maybe it just seemed put together in a different way. Like a puzzle there are two answers to.

He got the wrong door. Thought it was the front door, but it wasn't. A cupboard. With a skeleton hanging inside. No head, just all the bones from a body. Sewn on to black fabric. A suit of bones. His heart slammed against his ribs, it seemed for a moment they might crack. He closed the cupboard, pretended he'd seen nothing. He found the front door. This time he knew he was right because of the locks. There were four different locks and it was minutes before he could align them correctly. Each time he turned a knob, it clicked and, sooner or later, he felt sure, one of these clicks would reach the bedroom. That kind priest's voice behind him. That gentle hand on his shoulder. He didn't know why he was frightened. Yes, he did. That kimono, that suit of bones. Why? They were the first personal things he'd seen, that was why. The first things he'd seen that belonged to Reid. A vulture and a suit of bones.

He saw himself in a mirror outside the elevator. His hair in his eyes, his shirt ripped. He looked as if he'd been attacked. The night porter was dozing. He crept past on bare feet, his shoes in his hand. One last wisp of steam drifted up from the cooling cup of coffee at the porter's elbow. The clock behind his head said ten to five.

He walked down to the promenade and caught a cab at the all-night taxi-stand outside Belgrano's. The driver wore a cap and a leather jacket. He wanted to talk. He tried a couple of subjects, but Nathan didn't say much. He eyed Nathan once or twice in the mirror.

'You've been fucking,' the driver said, 'haven't you?'

Nathan turned and looked at him. 'What?'

'You heard me. Listen, I've been driving cabs for twenty-four years. I know who's been fucking and who hasn't. Know how I know?'

'How do you know?'

'It's five in the fucking morning, that's how I know. Right? And another thing. You've got the look of fucking about you. You've got that look people have when they've been fucking, know what I mean?'

Nathan smiled faintly.

'She all right, was she?' The driver was rubbing his lips. 'She nice?'

'Yeah,' Nathan said, 'she was great.'

ALL WINS ON LIT
LINES ONLY

The Towers of Remembrance dated from a time when many of the city's graveyards were full. A time of panic: suddenly there was nowhere for the dead to go. And then somebody said, 'Let people be buried high above the ground, not six feet under it; let people be buried closer to heaven.' It seemed like the perfect solution. The first high-rise cemetery in history. Original, dramatic, space-conscious. And also, unfortunately, doomed.

There had been a sudden reaction against the whole notion of burial on land. It was unhealthy, people said. It slowed the natural decay of the body. Hindered the soul's transition. Sins collected, fouled the earth. Result? Psychic unrest, evil spirits, disease. And so, after an initial rush of enthusiasm, the Towers were left to rot. Windows were smashed. Graffiti blossomed. Ever since Jed could remember, the place had been a sanctuary for runaways, vultures, junkies. A lost generation. Not gone, but forgotten. He climbed out of his car and locked the door. The South Tower had been his home for three years. His own ghosts were here, among all the others.

It was almost dark now. A wind blew off the ocean. It was a warm wind, but the sound it made as it lunged down the concrete corridors was cold. He stepped into the central plaza. Something landed on the ground next to his left foot. A white frothy medal of spit. He looked up. Two children peered at him from the walkway twenty feet above. A boy with a crewcut and puffy eyes and a girl with heart-shaped sunglasses and white-blonde hair. Project kids.

'Hey, mister,' the girl called down, 'why are you wearing that stupid hat?'

The boy grinned. 'So we can't spit on his stupid head.'

Their screechy laughter broke up in a sudden gust of wind.

Jed walked on.

He reached the foot of the South Tower. Steel doors slouched on their hinges, windows were holes with glass teeth round the edge. In the hallway the walls had been sprayed with the usual tangle of graffiti. The elevator was jammed open. He punched the button a couple of times, but nothing happened. He looked inside. Rectangular, for the coffins. A red smear on the dull metal wall. It could've been paint or blood. Blood, most likely: this was Mangrove East. He stepped back. Above the elevator was a notice: PLEASE SHOW RESPECT FOR THE DEAD. Bit late for that. He took a breath and started up the stairs.

By the time he reached the thirteenth floor he was winded. He leaned against the door until his heart slowed down, then he knocked. He waited, knocked again. At last he heard footsteps, the shooting of bolts. A woman's face appeared. She wore her hair tied back in a ponytail. A baby sat in the crook of her arm. Jed just stared.

'It's a baby,' the woman said.

Now Jed stared at her. 'I'm looking for Silence.'

The woman jerked her head. 'Come on in.'

He brushed past her. Stood in the corridor while she fastened an assortment of locks and bolts.

'Not a very high-class neighbourhood,' she said.

'I know,' he said. 'I used to live here.'

She pushed past him. He followed her down the corridor. Boxes stacked against one wall, almost to the ceiling. He turned his head sideways, read a label. Videos. There must've been fifty of them. All the same make. Silence the fence.

He passed through an archway and into what had once been the memory room. This was where the ashes would've rested. This was where the family would've gathered to pay their respects. Silence rose from a deep leather chair. He was wearing a bright rust-coloured suit with a pale-blue pinstripe. Ten years didn't seem to have aged him at all. He had the same round cheeks, the same slit eyes.

'Like the suit,' Jed said.

Silence smiled. They shook hands. Silence pointed at the sofa. They both sat down again, Jed on the sofa, Silence in his leather chair. Silence was watching a programme on TV.

Jed looked around. Silence had knocked through into the next grave suite, by the look of it, and turned the extra space into a kitchen and bathroom. He'd installed a cooker, fuelled by gas cylinders, and a hot-water heater. The electricity was being supplied by a portable generator. A bit of a change from the old days of fast-food and candlelight.

He touched Silence on the arm. 'Real nice job you've done.'

Silence accepted the compliment with another smile and a slight bow.

Jed turned to the woman. 'You live here too?'

'No,' she said, 'we're just visiting.' She opened the glass door to the balcony. It faced due north, towards the airport. 'Bob likes it here,' she said. 'He sits here for hours drinking his milk and watching the planes.'

Jed stared at the baby again. It looked like a tortoise.

Silence tapped him on the arm and handed him a business card. On the blank side Silence had written something in block capitals: IT'S BEEN A LONG TIME.

'No kidding,' Jed said.

He held the card out for Silence to take, but Silence made a tearing gesture with his hands and pointed at the bin. Jed tore the card in two and dropped the pieces in the bin. He noticed that the bin was half full of identical business cards that had been torn in a similar way.

'This all the things you say?' Jed asked.

Silence nodded.

'How long since you emptied it?'

Silence shrugged. ABOUT A MONTH, he wrote.

'You don't talk much, do you?' Jed said. 'I guess you never did.'

THERE'S TWO KINDS OF TALKING, Silence wrote. TALK-ING OUT LOUD AND TALKING IN YOUR HEAD.

Jed had to agree with that.

SO WHAT I CAN DO FOR YOU? Silence wrote.

'I need somewhere to stay.'

NO PROBLEM.

'Something else,' Jed said. 'I'm not here, OK? If anyone asks, don't tell them a thing.'

HOW AM I SUPPOSED TO TELL THEM? I'M A DEAF MUTE, REMEMBER?

'What if they tell you to write it down?'

Silence smiled and wrote, OW! I JUST HURT MY HAND.

Jed was given Tip's old room. Eight feet by eight (in the old days they'd christened it the Cell). Now it was used for what Silence called 'stock': two rowing-machines, a stack of cordless phones, ten microwaves, and a mountain bike. There was just enough room left over for a bunk bed. Jed took the top bunk. He went to sleep early that night and woke before morning. He rolled on to his belly, stared out of the window. Dawn had driven yellow wedges into the darkness along the horizon. The city lay below, cool as ashes. He could hear no traffic, only the wind murmuring. He remembered the night Tip OD'd. High winds, storm-force. Clothes swayed on their rails, water see-sawed in the goldfish tank. Tip had shot up and tumbled sideways, his face grey, words like rubber. Jed called the ambulance, then he hid behind the sliding doors that used to house the altar and waited. It didn't take them long. He heard boots on the floor, breathing, curses. And all the time the south wind moaning, like a choir of ghosts. That was where the ocean cemeteries were, south of the city, twelve miles out. When the wind blew from that direction, some people said it was the voices of the dead. The cops were so spooked that night, they didn't even think to search the place. Lucky for him. That was the last time he saw Tip. He laid his head back on the pillow, watched the walls turn grey. There were ashes in urns on the floor above. There were fourteen people sealed into the walls downstairs. But you could flip fear over like a coin and then it meant protection. He was glad to be this high up, it made him feel out of reach, safe. And the wind? That was like airport music, it was nothing, it was just there. He fell asleep again and slept till midday.

He left for the asylum at five that afternoon. One phone-call had told him all he needed to know: the visiting hours (between six and eight) and the address (somewhere in Westwood Heights). From Mangrove he cut through the old meat-packing district towards the tunnel. It was a narrow road that ran along the southern lip of the harbour. No restaurants or stores here, just the steel-roll doors of warehouses, wide enough for trucks, and cobblestones instead of tarmac, and deep gutters for the blood to run down. When he reached the Helix, it spun him round till he was almost dizzy, then he dipped down under the harbour and rose again for air in Venus. He headed west on Highway 12. It was the same route he'd taken from Mitch's place the day before, only now he was travelling in the opposite direction, away from the city. It was a gamble to be travelling at all, but it was one that he had to take, one that Mitch, for all his warnings, might understand. If anyone was going to understand what he was doing, it would be Mitch, he felt. He left the highway five miles further on, drove through Westwood and up into the foothills.

The location surprised him. He would've expected to find the asylum in one of the gloomier and more fetid sections of the city. But Westwood was a retirement suburb. Tree-lined streets, wrought-iron gates. Valets and video security. People died comfortably here, in monogrammed sheets, their heads wrapped in a soft cocoon of drugs. In fact, they didn't really die at all; they 'fell asleep', they 'joined their maker', they were 'called'. A death in Westwood was worth at least two or three in Mangrove. These had always been rich harvesting grounds for the Paradise Corporation.

It was dusk. He caught a glimpse of a building set high above the road and floodlit from beneath. That would be the place. He took a curve too fast and almost lost control. A black H showed in his headlamps. H for Hospital. He turned between stone gateposts. Another sign told him to go slow. After driving through acres of parkland, the grass turning blue as night came down, he saw a lawn. It was so neat, it frightened him. He'd met people like that. Suit on the outside, knife underneath. He reached into his inside pocket and took out a piece of candy. He tore the wrapper off and tossed it on the floor of the car.

In the lobby the girl behind the reception desk had fingernails that could have been his mother's doing. An inch long and frosty-pink. The girl ignored him for a while. He had time to admire her crisp white uniform, to notice the glittery gold belt she wore around her waist.

He took his hat off, smoothed his hair. 'I'm here to see Mr Gorelli,' he said.

She glanced up at him and then her eyes slid sideways and came to rest on his right shoulder. 'I'm sorry?'

'I'm here to see Mr Gorelli. I rang earlier.'

The girl lifted a white phone. 'There's someone to see Mr Gorelli.' She replaced the phone. 'Sister will be along in a moment,' she told him. 'If you'd like to take a seat.'

He crossed the polished marble floor and sank down into a soft pink sofa. There were three more soft pink sofas in the lobby. There was a white grand piano too, like something from a winter fairy tale. The girl with the gold belt was watching him. When the clock struck six, she'd change into a vulture. He let his eyes drift away from her and through the room. Money was seeds. People threw it around and places like this sprang up out of the ground. He wondered how Vasco could afford it. And then his chin jerked upwards like a fish on a line. Maybe Creed was paying the bills. He was perverse enough.

'Are you the gentleman who's come to see Mr Gorelli?'

One look at the Sister and he thought he'd better smile. She was about fifty. Her face seemed to hang from some invisible hook, all its weight gathered in the folds of her cheeks and the rolls beneath her chin. The skin under her eyes looked stretched. As if it was being pulled downwards. As if, at any moment, it might tear.

'Yes,' he said, 'I'm the gentleman,' and he rose to his feet.

'This way, please.'

'How is he?' He thought he ought to ask.

She eyed him over her shoulder. 'Pretty much the same.'

The same as what?

He tried to remember what Mitch had told him. All he could see was a man curled naked in a gutter. It didn't even look like Vasco.

Sister pushed through some swing doors that were muffled, like her shoes, in black rubber. Everything about her was precise, hygienic. If she ever farted, he thought, it'd probably sound like someone slipping a note under a door.

'Nearly there,' she said.

They pushed through more swing doors and entered a long room with a wooden floor. There were ten beds on either side and bars on the windows. The air smelt faintly of ether.

'Second bed from the end on the right,' the Sister said. 'Are you a relative?'

'I'm a colleague. We used to work together.'

She nodded. 'If you need me, I'll be in the office.'

'Thank you, Sister.'

Jed stood beside the bed, looking down. Vasco lay with his arms resting on top of the blankets, his hands loosely clenched. Those chunky rings he used to wear had been removed. But there was nothing anyone could do about the tombstones: two rows of blue tattoos that ran all the way from his shoulders to his wrists. And there was one, Jed remembered with a shiver, that covered almost the whole of his back. His eyes jumped to Vasco's face. Masklike. All the blood seemed to have drained from his skin, and his hair, still black, looked stiff, fake.

Jed sat down. 'Hey, Vasco,' he said, 'remember me?'

Vasco stared at the ceiling.

Jed shifted his chair closer to the bed. 'It's Jed,' he whispered. 'You know, Spaghetti. The ugly one.' He leaned closer still, spoke right into Vasco's ear. 'So fucking ugly, I'm hardly human.'

There was a murmur at his shoulder. He looked round. An old man stood behind him, clutching a hymn book. The old man's pyjamas had come undone and Jed could see his penis dangling like a piece of gristle in the gap.

'He ain't going to talk to you,' the old man said.

Jed frowned. 'What do you mean?'

'He's been here five years. He ain't talked to nobody.'

Jed turned away from the old man. Thinking back, he could remember other times when Vasco had seemed to go missing inside himself. On the mudbanks of the river once. Then that morning when they stood in the place where Scraper had been killed. And again the night they torched the construction site in Meadowland. It hadn't mattered then: he'd always come back. This time, though, he'd gone further. Further than ever before.

Jed bent close to his friend. 'I should've listened to you. You were doing the right thing. You were just clumsy, that's all.'

He sat back. Dinner at Vasco's house. A three-car garage, a flagpole on the lawn, a wife. Too many distractions. Vasco had tried to warn him that night, and he'd ignored it. He'd thought Vasco was being dramatic. But the drama only came later, when Vasco sold the story to the papers.

He bent close again. 'That story you leaked, it never would've stuck.' He shook his head. 'You must've been crazy to try and pull something like that.' He bent closer still. 'You should've asked me, Vasco. I always had ideas. We could've done it together.'

No, no. That was just dream talk. He'd already been drawn into Creed's magnetic field by then. He never would've taken sides against Creed. 'Listen, Vasco. I want to bring him down. I want to break him. But I need your help. You helped me before. A couple of times. You can do it again. We can get him, but we've got to move now. It's our last chance.' He eased back slowly, hands braced on his knees. He waited. But Vasco wasn't even there. Jed looked down. He didn't know what else he could say.

'You're not the first one who's tried.'

Jed spun round. It was the old man again. The old man took a step backwards, sniggered. 'Others've tried, don't make no difference.'

'Others?'

The old man nodded.

'Who?'

'Don't make no difference who. He ain't going to talk is all. Me, I talk up a storm. Don't get enough time for what I got to say. But him,' and he pointed at Vasco with his hymn book, 'he ain't got nothing he wants to say, not to nobody.'

Jed stared at Vasco. Sharon had told him a story once. It was one of her typical tall stories, it belonged with her magic bag. And yet it seemed to have come alive in his head, and he found that he could remember parts he didn't even think he'd heard.

It was about a man who lived in a small village on the other side of the world. This man had a pig that he wanted to sell. On market day he set out for the nearby town, but as he reached the gates of the town he fell down dead. His family buried him in sacred ground, which was up a mountain, Jed remembered, past some big trees.

Not long after being buried, the man rose up out of his grave and shook the earth from his limbs and walked through the big trees, back into the village. He told his family that he'd had a dream. In the dream he'd appeared at the temple of the dead, but the god who guarded the gate had denied him entry. 'You're not ready yet,' the god had told him. 'You must go back.'

How did the story go on? Something about the man turning strange. Something about him sitting outside his hut and staring straight ahead as if there was nothing in front of him, nothing for miles. Jed's eyes drifted down to Vasco, and he shivered.

At first the man's family let him be, but they soon got scared. They asked the wise men what to do. The wise men couldn't really help. They said that the man's soul had left his body while he was lying in the ground, and now he was trapped between two lives, just waiting to die. It was then that the mother had an inspiration. 'We must sell the pig,' she said. If they sold the pig, her son would have his last desire, and maybe then he'd find peace.

She put the pig up for auction. There wasn't much interest at first. A pig, after all, was only a pig. It wasn't even a very succulent pig; if anything, Jed remembered, it was kind of scrawny. But, all of a sudden, rumours began to fly through the village and the surrounding countryside. There was a pig for sale. The pig had some kind of magic power. Whoever owned the pig would never die. People came from far and wide, the bidding soared.

By the time it was over, the pig had fetched a huge price. The mother went to tell her son the news, but when she touched him on the shoulder he toppled sideways. She didn't know whether to laugh or weep. The family buried him again, and this time he stayed in his grave, and his body turned black and sank into the earth.

Jed looked into Vasco's eyes. Maybe the same kind of story had happened here. Maybe Vasco had asked for death, and been turned away. And so he'd walked naked through the big trees, and now he was sitting outside his house, waiting for some god to call his name. Jed felt like one of the family: invisible and scared. Like the mother, he had to think of something. He had to try and change where Vasco was.

'You recognise me, don't you, Vasco?' He was so close, he could smell the stale urine, the antiseptic. 'I can't believe you don't recognise me.'

The old man touched Jed on the shoulder and Jed looked round. 'You want to hear a song?' The old man was already fumbling through the pages.

'No,' Jed said. 'Just leave us alone.'

'I found a good one.' The old man was holding the hymn book in both hands and shifting hopefully from one foot to the other.

'I said, leave us alone,' Jed snapped.

The old man backed away across the ward, his eyes skidding on the floor, the hymn book dangling against his thigh like part of a broken limb.

Some of the anger was still with Jed when he turned back to Vasco. He'd tried everything and got nowhere. He could only think of one last way he might get through. He put his mouth close to Vasco's ear.

'I know who killed your brother,' he whispered.

He drew back. Nothing.

He leaned down again. 'Your brother, Francis,' he whispered. 'I know who killed him.'

He waited. Still nothing.

'It was me. I killed him.'

Suddenly those pale hands were fastened round his neck. The arms a blur of black hair, blue with all those deaths. Room for one more. Jed tried to break the hold, but the hands just locked and tightened. He was on the floor and Vasco was above him. He could see Vasco's face and it was blank. Then black ink began to seep in around the edges of his vision. The stench of stale urine. Like old Mr Garbett. The soiled yellow cardigan, the dusty brown bottle on the floor. The click-click-click of a spool still turning when the tape's run out. A pair of striped pants, an open fly. A shrivelled penis nodding in the gap. Moscow, Brussels, Helsinki. The click-click-click, won't someone switch that off? Oslo, Hilversum. The penis uncurling, lifting, swelling. The black ink flooding through his head.

'Are you all right?' The Sister was kneeling beside him.

He sat up, touched his forehead. 'My hat,' he tried to say, 'where's my hat?' but his voice didn't work properly.

The Sister spoke to a nurse. 'I think he wants his hat.'

The nurse handed Jed his hat. He took it, thanked her, put it on. Then brought one hand up to support his throat. He thought he could hear trees. Leaves rustling, leaves in wind. He looked up. Saw Vasco wrestling with three attendants. The struggle was taking place in near silence. That sound he could hear was the sound of their starched white uniforms. Vasco's limbs twisted and convulsed, but his face was still blank. His eyes, also blank, were pinned on Jed.

'It was Creed.' Jed was trying to shout, but his voice would only crack and squeak. 'Creed told me to do it.'

The Sister gripped him by the arm. 'This way, sir.'

'That's what I wanted to tell you, Vasco. That's why I came. I'm going to bring that bastard down, but I need your help – '

'That's enough.' The Sister steered him towards the door.

'He made me do it, Vasco,' Jed croaked. 'He made me.' The doors swung closed. He could still see Vasco's blank face framed in the square glass panel that made up the top half of the door. 'Would you like a song?' he heard the old man cry. A cackle, then he was round the corner, out of earshot.

The Sister took him to see the doctor on duty. After a brief examination, the doctor told him it was severe bruising, nothing more, and prescribed a course of pain-killers. The Sister had the prescription made up for him in the hospital dispensary, then she led him back to the lobby.

'I think it would be better,' she said, 'if you didn't visit Mr Gorelli again.'

Nobody was in when he got back to the tower. He went and stood in front of the bathroom mirror. The ghosts of Vasco's fingers had appeared on his neck. He stole a scarf out of Silence's bedroom and wrapped it round the bruises. He'd tell Silence that he had the flu.

He heated a tin of vegetable soup, but he had to leave all the vegetables. He couldn't eat, only drink. He couldn't even swallow the pain-killers he'd been given. It hurt too much. He had to grind the tablets up with the back of a spoon and swallow the powder in a glass of water. He went to bed early and lay on his back in the dark.

He had a dream that night. He was standing in a garden. There was an old man lying on the branch of a tree. Another, younger man stood below him, listening. Jed spoke to them; they both ignored him. He was just turning away when a strange machine lumbered through the air towards him. It looked like the inside of a radio, but it was the size of a helicopter. He watched it knock against a building and veer sideways, narrowly missing a tree. Everybody on the lawn was scattering.

Then the machine swooped down and plucked the old man off his branch. At first he seemed to think it was fun, a kind of fairground ride. The machine jolted, twisted, groaned. It collided with everything in sight, but it always lurched back into the air again. Only gradually did it become clear that this was the machine's way of killing people.

The old man's friends managed to pin the machine to the grass. As soon as they'd released the old man they began to attack the machine with anything they could lay their hands on. Some had iron bars, others had planks. One had an axe. When the axe struck, the machine let out a scream, as if it was a human being in pain. Then something even stranger started happening. One moment it looked like valves and pipes and fuse-boxes, the next it looked like a heart, intestines, lungs. It flickered backwards and forwards between the two, it couldn't seem to decide which one it really was. Still the blows descended, sometimes clanging against metal, sometimes splashing into flesh. Then, suddenly, it assumed its human form. There was even a head, though only the lower half could be seen. And with every second that passed less and less of the head was visible, it was as if it was escaping through a hole in reality, it seemed to be trying to draw its tortured body after it. One of the friends caught on. He swung the axe and severed the head from the body. A scream not of pain now but of rage and the body reared, stood up. It tottered across the lawn, blood spilling from its neck. It grew a new head, and the face was grey and mad. Blood fitted the scalp like a red skullcap. And then it saw Jed, he was hiding behind a tree, but it was no good, the tree was too narrow. It was turning now, it was bearing down on him . . .

He woke, the sheets cold with sweat. His neck pulsed. It was agony. He got up, went to the kitchen. Ground two more tablets into powder. Drank them down. He leaned on the window, still trembling from the dream.

He never dreamed, never. He thought dreams were bullshit, mumbo-jumbo, a waste of time. If somebody started telling him their dreams, he always switched off right away. That red giant, though. He was hard to shake.

The city lay below, a grid of orange lines, secret parcels of darkness between. He thought of his favourite slot machine. In the bar of the

Commercial Hotel in Adam's Creek. How long ago. All that had happened since. What did it say across the top? ALL WINS ON LIT LINES ONLY. It was the same here. The same now. He'd staked everything on this game. The lines were lit. The rest was up to him.

RED FLAGS

It was a battle to get in, the waves were strong, but soon he was lying on the other side of the water. The ocean cradled him. Moved him up towards the sky and moved him back again. The last twelve hours came to him in flashes. It had happened with such ease. Elation first, then pleasure. Lastly, fear. And there were gaps between, black enough to be unconsciousness. He remembered feeling he'd been taken by a current, remembered feeling he could wait for the next big wave and ride it to the shore; he remembered thinking he'd accomplished that. Now he wasn't so sure. He felt as if he might still be in that current's grip. Even now, he thought, those high-powered binoculars could be trained on him. He turned in the water. A wave lifted him and, looking back towards the city, he saw the grey turrets of the Palace Hotel. Even now, he thought.

When he walked out of the water, Harriet was standing on the beach holding his towel. She seemed to relish his surprise. He took the towel from her and began to dry himself.

'You shouldn't be swimming,' she said.

'Why's that?'

'The red flags are up. It's dangerous.'

'I'm a lifeguard,' he said, 'remember?' He rubbed his hair, then pushed it back out of his eyes. 'What are you doing here anyway?'

'That's nice,' she said.

He sighed.

'I've come to take you to lunch,' she said.

'I'm not hungry.'

'I want to talk to you,' she said and before he could reply she was walking away. 'I'll wait for you in the car.'

He took his time drying.

As soon as he got into the car, she started the engine and pulled out into the traffic. They drove along in silence for a while. Then, casually, like someone making conversation, she said, 'You came home pretty late last night.'

'It was pretty late,' he said, 'yes.'

'Where were you?'

'I was out.'

'Well, obviously.'

She turned the radio on. One of those easy-listening stations. All swooning strings and lush brass.

'You mind if I change this?' he asked her.

'I like it,' she said.

She tightened her lips, holding the smile inside. It showed only as a narrowing at the corners of her eyes, a kind of temporary roundness in her cheeks, as if she had fruit in there, or candy.

He looked out of the window. 'Where are we going?'

'A little place I know,' she said. 'It's in Torch Bay.'

Torch Bay. He might've guessed. It was just about the most pretentious suburb in the city. White yachts, beauty parlours, haughty blondes in foreign cars. Some people called it T B, for short. Like the disease.

They pulled up outside a place called Maison something. Shrubs in tubs on the sidewalk. Coachlamps. Valet parking.

'I'm not dressed for this,' he said.

She slipped her feet into black suede pumps, teased her fringe out in the mirror. 'You're fine.'

As they entered the restaurant a waiter took her hand and bent over it, his hair swirling into the crown of his head the way bathwater disappears down a plughole. They were led to a table by the window. Nathan looked around. A peppermint interior. Air-conditioning on Hi-Cool. A woman perched on a stool at the bar in a lime-green jumpsuit, amethyst lipstick and enough gold chains to get her elected mayor. He turned back to Harriet. 'So what was it you wanted to talk about?'

The waiter appeared at her shoulder.

'I think we should order first,' she said, 'don't you?' She didn't have to look at the menu. 'I'll have the avocado salad,' she told the waiter, 'and some mineral water.' She turned to Nathan. 'What about you, darling?'

'I told you already. I'm not hungry.'

'But you must have something.'

'I'll have some coffee,' he said, 'then I'd better go.'

'Will you have the coffee now, sir?' the waiter asked him.

'Yes,' Nathan said, 'now.'

'That'll be all, thank you,' Harriet told the waiter.

The waiter bowed once, backed away.

Harriet snapped her bag open. She took out a pack of cigarettes and lit one. 'You've lost all your nice manners,' she said, and she inhaled, her pale lips tightening around the filter.

He leaned back in his chair and folded his arms.

'You never had much respect for me,' she went on, 'but at least you had nice manners. Now they seem to have completely vanished.' She tapped her cigarette against the lip of the ashtray. 'I don't know what your father would've thought.'

She raised the cigarette to her lips, inhaled again. Then she turned her head to one side and blew the smoke across the restaurant. Her eyes never left his face. 'I imagine,' she said, 'that he would've been rather disappointed.'

He saw that she would always use his love for Dad against him. Almost as if she was jealous of it. 'Is that what you brought me here to talk about,' he said, 'my manners?'

She laughed, but there was no amusement in it. This was something new, this sourness. It told of her many disappointments. It was their residue.

The waiter was back. Salad, fizzy water, coffee with a dome of froth. Nathan reached for a sachet of sugar. There was an advertisement on the back. THE HOUSE OF SWEETNESS AND LIGHT, it said. YOUR PEACE OF MIND IS OUR SATISFACTION. So they were even advertising on sugar now. The House of Sweetness and Light. They probably had a monopoly on everyone who died of diabetes. He tore the sachet open, watched the granules sink into the froth. He liked the way the froth seemed to open, swallow the sugar, and then close again as if nothing had happened.

'Nathan?'

He looked up. 'Yes?'

'I've seen a lawyer.'

'Oh. What did they say?'

'They say the house belongs to you and Georgia.'

'That's what I told you.'

'They say Rona's got no claim. None whatsoever.'

Nathan waited.

'It raises a question.'

He lifted an eyebrow. 'What question?'

'The question of Rona's share of the money.'

'That's all taken care of,' he said. 'It's going to be invested. By the time she's eighteen, it will've doubled.'

Harriet pushed a sliver of avocado around with her fork. 'That's nine years away.'

'I know.'

'She needs the money now.'

'She can't have it now. You know that.'

Harriet's fork hit the edge of her plate. 'You're going to try and cheat her out of her money, aren't you? You want to make her suffer, just like you made your father suffer. Christ, Nathan, you're so selfish.'

For a moment he couldn't move. Not his hands, not his face; nothing. It was hard for him to believe that she'd actually said what she'd just said. She could summon her venom with so little effort; it surfaced in such neat, numbing packages.

He forced himself forwards in his seat. He kept his voice low. 'Dad left instructions in his will. He said the money was to be invested for her until she was eighteen. It's the law, Harriet. All we're doing is obeying it.'

She drank a delicate amount of mineral water and replaced the glass on the table. 'You could still release the money,' she said, 'if you wanted to.'

He looked down at his coffee. The dome of froth had collapsed. 'Why do you think Dad wrote it into the will in the first place?'

She speared a piece of asparagus. She held the fork just below her lips and waited for him to tell her.

'He didn't trust you with the money. Same as what you're accusing me of. That's pretty funny, isn't it?'

She didn't seem to think so. She placed the asparagus in her mouth and put her fork down. She chewed, she swallowed. She sighed. 'I'm afraid I've talked to Georgia.'

He stared at her blankly. 'What do you mean?'

'I told her what you did to me on the day of the funeral.'

'What I did to you?'

'What you did to me,' and she paused, 'against my will.'

'You're not serious,' he said, and he began to laugh. But then he looked into her face and his laughter left him and he was cold suddenly. 'You told Georgia that?'

'Yes.'

'Why?'

Harriet shrugged. 'She thinks she knows you. I thought I'd tell her what you're really like.'

'But it's a lie.'

She turned a leaf of lettuce over with the tip of her knife. 'Who says it's a lie?'

He stood up quickly. Her glass slopped over. Water fizzed on the white tablecloth and was absorbed.

Harriet raised her hand. 'Waiter?'

'You should be careful,' Nathan said, and his voice was quiet, uneven at the edges. 'You should just be careful.'

On his way out of the restaurant he passed the woman in the lime-green jumpsuit. He heard her chains clink as she turned to watch him go. He stood in the bright sunshine, trembling. He went through his pockets. He had about a dollar-fifty. Just enough for a bus to Central Station. He could walk the rest of the way. He would've walked all the way if he'd had to. Anything rather than stay in that place a moment longer.

It took him five minutes to reach the centre of Torch Bay. He sat down on a bench and waited for a bus. The inside of his head was so tangled, he couldn't get one straight thought out.

When the bus drew up, he moved all the way to the back and sat with his eyes fixed and the points of his knees wedged against the seat in front of him. I told her what you did to me. He watched the city pass in the window. Sky and buildings blurred under the swirly tinted glass. A city under the sea. What you did to me. Against my will. The bus lumbered on. It was so hot, he was sitting over the engine, his eyes seemed weighed down, down. Down. It was as if he'd toppled off a ledge and sleep was the drop. A long, sweet drop; a million miles.

Then somebody was shouting. 'Central,' they were shouting, 'Central Station.' And somebody knocked against his leg.

He hauled himself upright, stumbled down out of the bus, his hair sticky with salt, lunchtime seeming like a dream he'd just woken from. But it wasn't a dream. It was real. Downtown crowded in on him. Sirens, neon, liquor. Every time he saw Georgia's face he shut the picture off. He didn't dare imagine. He simply had to get to her. He took the quiet streets and almost ran. At last he reached the building. An old apartment block with a canopy, a doorman, a marble hallway. Georgia, she always landed on her feet.

'I'm here to see Georgia,' he said. 'I'm her brother.'

'Georgia?' The doorman screwed his face up, as if he was trying to shift the whole of one side of it on to the other side. 'Reckon she went out.'

Nathan sagged, his strings cut. 'When?'

'About an hour ago.'

'Any idea where she went?'

'Sorry, pal.'

'I've got to see her,' Nathan said. 'I'd better wait.'

'Whatever you say.'

Nathan sat on the steps. A tall building at the end of the street told him, in beads of golden neon, that it was 2:55. 103°. 2:55. 103°. 2:56. 103°.

'Hottest day for nine years.'

Nathan looked up to see the doorman standing behind him. 'Is that right.'

The doorman had a grey rag in his hand. He dabbed the back of his neck with it. 'Just said so on the radio.'

'Think it'll rain?' Nathan asked him.

There were clouds in the sky. Scalloped at the edges, like old postcards. Almost brown.

'Too hot to fucking rain.' The doorman tipped his face at the sky and slit his eyes. Then he shook his head and returned to the lobby.

No rain came. Only lightning, sheeting above the roof of the Hotel Terminal. As if some kind of press conference was being held in the next street.

Time went by, measured in golden beads. Dusty yellow curtains slouched in the open windows of the hotel. A lazy neon sign said V CANCIES. Couldn't even be bothered with the A.

3:25. 104°.

Then, looking up once more, he saw a figure that he recognised. The black top hat, the cracked black shoes. Unmistakable.

'Jed?' he called out. 'Hey! Jed!'

Jed stopped in his tracks, his body still facing forwards, and turned his head. Nathan ran across the street. When he reached Jed he didn't know what to say. He found himself staring at the scarf that Jed was wearing round his neck.

'You sick or something?' he said.

Light trickled off the rims of Jed's spectacles as he tilted his head towards the sky. 'Sick? Heh.' His voice creaked like a piece of wood furniture in an old house.

'So how're you doing?' Nathan said. 'Did you find a place?'

Jed nodded. 'I found a place.'

'Where?'

'Round here.' And Jed nodded again.

Nathan thought of the time he ran into Tip and Jed on Central Avenue. 'I remember when you used to live in the Towers.' He smiled. 'I went there once. I looked for you.' He shook his head. 'Couldn't find you, though.'

'Must've been years ago,' Jed said.

'The place was like a maze,' Nathan said.

'By the way.' Jed reached into his pocket and took out a bill. He smiled down at it for a moment, then he handed it to Nathan. 'Here's the money I owe you.'

Nathan stared at the bill. It was a hundred dollars. A hundred-dollar bill.

'But,' he said, 'but I only lent you eight.'

Jed was still smiling, but the smile had altered. 'Yeah, well,' he said. 'You were so kind, letting me stay and all.'

Nathan felt the change in that smile like a lowering in the temperature. He almost shivered.

'Well,' Jed said, 'better be going.'

Nathan watched Jed as he walked away. Jed stayed in the shadows, close to the wall, the way blind men do. When he reached the corner he looked back over his shoulder. He didn't make any sign or gesture, he just looked. Then he was gone.

Nathan returned to the steps and sat down. He looked at the hundred-dollar bill in his hand, could make no sense of it. Still, he felt easier now. Somehow his faith had been renewed. If Jed could come by, then surely Georgia could come by too. But he waited another hour and all that new faith drained away. It was 6:04. He left a message with the doorman, then he stood on the sidewalk, trying to remember Georgia's favourite places, trying to think where she might be.

He worked his way through the neighbourhood. The bars, the cocktail lounges. By the time he'd finished, it was almost nine. Then he suddenly remembered. There was a place she sometimes went when she was depressed. The Starlite Rooms, on the end of the pier. She liked to watch the old people dance.

It was years since he'd been along the pier at night. So much junk on sale. Coffin-shaped ice-creams, T-shirts that said things like MOON BEACH – THE CITY THAT PUTS THE FUN BACK INTO FUNERALS, midnight cruises to the ocean cemeteries. There was even a DATE-OF-YOUR-DEATH machine. You put 50 cents in the slot, then you placed your hand in the machine and it told you how much longer you were going to live. 'You'll die tomorrow. Have a nice day.' He kept walking. Up ahead he could see the pale dome of the Starlite Rooms. A white neon sign glowed above the entrance: DANCING NITELY. He could hear music now. An electric organ, a drum machine. A man's voice singing. Something about turning off the sunshine. It sounded blurred and he thought he knew why. It was all the old folks singing along. Late on their cues and out of tune. It was as if the music was a ship and it was leaving a wake behind it in the air.

The doorman had a pencil moustache and a wide fierce nose. 'Evening, sir,' he said. 'You dancing tonight?'

'I don't know,' Nathan said. 'I'm looking for my sister.'

The doorman sucked some air in past his teeth. 'How old is she, this sister of yours?'

'Twenty-three.'

'Ah, well. You won't find her in there.'

'How do you know?'

'No one under fifty in there.'

A waltz started up inside. The doorman's arms lifted away from his sides and curved to hold an invisible woman. He twirled her round the entrance hall. 'Never could resist a waltz,' he said, grinning over his shoulder.

'I think I'll just have a look, if you don't mind,' Nathan told him, and pushed through the mirror doors.

The place was lit like the inside of a fridge. A stage with a backdrop of spangled gold drapes. A horseshoe dance-floor. Hundreds of tables, all occupied. Nathan scanned the room, but the doorman was right. No one under fifty. Still, there was a chance she might turn up. It was only just after nine. He bought a drink and sat at a table with three old ladies in sleevelesss frocks. The waltz ended.

The man who was playing the organ tucked his chin into his right shoulder in a kind of shorthand bow. 'Thank you, ladies and gentlemen. I must say it's a great pleasure to be here in the famous Starlite Rooms tonight . . . '

Maroon suit, green skin. Hair as slick and black as liquorice.

' . . . my name's Maxie Carlo . . . I play, you sway . . . '

The three old ladies tittered, winked.

The organ had a built-in drum machine. Maxie Carlo twisted a couple of dials and a new rhythm began.

' . . . good to see a bit of spirit here tonight . . . I stick to lemonade, myself . . . '

Halfway through his second drink Nathan thought he'd try calling

Georgia again. He found a phone near the men's room. He dialled Georgia's apartment, but there was still no reply. On the way back to his table, he bought another drink. He sat down again. The music had stopped.

'Nathan, what a pleasant surprise.' The voice was rich and cool, and came from his right shoulder.

He looked round. It was Maxie Carlo. Black hairs bristled in his nostrils. A damp top lip. No neck.

'I would never have expected to see you here,' Maxie said. 'How are you?'

'Fine.' Nathan could feel the blankness on his face.

'I'm sorry, Nathan,' Maxie said, 'you don't remember me, do you? I guess you were kind of preoccupied last night.' Only his top row of teeth showed when he smiled. One of them was edged in gold, like a page from the Bible. 'I met you in that bar on the promenade. You were with Neville.'

'Neville?'

'Oh dear.' Maxie laughed. It didn't make a sound. 'Maybe you know him as Reid. That's what he calls himself when he doesn't call himself Neville. Except sometimes he calls himself Vince or Len. Or Eric. Once,' and he ran the tip of his little finger round the curve of his nostril, 'once he called himself Irv.' That soundless laugh again. That gilded tooth.

Nathan didn't say anything. He didn't like this man leaning over him as if he owned him.

'They're anagrams,' Maxie explained.

'Anagrams?'

'You know. Words you get out of another word.' Maxie looked down at Nathan and affected great concern. 'Dear, oh dear,' he said. 'I can see you've fallen for the whole thing.'

There was a slow turning in Nathan's stomach, a sense of unease that was massive and inexplicable, like the movement of galaxies. He felt slightly sick.

'Well,' and Maxie took his hand off Nathan's shoulder and held it out, palm up, 'the organ calls.' And with another soundless laugh he slid away between the tables as if he'd been greased.

One of the old women reached across and touched Nathan's arm. 'You know Mr Carlo, do you?'

'Not really,' Nathan said.

'He's very good, isn't he?'

'Yes, he is.' Nathan looked towards the dance-floor. A man of about sixty stood in the spotlight, alone and blinking. He wore old brown chinos and a mustard-coloured cardigan.

'Clive's going to sing for us now,' Maxie said, 'aren't you, Clive?'

Clive ducked his head.

'What are you going to sing for us, Clive?'

Clive mumbled something.

'Clive's going to sing an old music-hall number for us.' Maxie raised an eyebrow at the audience. 'I can hardly wait.'

The drum machine started up, the organ came in. Clive shifted, crouched, found the position. Legs apart, eyes closed, one hand splayed, waist-level, in the air. He had the gestures down. The only trouble was, he couldn't sing. It would've made a great comic act, Clive in his mustard cardigan, eyes closed, hand splayed, fucking terrible voice.

As Nathan walked back down the pier he heard a few whistles, some brittle applause. Clive must have finished his song. The ocean sighed and shifted under his feet. He'd only had three or four drinks, but his mouth felt loose and he was talking to himself.

He leaned on a railing. 'It's an anagram,' he said. 'An anagram.' He laughed. 'You know.'

He stared down at the tilting black sheets of water. 'Once he was Irv,' he said, and laughed again. When he stopped laughing he took a deep breath and called out, 'George?'

He passed the gardens on the promenade. The strips of neat mown grass. The tight, bright symmetries of flowers. He walked on. There was a strange hollow rattling sound. A white car cruised by with a skeleton tied to its rear fender. The bones jumped and twitched on the road, as if possessed by fever. Then he was looking up at the façade of the Palace Hotel. He suddenly felt like talking to that man. Like being listened to. That man who acted like a priest. That man with all the names. He certainly didn't want to go home. He saw a phone-booth on the corner of the street. He'd try Georgia one last time.

As he walked towards the phone-booth, the phone started ringing. He stopped, looked around. But there was nobody in sight. The phone was still ringing. He ducked into the booth and picked up the receiver. He didn't say anything. He just listened.

'You took your time.'

'Who's this?' Nathan said.

'One guess.'

Still holding the receiver, Nathan turned and looked up at the hotel. 'Is that you?'

'I saw you passing. Thought I'd give you a call.'

Nathan smiled. 'Where are you?'

'Where do you think?'

'It's funny, but I wanted to come and see you. It's just I didn't know how.'

'You don't remember?'

'No.'

A laugh. 'I'm not surprised. It's the fourteenth floor. Apartment 1412. Got that?'

'I've got it.' Nathan hung up. He left the booth and walked towards the hotel, the ocean crackling behind him like a policeman's radio, like the scene of a crime.

YOGHURT, ICE-CREAM, MINESTRONE

Jed couldn't even swallow his own saliva. He had to keep a bowl beside the bed. He lay on his back all day, he saw the sun rise and fall in the window, he felt such anger that he hit the wall with his fist and burned the skin off his knuckles. He had to make that phone-call, and he had to make it soon, but he couldn't do anything till he had his voice back.

At about midday somebody knocked on the door. Jed quickly wrapped the scarf around his neck. Silence stood in the doorway, wearing a pair of pyjamas and his suit jacket. He handed Jed one of his cards: ARE YOU ALL RIGHT?

Jed nodded. 'It's just a really bad cold.' He couldn't speak so he just mouthed the words. Not that it made any difference to Silence.

Silence produced another card: DO YOU NEED ANYTHING?

Jed shook his head. 'I'll be OK.'

One more card: YOU SURE?

Jed nodded. 'I'm sure.' Then he thought of something. 'If you go out, could you get me some yoghurt?'

Silence looked puzzled. Maybe he hadn't understood. Maybe the word was hard to read.

'Yoghurt,' Jed whispered. 'Yog-hurt.'

After Silence had left the room, Jed lay back. He was curiously touched. Silence had prepared those three cards in advance. That was a lot of words for Silence. Maybe even a whole day's worth.

He turned his thoughts back to Creed and, reaching into his jacket, took out his wallet. Inside the wallet was a newspaper article. He unfolded it and laid it flat on the pillow. And though he knew the article by heart he began to read it through once more:

RIDDLE OF MISSING STUDENT

A medical student was abducted from his Los Ilusiones apartment last night by several armed men.

Mr Francis Gorelli, 19, worked as an intern at
the Moon Beach General Hospital, and was due to
take examinations later in the year.
    One of the armed men was about 25, white, and
he was wearing a black suit and a black top hat. A
dark car was seen leaving the area and police are still
trying to trace the vehicle.
    The family of the missing man refused to com-
ment today. The abduction of Mr Gorelli is only the
latest incident in a wave of violence that has been
sweeping the notorious eastern suburbs of the city.

A pretty accurate description, considering. But maybe the shock
had burned his image into that girl's memory. Certainly he'd never
forgotten her: her long black hair, her yellow dress; her screams.
Creed had sent him into the building knowing that he'd be seen.
Knowing also, possibly, that he'd be remembered. His face twisted in
a sour smile. Even six years later it'd been something of a gamble,
perhaps, to drive back to the city in a black suit and a black top hat,
to drive back to the city in the same dark car.

    Every time he read the article he had to admire Creed's strategy.
Two things. One: the murder of Francis Gorelli had driven Vasco
insane, and insanity, surely, was a far more effective, far more exquisite
punishment than death. Two: the killing (or, as the papers understood
it, the abduction) of an innocent man was a crime with no motive. It
forced the police to generalise. Their conclusion only scratched the
surface of the truth. The crime was part of 'a wave of violence'. Its
context had become its cause. Nor had the body (or, for that matter,
any other evidence) been discovered. Not even a murder then. Not
necessarily. Just another missing-persons case. A poster in a police
station. An appeal on the back of a carton of milk.

    Jed dozed through the afternoon. By the evening he needed more
pain-killers. When he left his room he noticed that all the videos had
gone; Silence must've been busy. He heard voices in the kitchen, and
went and stood in the doorway. Silence was sitting at the table with a
man. There were small transparent plastic bags scattered all over the
formica. Inside were watches, lighters, rings. Sensing something
behind him, the man swung round. 'Who the fuck's this?'

    Silence showed him a card: FRIEND.

    'OK,' the man said, 'OK,' and he turned to Jed and said, 'Sorry
about that.'

    Jed nodded. He didn't want to risk speaking. Not yet. He shook two tablets on to a piece of silver foil and began to grind them up with the back of a spoon.

The man had sandy-gold hair and tiny red veins below his side-burns. His hands shook. He was smoking menthol cigarettes. 'What's this you've got?' he said, tapping a maroon box with one finger.

Silence snapped the lid open. He took out a gold pocket watch and handed it to the man. Jed saw the watch over the man's shoulder. Its face was ringed with gems.

The man nodded. 'Nice piece.'

Silence reached over. He flicked the back of the watch open with his thumb and held it to the man's ear. It played 'As Time Goes By'.

'Ain't that something.' The man stared at Silence. 'How'd you know it played a tune, Silence, you being deaf and all?'

Silence wrote, SOMEBODY TOLD ME.

The man guffawed. 'And you trusted them?'

Silence wrote, DID YOU HEAR THE TUNE OR DIDN'T YOU? 'I heard the tune.'

I MAY BE DUMB, Silence wrote, BUT I'M NOT THAT DUMB. Then he tucked the rest of his cards back into his pocket. Clearly that was all he was going to say on the subject.

Jed opened the fridge. There was a six-pack of plain yoghurt on the top shelf. Silence had come through for him. He stirred his crushed tablets into a yoghurt, then he found a piece of paper and wrote, THANKS FOR THE YOGHURT. On his way out of the room he handed Silence the message.

Silence smiled. YOUR'E WELCOME, he wrote.

'You're weird, you are,' the man said. 'Just plain weird, the lot of you.'

Jed went back to bed.

The next day he left the apartment at noon. He stood at ground-level and looked around. Heat rippled on the concrete, the horizon seemed alive with snakes. He walked past his car and out through the housing project. Smells came to him: warm garbage, tar melting, dead fish. There was nobody about. Days like this most people stayed home and stood in front of the fridge with the door open or something.

He was heading for the thrift stores in Mangrove South. He'd decided that if he walked he'd be less visible. It was only twenty minutes. He took shortcuts and kept to the shadows. Every now and then he spoke to himself. He was testing his voice. There was no danger in it. He was east of downtown and the only people on the streets were old men with bottles of sweet red wine. They talked to themselves all the time. He fitted right in. Christ, it was hot, though. He could feel the heat of the sidewalk through the soles of his boots.

He was almost there when he heard somebody call his name. He ignored it. Then somebody came running out of the sunlight towards him. It was Nathan.

'You sick or something?' Nathan said.

Jed touched the scarf at his neck. 'Sick? Heh.' That was one way of putting it.

'So how are you doing? Did you find a place?'

There'd always been something manic about Nathan. Behind those green eyes, that blond hair. Behind that tan. He was like a dog with training that nobody can use.

Jed nodded. 'I found a place.'

'Where is it?'

As if he was going to tell him that.

'Round here.'

Then Nathan said, 'I remember when you used to live in the Towers.' Straight out. As if he could see right into the hooded part of Jed's brain.

Jed stared at him. But Nathan's eyes had misted over; he seemed to have lowered himself into his own memory.

'I went there once. I looked for you.' He smiled. 'Couldn't find you, though.'

'Must've been years ago,' Jed said, still watching him closely.

'The place was like a maze,' Nathan said.

Still is.

Jed chipped at the wall with his boot. And began to smile, because he'd thought of something.

'By the way.' He took out one of Mario's hundred-dollar bills and smiled down at it. He'd kept it as a kind of souvenir. But now he had a better use for it. He held the bill out to Nathan. 'Here's the money I owe you.'

It was worth $100 just to see Nathan's face.

'But,' he was stammering, 'but I only lent you eight.'

'Yeah, well,' Jed said. 'You were so kind, letting me stay and all.'

And his smile began to twist on his face, he just couldn't keep the sneer out of it. 'Well,' he said, 'better be going.'

And just walked away.

When he reached the corner of the street he glanced over his shoulder. Nathan was still standing on the sidewalk staring at him. Had Nathan guessed where he was living? No, he was thrown by the money. That was all it was. Jed shifted his shoulders inside his jacket. So he used to live in the Towers once upon a time. So what. He hadn't told Nathan anything, had he?

He walked on. Two blocks west he found the thrift store he'd been looking for. Inside he moved from rail to rail. He began to assemble a wardrobe. It wasn't easy. These were all dead men's clothes. Why was everyone who died so fucking fat? You'd think a few thin people would die sometimes, but no. It took him fifteen minutes just to find a pair of pants and even then they were three inches too big around the waist and he needed a belt to hold them up. Still, it was a start. In half an hour he was standing in front of a full-length mirror. This was what he had on: a pale-blue turtleneck (it hid the ghosts); a pair of chinos in a kind of rusty ochre colour; brown leather sandals with rubber soles (he'd learned a thing or two from that Sister in the hospital); a grey fake snakeskin belt; and a maroon leather jacket with black buttons and scoop lapels.

'A bloody Christian,' he whispered. 'A missionary.' And laughed to himself. Because, after all, he *was* on a mission, wasn't he? A mission of a kind.

He heaped his own clothes on the counter and explained that he wanted to trade them for the clothes he was now wearing. The woman who ran the place wore a cardigan draped over her shoulders. She shifted her arms inside the cardigan and looked at him sideways. Her jackdaw eye swooped on his most valuable possession. 'What about the hat?'

He wedged the hat under his arm. 'Not for sale.'

The woman shrugged. She began to sort one-handed through his clothes. Held a boot up between finger and thumb. 'Don't suppose you ever heard of polish, did you?'

'They're all black, the clothes,' he said. 'You should be able to shift them pretty quick in a town like this.'

'That may be so, but look at the state of them.' The woman lifted his frayed jacket and let it drop again. 'All right,' she said, 'you leave your clothes plus fifteen dollars, on account of that coat you got there's leather,' and her eye hovered, gleaming, above his hat once more, 'unless of course – '

He paid the $15 and left. On his way back to the Towers he had to stop in a supermarket and a pharmacy. By the time he reached the thirteenth floor he was drenched in sweat. Silence let him in. He went straight to the kitchen. Silence followed him, stood in the doorway. He began to unpack the bags he was carrying. A block of ice-cream.

A tin of minestrone soup. A box of COLOR-U-BLONDE hair dye. A roll of silver foil. And two six-packs of yoghurt (one plain, one assorted-fruit flavours).

He turned. Silence was still watching from the doorway. Silence handed him a card: I WAS WORRIED FOR A MOMENT. I THOUGHT YOU MIGHT'VE FORGOTTEN THE YOGHURT.

Jed had to grin.

WHAT'S WITH THE SOUP? Silence wrote.

'It's my throat,' Jed explained. 'Yoghurt, ice-cream, minestrone. They're the only things I can get down.'

Later that evening, when Silence had gone out, he locked himself in the bathroom. He took off his new blue turtleneck and wrapped a towel around his shoulders. He opened the COLOR-U-BLONDE, pulled on a pair of rubber gloves and slowly, meticulously, applied the peroxide solution to his hair. Afterwards he covered his head in silver foil. Almost immediately his scalp began to burn. This reassured him. No change is possible, he thought, without pain. No change is real unless it hurts.

He walked out on to the balcony as the sun set. The city lay in its own haze, buildings dipped in spun sugar, they could melt on your tongue. The sting of peroxide balanced the ache in his throat, almost cancelled it. Tomorrow, he decided. Tomorrow he would make the call.

The evening passed. He stood on the balcony eating fruit yoghurt and watching the planes. A calmness eased into his bones. His blood slowed down. That tortoise, Bob, he was smarter than he looked.

Towards midnight he heard Silence return. He left his bedroom and joined Silence in the lounge. Silence was smoking a joint and watching TV. He offered Jed the joint. Jed turned it down. Silence was staring at him now. Silence put the joint down in the ashtray so he could stare better. Then he wrote on a card and handed it to Jed. Jed read the card and smiled. There was only one word on it:

EERIE.

The next morning he walked into the bathroom and saw a blond stranger in the mirror. 'Jesus,' he said. His voice didn't sound bad. A bit croaky, but OK. He undid the scarf. The ghosts had changed colour. They'd achieved a curious yellow-brown. It reminded him of crème caramel, old banana skins. Or the thin band of pollution that sometimes circled the horizon.

He borrowed one of Silence's cordless phones and stood on the balcony. The city was making that sound that cities make. Like if you're told to breathe out slowly through your mouth. He sensed the first drop of rain on his shoulder, he felt it burn into his skin like acid, he heard it telling him that he was special, special. The sound of the rain in that word. The meaning of that word on his skin.

He dialled the Paradise Corporation.

The receptionist put him through to the chairman's office. A secretary answered. 'Mr Creed's at home today. Can I take a message?'

'No message,' Jed said, and cut her off.

He dialled the Palace Hotel. 'Apartment 1412, please.'

'One moment.'

He could hear the phone ringing in Creed's apartment now. Then it was picked up. 'Yes?'

'Mr Creed, please.'

'Who's calling?'

Jed recognised the voice on the other end. It was the Skull. Michael The Skull McGowan. So they were still working together. If that wasn't loyalty.

'Who's calling?' the Skull said again.

'It's Jed Morgan.' There was a pause, then Creed was on the line. Jed could tell by the silence. He'd know that silence anywhere.

'Creed?'

'Spaghetti. How nice. I've been expecting your call.'

Jed's hand tightened round the phone. You could never tell whether Creed was bluffing. 'What do you mean?'

But Creed just laughed. 'Your voice sounds terrible.'

'I've had a cold.'

'It doesn't sound like a cold. It sounds more like someone tried to strangle you.'

His heart beat hard, the air thickened around him. He gripped the balcony with his free hand. How did Creed know all this? Did he know everything?

'What do you want, Spaghetti?' Creed was saying. 'I'm a busy man. I haven't got all day.'

He hadn't thought this out properly. He hadn't imagined the way it might go. He jumped at some words as they came into his mind. 'I need some money.'

'I didn't think you were interested in money.'

'I want half a million.'

'You'll only start throwing it around. Remember last time.'

'Half a million. And I want it tomorrow night.'

'What makes you think you deserve anything?'

'I've got a tape. You want to hear it?'

'What is it? Violins?'

Jed picked up his pen recorder and pressed PLAY. He held it over the phone. 'You want me to kill Vasco's brother? . . . That's right . . . How? . . . Don't worry about that . . . It's taken care of . . . It's nice . . . ' He pressed STOP. 'There's your violins, Creed. Did you like them?'

'Tape doesn't stand up in court, Spaghetti.'

'How about the papers, Creed? Does tape stand up in the papers?'

A silence.

He had him. At last he had him.

'How would it look on the front page, Creed? I can see the headline now. Funeral baron held on murder charge. Headline like that, you could sell a few papers, I reckon.'

Don't give him time to think.

'Midnight tomorrow. The West Pier. Just you and me. You got that?'

Another silence.

'Jed?'

'What?'

'You're still driving the same car.'

'So?'

'Bit risky, isn't it, driving the same car? I mean, it could be seen as evidence, couldn't it?' A pause. 'You know what they say about evidence. They say destroy it.'

'What are you talking about, Creed?'

'I thought I'd do a friend a favour, that's all.'

'What the *fuck* are you talking about?'

'Why don't you look out the window?'

'I am looking out the – '

His car exploded with a dull thump. One hand on the balcony, he felt the building shake. Bits of chrome and glass scattered over the parking-lot. Flames reached arms out of the windows, clawed their way across the roof. The flames sounded like rain, he thought. Like rain. Then a fire alarm jangled and a baby started crying.

He dropped the phone and ran inside. Silence was standing outside his bedroom door in his pyjamas. The explosion must've woken him.

'It's my car,' Jed said. 'They blew up my car.'

He ran down the stairs, all thirteen floors. By the time he reached the ground his car was surrounded by kids from the project. Some

were pointing, chattering. Others scoured the concrete, collecting bits
of headlamp and mirror. He pushed to the front. You could no longer
tell what colour the car had been. You could only just read the
numberplate: CREAM 8. He'd had that numberplate since he was
sixteen. He'd paid a fucking hundred dollars for that numberplate.
He dashed towards it, hands outstretched, but a blast of heat threw
him back with no eyebrows.

'This your car?' one of the kids shouted.

He didn't answer. He could hear sirens whooping on Ocean
Avenue. Weee-ooo Weee-ooo Weee-ooo. They'd be arriving any
moment. He turned and made off in the direction of the project.

He ran up a flight of stairs and along a walkway, putting solid
concrete between himself and his burning car. He glanced up once
and saw the boy with the crewcut and the puffy eyes standing on a
balcony above him.

The boy shouted something.

He didn't hear it the first time.

The boy shouted it again. 'Where's your hat, mister?'

THE OCEAN BED MOTEL

When Nathan woke in the morning, the bed was empty. Through the open door he could hear Reid talking.

'You know what they say about evidence.' A pause. 'They say destroy it.' Another pause. 'I thought I'd do a friend a favour, that's all.'

He could hear no second voice. It must be a phone-call. He eased out of the bed and pulled on his jeans. In the lounge the sun pressed against the drawn blinds. A few bright ribs of light thrown on the floor.

'Why don't you look out the window?' Reid said, and then he hung up.

Strange way to end a phone-call.

Reid put the phone down with a smile. When he looked up and saw Nathan standing in the doorway the smile remained. Or rather, the shape of the smile remained. The content had altered. Where the first smile had been poisonous, the second was benign. And the transition was so effortless, so deft. Nathan knew he was supposed to be smiling back, but found that he could only stare.

'I'd almost forgotten you were here,' Reid said.

'How could you forget?' Nathan murmured. He wasn't sure whether or not he was joking.

He watched as Reid rose from the sofa and moved towards him. He closed his eyes. He felt one gloved hand brush the hair back from his forehead.

'You time things just right,' he said.

He felt one gloved finger trace the outline of his top lip.

'Like when you called me,' he said. 'Last night. On the street.'

Then he heard Reid's voice, close to his ear: 'I'm going to take you somewhere.'

'Where?'

'Somewhere special.'

Nathan opened his eyes again. Part of the wall seemed to move behind Reid's shoulder and a second man moved across the room towards them. Nathan hadn't even noticed him. But he must have been there the whole time. Must have heard them talk. Seen them touch.

He had a shaved head and mirror shades. An M-shaped vein pulsed high up on the left side of his forehead. Nathan looked at the man and saw himself twice.

'This is McGowan,' Reid said. 'Otherwise known as the Skull.' He laughed. 'You can probably see why.'

The Skull tipped his head back a fraction.

Nathan nodded. He could see.

Putting his hand on the Skull's shoulder, Reid steered him towards the door. Nathan went to the window. He picked up the binoculars and stared down at the promenade. He heard Reid say, 'Me too,' and then he heard the word, 'Eight,' then the door clicked shut. He watched a man and a boy playing football in the sunshine. The boy swung his leg and kicked the ball. The man trapped the ball and kicked it back again. The boy swung his leg again. This time he missed, the ball rolled past, he scampered after it. The man lay down on the bright grass. Nathan felt Reid behind him. Not a sound exactly. More like a displacement of the air.

'Are you ready?'

Nathan put the binoculars down.

They took the elevator to the underground parking-lot. A black car crouched in the shadows on fat tyres. Nathan slid into the hard leather seat and pulled the door shut after him. It made that sound, he remembered it from before, somewhere between a crunch and a click. Such luxury in that sound.

But the unease was still with him. He felt robbed by that man's presence in the apartment, and he couldn't rid himself of the feeling. When he thought back he could sense the man gloating from the far side of the room. And then that supernatural moment when he detached himself from the wall and moved forwards.

'Is something bothering you?' Reid asked.

'I didn't see him,' Nathan said.

Reid eased the car up the ramp and out into the sunlight. 'I don't follow you.'

'That man,' Nathan said. 'I didn't know he was there.'

'Did it upset you?'

'I just felt he saw everything.'

Reid reached for his dark glasses. 'Well,' he said with a smile, 'there's nobody to see us now.'

The knitting-needle click of the gears as he shifted into third for the slip-road that led to the expressway.

'We'll be there soon. You should take this.' He passed Nathan a white capsule.

'You really think I need it?'

Reid shrugged. 'It's up to you. It might relax you.'

'I don't know whether I want to relax.'

'Please yourself.'

Nathan closed his hand around the capsule. He held it in his fist like a dice he might throw.

'Where we're going,' he said, 'is there a phone?'

Reid looked across at Nathan. 'Where we're going,' he said, 'there's a phone with fish inside it.'

This brought a smile to Nathan's face. He shook off his misapprehensions. Put the pill into his mouth and swallowed it.

The car skated across three lanes, one crisp diagonal at eighty miles an hour, fast lane to slow. Out through Exit 6: Moon Beach East. In five minutes they were passing under a pale-blue archway. White letters on the curving crossbar: THE OCEAN BED MOTEL.

'You been here before?' Reid asked him.

Nathan shook his head. 'I've never even heard of it.'

You approached the motel from above, along a road that snaked through a landscape of spindly palms and boulders. It was a pale-blue building, two storeys high. There were waves on the roof, sculpted out of poured concrete. It looked like a cross-section of the ocean.

While Reid registered, Nathan looked round. There was a strong smell of seaweed in the lobby. This, he soon found out, was emanating from the motel restaurant where Today's Special was Charbroiled Shark Steak with Hot Seaweed Salad. Someone had gone to a great deal of trouble with the décor. There were racks of pink coral and treasure chests half buried in drifts of sand. There was dim, fathoms-down lighting. There were bits of ships lying about, rusting. The ocean bed. Replace the air with water and you'd be there.

'What do you think?' Reid asked him.

But he couldn't answer. The drug was beginning to rush through him now and he was finding it hard to distinguish reality and hallucination. For instance: he was seeing mermaids everywhere. Cascades of blonde hair, bodies sheathed in silver scales from the waist down. Mermaids. There was something he ought to be doing, but it was as if he had his ear to a shell: he could hear the sea and all his other thoughts escaped him.

He saw the car that he'd left on the promenade. He saw it in detail – a city map on the dashboard, the groceries on the back seat. It had been there for at least twenty-four hours. The milk would be sour by now, he thought.

They were following a mermaid down dark-blue corridors with dark-green doors. Her sequins chinked and glittered.

She touched him on the shoulder. 'Hear that?'

'What?' he said.

'Listen.'

He listened. It sounded like doors being opened very slowly. Or the noise people make when they stretch. 'What is it?' he asked her.

'It's whales,' she said. 'It's for atmosphere.'

Reid turned to him and smiled.

He keeps doing that, Nathan thought. Turning and smiling at me. Running his eyes over me like hands.

The mermaid stood by an open door, her nipples hidden in pale-pink shells. Smiling, she showed him into a room. One entire wall was an aquarium. The rest seemed plunged in darkness. But he could just make out a bed sunk in the floor. And there was a telephone beside the bed. It was made of clear plastic. There were goldfish swimming in the receiver. He bent down, watched the goldfish. Now he was smiling too. He could no longer remember what was so important about the telephone. All he knew was that Reid hadn't lied to him. There was a telephone and it had fish in it. Reid had told the truth. That was the main thing.

Reid turned the key in the door.

'Take off your clothes,' he said.

Nathan looked across at him. 'What about you?'

'You first. I want to watch.'

Nathan began to undress. Soon he was naked except for a pair of white boxers. So white in the mauve light shed by the aquarium. He slipped his thumbs inside the elastic and was about to draw them down when Reid said, 'Leave those on.'

Reid moved across the room. He covered distance the way other people altered the angle of their heads. He accomplished it with such tact, such grace. There were only two positions: over there and here, now. Nathan felt Reid's clothes, the fabric coarse against his bare skin, and he was glad that Reid had told him to undress first.

'You've been here before, haven't you?' Nathan murmured.

Reid nodded. 'Many times.'

'Always with boys?'

'Always.'

He could hear the whales again. It sounded like something familiar slowed down. It sounded like curiosity.

The gloves lingered on his ribs, slid down his spine.

Only the rush of waves now. They rolled towards a reef, ripped open, spilled their foam. And then a wall built out of water, and fish trailing wakes of red and blue and gold.

There was a click. So precise in the haze of everything else that he was almost startled. He looked round. Reid was shutting his briefcase.

Reid handed him a mask. 'I want you to wear this.'

He took the mask.

It was black leather, the shape of a head. Two holes to breathe through and a silver zipper for a mouth. No eyes.

'I won't be able to see,' he said.

'Just feel.' Reid smiled. 'Would you do that for me?'

He pulled the mask over his head and found that he could breathe quite easily. He lay back on the bed. The sheets were satin, cool against his forearms. The bed began to tilt and rock.

He reached out, found a body, touched it. Ran the tip of his finger all the way from the armpit to the anklebone. The same speed as a plane crossing the sky. He thought maybe you could learn to read a body blind. By touch. Like braille.

A moment of clarity, and he said, 'I don't know your body at all.' And then, when there was no reply, 'Are you there?'

'I'm here.' A pause. 'Your skin, it's so soft.'

'How can you tell?' he said. 'You're wearing gloves.'

'You're forgetting something. There's my mouth.'

He felt his boxers being eased down, over his thighs, down to his ankles. His cock on a spring. This contact with the air was almost friction enough. Then the sudden warmth. A mouth.

His head locked in darkness, his body twitching like one of those fish you place on the palm of your hand to tell your fortune, they curl, they arch, sometimes they flip right over, but they're never still, not unless you're very cold, not until your fortune's told.

He felt something push through the zipper and into his mouth.

'Make it tighter.'

He did as he was told. It was taking a long time.

'Use your teeth.'

And Reid's body heaved and a sound was dragged out of him, it had notches, like a rack, and Nathan rolled on to his back and lay there, swallowing.

Soon afterwards he took the mask off. The room, it was so bright, it was like being inside a jewel. Reid stood by the window, parted the curtains an inch. Outside it was dark. The room was wearing a mask. Reid began to laugh.

'What's so funny?' Nathan asked.

'Private joke.'

'You're not going to tell me?'

'No.' Reid had this way of standing so his face was always in shadow. When Reid turned to look at him, he could read nothing there. He just heard that soft laughter and felt a surprising lack of curiosity about its source.

'I don't want to know,' he said, 'I really don't. I'm not interested.'

Reid laughed again. 'That's my girl.'

'If I was a girl,' Nathan said, 'you wouldn't look twice.'

Reid came towards the bed, both hands on the buckle of his belt. 'Maybe not even once.'

Nathan watched him approach. 'I thought you'd finished.'

'I'm starting again,' Reid said.

Afterwards he must've slept because everything went still, that stillness that seems sudden, that tells you time's gone by.

'We'll need a boat.' A silence. 'Good.'

Reid was talking on the phone again. Nathan watched through half-closed eyes.

'Just make sure it's there. The West Pier, midnight.'

Nathan walked to the window. A flicker of silver on the ground outside. Like a thrown rope, a lasso. It took him a moment to realise that it was a reflection, that there was water out there. A pool.

He slid the window open and crossed the patio. When he dived in he hardly felt the transition from air to water. It was as if he was moving from one kind of air that was warm into another that was cooler. He surfaced, lay on his back. The palm trees were black silhouettes against a bright brown sky. We'll need a boat. The West Pier. Midnight. He saw Maxie Carlo's face close up. Maybe you know him as Reid. That's what he calls himself sometimes. Maxie's top teeth showed as he smiled, one tooth edged in gold like a page from the Bible. But which page? Not the Ten Commandments, that was for sure. Something from Revelation, maybe. The sound of a plane in the sky like paper being torn slowly. The red light winking on its wing-tip. Know what I mean?

He walked back through the sliding window just as Reid put the phone down.

'How do you feel?' Reid asked him.

'Fine.' Nathan sat down on the bed. 'I ran into a friend of yours the other night.'

'Really? Who?'

'Maxie Carlo.'

'Old Maxie. How is he?'

'He said your name's Neville.'

'That's my professional name.'

'Professional name?'

'I told you I was a hand model, didn't I?' Reid looked at Nathan, then he lit a cigarette. His face so smooth and still, the flame seemed nervous.

Nathan remembered a grey day on South Beach. This was a few months back, before Dad died. A storm was on the way and the red flags were up. Nobody was swimming.

Towards lunchtime a woman strode on to the beach with a towel and goggles. He hadn't seen her before, but he knew the type. He knew she probably wouldn't listen to him.

'I'm sorry,' he said, 'but you can't swim today.'

She continued buckling the strap of her bathing cap under her chin. 'Oh? Why not?'

'The flags are up.'

She smiled at him. 'It's all right, I'm a swimming instructor.'

In a strange way she reminded him of Yvonne so he was patient with her. 'Listen,' he said, 'it's my lunchbreak. If anything happens to you while I'm away it'll be my responsibility.'

'You go and have your lunch,' she said. 'I'll be fine.'

Sometimes you have an instinct for what'll happen next. He knew this woman was going to get into trouble. He knew that if he left the beach she might even drown. He also knew that she had to find out for herself.

He waited at the top of the beach, under the awning of the kiosk that sold candy bars and soda. He watched her run towards the water. He saw the short arc her body made as she met the first wave.

It took a while. But then he saw one arm reach up, pale against the charcoal waves, pale against the sky, like a child asking a question in class.

When he brought her out of the water, she wouldn't look at him. 'I was wrong,' she said. And then she said, 'Thank you.'

He gave her a smile. 'It's my job.'

Almost every day after that she'd arrive with offerings at lunchtime, sandwiches or fruit or cold drinks, but that wasn't the point of the story. The point was, he'd seen through something, and he'd been ready. He had the same feeling now. The feeling that he couldn't go to lunch. Except there were too many people on the beach and he didn't know which way to look.

'What's wrong?' Reid said. 'Don't you remember?'

Nathan lay back on the bed. 'I remember.'

He drifted off to sleep. He woke suddenly and his mind had jumped tracks. Georgia. It was a whole day later and he still hadn't got through to her. He glanced at his watch. 5:45 a.m.

He reached out, picked up the phone. He dialled her apartment first. No reply. He dialled the house. He let it ring and ring. He was about to hang up when somebody answered.

'Who's that?' he said.

'It's Georgia.'

'You sound strange, George. Did I wake you up?'

'Nathan?'

'George, what's wrong?'

'I took some pills.' Her words were slurred. It was hard to understand her.

'What pills?'

'Dad's pills,' she said. 'You know. He's got lots. I took some green ones, then I took some red ones, then I think I had a blue one – '

'Where are you, George?'

'I'm in Dad's bedroom. On the bed. There's bottles everywhere. Tiny little bottles – '

'How many did you take?'

'Don't know. Didn't count.'

'George, listen. Don't go to sleep, all right?'

'Yeah. OK.'

'I mean it. Don't go to sleep.'

'OK.'

He stood still for a few seconds, then he put the phone down and turned the light on. Reid's eyes opened wide, as if he'd only been pretending to be asleep.

'What are you doing?'

Nathan was already dressing. 'I've got to leave.'

'Is there a problem?'

'It's my sister. She's taken some pills.'

In five minutes they were walking out of the motel, the rising sun driving a thin wedge of orange light into the bank of dark cloud on the horizon.

MACKEREL STREET

That awful smell, it was his eyebrows. He touched one. It crumbled on the tips of his fingers like a kind of wiry dust. He could smell his own eyebrows, for Christ's sake.

He couldn't think about it, what was in that car. The sheet, his back-up copy of the tape. The numberplate. He just couldn't think about it. His top hat was on the thirteenth floor. His wallet too. But he wasn't going back, not now. Not with those flames crackling in his ears like rain, not to that mass grave. Even now, maybe, he was being watched. That kid with the puffy eyes and the crewcut, he was everywhere you looked. Maybe he even worked for Creed. Creed had kids all over the city. A line of speed, a limo ride, a smile, and they were his. Sometimes he used them for sex, sometimes for information. Sometimes for both. Jed looked round. The kid was still standing on the balcony, his face turned in Jed's direction. A pale blotch, no features. The kid was still watching. Where's your hat, mister?

He walked to the bus station in Mangrove East. He bought half a pound of Peanut Brittle on the way. It was how he felt. The wind moved past his ears and he thought of nothing. Rage filled him full, his skin felt tight with it. Instead of standing in line, he eased back against the wall, next to a fruit machine. Nobody came near him. Half a pound of Peanut Brittle and a head tight with rage. People know a force-field when they see one. He felt in all his pockets, pooled what money he had in the palm of one hand. Four dollar bills and some loose change. It would do. He waited till the Rialto bus pulled in, then he pushed through the crowd and climbed on board.

In ten minutes he was walking into TATTOO CITY. The walls were papered with the usual designs: anchors, roses, skulls. Nobody had numbers like he had. He could hear the buzzing of Mitch's needle-gun. He stamped down to the workshop at the back. Mitch was working on a boy's left shoulder. Jed waited for silence, then he bit off a piece of Brittle. Crisp as a bone snapping. It almost took his front teeth out. Then he said, 'You set me up, Mitch.'

Mitch looked round. 'Can't you see I'm busy?'

'You fucking set me up. Admit it.'

The boy peered at Jed, mouth hanging open. Jed wanted to fill it with something. Liquid concrete. Manure. Glue.

Mitch spoke to the boy. 'Give me ten minutes.'

The boy nodded.

Mitch put his needle-gun down and crossed the room. He stood in front of the door to his house, hands dangling against his thighs. 'You want to talk or don't you?'

Jed led the way into the house. One dark corridor, all the rooms on the left. He passed the kitchen. Mitch's old lady was sitting at the table, hands clasped together as if in prayer. Wisps of black hair veiled her eyes. Jed paused, but Mitch pushed him between the shoulderblades.

'In the study.'

The study was in the back. One small window looked on to the verandah where they'd drunk beer the week before. One wall was lined with shelves. Books, model boats, clocks.

Mitch took a pipe out of the rack on the mantelpiece and began to pack it with tobacco. Jed counted the clocks, trying to keep his anger down. There were eleven. Mitch sank into a leather armchair. Jed counted the clocks again, just to make sure he hadn't missed any. He hadn't.

'You look pretty strange,' Mitch said. 'You look so strange, I didn't hardly recognise you.'

'I could be looking even stranger,' Jed said. 'I could be fucking looking dead.'

Mitch lit his pipe. He leaned forwards, tossed the match into the fireplace, leaned back again. 'Well,' he said, 'you can't say I didn't warn you.'

'Why did you do it, Mitch? Why did you set me up like that?'

Mitch moved his eyes on to Jed's face and left them there. 'How do you know it was me?'

'It must've been you. You were the only one who knew.'

'You might've been followed.'

'I wasn't followed. I know enough about driving to know that.' Jed looked into the fireplace. All Mitch's dead matches. All at different angles. Celia would've found some kind of omen in those matches.

Celia.

And his voice became patient, as if he had time, plenty of it. 'When

I called them this morning, they knew where I was. They knew *exactly* where I was.'

'How do you know they knew?' Mitch said. 'What makes you so sure?'

Jed's temper flared. 'Because they fucking blew my car up, that's how.' He catapulted out of his chair and kicked the wall. A black half-moon appeared on the faded paint.

'Sit down, Jed.'

He did as he was told. All the air drained out of him. Suddenly he could've cried.

Mitch sucked on his pipe. Smoke moved through the room. It seemed to be constantly on the point of turning into something, of assuming some recognisable shape, but it would never quite commit itself.

'You're right,' Mitch said finally. 'I told them. But you know what? They already knew.'

Jed stared at him. 'They already knew? How?'

'Beats me. But they did.'

'But you still told them, Mitch. How could you do that? How come you even *talked* to them?'

Mitch sighed. He put his pipe down on the hearth and rose to his feet. He unlocked the top drawer of his desk and took out a polaroid. He handed the polaroid to Jed and returned to his chair.

It was a picture of Mitch's old lady. She was lying in a coffin. Her face was white, her eyes were shut. Blood had trickled out of the corner of her mouth and then dried. She looked dead. Jed turned the polaroid over. On the back it said CO-OPERATE AND IT WON'T HAPPEN.

He looked at the picture again. Nice make-up job. It was Morton's work, no question about that.

'What would you have done?' Mitch said.

Jed looked up. 'Is she all right?'

Mitch shrugged. 'They held her for twenty-four hours. What do you want to hear?'

A silence. The ticking of eleven clocks.

'You've got to be fucking out of your mind messing with those people,' Mitch said.

Jed scowled. 'I know what I'm doing. I worked with them.'

'Worked with them?' Mitch scoffed. 'You drove.'

'What's the difference?'

'You were nothing.'

'I was NOT NOTHING.'

Mitch sighed. 'You were nothing to them. That's what those people do. They hang you on their Christmas tree, they put you where you look right, like one of those coloured balls, but pretty soon they get bored with you, your time's over, they throw you out. Or maybe you break first. You've got some kind of shine, that's why they choose you in the first place, but under that shine you've got you're pretty fragile, pretty hollow. So you don't last long. And people like that, they're the ones that know it.'

Jed watched Mitch lean down and knock his pipe against the hearth. He eased out of the chair.

'Look, I'm sorry about Anne-Marie,' he said. 'I'm going now.' He stood in front of Mitch. 'Can you loan me ten dollars?'

Mitch laughed.

'What's so funny?' Jed asked him.

Mitch was still laughing. 'Loan,' he said.

'It's all right,' Jed said. 'I'll pay you back.'

'Pay me back? Sure you'll pay me back. What are you going to do, leave me ten bucks in your will?'

'Where's your faith, Mitch?'

Mitch shook his head. 'Not only dressed like a fucking preacher, talking like one too.' He reached into his back pocket, snapped a twenty-dollar bill out into the air. 'Here.'

'I only asked for ten,' Jed said.

'Twenty's all I've got.'

'Thanks, Mitch.' Jed stopped in the doorway. 'I'll see you around.'

'Yeah,' Mitch said, 'sure you will.'

Jed stood on the main street that ran through Rialto. The clouds that piled above the rooftops were veined like marble, almost green. The heavens would open before long. His lips tightened, taut as a drawn bow. He aimed a queer, crooked smile at the sky. It was the rain that had started it. It was the rain that told him he was special. So he'd lost everything. The car, his hat. The shirt off his back. So they knew his every move. So what. A fizzing began between his ribs. A fizzing that was like a lit fuse. He'd been underplaying it. He'd needed some final twist. And Mitch had handed it to him; he hadn't meant to, but he had. Those people, they took blackmail and faded it to grey. It was a game for them. But he could use that game to draw them in. Then he could settle it, once and for all.

With Mitch's $20 he could afford to catch a taxi to his mother's place. He asked the driver to drop him at the top of Mackerel Street. It was habit, a ritual, left over from the days when he used to leave transistor radios playing in her front garden. Like fingers pointing. Like ghosts come back to haunt her. He'd always have a taxi waiting at the top of the street so he could make his getaway.

He began to walk down the hill. He could feel his right heel, the birth of a blister there. The new sandals didn't fit quite as well as he'd thought. He turned the corner, into the part of the street that was dead-end. Houses the same colour as ice-cream. Lemon, peppermint, raspberry. Every flavour you could imagine. No trees, just streetlamps. And sidewalks inlaid with neat strips of grass. He was back in Mackerel Street, he was actually back. He wondered how long it had been. Curiosity, not sentiment. Was it twelve years? No, thirteen. Almost half his life ago. It was hard to believe. He looked up and found that his calculation had taken him all the way to his front gate.

He was just reaching for the latch when a movement in the corner of his eye distracted him. He turned in time to see the curtain swing back into place in the window of the house next door. It was that kind of neighbourhood. Every house hid the same voyeur. He was glad he looked so different. With his blond hair and his Christian outfit, there was little chance of being recognised by anyone. They would peer at him from behind their lace curtains and think: Stranger. The same way they had always peered at his mother and thought: Whore. He smiled grimly. In those days he would probably have agreed with them; he'd had good reasons for seeing her in that red light. Now? Who she was fucking was her own affair. He didn't even care what colour their shoes were.

He brought his eyes back into focus. Noticed casually, almost incidentally, that his mother was standing in the downstairs window looking at him. There followed a curious interval during which they both stared at each other without any change of expression. Then, almost with a jolt, they came alive again and he saw her say, 'Jed?'

He watched her approach, blurred and unidentifiable, in the frosted glass of the door. He couldn't imagine what he was going to say to her. When the door opened, they both held their ground. They were searching each other's faces, searching for words.

She found some first. 'What were you doing,' she said, 'skulking in the road like that?'

He shrugged. 'I don't know. Just thinking.'

'I thought you were going to go away again.'

'Would you have liked that better?'

'Jed.' The word came out sounding like cream poured over a spoon. That tone of voice, how well he remembered it.

'Well,' he said, 'would you?'

She sighed. 'Are you going to stand on the doorstep all afternoon,' she said, 'or are you going to come in?'

It smelt synthetic in the hall. It was her own smell, she carried it around with her. If you boiled her down, reduced her to her essence, it would smell of air freshener, nail polish, fashion magazines, he was sure of it. He waited for her to close the door, then he followed her down the corridor and into the kitchen. She wore the same kind of clothes she'd always worn: a pink velour sweatsuit and a pair of sneakers with plump white tongues. Her dry blonde hair tucked under her jawbone, curled into the nape of her neck.

'How about some coffee?' she said. 'It's fresh.'

'Sure. Great.' He sat on a stool while she poured. He looked around. A lot of red and pink, a lot of stripped pine. The same old bric-à-brac above the sink: a china doll, a dog with one paw raised, a matador. A small colour TV on low volume. The early-evening news.

She placed a cup of coffee in front of him with a waitress smile, then she sat down opposite him, on the other side of the breakfast bar. She held her own cup in both hands, just below her mouth. He could see that she had aged, even through the veil of steam. There were two faces, and one of them had slipped. A curious, smeared look. And nothing left of her eyebrows except two lines sketched in brown pencil.

But she didn't want him scrutinising her. 'You look so,' and she quickly sorted through words, as if they were dresses, and chose one, 'different.'

'That's the idea,' he said.

She eyed him thoughtfully over the rim of her cup. 'You should do something about your hair.'

He laughed, slopping his coffee over. 'I'm not one of your fucking clients, mother.'

She went to the sink and came back with a damp cloth. 'I'm running the place now, you know,' she said. 'It's going very well.' She lifted his cup and wiped the base, then she wiped the wood surface underneath.

'That's great.' He couldn't keep the sneer out of his voice. She was folding the cloth. Once, twice, three times. If she folded it much more, he thought, it might disappear altogether.

'Did you come here to insult me, Jed?' she said. 'Is that why you came? Or was there something you wanted?'

A plane went overhead, almost scraping the tiles off the roof. Cups nodded on their red plastic hooks. When the noise had died away, it seemed as if another layer had been stripped from the silence.

'You must have a reason,' she said, 'after all these years.'

'It's nothing to do with all these years,' he said.

'You were always so calculating. You never did anything without a reason.'

'How come I need a reason?' he said. 'I've been away. I was away for a long time. I couldn't've come to see you even if I'd wanted to.' He thought of the phone-call he'd made from that booth on the highway. Six years ago. Henry, is that you?

She came and sat down. 'You got into trouble again, I suppose.'

'I went and lived in a town called Adam's Creek,' he said. 'The name was a joke. There wasn't any creek, never had been.' He turned his cup on its base. 'There wasn't even an Adam.'

'Adam's Creek?' she said. 'I never heard of it.'

'It's in the middle of nowhere.' He told her about the Commercial Hotel and THE WORLD OF 45 FLAVOURS. But he looked at her once and her chin was propped on the flat of her hand as if it was about to be served by a waiter and she was looking out of the window. She wasn't listening, he could tell, so he just stopped. She looked back at him and sighed, a sigh that didn't seem to have anything to do with him.

'I think I'll go and lie down,' he said. 'I'm really tired.'

She took his empty cup, put it in the sink with hers. 'You can use your old room.'

He stood up, stretched.

'Do you want me to wake you?' she said.

'It's all right,' he said. 'I'm just going to sleep for an hour.'

At the top of the stairs he stood by the window and looked out. This neighbourhood where he'd grown up, it was another world to him now, a world he had to search his blood for. This house was his home, that woman in the kitchen was his mother. He knew it, but it was a long time since he'd felt it. The feeling had gone, only the facts remained.

When he opened the door to his old room he found himself nodding. It was exactly what he might have expected. There were two twin beds. There was a lamp with a white shade. There were small bowls of dried flowers. It was immaculate, anonymous; neutral as a motel room. There was nothing to suggest that he had ever slept there, not a trace of his presence. There wasn't even the ghost of a radio.

He took his jacket and his sandals off, and lay down on his side with his knees drawn up to his chest. He closed his eyes. Listened to the planes go over. That long slow rumble. His ribs vibrating gently. And he rose up over the rooftops of Sweetwater and beyond Mario's handkerchief factory, beyond the river, he could see the tall white buildings of the city clustered tight as skittles, he could see Death Row and the slim black shape of the Paradise Corporation, like the shadow of a building, and the factory and the river vanished, and there was golden wood where they had been, a corridor of polished golden wood with gutters on either side, and he looked down at his hand and saw he was holding a huge black ball, and he took three steps forwards and swung his arm and let the ball go, and that long slow rumble in the sky, that was the sound of the ball rolling down the corridor of golden wood, rolling towards the cluster of tall build-ings, plane after plane, and always that black ball rolling until at last he saw it slowly smash into the buildings, he saw the buildings stagger, topple over, every one of them, and there was no city any more, there was only a game that he had won, and the planes going over, they were the applause, a standing ovation, and he was turning away from that corridor of golden wood, one hand raised, a kind of hero now.

When he woke, it was almost dark. He could hear music downstairs, dance music. He had no idea where he was. Propped on one elbow, he saw a jacket and a pair of sandals that some stranger must've left behind.

And then he remembered; it all came back together slowly, like an explosion played in reverse. That music downstairs, that would be his mother's radio. She always tuned in to Latin stations at night. She used to cook to the rhythms of the tango and the rumba, she'd snap her fingers, tilt her hips, and he'd be watching, embarrassed, through a jungle of fingers. This was no motel, this was his old bedroom, this was home, and as for that stranger with the jacket and the sandals, that stranger was him.

One of his knees had seized up. He eased both legs on to the floor and sat still. Then he buckled his sandals, wincing as the straps bit into his heels. He limped downstairs and into the kitchen. His mother was perched at the breakfast bar with a drink and a cigarette.

'What's that?' he asked her.

'Scotch and soda. You want one?'

He shook his head. 'I don't drink.'

'Did you sleep well?'

'I woke up,' he said, 'and I didn't know where I was.'

'That's not surprising when you think how long it's been.'

'I heard the radio, and I remembered how you used to cook with that music on, and then I knew.'

She smiled. 'I still do.' She folded her cigarette up in the ashtray. She'd smoked less than half of it. 'Talking of that, are you staying for dinner?'

'I need to stay the night.' He watched her face. 'Don't worry, it's only tonight. Then I'll be gone.'

'Need to?'

'Yes,' he said. 'Need to.'

She took another cigarette out of her pack and looked at it as if she thought she might learn something from it. They were exactly the kind of cigarettes he would've imagined she smoked. Extra slim, extra mild. 100s. A delicate garland of flowers encircling the cigarette just below the filter.

'You never told me anything, did you?' she said.

'You don't want to know,' he said, 'you really don't.'

'That's not giving me much say, is it?'

'You lost the right to that a long time ago.'

This time she stubbed her cigarette out as if it was alive and she wanted it dead. 'You'll never forgive me, will you, for throwing your stupid radios away.'

'I'm not talking about radios,' he said. 'I'm talking about you pretending I didn't belong to you, you being ashamed. You still feel guilty about it. If you didn't feel guilty, you'd already've thrown me out. But you haven't and you won't,' and he looked at her, 'because you're guilty.'

She banged her glass down so hard it cracked. And she held on to it, the skin stretched tight between each knuckle. 'Stop telling me what I feel and what I don't feel, for Christ's sake. What do you know about what I feel? You don't know a thing.' She let go of the glass, looked down at her hand. She'd gashed the mound at the base of her thumb. Blood slid along the fine grooves on the inside of her wrist.

She stood at the sink and ran cold water on to the wound. 'I'm making hamburgers for dinner,' she announced suddenly, without turning round.

She dabbed at her cut with a piece of paper towel. He couldn't remember seeing her bleeding before, or hurt, not ever. Dealing with this damage to herself, she seemed tentative and clumsy. There was a despair about her, a kind of fatalism, as if she might at any moment throw in the paper towel and sit down on a chair and simply bleed. He stood up and fetched the first-aid kit from the cupboard. He placed it on the draining-board beside her.

'Thank you,' she muttered.

He watched her opening the kit and thought: I know a thing about you. Her drinking, her smeared face. A looseness in her head that could only be tightened by love. You've always chosen the wrong men, or let the wrong men choose you. Your life's been one mistake after another. I'm only one of them.

She stuck a plaster over the cut and moved to the chopping-board. She lit a cigarette and put it straight in the ashtray. Then she began to chop onions. The cigarette burned all the way down to that delicate garland of flowers, she didn't touch it once. When she'd finished the onions she reached for the whisky bottle and held it up to the light. Half an inch left. She tipped it into her glass, no soda this time. She stood the empty bottle on the floor.

'If you want something to drink, there's wine in the fridge,' she said.

'I told you,' he said. 'I don't drink.'

The smell of meat and onions frying began to load the air. He realised he'd eaten nothing all day.

'Smells good,' he said.

She crossed the room and opened the patio doors. She didn't seem to have heard him.

They ate at the kitchen table. Afterwards they watched a movie on TV. It was about killer ants. There was one part where the ants were swarming across a blonde girl's thigh while she was sleeping. A man, the hero, presumably, was standing on a beach with a gun in his hand.

Jed turned to his mother. 'You seen anything of Pop?'

'Oh, you know. He drops in from time to time.'

'If you can call smashing the door down dropping in.' Smiling to himself, Jed looked across at his mother and was surprised to see that she was smiling too.

They were both smiling, both at the same time.

She poured herself another glass of wine. 'You know, you weren't really a mistake.'

He was looking at the TV again. The blonde girl had just woken up. She was screaming.

'You weren't,' she said. 'We wanted you.'

'Maybe I wasn't,' he said, 'but you made me feel like one.'

She sighed and sipped her drink. 'I was too selfish, but that still doesn't mean you were a mistake.'

He nodded.

The hero was running up the stairs, but it was too late.

The blonde girl was dead.

His mother cleared the plates away, then she went and stood in the doorway looking out into the night. The wind swelled and the trees in the yard shook like tambourines. One of the patio doors slammed against the outside wall.

'It's going to storm,' she said.

The wind pushed at her hair. A silence seemed to swoop down, and lightning burned the air behind her white. She seemed to have been drawn round haphazardly in black pencil. It made her look as if she would never move again. As if she would always be alone. In that moment he could see why they might laugh together, and why they might cry. Then she was pulling the doors shut, reaching up to fasten the bolt at the top, bending down to fasten the other bolt near the floor. She turned to him, her face dark with the effort. 'I'm going up to bed now.'

'What time do you go to work?'

'About eight.'

'Could you wake me?'

She nodded. 'Goodnight, Jed.'

'Goodnight.'

That green sky he'd seen earlier, it was over the house now, loud and poisonous. He was drawn to the window. Thunder hid the sound of planes. (Or maybe they weren't taking off tonight, maybe the weather was too bad.) Lightning flattened itself against the glass, a face with no features only inches from his own, a boy shouting from a balcony. He stepped back into the room.

There was nothing much on TV, but he watched it anyway. Like water, it ran into every compartment in his head and left no room for anything else.

He went to bed at eleven. As he climbed the stairs, the rain came with a sudden loud sigh. The roof shook under the weight of it. He passed his mother's bedroom. There was no strip of light under the door. She must already be asleep.

At three his eyes clicked open. He dressed in darkness, crept downstairs. The storm had passed on. It was quiet. A thick grey light lay on the furniture like a coat of dust. He felt his way into the lounge.

There, in the corner, was the bureau desk that had belonged to his father. If he remembered right, the gun would be in the bottom drawer. He tried the drawer. Locked. Somehow that was encouraging. He reached underneath to see if the bottom could be removed, but it seemed solid. He'd have to force the lock. But what with? He crossed the hallway to the kitchen, returned with a pair of scissors, a chisel, some garden shears. He tried the scissors first. They bent. The shears next. Too big. He inserted the chisel into the gap and worked it back and forwards until he had leverage, then he began to push the handle of the chisel downwards, away from the desk. He could feel the sweat all slippery on his forehead and his throat. A crack suddenly, and he fell back. He thought the chisel had snapped, but it was the lock. He put the chisel down, pulled the drawer open and began to feel around inside. A pile of papers. A roll of Scotch tape. More papers. It had to be there. Then his hand closed around a rectangular box.

He lifted the box out of the drawer and carried it to the window. He opened the lid. Grey light spilled along the smooth, tooled grooves of the gun. It had belonged to his brother, Tom. Tom had brought it round during the days when Pop kept showing up outside the house at night and shouting threats.

'Taste of his own medicine,' Tom had said. It was one of the few things Tom had inherited from his father, this love of guns; his mouth bent when he talked about them, the same way it bent when he talked about certain types of women.

Their mother was giggling nervously. 'I can't.'

'Take it.' Tom seized her hand and wrapped her fingers round the gun. One off her nails caught on the butt and snapped. But the gun was a piece of witchcraft and she hardly noticed. Her fingers opened again, slowly, like a door finding its natural position on its hinges, and they all stared down at the gun. Too big for her hand, too big and dark and blunt. When they looked up again, looked at each other, their eyes seemed to be the same colour as the gun, and capable of the same violence.

She did take it. But, as soon as Tom had driven away, she locked it in the desk. 'I could never,' and her shoulders rippled with disgust, '*never* use something like that.' Standing at the window with the gun in his hand Jed supposed he'd been relying on her to hold to that.

Suddenly the darkness shrank and he was blind. He turned, blinking. Saw his mother standing in the doorway, one hand on the light switch. She was wearing a nightgown with short, puffy sleeves. A knife glimmered in her other hand. She ran towards him and he felt the knife slide through the cheap leather of his sleeve, scorch the muscle of his forearm. He twisted sideways, snatched at her wrist. The knife dropped to the carpet. He pushed her away from him.

'What're you doing?' he said.

She began to speak and her voice was thick as the light in the hallway, thick with pills. 'You get out, you get out of here, get out – '

'You could've killed me,' he said.

' – you get out of my house, just get out,' and then her voice lifted in pitch and volume, and she was screaming at him, 'GET OUT, GET OUT, GET – '

He slapped her hard across the side of her head, and she stopped, right in the middle of a word, as if he'd switched her off. 'You don't know what you're doing,' he said.

She stood in the room, her shoulders hunched in the nightgown, her mouth wrenched out of shape.

'I'll take you up to bed,' he told her, 'then I'll go.'

He took her by the arm and, turning her round, led her back upstairs. He helped her into bed and pulled the covers over her. 'I'm going to turn the light off now,' he said. He turned the light off and stood by the door, listening. Her breathing was steady; she was asleep. He wondered what she'd think when she found his empty bed in the morning. He wondered whether she'd remember.

Outside it was still dark. Rain scuttling in the gutters. When he reached the top of Mackerel Street he stopped and glanced up at the house on the corner. One light shining in an upstairs room made him feel that he was floating on an ocean, cut loose and drifting, but then he felt the weight of the gun in his jacket pocket, and it was a good purposeful weight, it was like ballast. There would be no drifting.

He eased his jacket off and inspected his arm. He'd been lucky. It had taken all the knife's strength just to slice through the sleeve so the wound was superficial. A thin, dark line of drying blood, more of a scratch than a cut. He lifted his arm to his mouth, licked the wound clean.

He put his jacket back on. No lightening of the sky yet, but dawn could only be an hour away. There were blue flashes in the east, as if someone further down the coast was watching a giant TV. He decided to walk to the train station in Sweetwater. There used to be an all-night café under the platforms. He'd sit in the café and drink a cup of coffee and wait for the first train to the city. He searched his pockets for candy. Just a few fragments of Peanut Brittle and a handful of empty wrappers.

It was two miles to the station and as he splashed along in his sandals he could taste blood in his mouth. Sharon's lazy voice came back to him: You won't like it. Men don't.

She was high that night, almost gone, otherwise she never would've let it happen. It was one of his rare nights off, and she'd come round to his two rooms under the Palace with a litre of mescal in a brown paper bag and half an ounce of grass in her bra. They were sprawled across his single bed, most of their clothes on the floor.

'It'll get everywhere.' But she had this grin draped over her face.

'It's my place,' he told her. 'I don't care where it gets.'

'Well, all right. But don't make a habit of it.'

He put his mouth to her cunt. People think blood always tastes the same. That's because they don't know. There's sweet blood and there's sour blood. There's blood that's old and blood that tastes brand-new. Sometimes blood tastes cheap, like tin cans or cutlery, other times it tastes as rich as gold. Sharon's blood tasted sugary that night. But with an edge to it, like fresh lime. He was down there so long that she came twice just from his tongue. She said nobody had ever done that to her before. Then they fucked and she was right, it did get everywhere. The next day he had to throw half his bed in the garbage. It was only later, with Celia, that he took to keeping the sheets. That had been her idea. Towards the end she became almost religious about it. Blood as sacrament, an emblem of their union. Blood as affirmation. Blood as power.

The café was open. He drank a coffee and watched the clock go round. 4:55. 5:10. 5:23. Someone had left an early edition of the paper on the table next to him. He read it from front to back. 5:41. He thought of Sharon and her cunt brimming with that sweet dark blood. Then he remembered how she'd rationed him. They'd been on and off for almost three years, and yet he could count the times. Once in the Palace, once in the storeroom. That was it. He wondered if Max liked it. Probably not. Men don't.

The city train came in at 6:05. It was crowded. Hundreds of people with sleep in their eyes and their heads nodding on their necks. The train rattled over the river. Between the grey metal struts he caught glimpses of the Witch's Fingers glistening in the grainy light. Sometimes Celia's body had looked like that, when it was hot, a silvering along the edges of her skin. Don't make a habit of it. Of course, with Celia, that was precisely what it had become. A habit. Same time every month. And that evening when she turned to him on their sheet that was stained with roses, the power station lit up behind her like a twisted heap of pearls, and she said, 'You know the really weird thing? It takes the pain away.' Something went through him in that moment, it moved so fast he only saw its heels, but now, thinking back on it, he thought it might've been the closest he had ever got to love.

A man fell against him, muttered an apology. He must've fallen asleep on his feet.

The train dipped underground at Y Street. The lights flickered on, they trembled on and off, like the eyelids of someone who's dreaming. Three minutes later they were pulling into Central Station. One screech of the brakes, and a lurch that sent people staggering.

He bought two bags of Iceberg Mints at the news-stand, then he took the escalator up to the street. He thought he'd stroll down to the ocean, find himself a deck chair and a piece of shadow, doze for a few hours. Later he could breakfast at the Aquarium Café. He took the direct route, south from Central, through the M Street mall and down the hill past the Palace Hotel. He hadn't meant to pass the Palace. He didn't want any memories this morning. Not memories like that, anyway. They were knots in the smooth grain of a wood. They made the saw jump. You could lose a finger that way. He stared up at the building as he passed and knew why Creed had chosen it. The respectability, the grandeur, the sheer weight of that façade, they all told lies about him.

Lies.

His gaze dropped back to ground-level. The revolving doors began to spin, flick over, like the pages of a book, and out of the book stepped two figures, men.

Jed edged back into the shade of a tree. Without taking his eyes off the doors, he unwrapped a mint. Fed it into his mouth, crushed it to fragments with his teeth.

'My Christ,' he whispered.

One of the men was Neville Creed, the other man was Nathan Christie. They knew each other. They not only knew each other, they slept with each other too.

He remembered Mitch's words: I told them. But they already knew. *They already knew.*

'No wonder,' he whispered. 'No fucking wonder.'

And his mind leapt across seventeen years, a spark jumping between two terminals. The shark run. Nathan Christie had been found guilty in that dark corner of the harbour. If he'd been innocent he would've drowned, and Jed would never've seen him again. Only the guilty came back.

He should've known.

And this knowledge, so late in coming, burst through his head, one explosion, then another, then another, it was like a match dropped in an ammunition dump, and he reached into his pocket, and his hand tightened round the gun.

3UR 1AL

It even looked as if something was wrong. When he ran up the stairs he saw that Dad's bedroom door was open. All through his childhood he'd been taught to close that door. Pull it until it clicks, Dad used to say, he couldn't sleep if he thought the door wasn't closed properly. And now it was open, wide open, like a raided tomb.

'George?'

She was lying stretched out on the bed, her head propped on a mass of pillows. She was watching TV. There were no other lights on in the room. Her face was flickering: bright, dark, bright, dark. The whites of her eyes were luminous and fierce. They looked washed clean, somehow. He had the feeling that she'd been crying.

He moved to the side of the bed. 'Are you OK?'

'I'm fine,' she said, 'fine.'

'You're not dead or anything?'

She smiled faintly. 'Look at this. It's the wedding.'

'Wedding? What wedding?' He sat on the edge of the bed. She was surrounded by bottles of pills. The bed clicked and rattled every time he moved. 'Where did you get all these pills?'

'They're Dad's. They were in his drawer.'

'How many have you had?'

'Not many.'

'How many?'

She shrugged. 'About fifteen.'

'Fifteen? Which ones?'

'All different.' She looked at him. 'It doesn't matter anyway. They're mostly stale. They don't do much.'

'Stale? How can you tell?'

'The dates on the bottles. Some of them are ten years old.'

He looked at her dubiously.

'For Christ's sake, Nat,' she said, 'I'm ALL RIGHT.'

'You sounded so strange on the phone. Like one of those movie-stars who takes an overdose and then they start making phone-calls.'

'You called me, remember?'

'I know. But, you know.'

'Well, I'm sorry. I certainly didn't mean to sound like one of those movie-stars.'

It was so unlike her to be sarcastic, her face took on a shape he didn't recognise. Waves of anger, and hurt under the anger like a reef. Uncomfortable, he turned to the TV.

City Hall on a bright day, the shadows almost purple. A scrap of paper went tumbling across the wide, stone steps. He could see Dad and Harriet standing just inside the entrance, Dad agitated, smoothing his hair. A chip of white flashed in the gloom. Harriet's teeth. She must've been saying something. Then they emerged, arm in arm. Into the sunlight, blinking. Dad took her hand. Their smiles seemed slowed down. The veins showed on the back of Dad's hand, stood out like weak ropes. Moored in his body, but only just. Dad and Harriet turned to face each other, they were supposed to kiss. A moment's hesitation.

The tape ended suddenly.

'There's another one somewhere,' Georgia said. 'I've been watching them all night.'

'So where've you been?' Nathan asked her.

'I don't know. Around.'

'I was trying to find you. Yesterday, it was.'

'Yesterday?'

'No, wait. It was the day before. I waited outside your place all afternoon.' He put his hand on hers. 'I wanted to see you. It was after I had lunch with Harriet.'

'Talking of Harriet.' Georgia reached down beside the bed and pulled out another video. 'Here,' she said. 'Why don't you put this on.'

'What is it?'

'Put it on.'

He took the video from her, pushed it into the machine, and pressed PLAY. He sat back on the bed. He glanced at her, but she wouldn't look at him. He faced the TV again.

The back garden. A hot day. Every blade of grass caught the light. The lawn looked sharp, almost metallic. A bed of nails. Harriet lay in the distance, sunbathing.

And then close-up suddenly, everything tilting, seasick. Harriet was sitting on a blue towel in her bikini, a can of Coke beside her, a radio. She said something, then smiled. Then said something else.

There was tanning oil trapped, like mercury, in the crease that ran across her belly.

Nathan turned to Georgia. 'Why do you want me to watch this?'

'Just wait,' Georgia said.

Darkness now. Inside the house. The view from the hallway, looking up the stairs. He noted the banisters, the moon painting that Yvonne had given him, and, high up, the pale oblong of the landing window. The darkness was blue, as if lightning had struck and left a low electric charge behind.

And then a shadow passed the window, coming down the stairs. It was Harriet. At first he thought she was wearing that white silk underwear of hers. Then he realised she was naked. The white areas were the parts of her body that hadn't been exposed to the sun. She came down the stairs, a smile held awkwardly on her face, as if balanced, her eyes lit with a strange glitter. He couldn't take his eyes off her breasts, her groin. So white, raw somehow, almost painful. That smile, her nudity, the blue gloom of the house. He turned to Georgia. 'I don't think I want to watch this.'

She didn't take her eyes off the screen. 'It's nearly over.'

'I don't want to watch any more.'

She looked at him. 'I thought you liked her.'

He shook his head slowly, a sad smile on his face. 'That's not why it happened, George.'

'Why didn't you tell me? I thought,' and her voice shrank, 'I thought we were brothers.'

'We are brothers.'

'So why didn't you tell me, Nathan? Why did I have to hear it from her?'

He began to explain it to her. It had started so long ago, he said, long before they became brothers. He told her everything, and she listened carefully, her head lowered, her fingers wandering among the beads of her necklace.

'It wasn't like sex,' he finished by saying, 'not really. It was more like an exorcism or something. She'd screwed me up for so long. I had to get her out of my system.'

Georgia was silent for a while, then she lifted her head and a smile tiptoed on to her face. 'You know what she told me?'

'No. What?'

'She told me you were lousy in bed.'

'Yes,' he said, 'I suppose I was.' Then he began to smile.

'What's so funny?' she asked.

'I was just thinking. She'll never know.'

'Never know what?'

'How good I am in bed.'

She stared at him. 'But I thought you said you – '

'We did. But not in bed.'

'Where then?'

'In the summerhouse.'

'You didn't.'

'We did.' He looked at her and saw that she was laughing, and then he knew he had her back again.

But he hadn't finished yet, he had to go on. This laughter of hers, it would seal her return to him.

'In the summerhouse,' he said, 'with all those flowerpots and bicycle pumps. With all those watering cans.' He shook his head. 'I was just about to come and I knelt on a tomato.'

Tears were sliding down her cheeks. All the tiny bottles of pills tumbled off the bed and rolled across the floor.

'I was lousy,' he said. 'I was really lousy.'

Towards midday she dropped into a deep sleep. He didn't want to risk losing her again so he stayed beside her. Those jets were circling in the small sky of the room, circling like vultures, and he took her hand and held it while she slept. He watched TV, he listened to her breathing change. Then, as dusk fell, he grew tired too. He lay down beside her and soon he was asleep.

He woke once, sat upright. 'What's that?' he said.

'What?' she murmured.

'I thought I heard something.'

She turned over. 'You're getting as bad as Dad.'

He lay down again, and slept.

The next time he woke, his watch said eleven. He couldn't believe he'd slept so long. He left the bed and crossed the landing to his old room. He switched the light on, and jumped. A thin man was sitting in the chair by the window. Blond hair, glasses, dark-red leather jacket. The man reached up and scratched his neck, just to the left of his Adam's apple, with the first two fingers of his right hand. A few flakes of dry skin trickled down through the yellow air.

'Jed?'

Jed just stared at him.

'I didn't recognise you,' Nathan said.

Jed looked down at himself, as if he'd forgotten, then he looked up again. 'So what's new?' His voice was thin, whittled to a point, like a stick.

He was wearing different clothes. No black top hat, no black jacket. He looked like one of those street preachers, the ones who come by in the daytime and stick one foot in the door and tell you what hell's like. Mostly they look like they've been there. They're not easy to get rid of either. If you slam the door in their faces, they just walk right through the wall.

'Who let you in, Jed?'

'Nobody let me in. I broke in.'

'What's the idea?'

Jed reached into his pocket and took out a piece of candy. He unwrapped the candy and put it in his mouth. He dropped the wrapper, watched it see-saw to the floor. He smiled. 'How's Creed?'

'Creed?' Nathan swallowed.

'How's Neville?'

'I don't know what you're talking about.'

'You don't listen too well, do you?' The candy grated against Jed's teeth. 'The first night we met I told you I used to work for a guy in the funeral business. I told you I did a job for him. I told you his name too. Creed.'

Nathan still didn't see it.

'Neville Creed,' Jed said. He leaned back in the chair. 'When I told you I'd killed someone, it didn't seem to bother you much. I thought it was the coke, but it wasn't that. You'd heard it all before, hadn't you? You knew all about it.'

Jed stared at Nathan. There was a splintering as Jed bit clean through the piece of candy in his mouth.

'It's no use acting innocent. I know you're sleeping with him. My hunch is, you're working for him too. You've been working for him all along. You didn't just happen to be in that bar that night. You'd been planted there. Old friend, small world, fuck,' and Jed laughed, it was a bitter laugh. Nathan had heard Dad laugh like that on the night of the spaceship.

'You're not making any sense, Jed. I didn't even know his name was Neville till a couple of days ago. I didn't know he worked for a funeral parlour. He said he – ' And the whole thing came tumbling down, a set of dominoes stretching back into the past: that meeting on the promenade, the grey man under the umbrella, Reid's casual questions about his 'friend'. Maxie Carlo and his anagrams. All he could hear was one long, rippling crash as the dominoes fell. He'd been so fooled, so used. He stared down at the carpet. 'Oh shit.'

'Yeah,' Jed said. 'Oh shit.'

'He really works for a funeral parlour?'

'Look,' and Jed's voice softened with leashed rage, 'I don't want to listen to any more of your stories. It's showdown time tonight. I'm meeting up with Creed and you're coming with me.'

Nathan took a step backwards. 'No,' he said, 'I don't want anything to do with this.'

Jed reached into his coat. He pulled out a gun and laid it casually across the palm of his left hand. 'Yes, you do.'

Nathan sat down on the edge of the bed.

'What's the time?' Jed asked.

'About eleven.'

'All right. This is what we're going to do. We're going to get in your car and we're going to drive down to the West Pier and then we're – '

Suddenly Nathan remembered Creed's phone-call. 'Listen, Jed, when I was with Creed last night – '

'Where'd he take you? The Ocean Bed Motel?' Jed leered. 'Christ, I've seen a million like you.'

'He made a phone-call late last night. He said something about the West Pier. You be there with the boat, he said. I think it was – '

Jed uncoiled from the chair. 'I said no more stories. We're leaving.'

It was dark on the landing, and Nathan didn't bother to turn the light on. He thought of Harriet walking down the stairs in that movie Dad had made. His movements seemed like some kind of replica or echo. He saw himself naked, bars of thick white paint splashed across his chest, across his groin, as if he was taking part in a tribal ceremony, an initiation, even, perhaps, a sacrifice, and he saw Jed behind him, dressed in his true clothing again, the clothing he wore under his skin, that black suit with the shiny elbows, shiny shoulderblades, that voodoo hat perched on this head, a medicine man whose medicine made you ill, not well.

They left the house by the back door. As Nathan unlocked the car, a bird called from a nearby tree. One low, reverberating call; a rolled R. If nostalgia had a sound, that would be it. It reminded him of Dad, and he wondered what Dad would've thought if he could've witnessed this scene. The mere fact of driving somewhere at midnight. Mad. And yet they'd been deceived in such similar ways. A different setting, that was all. A difference of scale. Like father, like son. And suddenly he relaxed, stopped caring. He smiled as he reached across and unlocked the door on the passenger side.

Jed slammed the door. 'What's so funny?'

'Nothing.' Nathan fitted the key in the ignition. 'What happened to your clothes?'

'I sold them.'

'You think if you change your clothes people aren't going to recognise you?'

'Shut up.'

'They'll still – '

Jed touched the gun to Nathan's ear. 'Drive.'

Nathan shrugged. He reversed out to the street. He looked left and right. No grey man tonight. They didn't need any grey men any more. All thoughts were read, all movements known.

Blenheim slept. Only one take-out place was still open: HOT CHICKENS. COLD DRINKS. White neon and stainless steel. Two drunks in the doorway, sucking on bones. A faint rasping in his ear and he glanced sideways. Only Jed scratching again. The inside of his forearm this time. His nails left long red smears on the pale flesh. Jed had swopped his clothes and dyed his hair. Nothing he could do about his skin, though.

He drove through Blenheim towards the bridge. Towards what, though, really? He saw the dead skin falling in the car, falling as softly as snow. He'd have to vacuum in the morning. He kept his thinking light, skimming thoughts like stones across the black water of events, but he knew that sooner or later, no matter how many times they bounced, they'd sink into those depths, depths that held the unknown, the unforeseeable, they'd sink and maybe they would never rise again.

They'd turned all the lights out on the bridge. After midnight then. He saw the last ferry creep towards the M Street Quay. As he came down off the bridge he took the South Side Highway to the promenade. The West Pier lay off to the right, crouching over the ocean, unlit. It had been years since there had been any life on the West Pier. He looked across at Jed and knew that it was Jed who'd chosen the place.

The turnstiles were shackled with chains, so they had to climb over. The city council had put up a sign: WARNING. DANGEROUS STRUCTURE. DO NOT PROCEED BEYOND THIS POINT.

They proceeded.

Nathan looked down through the gaps between the wooden slats. The ocean unrolled on the beach fifty feet below. He saw the water shatter into froth and then slide backwards fast, sucking at the metal pillars. He thought he felt the pier shake, but it was probably just that notice, the drugs still running in his blood, imagination.

'Hands behind your back,' Jed said.

Nathan stared at him. 'What?'

'You fucking deaf? Hands behind your back.' Jed began to unbuckle his belt.

Nathan clasped one hand with the other, held them against the small of his back. Jed stood behind him. Nathan felt Jed knotting the belt around his wrists.

'Why are you doing that?'

Jed slid the barrel of the gun against Nathan's cheek. It was cold as toothache. It smelt of oil, his sleepwalking days. 'We're going to meet your lover,' Jed hissed. 'Don't want you getting carried away.'

'Oh for Christ's sake,' Nathan said. 'You still don't get it, do you? I'm on your side in this.'

'Oh yeah,' and Jed smirked, 'I forgot.' Then the smirk vanished and he slammed Nathan against the wall of the ticket booth. 'Now listen, golden boy, and listen good. I don't want another squeak out of you. Do you understand?'

Nathan nodded. There was no way of getting through to Jed. He knew that now.

They began to edge down the left side of the pier, Nathan in front, Jed just behind. DANGEROUS STRUCTURE was right. All the paint had flaked off or worn away, and most of what lay beneath had either rusted or rotted through. If you stood still you could feel the metal pillars totter, you could hear them wince and groan. It was no illusion after all. Nathan had to test every footstep before he took it or he could be plunging fifty feet into the ocean with his hands tied. Nor were the safety railings to be trusted. In some places they had buckled or bent. In others it looked as if someone had hurled themselves towards the ocean with such force that they had burst clean through; each gap had the ominous allure of a successful suicide atttempt. The West Pier was up for sale, he remembered. The asking price: $1. The catch was, whoever bought it had to spend a million restoring it to its original condition.

Nathan looked east, towards the City Pier. The casino was still open. Lights reached out across the water. If he slitted his eyes, the pier looked as if it was balancing on half a dozen golden springs. He wondered if Maxie Carlo was playing tonight. He stopped, cocked his head. Listened for the organ's drone, the clip-clop of the drum machine. Instead, he thought he heard coins pulsing into a metal slot.

A jackpot, by the sound of it. Somebody, at least, was winning tonight. Jed shoved him in the back and he moved on.

Halfway along the pier they passed close to a children's funfair. They were about a hundred yards out now, and a warm breeze blew off the land, threading its way through the abandoned machinery, shifting anything that had come loose. The last curve of the helter-skelter had snapped off; it hung at a curious angle, bent backwards, like a badly broken limb. The roundabout turned slowly, all by itself, as if ghosts were riding it.

At last they reached the end of the pier. An area of wooden slats with metal railings on three sides. On the fourth side, the side nearest the land, there was a weatherboard wall, once white, with a flight of steps rising to a balcony. This would be the back wall of the old ballroom. Nathan looked at Jed. Jed's pants were too big in the waist. He had to hold them up with one hand.

'Sure you don't want the belt back?' Nathan said.

Jed glared. 'I told you to shut up.'

Nathan shrugged. He looked over the railings. There was a platform of studded metal below, and a winch that leaned out over the water. This was where you would've waited for your speedboat ride in the old days. Beyond that, just ocean. He turned back again, leaned cautiously against the railings, his numb fingers touching metal. Jed was standing with one hand in his pocket now. The other dangled next to his thigh, rose from time to time to scratch his neck, his ribs, the side of his face. Ten minutes went by. A clock struck something. One, probably. And as the last note warped in the air and faded, Nathan heard a faint clatter. Jed heard it too, and stiffened. Nathan eased forwards, away from the railings.

'I thought you said it was just you and me.'

The voice had come from above. They both looked up.

A skeleton was standing on the balcony. It was Creed. He was wearing the suit of bones.

'You must be out of your mind.'

Jed still hadn't spoken.

'To come back here?' Creed slowly turned his head from side to side. 'Out of your mind.'

He began to descend. The steps, though rotten, held. His eyes never left Jed's face, not once. The bones clicked as he moved, like dice in a gambler's hand. One throw. Death if you lose. Nathan glanced at Jed. Jed's head moved in fractions of an inch, keeping Creed in his sights. He was shivering.

At the foot of the steps Creed stopped. He turned his eyes on Nathan. 'This is a surprise.' He didn't seem surprised. But then nothing got to Creed's face, not unless he wanted it to.

Nathan spoke up. 'He thinks I'm working for you. He tied me up.' And he turned his back, showed Creed his hands.

Creed just laughed.

Jed cut across the laughter. 'Did you bring the money?'

Creed opened his briefcase and showed the inside to Jed. The money was stacked in neat, sarcastic piles.

Jed sneered. 'You really think you can pay for what you did?' He drew his gun.

Suddenly a hand reached through a gap in the slats and locked round Jed's ankle. Jed tripped, fell. Creed stepped backwards, closing the briefcase, smiling. Then a man leapt over the railings, something black and springy in his hand. Jed twisted on the ground and fired at Creed. The sound of the shot was loud, contained, as if the night had walls. Then the wind snatched the sound away. Creed's smile had shrunk, but he was still standing. The man struck Jed on the neck. A grunt and Jed's head hit the wood. The hand holding Jed's ankle vanished. A second man climbed through a gap in the slats. He was wearing a leather jacket and army boots. Nathan recognised him straight away. The Skull.

'Hey, Angelo,' the Skull said. 'He dead?'

Angelo crouched over Jed's body. 'No. He's just stunned.'

'Good.' The Skull reached into the bag that was slung over his shoulder. He took out a syringe. He tested it for air, then he rolled Jed's sleeve and injected him in the arm. 'That'll keep him quiet.' He looked up at Creed. 'You all right?'

Creed was smiling, in a kind of trance. 'I saw the bullet go by,' he said. 'It didn't have my name on it.'

'No bullet's got your name on it,' Angelo said. 'He should've known that.' Bending down he prised the gun out of Jed's fingers and tossed it over the railings. A clang of metal on metal. A splash.

'Smelt it too,' Creed said, 'just for a second. Like when you're driving along the highway and there's a dead animal.' He was still smiling. 'Someone else's death, not mine.' He stepped forwards, the bones on his suit clicking, loaded dice. His eyes passed from the Skull to Angelo and back again. 'My bodyguards,' he said. 'My executioners.'

Angelo stood in front of Nathan. 'Who are you?' But there was nothing in his dark eyes, not even curiosity, and his voice was cold as lilies.

Creed answered for him. 'He's coming on the boat with us. He ought to see this.'

So there *was* a boat. Nathan looked down at Jed, his buckled limbs, his drugged blood. You should've listened. Now look at you.

'We better get going,' the Skull said.

'Yeah,' and Angelo scanned the air above his head, 'maybe someone heard the shot.'

Nathan watched as they hauled Jed's body down to the metal platform, then he turned to Creed. 'See what?'

Creed didn't answer. He just pushed Nathan down the stairs ahead of him. When Nathan reached the platform he saw another metal staircase, four flights down into the ocean. A white motor launch rocked on the black water.

The Skull and Angelo went first with Jed. They were none too careful. Blood ran from a gash on Jed's left hand where it had caught on a nail. They laid him in the back of the boat, the place where you'd sit with a crate of beer and wait for the reel to spin, that whine and roar as your line payed out. Angelo climbed the ladder to the top deck and started the engines. The water churned into cream at the stern. Nathan sat down, his feet just touching Jed's shoulder. Angelo opened the throttle and the note of the engine lifted an octave. Nathan looked round. Down here, under the pier, it was like a forest of metal. The boat slipped between two rows of pillars, evenly spaced, studded with barnacles and limpets, and wrapped in scarves of seaweed at the base. Then suddenly they were clear. In the open, the uncluttered darkness. The Skull stood next to Angel on the top deck, his forehead sloping. Angelo spun the wheel one-handed, his black curls swirling in the breeze. They were heading out to sea.

Creed was going through Jed's pockets.

'Could you undo my hands?' Nathan spoke in a low voice so the others couldn't hear.

'I think you should stay like that,' Creed said. 'I like you like that.'

'This is no joke,' Nathan said. 'My hands are numb.'

'I said I like you like that.' Creed was staring at Nathan as if he'd never seen Nathan before. This sudden detachment, a withdrawal that was both rapid and absolute, made Nathan feel almost dizzy, silenced him.

He watched Creed find something. Candy wrappers. Creed opened his hand and the wrappers fluttered away, swarmed up into the dark air, like butterflies, like dead skin, like fragments of Jed's soul, and

Creed looked at the sky, then at his hand, it was as if he suddenly regretted having let them go.

The Skull clambered down the ladder in his heavy boots. 'You found the tape?'

'Not yet.'

The tape was in Jed's inside jacket pocket. Creed held it up for the Skull to see, and the Skull nodded and grinned.

'Half a million dollars.' Creed snapped the tape and fed it out into the wind. A thin streamer flickering behind the boat. Then he just flipped the whole thing over the side.

'He had a question,' Creed said. 'He wanted to know how I knew.' That soft laugh again. You might've confused it with a breath of wind. 'He held no secrets from me. I put the food on his tongue. I put the dreams in his head. Everything he did was written in my book.'

It sounded like an epitaph. Nathan had a question too, but he was afraid that Creed's short speech had answered it.

'He called himself the Leech,' Creed was saying. 'Did you know that?'

Nathan shook his head.

'He was going to bleed me dry,' Creed said. 'Now who's doing the bleeding?'

The Leech, Nathan thought. He hunched over. Jed was still out cold. Some blood seeped from his forehead, from his hand. Not much blood, though, considering his name. It hardly stained the bottom of the boat. Not much of a leech.

In the end Nathan had to ask. 'What are you going to do with him?' And when Creed didn't answer, he looked up. 'You're going to kill him, aren't you?'

Creed was staring out into the darkness. 'He already did that himself. All we're going to do,' and he smiled, almost wistfully, 'is bury him.'

'That's murder,' Nathan said.

Creed shook his head. 'Burial.'

They stared at each other until Nathan had to look away. He couldn't look into those eyes any more.

The boat lifted, spliced a wave. Spray flew past and nicked his cheek. His upper arms and shoulders ached as if his bones had turned to metal.

He faced into the wind. And there, across the water, less than a hundred yards away, he saw a white light glowing. At first he didn't recognise it. Then, as they edged closer, he realised with a shiver where they were. They were approaching one of the ocean cemeteries, and that white glow would be a memory buoy. They shouldn't be here, he was thinking, not after dark. These were the sacred territories, these were the pastures of the dead. He found himself remembering the shark run he had undergone all those years ago, the moment when he grew tired and his legs dropped. That deepness where anything you thought of became real.

They passed within a few feet of the buoy, their engines idling now. An angel knelt beside a cross, the whole tableau lit from the inside. Nathan leaned forwards to read the inscription: ANGEL MEADOWS. And then some quotation from the Bible, but he could only make out one word: SLEEP.

The Skull stood in front of Creed, hands on his hips. 'I guess this'll do, won't it?'

Creed nodded.

Angelo flicked a switch inside the cabin and the lower deck lit up. There were colours where there'd been none before. The green and brown of the Skull's fatigues. The red of Jed's blood. The white of Creed's face, the black of his eyes.

Angelo and the Skull began to load clear plastic bags of white stones into Jed's pockets.

The Skull noticed Nathan watching. 'We cleaned out the ovens yesterday,' he said. 'These are what you might call,' and he grinned, 'the leftovers.'

When they'd used up all the bags they hauled Jed's body down to the stern.

'Anyone want to say anything?' the Skull asked.

Creed turned away. 'Just drop him.'

There was a moment of stillness, unintentional, then the two men heaved the body over the side. Spray rose into the air and flopped on to the deck. Nathan watched as Jed floated just below the surface in the part of the water that was green, almost transparent, lit by the boat's bright lamps. He saw Jed's eyes flicker open, close, flicker open again.

He woke up and he was drowning.

It was as if he'd been born into a world where the only element was water. He struck out with his hands, kicked with his feet, but the water wrapped all his movements up, stole all their strength. He struck out, kicked again. Rose to the surface. Drank the black air down. Drank some water too. He could see lights, hear voices. They were talking about him. They were saying goodbye. Was he leaving?

'Goodbye, Spaghetti.'

'Spaghetti.' A laugh. A laugh he recognised. 'Place in lightly salted water. Cook for ten minutes.'

'Lightly salted water?' Another laugh. A different laugh.

And then another voice: 'Place in lightly salted water. Cook for ever.'

It was like being food. And the cooks were all laughing, they were jolly men with big faces, they were in a good mood.

Then the waves swirled in his ears, and he was falling back. He reached for the surface again. Drank black air and water mixed. Drank it down like medicine and choked on it. He wanted to call out, but he had no space in his mouth for words. He began to see images. One flowed into the next, as if they were made of water, water of many colours, water that held shapes.

He saw a man rise up out of the ground like something growing. Rise naked from the ground, mud tumbling off his shoulders, off his belly, off his thighs. Stumbling back through the big trees, back into the village. He heard a woman's lazy voice. 'They didn't have no room for him,' she was saying. 'It was like, wait for the next bus, you know?' And her head tipped back, she was laughing. A glimpse of all her cavities. One molar filled with amethyst. He wanted to warn her. They'd lift that in the morgue.

He had other things to say, about the naked man, about the bus. He tried to shout, but his body turned over. He was under the water, his body rolled like gas. His ears were loud, his mouth was stopped with earth. He was heavy, dreamy, deaf.

He made one last effort to rise up, to throw off this cloak of water, cloak of mud. He was standing at the temple gates. He couldn't see the guard, except as a shape. There were gloves on the guard's hands. It must be cold in heaven. Then a still, calm voice. A voice you couldn't disobey. 'Enter.'

He found words. 'I'm not ready.'

'Why would you be here, if you weren't ready?'

'Tell me I'm not ready,' he begged. 'Send me back.'

'It's too late for that.'

'Please let me go back. I'll sit outside my hut. I won't speak to anyone. I'll be mad. Just send me back.'

'It's too late. You're here. It's your time.'

Then he was high up, on Blood Rock. The wind draped flags across his back, and Celia lay below him. Warm dust blew into her hair, her armpits, the corners of her eyes. He brushed the dust away. The blood had dried in brown streaks on the inside of her thighs. He moistened the blood with the tip of his tongue. Her hand flexed in his hair. He moved back up her body to her face. She gazed up at him with so much distance in her eyes that he felt like the sky, he felt that far away, he felt she loved him.

'You're doomed,' she whispered. Her lips were hardly moving on her broken teeth. 'You're doomed.'

'And you,' he said, 'what about you?'

'That's just the thing.' The same whisper, the same slow-moving lips. As if she was very tired or weak. 'I know I am. I've known it all along. But you. You don't know, do you?'

He wanted to make light of this, he wanted to laugh like some brave warrior. Not even a smile came.

'You don't understand,' she whispered, 'do you?'

He was standing, he was walking in sand, he was standing still. He saw the drop of rain on his shoulder, crouching on his shoulder like a spider. He tried to brush it off, but it wouldn't go. He ran, but it clung to him. He saw the drop of rain, as if he was outside himself, and suddenly he knew the truth about it.

It had never told him he was special, it had never told him that at all. He hadn't listened properly, he hadn't understood. He heard it speaking now, he heard it for the first time, the voice in the rain.

'What are you doing here?'

That finger on his shoulder. You. You're trespassing. You don't belong.

You're doomed.

A man walked towards him. Dark hair, black eyes, gloves. That still, calm voice again.

'You'd do anything for me, wouldn't you?'

And his own voice, passive, 'Yes.'

'You'd lie.'

'Yes.'

'Steal.'

'Yes.'

'Kill.'

'Yes.'

'Die.'

His eyes were open now, and he was falling away. It was the clearest it had ever been. He could see a light, but he was staring up through dark air, air like green glass, the light seemed warm, it seemed to glow like the dial of a radio, but it was an old radio, someone had just switched it off, the light was slowly shrinking, the light was fading, slowly, slowly, he knew how they worked, he'd watched it happening so often, soon there would be nothing.

One moment Jed was floating in that transparent, green water, the next he sank out of sight, into water that no light could penetrate. It was as if he'd been sucked down by some immensely powerful magnet.

'Goodbye, Spaghetti,' the Skull said.

Creed consulted his watch. 'We should be getting back.'

Angelo climbed back up to the top deck. He started the engines and swung the boat round in a tight circle. All Nathan could see, even when he closed his eyes, was Jed's face in that lit water, Jed's face held fast, as if in gelatine. There one moment, as if preserved for ever; gone the next, as if it had never been. Jed had done it all wrong. He should've slipped in like a dagger, between the ribs of the city. But no, he'd creaked and crackled his way down V Street, he'd swaggered along in his top hat and black suit, his purple car, and all the vultures there. Everything that happened afterwards had started in those first few moments of defiance: 'It's me. I'm here. I'm back.' He'd worshipped Creed too long; the suicide was so deep in him, he didn't even know it was there. In a way Creed was right when he said that Jed had killed himself. A sudden scratching sound. An echo of Jed's fingers on some part of his pale, pocked body. He turned. But it was just the Skull scrubbing the deck, removing the last traces of Jed's blood.

'Nathan?' Creed stood in the doorway to the cabin. He'd taken off the suit of bones. He was wearing his usual dark clothes again. The ceremony was over.

'Come here, Nathan.'

Nathan stood up, walked across the deck. It was hard to balance without the use of his arms. The bones in his legs ached, the way they used to when he was fourteen. He wanted sleep.

Creed gripped him by the shoulder and steered him into the cabin.
Once they were inside, he locked the door, then he turned. 'You've
been holding out on me.'

'I don't know what you're talking about.' Nathan took a step
backwards, and felt the wall of the cabin with his wrists.

'Lie down,' Creed said. 'Face down.'

Nathan didn't move.

'You want me to get help?' Creed said.

Nathan lay down on the bunk bed. He tried to focus on the sound
of the ocean, he tried to use that sound as a key to open the cabin
door, to rise into the air, to be somewhere else while this was
happening. Because it was going to happen.

Cushions were placed under his head and chest so he was almost
kneeling. The top cushion was a kind of green. A kind of blue. What
did they call it? Turquoise. It was all he could see, this turquoise
cushion, as it pressed against his left cheek. That and the fake teak
of the cabin wall.

He gasped. That feeling of being filled in a place he'd never thought
of as being empty.

Through the door, somewhere else, quick.

Somewhere far away. He saw black children dancing on sand. They
were Twilight's children. They had names like Morning, Noon, and
Siesta (she was the lazy one), because that was where they were in
their lives. And even though it wasn't raining, even though there
wasn't a cloud in the sky, he could hear the old woman playing her
flute. And there were children dancing on sand, and their hair was
tied back with ribbons and string, and they were pure.

It was only the burning that suddenly spread through him like
something spilt that told him it was over. He curled up on his side,
facing the wall. That safe, fake teak. A wetness spreading under him.

'You're lucky,' Creed said. 'I did it the nice way.'

Nathan didn't answer.

'You're lucky I didn't let the Skull loose on you.' Creed unlocked
the cabin door. 'Skull?' he called out. 'Hey, Skull.'

The Skull's shaved head appeared in the doorway. He grinned at
the sight of Nathan, naked from the waist down.

'He doesn't think he's lucky,' Creed said. 'Tell him how lucky he
is,' he said, 'that I didn't hand him over to you.'

'No point you handing him over to me,' the Skull said.

'Why not?'

'I had him already.'

'That's right. I forgot.'

Nathan spoke to the Skull. 'What do you mean by that?'

'In the motel. You did it for me there.'

'Did what?'

'You know. Did it.'

'But,' and Nathan was talking to Creed now, 'that was you.'

'How would you know,' the Skull leered, 'with that mask on your head?'

'That was you,' Nathan repeated, appealing to Creed.

Creed snapped his lighter open, lit a cigarette. 'Me once, him once.' He snapped the lighter shut again, tucked it into his pocket. 'Fair's fair.'

The Skull was still grinning, knots of muscle standing out on his jaw, his teeth slick with saliva. It was true. That was what the truth looked like.

'Creed?' It was Angelo, up on deck. He sounded alarmed. 'There's a patrol boat coming.'

Creed spoke to the Skull. 'Keep him quiet.' He left the cabin, closing the door behind him.

A police voice came through a megaphone. 'Cut your engines. We're coming aboard.'

The Skull sat on the bunk opposite Nathan. He drew a four-inch knife out of his boot and tapped the blade against his palm. He tilted his head towards the roof. A vein pulsed in his temple.

The engines died. Only the slapping of waves and then a bump as the patrol boat tied up alongside.

Creed spoke first. 'Good evening, Sergeant.'

'What's your business out here, sir?'

'We had a report that one of the buoys had come loose in Angel Meadows. We've just been out to check on them. Here's my licence.'

A silence.

'That seems to be in order.'

'If you need verification, just call Lieutenant Gomez down at O Street. He's got the details.'

'I don't reckon that'll be necessary. Sorry to trouble you, Mr Creed.'

'No problem, Sergeant. Good night.'

'Good night.'

Nathan heard the sudden growling of engines as the patrol boat swung away. He listened to the growling turn to purring and then nothing. The police had been tamed.

'You've got the fairy dust, Creed,' came Angelo's voice. 'You've got the fairy dust all right.'

'Those water cops,' Creed said. 'You could tell them it's Tuesday, they'd believe you.'

Then Angelo's voice. 'It *is* Tuesday.'

And Creed's laughter.

The cabin door opened and Creed looked in. 'Dress him, Skull,' he said, 'then bring him out.'

The Skull hauled Nathan to his feet, then he pulled up Nathan's pants. 'You don't smell too good.'

He brought Nathan to within two inches of his face. Nathan could see himself twice in the mirrors of the Skull's eyes, he could smell the Skull's bitter breath. He saw one corner of the Skull's mouth lift, as if the Skull had been hooked, as if someone was pulling on a line. Then he was pushed through the cabin door and up the stairs and out on deck.

They were already in the harbour, no more than a couple of hundred yards offshore. He tried to get his bearings. A passing sign said VENUS ENGINEERING. It must be Venus Bay then. One of the remote backwaters. Angelo steered into the flat black water of a boatyard and threw the engines into reverse to bring the port side flush with the quay. The Skull jumped ashore. Once he'd secured the ropes, Creed and Nathan followed.

They walked down the quay and out into a parking-lot. Creed's black car waited by a high, wire-mesh fence. The Skull tossed a set of keys to Angelo, who bounced them on his palm. Angelo walked to the car on feet that seemed alert. Angelo would be the one to follow through a minefield; he'd always find the magic route. Nathan watched him unlock the car and climb inside. The engine crackled and spat, the headlamps lifted like eyes and lit the gravel. Nathan thought of Jed's bad skin.

Creed put a hand on his shoulder. 'I'm afraid you're going to have to find your own way back.'

'So you're not going to kill me?'

Creed smiled. 'You'll keep your mouth shut. You've seen what happens to people who don't.'

The car drew alongside. The tail-lights turned their faces red. For the first time Nathan noticed the numberplate:

3UR 1AL

Creed saw where he was looking. 'You like it?'

Nathan didn't answer.

'Numberplates,' Creed said. 'It's a little hobby of mine. Maybe you should come and see my collection some time.'

Nathan took a step backwards.

Creed laughed, slid into the car. The door clicked shut. The car trickled over the gravel to the gate.

'What about my hands?' Nathan shouted.

The car turned left on to the road and vanished behind a warehouse wall. The sound of the engine faded.

He walked to the gate. On the other side of the road there was a small park with trees and benches. That would do. All he could think of now was sleep. He crossed the road and lay down on the first bench he came to. The world went black, the stars shrank and vanished, his heart blew through his body like a bomb, again, again, again. He heard the shrapnel land on the ground around him, it came showering down like rain. He was so cold inside, and burning too. But he was feeling less and less. His eyelids closing, it was like dust settling, soon there was nothing.

He woke, and it was light. He sat up. He wanted to rub his eyes, but he didn't have any hands. He looked up and saw a policeman standing in front of him. A big solid policeman.

'What's the time?' he asked the policeman.

The policeman was wearing a big solid watch to go with the rest of him. 'It's seven-thirty.' He seemed slightly annoyed Nathan had asked the first question. Policemen are supposed to do that. He had to be satisfied with the second question. 'What are you doing here?'

'I was just waiting till daylight,' Nathan said. 'Then I was going to hitch a lift home.' Though how would he hitch, he wondered, with no thumbs?

'Couldn't you get home last night or what?'

'No money.' Nathan wanted to spread his hands in the air. Couldn't, of course. All he could manage was a kind of shrug, a kind of grin.

The policeman slowly leaned sideways, like a falling tree. 'Something wrong with your hands?'

'You guessed it.' Nathan couldn't help sounding smart. It was just to keep his head above water. If he didn't say stuff, if he stopped and looked at his boots, he'd sink for sure. 'I'm all tied up.' He turned round, showed the policeman his hands.

'How do you explain that?' the policeman asked.

'It was a joke,' Nathan said. 'Some friends of mine.'

'Nice friends,' the policeman said and, walking round behind Nathan, he began to untie the belt.

DEAD ENDS

He woke up and he was drowning. It was as if he'd been born blind into a world where the only element was water. He struck out with his hands and kicked with his feet, but the water wrapped all his movements up, stole all their strength. He struck out, kicked again. Rose to the surface. Drank the black air down. He wiped at his eyes with the back of his wrist. Now he could see. Black trees crowding over him. The night sky, one shade lighter, just behind. He turned in the water. A glimmer of white. Windows hooded like the eyes of owls. The house. He swam to the side of the pool and hauled himself out. He crouched, his head between his knees, retching.

When the water had finished spilling from his nose and mouth, he huddled at the end of the pool, his toes hooked over the edge. A warm wind blew across his shoulders, drying him. He could only think of one explanation. He must've been walking in his sleep. He must've walked right into the deep end.

Ever since that night on the boat he'd been buying the Moon Beach papers every day, scouring their pages for some mention of the name Jed Morgan. He wasn't expecting front-page news. He knew Creed well enough to realise there'd be no mistakes, no clues. That was why Jed had been dumped in Angel Meadows and not some stagnant harbour bay. When those deep waters took you they took you for ever. But there had to be a paragraph somewhere, even if it was only six lines tucked away at the bottom of a page: MAN, 27, MISSING. Something like that. Surely *someone* would report him missing. He felt he needed evidence of what had happened. Some kind of proof. But almost a month had passed, and there'd been nothing.

And now he was walking in his sleep again, for the first time in almost fifteen years. He remembered the rumours it had spread about him, the tall tales it had told. And yet he'd never said anything about it. That was the way he'd been brought up. You kept all your worries locked inside, in some attic in your head, like mad relations. Sometimes you met people who could hear the screams. You tried to cover up.

Scream? you said. I didn't hear a scream. Must've been the wind. Sometimes he thought that all his pain had come from biting his tongue, all his pain had come from silence. And silence, once established, bred a new pain of its own.

He remembered how Georgia had appeared behind the reinforced glass of the police-station window. Her face still smeared with sleep, it had been so early. Her eyes moving from his torn and filthy clothes to his scorched wrists.

'Nathan,' she said, 'what happened?'

It was in his head to say, 'I'm all right, don't worry, I'm all right, really,' but that was what he'd been taught, white lies and twisted courage. There were no apologies to give her, no reassurances. Not this time.

Her eyes silvered over with tears. 'But,' and she didn't know quite how to put it, 'but it's me who's supposed to do things like this.'

'Just take me home,' he said.

She was right. In the past it had always been her who needed saving. Now, suddenly, it was him. He could hear the shock in her voice, it sounded almost petulant, like indignation. He could hear the fear.

But she took him home. Ran a hot oil-bath for him. He sank into that water with such gratitude. He felt his body slow, his thoughts cut out. He lay back, let the seconds ripple, drift. Through the perfumed steam and the half-open door he saw clean sheets billowing across a room.

Later, as she tucked him into bed, she said, 'We've got to look after each other. Like that dream you had. Like the jets.' He smiled. She had the measure of the simple things. She knew what they were.

Time passed, and that simplicity attached to everything. They sat down at the kitchen table and made decisions. First they arranged for the bank to execute Dad's will on their behalf; it would put Nathan out of Harriet's reach. Next they accepted an offer on the house. It meant they had just one month to clear the place, but to Nathan that kind of urgency seemed welcome now, intended, even crucial. Apart from anything else, it took his mind off the continuing silence of the newspapers. Working together, they began to sift the past, and they sifted it with an exuberance that bordered, at times, on delirium. One afternoon they built a fire out of all the worst things they could find: carpets, mattresses, hose-pipes, tyres. Black smoke gushed into the air, it looked as if a plane had crashed in their back garden, and some neighbour called the fire department. But they just laughed when the red trucks lined up in the road, it had the look of a joke, they were children answering to nobody. The days ran like clean cold water from a tap. Not even Harriet had any power any more.

Though she made one last attempt to wield it.

It was late one afternoon. The distant beat of helicopters circling above the harbour bridge. A fringe of shadows on the lawn. He was down in the empty pool, scrubbing the tiled sides, when he heard footsteps behind him. He turned round. Harriet was standing in the shallow end. She was smiling with her crimson lips. She thought she'd made an entrance.

'Well?' she said, and the empty pool took the word and played ball with it. 'Have you been thinking about what I said?'

He smiled. 'Yes, I have.'

'What did you decide?'

'If you have any questions about the will,' he said, 'you'd better contact the bank. They're dealing with it now.'

He watched her lips tighten on her teeth. He had to be careful or she would turn him into someone like her. That was the one power she still had left. And so he bore her no ill will, he showed no malice. He simply told the truth. And smiled.

'I thought they might do a better job,' he said. 'I thought they might be more,' and his smile widened, 'trustworthy.'

She walked back up the steps, her head set so stiff on her shoulders that it might've been glued. It's hard to make a dramatic exit when there isn't any door to slam. She had to be content with the screeching of her tyres on the drive. That was the last they'd heard of her.

Within hours of Harriet's departure, Yvonne called. She asked if she could come and say goodbye to the house. And take some of Dad's paintings to remember him by.

'As if you need to ask,' he said.

She drove down the next day in her station-wagon. When she opened the car door, clouds of smoke poured out as if she'd been lighting fires of her own. She stood on the driveway with her legs astride and a cheroot stuck in the side of her mouth, her copper hair tied back with a piece of paint-stained silk. They ran to her and wrapped their arms round her. She smelt of the inside of cupboards, long journeys, kindness.

Nathan spoke for both of them. 'We've missed you.'

Later that day, walking in the garden, she said, 'It's funny, you've risked your life so many times saving all these people you don't know, and all along the only person you ever really wanted to save,' and she looked at him, 'but you know that, don't you?'

He nodded. 'I know.'

In that moment he also knew that he'd been asking the impossible of himself. He couldn't have saved Dad. He couldn't even save Jed. You lose people sometimes. It was one of the laws of the surf. The captain had told him that. Sometimes the ocean's just too strong, the captain had said. Spring tides, a rip, whatever. There's someone in trouble, you go after them, they're there, they're still there, and he snapped his fingers, then suddenly they're gone. Don't pretend it never happened. They were there, you did your best. You live with that. You carry on.

Nathan looked at Yvonne. Her bent teeth stained by cigars, her hair as crunchy as a horse's mane.

'You loved him, didn't you?' he said. 'Harriet was right about that.'

She looked away into the lowest part of the sky. It was a look that was both longing and resigned. It was as if she could see all the things that had never happened to her.

'Love?' she said. 'I don't know. There was just a feeling I got sometimes, when I looked at his hands.'

He took her arm and they crossed the bright grass without another word. They walked up the stone steps and back into the house. It's one of the hardest things, he thought, when life is miserly to those you care for.

On her last night they barbecued some chicken by the pool. It was so still; they lit candles and ate their dinner under the stars. Yvonne had brought some wine down from the Cape. It was that pale white wine that looks almost green in the glass. They drank to the future of the house without them. They drank to Dad and to themselves. They drank to so many things that Yvonne had to open a third bottle.

'So tell me,' she said finally, 'what are your plans?'

Nathan and Georgia looked at each other. They'd hardly discussed it. It had been enough to move from one day to the next, to feel the days forge links and pick up speed.

'Summer's on the way,' she said. 'Maybe you should come and stay at my house for a while.'

He didn't have to look at Georgia this time to know the answer. They watched Yvonne drive away the next day, the back of her station-wagon stacked with paintings, Dad's red chair strapped to the roof, and knew that they would see her soon.

He leaned back, stretched. It was almost morning. The wind blew some pale blossoms against his thigh. He'd been through hard water all his life, but there was no water harder than the water of the last few weeks. He'd come through, though, he'd been strong enough, and he could build on that. He could learn from Dad too. Not the carefulness, the wariness; not the silence. But the sheer determination, that iron grip on life. Death had brushed past, snatched half each lung and a handful of ribs. But Dad had clung on. What had that nurse at the hospital said? 'Your father's been living on borrowed time.' Crap. Dad didn't borrow it. He took it. He laid his hands on it and said this is mine. That's what you do with time. The thought of Dad as some kind of thief brought him to his feet with a smile. He walked towards the house, the lawn warm under his heels, still warm from the day.

The next morning he left the house at around eleven. He was halfway down the hill when he met Mrs Fernandez, the lady who used to clean for Dad sometimes. She put a hand on his wrist. 'I was so sorry to hear about your father,' she said. He thanked her. There was sweat on her top lip, he noticed. It was a hot day, but not the thick, wet heat of summer. Not yet. He said goodbye to her and walked on down the street towards the newsagent's. A breeze picked up. The dry branches of the palm trees clicked and scraped. It was a Tuesday.

He only bought one newspaper that morning. As he left the store he tore the front page out of the paper and dropped the rest in a trash bin. He walked back to the house without lifting his eyes from the front page once. And by the time he did he was home again, sitting at the kitchen table, and he put the page down and moved his head slowly from side to side, all the blood drawn out of his face. Then he picked the page up again and read it through once more:

DEATH KING BRUTALLY MURDERED

Escaped mental patient found
in victim's apartment

Mr Neville Creed, chairman of the prestigious Paradise Corporation, was found dead in his apartment in the Palace Hotel last night.

In what is already being called the 'John the Baptist' murder, Mr Creed, 43, was stabbed fourteen times and then decapitated.

Police have arrested Mr Vasco Gorelli, who was found in Mr Creed's apartment. Mr Gorelli escaped

from the Westwood Hill Clinic last Friday where he
was held in a ward for the dangerously insane. He
was still unavailable for comment yesterday.

Mental

The ferocity and bizarre nature of the killing have
drawn comment, even from police working on the
case.

'It's a horrific crime,' said Det. Sergeant John
Lopez of Moon Beach Homicide. 'I understand the
suspect has a history of mental illness and maybe
that explains it.'

The body was found by Mr Al Cone, a night
porter at the Palace Hotel, when he received com-
plaints of a disturbance on the fourteenth floor and
went up to investigate.

A visibly shaken Mr Cone told reporters how he
had found Mr Gorelli sitting in an armchair covered
in blood while the headless body of Mr Creed lay
beside him on the floor. Gorelli had smashed the
television screen and put his victim's head inside.

Mr Cone went on, 'He was watching it, like it
still worked. You know what he said to me when I
came in? "Ssshh," he said, "it's the news."'

Charmed

Neville Creed was one of the city's most distinguished funeral directors, with a record few could
match. Marble Grove, his uncle's funeral business,
was on the brink of receivership when Creed took it
over, at the age of 22.

Seven years later he merged with the Paradise
Corporation, who bought Creed's company for an
estimated $30m. Creed was made a member of the
board.

'It was a meteoric rise,' said an old partner of
Creed's. 'Some people truly seem to lead charmed
lives.'

Private

Like many rich people, Creed was intensely private.
He didn't mix in Moon Beach society and he had
few friends. He lived a life shrouded in mystery in
his penthouse apartment on the top floor of the
exclusive Palace Hotel.

The circumstances of his death are no less mysterious. Police are still trying to establish a motive
for this seemingly senseless killing, but, so far, they
have come up against nothing but dead ends.

Nathan folded up the front page and looked round for the waste
bin. His eyes moved through the empty room, found nothing. They
must've already thrown it away. He looked out of the window. A thin
column of black smoke rose above the hedge. Georgia must have built
another fire early that morning. One last fire. The neighbours would
be complaining again.

He left the house and walked to the end of the garden. He stood
looking down into the fire. He could identify various objects. An
empty box of cheroots, the video of Harriet. Several dozen bottles of
stale pills. Smiling, he dropped the newspaper article into the core of
the blaze. He stood over it, watched it begin to turn yellow, then
brown, watched it begin to burn. Then stepped back, startled, as it
rose out of the flames, rose past his face, and flapped away through
the clear blue air, its wings black at the edges, its body still on fire.

A NOTE ON THE TYPE

The text of this book was set in Ehrhardt,
a typeface first released by The Monotype
Corporation of London in 1937. The design
of the the face was based on a seventeenth-
century type, probably cut by Nicholas Kis,
used at the Ehrhardt foundry in Frankfurt.
The original cutting was one of the first
typefaces bearing the characteristics now
referred to as "modern."

Printed and bound by Fairfield Graphics,
Fairfield, Pennsylvania

Title page and binding design by
George J. McKeon